Classical Chinese Love Stories
中国古代爱情故事

GW00372137

The Peach Blossom Fan

桃 花 扇

Kong Shangren

孔尚任（清）

Adapted by Chen Meilin

陈美林 改编

New World Press
新世界出版社

First Edition 1999
Second Printing 2001

Translated by Kuang Peihua, Ren Lingjuan and He Fei
Edited by Zhang Minjie
Book Design by Li Hui

ISBN 7 – 80005 – 432 – 2

Published by
NEW WORLD PRESS
24 Baiwanzhuang Road, Beijing 100037, China

Distributed by
NEW WORLD PRESS
24 Baiwanzhuang Road, Beijing 100037, China
Tel: 0086 – 10 – 68994118
Fax: 0086 – 10 – 68326679

Printed in the People's Republic of China

李香君

侯朝宗

柳敬亭　　　　　　　　　苏昆生

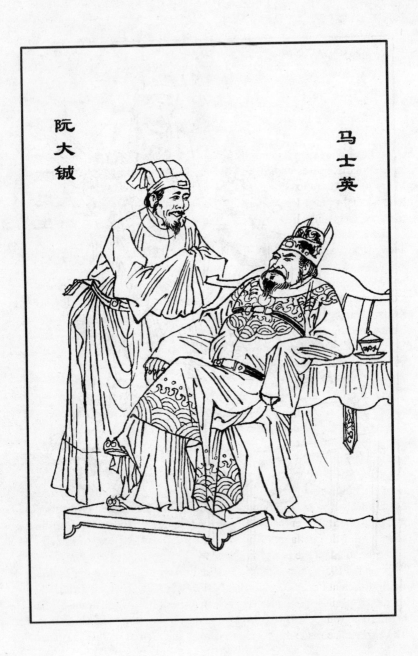

阮大铖　　　　　　　　　　　马士英

FOREWORD

Love is an eternal theme. Since ancient times the arts the world over have sung its praises and love stories make up a vast body of literature. Many of them are excellent, portraying spirited and worthy characters, lofty ideals, and the love shared by men and women. They allow readers to renew their souls, lift their spirits and appreciate the meaning and value of life. Readers are inspired to lead a more fulfiling life. At the same time a love story must be influenced by the author's life and environment, his economic circumstances, the existing political and social system, his philosophical and cultural background and moral concepts. Reading love stories acquaints readers with such external factors and helps them to realize their significance, thus promoting changes in society and progress. Hence reading and reviewing good love stories is most important.

Ms. Zhou Kuijie and Ms. Zhang Minjie of the New World Press have asked me to adapt the traditional love dramas *The Peony Pavilion*, *The Palace of Eternal Youth* and *The Peach Blossom Fan*, whose English-Chinese editions are to be published. In the 1980s, Ms. Zhou Kuijie, who worked for the Foreign Languages Press, caught sight of my book *The Collection of Zaju Stories of the Yuan Dynasty* (*zaju* is a poetic drama set to music, a form that flourished in the Yuan Dynasty) written under my pen name. She liked it and thought that it should be introduced to readers overseas. She contacted me through Mr. Wang Yuanhong of the Jiangsu People's Publishing House. Thanks to the efforts of Ms. Zhou Kuijie, Mr. Chen Yousheng and Ms. Yang Chunyan, the English edition of this book was published at the end of 1997, and the French edition will be published soon. After this collaboration, though I was busy, I was determined to find time to adapt the books for New World Press.

In the 1950s when I taught ancient literature at a university I started writing ancient Chinese dramas as stories. With few teaching materials, I found it especially difficult to lecture on ancient stories and dramas. I had to briefly introduce each drama to students who knew nothing about them. The experience made me decide to rewrite the dramas as short stories or medium-length stories for my students. In the early 1980s Mr. Wang Yuanhong thought these stories should be published. The collections, *zaju* stories of the Yuan (1279-1368), Ming (1368-1644) and Qing (1644-1911) were published in 1983, 1987 and 1988, a total of 700,000 words. In the summer of 1995, Mr. Liu Yongjian, deputy editor-in-chief of the Jiangsu People's Publishing House suggested to Mr. Wang Yuanhong that the legends that I had put aside be published. After several discussions with the publishing house, *The Collection of the Chinese Opera Stories* which included some stories based on *zaju, The Story of the Lute, The Peony Pavilion, The Palace of Eternal Youth,* and *The Peach Blossom Fan* was published.

When I write a story from an ancient drama I stick to the original plot and themes. The story is a different form of expression but I abide by the artistic rules and follow designated aesthetic standards. Re-writing dramas as stories is a creative process although it may appear simple.

The original versions that I adapted from the dramas *The Peony Pavilion, The Palace of Eternal Youth* and *The Peach Blossom Fan* range from 30,000 to 50,000 words. However, the New World Press asked that each story be about 80,000 words, and include several chapters, each with a subtitle. After careful consideration I decided to rewrite the stories from the original drama rather than extend the adapted versions. I chose this method because the extra length meant that I had to reconsider the form of the stories, re-evaluate their plots and roles. I am not sure if this new version is satisfactory and sincerely welcome comments or suggestions from readers.

Written on August 9, 1998
at the foot of the Qingliang Mountain
by the Stone City

序

爱情是文学艺术的永恒主题，在古今中外的文艺创作中歌颂爱情的作品如恒河沙数，其中为人称道的优秀之作，大都能通过对爱情的描写，肯定和赞扬人的美好心灵和高尚品德。读者在阅读这些作品时，常能经受一次灵魂的洗礼和精神的升华，认识到生命的价值和人生的真谛，从而萌发对美好生活的憧憬和追求。同时，由于作者所描写的爱情故事，离不开他们所生活的时代和生存的环境，因而必然受着一定的经济基础、政治状况、社会制度、哲学思潮、文化背景以及道德观念等等因素有形无形的制约，读者在阅读这些作品时，还可以明白造成男女爱情悲欢离合的外部因素，认识到这些外部因素的实质，从而促进社会的变革和人类的进步。因此正确地阅读、评述优秀的爱情之作，也是一项极有意义之举。

新世界出版社周奎杰、张民捷先生约我为他们改写爱情剧《牡丹亭》、《长生殿》和《桃花扇》，出版英汉对照本。早在八十年代，当时在外文出版社工作的周奎杰先生，见到笔者用笔名出版的《元杂剧故事集》一书，认为可以介绍到海外，便通过江苏人民出版社王远鸿先生与笔者联系，在周奎杰以及陈有昇、杨春燕等先生努力下，此书英文版已于 1997 年年底出版，法文版不日亦将出版。有此渊源，尽管手边任务甚繁，也排除万难，接受新世界出版社的约稿。

笔者尝试改写工作，起初完全是出自工作需要。五十年代在高校讲授古代文学，并无现成教材可资凭借，需要自编自讲。尤其是讲授古代小说、戏曲时，很多作品不易寻觅，学生无法知其内容，教师便无法进行评述，只能在评述之前先介绍作品的故事情节。为此，当年曾将古代戏曲的名作，效法《莎氏乐府本事》，写成一类似短篇、中篇的小说，以应付教学之需。八十年代初期，王远鸿先生认为此可发表，便先后于1983年、1987年、1988年分别出版了元、明、清三本杂剧故事集，总计七十万字。1995年夏，王远鸿先生告知该社副总编刘勇坚先生认为当年延搁的传奇部分也可出版。几经磋商，先行将部分杂剧以及《琵琶记》、《牡丹亭》、《长生殿》、《桃花扇》四部传奇合为一集《中国戏曲故事选》先行出版。

将戏曲改写成小说，虽然题材不变，故事情节相同，但体裁不同，表现手段各异，改写者必须遵循不同体裁的艺术规则和特定的审美要求从事。尽管如此，这其实是一项看似容易却实不易为的工作，因此有识之士认为这样的改写其实也是一种"创作"。

笔者对《牡丹亭》、《长生殿》、《桃花扇》三剧原有改写本，分别为三、五万字不等。此次新世界出版社约稿，要求每本在八万字左右，同时要考虑海外读者阅读习惯，需分章立节、出小标题。为此，笔者斟酌再三，只能放弃在原改写本上增加篇幅的打算，而是按照原剧重新改写。因为篇幅的增加并不意味着简单地增加一些文字，这牵涉到全书的结构布局、故事情节的演变、人物性格的发展，甚至人物活动的场所与时序的变化等等，都需重新做全盘的考虑与安排。因此，这次改写工作不是对原改写本的简单增删，而是对原剧的重新改写。当然，改写得是否尽如人意，笔者亦不敢自信，敬希广大读者有以指正。

1998年8月9日，时届立秋，而暑热未退，
于石头城畔清凉山麓挥汗为序

ABOUT THE ORIGINAL PLAY
The Peach Blossom Fan

Kong Shangren (style name of Pinzhi), the author of *The Peach Blossom Fan*, was born in Qufu, Shandong Province, in 1648. He died in 1718.

A grandson of Confucius (64 times removed), Kong Shangren came from a landowning and intellectual family. In 1667 he passed the county examination to earn the title of *xiucai**. and enrolled in the Imperial Academy in 1681. During an inspection tour of south China, Emperor Xuan Ye of the Qing Dynasty traveled to Qufu to make sacrifices to Confucius, the Great Master. Kong Shangren was chosen to give a lecture on Confucianism to the emperor and was appraised. The following year he went to the capital and became a master of the Imperial Academy.

In 1686 Kong Shangren took part in a conservancy project at the mouth of the Yangtze River and he spent three years in Yangzhou where he met many adherents of the former Ming Dynasty, survivors of the great upheaval during dynastic change. Through activities such as ascending the Meihua Mountain and visiting the grave containing the dress of Shi Kefa, Kong Shangren gathered raw material for his drama *The Peach Blossom Fan*. He also went to Nanjing where he visited the Ming imperial palace, the Emperor Xiaozong's Mausoleum of the Ming Dynasty, Qinhuai River, Sanshan Street, etc. He made a special trip to the Baiyun Temple on Qixia Mountain, where he met Zhang Yi, a Taoist priest, who was formerly a commanding officer during the Ming Dynasty.

Kong Shangren started to write *The Peach Blossom Fan* before he became an official. He continued writing when he was in Yangzhou and Zhaoyang (now Xinghua, Jiangsu Province). It took him over ten years to complete the famous romance. Having revised it three times, he finished

---

*Xiucai means one who passed the imperial examination at county level in the Ming and Qing dynasties.

it in June 1699.

After its publication, Kong Shangren assumed office as a vice-director of the Ministry of Revenue in March 1700, but was dismissed from office soon after. No reason was recorded for the dismissal. In the winter of 1702 he returned home from Beijing. He toured Shanxi, Hubei and Huaiyang, and then returned to Qufu, where he died at his home.

Kong Shangren also wrote many poems and prose works. But only *The Peach Blossom Fan* won him great renown and was his greatest work.

The play, ostensibly a love story, outlines the history of the downfall of Emperor Zhu Yousong of the Ming Dynasty in south China. The principal characters are Hou Chaozong and Li Xiangjun. Hou was a man of letters and Li an educated and famous prostitute. The separation and reunion of the lovers allowed the author to dwell on emotions associated with the rise and fall of a dynasty. The drama is set in the period 1643 to 1645.

In 1643 Li Zicheng, a leader of a peasant uprisings, invaded and took Beijing resulting in the suicide of Emperor Chongzhen of the Ming Dynasty on the Coal Hill, now Jingshan Park. In 1645 Emperor Shunzhi of the Qing Dynasty issued an invitation soliciting opinions from hermits and adherents of former regime. The play realistically reflects the complex contradictions of this historic period, giving reasons for the downfall of the empire and it serves as a lesson in history. This is what the author means when he says: "It not only affects the audience with deep emotions. It also makes them profit from the salvation of the state."

The play specifically describes Emperor Zhu Yousong indulging in wine and women and ignoring the business of state. Corrupt officials seize power forcing honest officials and loyal state servants out of office.

The officials who hold sway, welcome the emperor to the throne and, thinking that they have earned great merit, throw many into prison. They resent critics and repress people with differing views. This leads to the collapse of the empire. The author's grasp of the circumstances gave him the ability to reveal as much as possible of the true situation.

Kong Shangren lived in the Qing Dynasty, which replaced the Ming. He was born into a landlord family. He would not have had a comprehensive or objective view of history, nor would he have been able to give a full account of the reasons for the collapse of the Ming or sum up its fall.

Kong Shangren said that the fall of Ming was due to vagrants and bandits. This view owes much to the attitudes at the time and his class background. The author had formed an opinion of the Qing Dynasty but he could hardly give it openly. He could, at best, imply.

Yet the social outcasts in the drama, such as Liu Jingting, Su Kunsheng and Li Xiangjun were portrayed positively, as people with integrity and a concern for the safety of the state; they showed courage in the struggle against corrupt officials and gave support to a just cause; they knew the difference between right and wrong. All this demonstrates the author's progressive thinking.

When *The Peach Blossom Fan* appeared in print in Beijing, it had a great impact on society. It was read by princes and wealthy merchants alike. Many copied the drama resulting in a huge increase in the price of paper. It was reported that when Emperor Kang Xi of the Qing Dynasty read the extracts on the court hearing and choosing beauties, he stamped his feet, frowned and said that although Emperor Zhu Yousong did not want to perish, he could not escape his fate. *The Peach Blossom Fan* had great impact on readers.

As an artistic achievement, *The Peach Blossom Fan* is universally proclaimed for its values, and its wholesome and orderly composition. The verses are fluent and the dialogue polished, which gives life to the characters. The play's plot deserves attention. It does not have a traditionally happy ending. The romance is a unique piece of writing with a unique place in the history of Chinese drama. That is why Kong Shangren's reputation is similar to that of Hong Sheng, the author of *The Palace of Eternal Youth*.

Hong Sheng is regarded as the best playwright in south China while Kong Shangren is regarded as the best in the north.

原作简介

《桃花扇》为孔尚任所作。

孔尚任，字聘之，山东曲阜人，生于清顺治五年（1648），卒于康熙五十七年（1718）。

孔尚任出身于诗礼之家，为孔子第六十四代孙。早年用心举业，大约在康熙六年（1667）左右考取秀才，康熙二十年（1681）为国子监生。康熙二十三年（1684），玄烨南巡，返经曲阜祭孔，孔尚任被推为玄烨讲经并得到赏识，次年入京为国子监博士。

康熙二十五年（1686）曾赴扬州参加疏浚长江海口工程，得以接触社会现实。在扬州三年，结识不少明代遗民，还登梅花岭，凭吊史可法衣冠冢；并曾去南京，凭吊明故宫、明孝陵，游览秦淮河、三山街，又特地去栖霞山白云庵拜会了曾任南明锦衣千户的道士张怡，这些活动，为他创作《桃花扇》提供了丰富的资料。

《桃花扇》传奇的创作，开始于作者尚未出仕之前，此后又在淮扬、昭阳（江苏兴化）等地继续撰写，大约历经十余年，三易其稿，终于在康熙三十八年（1699）六月完成。

《桃花扇》面世不久，即康熙三十九年（1700）三月，孔尚任升任户部员外郎，但旋即罢官。何以获罪，现存资料无明确记载。康熙四十一年（1702）冬，他从北京回到家乡。先后又出游山西、湖北、淮扬等地，后返故乡山东曲阜，卒于家。

孔尚任一生创作了不少诗文，有《石门山》、《出山异数记》、《湖海集》、《享金簿》、《岸堂文集》等，但使他久享盛名的却是传奇《桃花扇》。

中国明朝末年政治腐败，人民处于水深火热之灾难中，李自成、张献忠等农民起义军群起反抗明王朝。崇祯皇帝在农民起义军攻陷京城时于煤山自缢。江南一带明王朝官僚们为了自身利益，拥戴福王称帝，这就是南明弘光朝。弘光朝成立之际，北方满族入关，攻陷北京，赶走农民起义军，整个北中国由清王朝所取代。造成"北兵"（清军）、"流寇"（农民军）、南明官兵三支政治军事力量的争斗局面。

《桃花扇》一剧通过复社文人侯朝宗与秦淮名妓李香君的爱情故事，反映了南明弘光朝覆亡的历史，所谓"借离合之情，写兴亡之感"。此剧根据的史实大约从明朝崇祯十六年（1643）起，到清朝顺治二年（1645）止，以李自成起义攻下北京、崇祯皇帝自缢煤山始，以清朝顺治皇帝征求山林隐逸结，比较真实地反映了这一历史时期的各种复杂矛盾，意图揭示弘光王朝覆亡的原因，使广大读者明白弘光朝覆亡的历史教训，即所谓"不独令观者感慨涕零，亦可惩创人心，为末世之一救矣"。

从剧作中的具体描写来看，作者显然认为弘光皇帝在民族危机极其严重的关头，不理政事，沉湎酒色，而权奸小人，又以迎立之功，把持朝政，排斥忠良，大兴党狱，挟嫌报复，是南明覆亡的原因。这样的认识在一定程度上也反映了当时的社会现实。

当然，孔尚任毕竟生活在取代明王朝的清王朝社会中，又出身于地主世家，当然还不能全面地、客观地总结南明王朝覆亡的本质原因，甚至认为"明朝之亡，亡于流寇也"（《总批》），这正是时代和阶级所限。但剧本最后两出，对清朝统治者似颇有微辞，这表明作者心有依违，颇有难言之隐。

至于剧中出现的一些下层人物，如柳敬亭、苏昆生、李香君等，作者均是将他们作为正面形象来表现的，肯定和赞扬了他们关心国家安危、敢于与权奸斗争、勇于支持正义，是非分明、临危不惧的品格，又充分显示了作者进步的思想观念。

《桃花扇》一面世，就产生了极大的社会反响，首先在北京流传，"王公荐绅，莫不借抄，时有纸贵之誉"。据说康熙索取此剧观看，当看至[设朝]、[选优]等出时，皱眉顿足地说："弘光弘光，虽欲不亡，其可得乎！"，可见其影响之大。

至于《桃花扇》的艺术成就，也为世人所称道，艺术结构极其严谨、完整；曲词流畅，宾白典雅，使得人物性格十分鲜明，这些成就都是极其显著的。它的结构尤其值得注意，一改大团圆的安排，突破了传统模式。凡此，都使得这部传奇成为中国戏剧史上不可多得的佳构，使得作者在当时就获得与《长生殿》作者洪昇同样的名声，一时有"南洪北孔"之称。

Contents
目次

CHAPTER ONE

Hou Stays in Nanjing

"Nanjing in southeast China is a land of beauty, and the capital of many dynasties." Because of its strategic importance, Nanjing served as the capital for eight dynasties in Chinese history. They included the State of Wu during the Three Kingdoms Period (220-280), the Eastern Jin (317-420), Song (420-479), Qi (479-502), Liang (502-557), Chen (557-589), later Tang (923-936) and Ming (1368-1644) dynasties. Of them only the Ming Dynasty re-unified the country and turned Nanjing into a national political center under the leadership of Zhu Yuanzhang, the first emperor of the Ming. Nanjing became a magnificent city after more than two decades of renewal. Later Emperor Zhu Di of the Ming made Beijing the capital, but Nanjing still preserved the central organizations — the Six Boards (the Boards of Personnel, Revenue, Rites, War, Justice and Works). It was an important southeastern Chinese city, prosperous, commercially active, and with arts and handicrafts as good as those in Beijing. Nanjing was also first in the country in terms of learning, talent and civilized living. It attracted many Chinese and foreign scholars and was the place where the provincial examination was held once every three years. Scholars from east China gathered there during the examination period.

In the imperial examination of the 14th year of the Chongzhen reign (1641) some lucky scholars passed and many failed. Among those who failed was a young man called Hou Fangyu (styled Chaozong), a native of Shangqiu in Henan Province. He was a descendant of Hou Ying, a distinguished person of the Warring States Period (475-221 B.C.). His grandfather Hou Zhipu once served as chief minister of the Court of Imperial Sacrifices; his father Hou Xun was imperial secretary of the Board of Revenue and later joined the Donglin Party.

In the later Ming Dynasty a group of eminent scholars in southeastern China renovated the Donglin Academy in Wuxi, Jiangsu Province, which was originally founded by Yang Shi, a philosopher of the

第一章
流寓南京

"江南佳丽地,金陵帝王州"。然而历代建都南京的政权,大都是半壁江山,东吴、东晋,南朝的宋、齐、梁、陈所谓六朝自不必说,其后的南唐,也是残局一副。惟有明太祖朱元璋南征北战,推翻元王朝,建立明王朝之日,定鼎金陵,南京方成为全国的政治中心。经过二十余年的修缮,建成一座宏伟壮观的城垣。明成祖朱棣迁都北京后,南京虽然不是朝廷所在,但中央机构六部*同样设置。当时,南京已发展为东南地区的大都市,城市之繁荣,商业之兴盛,手工业之发达,丝毫不亚于京师北京。至于学术的发展,文明的昌盛,人才的众多,更是居于全国之先列,各方士人乃至海外学者来游南京者不知几多人数。尤其是南京为江南贡院**所在,三年一科的乡试就在此处举行,大江南北、上江下江来应试的文士更是济济有众。

且说崇祯十四年(1641年)开考之后,有考取的幸运儿,也有落第的失败者。在名落孙山的士人中有一才子侯方域,河南商丘人,字朝宗,出自名门贵胄,为战国时名人侯嬴的后裔。祖父侯执蒲,官至太常寺卿。父亲侯恂,官至户部尚书。侯恂曾为东林党人。

明代后期,江南一带有正义感的文人,修复了宋朝理学家杨时在江苏无锡的东林书院,于其中讲学、评议时政,抨击以魏忠贤

---

*中央机构六部:从隋唐开始,中国封建王朝的中央行政机构一般分为吏部、户部、礼部、兵部、刑部、工部,统称六部。

**贡院:科举时代举行乡试或会试的场所。

Song Dynasty (960-1179). They gave lectures in the academy and not only spoke candidly about current affairs, but criticized contemporary leaders as well. They denounced the exploitation and brutal rule of the eunuch group headed by Wei Zhongxian and advocated protection of the interests of landlords, industrialists and merchants in southeast China. They were called "Men of the Donglin Party".

Later many societies carried on the party's traditions and showed the same spirit. The most famous of them was the Restoration Society. Hou Chaozong was a member of the Restoration Society. In his early years he was well known for his literary gatherings and he considered his prose poems as good as those of Ban Gu (A.D. 32-92), a famous historian and writer of the Eastern Han Dynasty, and Song Yu, a famous prose poet of the Warring States Period. His articles were as good as those of Han Yu (768-824) and Su Shi (1037-1101), two great writers in Chinese history. However, to his great surprise, he failed in the provincial examination and was most disappointed.

Instead of returning home, Hou Chaozong rented a house near the Mochou (Not-to Worry) Lake in the west of Nanjing and stayed in the city. Mochou Lake is a famous scenic spot in Nanjing and a place where men of letters often gathered. Legend has it that during the Southern Song Dynasty (1127-1279) a girl, Mochou, from Luoyang in Henan Province, was married to a rich and powerful man in Nanjing whose surname was Lu and whose home was by a lake. Soon after the wedding, her husband went to fight in a war. Though lonely and distressed, she was kind and warm and always ready to help those in difficulty. To show their love and respect for this woman, people later named the lake after her. Hou Chaozong often invited friends to drink wine and compose poems in his house where they could enjoy the beautiful scenery through the window.

In February 1643, the 16th year of the Chongzhen reign, Hou Chaozong stayed at his house. He had been going to bed early and getting up late; he was bored. There was a war in north China which stopped him receiving letters from home. Worry contended with boredom and he had not realized that the rainy season had arrived. Standing by the window looking at the lake in the rain, he sighed deeply and said, "I must not worry, I must not worry. I can't help worrying!"

Fortunately he had close friends living nearby. Chen Zhenhui (styled Dingsheng), a native of Yixing, Jiangsu Province, and Wu Yingji (styled Ciwei), a native of Guichi in Anhui Province, lived in the famous Cai

为首的宦官集团（即所谓的阉党）对江南人民的残酷剥削和暴虐统治，主张保护东南地区兼营工商业的地主的利益。这些士大夫就被称之为东林党人。

稍后于东林党的社团甚多，其中佼佼者有复社、几社等。他们继承了东林党的传统，具有类似东林党人的气骨。侯朝宗就是复社成员之一，早年曾在江苏南京一带以文会友，颇著声名。他自诩辞赋近似班固、宋玉，文章不亚韩愈、苏轼，自视甚高。岂料三年一科的江南乡试，他却未能顺利通过。自然出乎意外，未免懊丧万分。

侯朝宗落第以后，并未返回故乡，仍然留居南京，寄寓在城西莫愁湖附近。相传南宋时有河南洛阳少女莫愁远嫁于江东富豪卢家，曾在此湖之滨居住，因而湖名莫愁。湖面宽阔，周长十余里。沿湖有楼、厅、阁、亭，林木葱葱，绿荫幽幽。明太祖朱元璋曾与中山王徐达在湖中对奕，胜棋楼就是朱元璋赐给徐达的。莫愁湖附近还有东晋著名诗人孙楚故居即孙楚楼，唐代大诗人李白曾与友人于此痛饮。这一带自来就是南京的名胜区域，是文人聚会游览的处所。青年才子侯朝宗寄寓于此，正可也三五文友诗酒唱和，流连江南风光。

崇祯十六年（1643 年）二月，正是春寒料峭的时候，侯朝宗蛰居在一室之中，每日早睡迟起，客愁乡梦，扰人神思，加之北方战乱，烽火未靖，家信难通，倍增忧虑。不知不觉又到仲春季节，连城晓雨。每每独立窗前，面对湖天，长吁短叹："莫愁，莫愁，叫俺如何不愁！"

幸亏他在南京还有不少复社文友，如江苏宜兴人陈贞慧，字定生；安徽贵池人吴应箕，字次尾。他们此际也寄寓在南京三山街著名的蔡益所书坊中，离他的住所不远。他们三人时常住来，倒破

5

Yisuo Study in the Sanshan Street, not far from Mochou Lake. They were all members of the Restoration Society and frequently visited one another. One day they decided to go to the Mount Yeshan Taoist Temple near Mochou Lake to view the plum blossoms. Hou Chaozong rose early in the morning, got things ready and waited for his friends.

On the way to his house Chen Dingsheng asked, "Brother Ciwei, what do you know about the activities of the 'rebellious troops' these days?"

Wu Ciwei sighed heavily and said, "I read some articles in a newspaper yesterday. They have gradually moved on Beijing. The troops under Marquis Zuo Liangyu, who fought against Li Zicheng and Zhang Xianzhong (the leaders of the peasant uprisings of the Ming Dynasty), have retreated to Xiangyang. No troops in central China can resist them."

When they came to Chaozong's house, Wu Ciwei said that they should forget about the war and enjoy the beautiful spring scenery. Chaozong came out to greet them. "Please come in. My brothers have arrived really early today."

"We dare not be late when you invite us!" Wu Ciwei replied.

Chen Dingsheng said that he had sent a servant boy to prepare the temple and the wine.

CHAPTER TWO

Visit to a Storyteller

After they set out they ran into the servant who said, "Master, you're too late. You may as well return home."

"Are we late?" Chen Dingsheng didn't understand.

"Master Xu, the duke of the State of Wei, chartered the temple for his guests to view the plum blossoms."

Chen Dingsheng flew into rage and Hou Chaozong suggested that they went to the brothels by the Qinhuai River instead. "It will be fun to

除不少寂寞之感。今日三人约好前往莫愁湖附近的冶山道院去赏梅。侯朝宗便早早起床,梳洗已罢,专候陈定生、吴次尾到来。

陈定生与吴次尾相约而来,一路闲步,边走边谈。定生先问道:"次尾兄,可知'流寇'近日动静?"

吴次尾长叹一声,答道:"小弟昨日看了邸报,'流寇'连败官兵,渐逼京师。与李自成、张献忠屡屡作战的宁南侯左良玉,也全军退守襄阳。中原已无抵抗之人,朝廷大事也不可问了。我辈书生,又有何用?"说罢,彼此叹息不已。

不觉已走近朝宗寓所,吴次尾转换一个话题:"不说这些了,我们还是流连春光吧。"说着,两人进了侯寓。朝宗迎了出来:"请了。两位社兄,果然早到。"

吴次尾连声说道:"承兄台相邀,岂敢爽约!"

陈定生接着说:"小弟已使人去道院打扫,沽酒相待。"

第二章
访柳听书

侯朝宗与陈定生、吴次尾三人一同出了门。走不多远,迎头撞上去道院打扫的家僮,未等主人询问,家僮先行说道:"禀报相公,来迟了。诸位请回罢。"

陈定生未免诧异:"怎么来迟了?"

家僮回道:"魏国公府上徐公子邀请客人赏花,一座大大的道院,全被徐府包了。"

听见如此,陈定生不禁有些恼怒。侯朝宗见状,连忙转圜:"既是这样,不如去秦淮水榭,一访金陵佳丽,倒也有趣。"

chat with beautiful girls of Nanjing."

Wu Ciwei, who didn't want to go to the brothels, said, "It's a long way to the bank of the Qinhuai River, Brother Hou. Have you heard about Liu Jingting from Taizhou? He is a wonderful storyteller. Even the former high-ranking officials, such as Ma Jingwen and He Ruchong, thought highly of him. He lives near here. His stories would be a great diversion."

"That sounds good," said Chen Dingsheng.

Hou Chaozong became very angry. "Liu Jingting is a hanger-on of Ruan Dacheng, an adopted son of an eunuch. We should not listen to such a person."

Hou Chaozong did not actually know Liu Jingting. Wu Ciwei said, "Brother Hou, you are not familiar with Ruan Dacheng, an evil man who refuses to step down from public view. He has recruited female entertainers in Nanjing to ingratiate himself with gentry and officials and I have written an article that exposes his crimes. Before I wrote it Ruan's hanger-ons did not know that he belonged to the eunuch clique headed by Wei Zhongxian and Cui Chengxiu. Soon after they all left, one after another. One of them was Liu Jingting. I think we should take that into account when we judge his character and morals."

Hou Chaozong was very surprised and said ruefully, "I didn't know there was such a hero among the hangers-on. We should pay him a visit." The three young men walked towards Liu's home, and stood before it as the servant boy stepped forward to knock on the door, "Is Liu Jingting home?"

"He is a famous person. You should call him Master Liu," Chen Dingsheng said.

The boy called, "Please open the door, Master Liu."

Liu Jingting, a white-bearded man wearing a hat and a dark blue robe with wide sleeves, came to the door. "Hello, it's Master Chen and Master Wu. It was remiss of me not to come out to greet you." He turned towards Hou Chaozong and asked, "Who is this young man?"

"This is my friend Mr. Hou Chaozong, a distinguished scholar from Henan," Dingsheng said. "He knows of your illustrious name and we have come to listen to your story telling."

Liu invited them in to sit down and drink tea. "You are very familiar with *Records of the Historian* and *History of China*. Why do you come here to listen to my folk stories?"

Hou Chaozong, who had never heard his stories, urged him not to

吴次尾并不高兴去秦楼楚馆,说道:"依我说,不必大老远赶到秦淮河畔去。侯兄,你可知道泰州柳敬亭,说书最妙。连范大司马景文、何老相国如宠二公,都十分赏识。他的寓所就在附近,何不同往去听他说书,借此排遣春愁?"陈定生随即同意:"这样也好。"

侯朝宗却闻言大怒:"那柳敬亭新近做了太监的干儿子阮大铖的门客。这样的人品说书,不听也罢了!"

吴次尾知道侯朝宗并不了解柳敬亭的为人,向他解释道:"侯兄,你还不知道,阮大铖漏网馀孽,不肯退藏,依然在南京城里蓄养声妓,以此结纳官绅。小弟特地写了一篇文章,就是《留都防乱揭帖》,公开暴露阮大铖的罪行。他的那班门客才知道阮大铖原来与阉党魏忠贤、崔呈秀是一路货色,不等曲终,个个拂袖而去。这柳敬亭也是散去的门客之一。他的人品,难道不令人钦敬!"

侯朝宗这才明白自己错怪了柳敬亭,在惊异之中也夹杂着些许歉疚,说道:"啊呀!小弟竟然不知道此辈中有这样的豪杰,该去拜访的,该去拜访的。"于是,三人一同向柳寓走去。行不多时便到了柳寓,家僮上前一步,拍门叫道:"柳敬亭在家么?"

陈定生喝住家僮:"他是江湖名士,称他柳相公才是。"

家僮方才改口继续呼叫:"柳相公开门。"

柳敬亭戴了一顶便帽,身着一袭深蓝色的宽袖长袍,一绺白须,出来开门迎客:"唉呀,原来是陈、吴二位相公,老汉失迎了。"又对着侯朝宗问道:"此位何人?"

陈定生代为介绍:"这是敝友河南侯朝宗,当今名士。他久慕你的说书本领,特来领教。"

"不敢,不敢!请坐献茶。"柳敬亭说:"诸位相公都是读书君子,什么《史记》、《通鉴》,哪一位不是烂熟于胸,倒要来听老汉的俗谈?"

侯朝宗未曾听过,先开口请求:"不必过谦,就求赐教。"

be modest and to allow them to hear them.

Liu Jingting knew that it would be hard to turn them down and said, "Thank you for coming. I dare not decline. I expect that you are not interested in historical stories and folk tales. Let me tell you a section from *The Analects of Confucius*, something that you would be familiar with."

This surprised Hou Chaozong who said, "That is strange. How can you tell a story about *The Analects of Confucius*?"

"If you can read it, why can't I tell it?" Liu Jingting replied with a smile. "Today I will act as a cultured person and tell the story." He went to his special seat, stroked his wooden clapper on the table and began. "Today I would like to relate to you how the three Sun brothers cheated the king of Lu State and to speak of the great deeds of Confucius...." The three young scholars found the story interesting, vivid and easily understood.

"Bang!" At the sound of his wooden clapper, Liu Jingting stood up and made a bow by cupping his hands on his chest. He said, "I have made a fool of myself!"

"Wonderful! Wonderful!" Chen Dingsheng cried. "You explained ancient Chinese history so well. It's a unique skill indeed."

Wu Ciwei interrupted to say, "Brother Liu did not try to find refuge with anybody after he left Ruan Dacheng. Now he tries to advise others by using his own experience as an example."

After hearing Liu Jingting, Hou Chaozong felt that he knew him better. He could not resist saying, that he was a moral and liberal person who shared their views. Storytelling was just one of his skills.

The three young scholars voiced their approval and Jingting said modestly, "You are welcome to come again."

Hou Chaozong asked Liu about the others who left Ruan Dacheng when he did.

"They have all left Nanjing," Liu replied. " Only Su Kunsheng lives nearby. He is good at singing *kunqu*. I heard he is teaching the adopted daughter of Li Zhenli, a famous prostitute, to sing *kunqu*." (Melodies that originated in Kunshan, Jiangsu Province, in the Ming Dynasty.)

Chaozong said, "We'll see him too. I hope he and Brother Liu will come to visit us."

"I'll pay you a visit," Liu Jingting promised. Then he bowed and saw them off.

　　柳敬亭知道这是推辞不得的，也就爽快答允："既蒙光降，老汉也不敢推辞。只怕通常俺说的演义小说、民间传说，难入尊耳。这样罢，俺把相公们熟悉的《论语》说一章！"侯朝宗十分惊讶，闻所未闻，问道："这也奇了，《论语》如何能编成说书？"

　　柳敬亭倒也不气馁，微笑着说："相公读得，老汉就说不得？今日偏要假斯文一番，说它一回。"说罢，他也不再谦让，上位坐定，把醒木一拍，滔滔不绝地说道："今日所说不是别的，是申说春秋时鲁国仲孙、季孙、叔孙三家欺君之罪，表彰孔圣人正乐之功……"三人听了下去，原来柳敬亭倒真有些手段，将《论语》"微子"一篇敷衍成故事，把殷商末年仁人微子离暴虐的纣王而去的故事说得有板有眼，绘声绘影，倒也通俗易懂。"啪"的一声，随着醒木响后，柳敬亭立起身来，向三位拱手道："献丑，献丑！"

　　陈定生赞不绝口地说道："妙极，妙极。那般八股讲义，哪能说得如此痛快！真是绝技！"

　　吴次尾联系这一故事说道："敬亭才离开阮大铖家，不肯别投主人，故此现身说法。"

　　侯朝宗听了他的说书，对他的人品有了更进一步的认识，不禁赞道："俺看敬亭人品高绝，胸襟洒脱，是我辈中人，说书只不过是他的末技耳。"

　　三人你一句我一句地赞不绝口。柳敬亭则不住口的逊让，一再表示："欢迎再来。"

　　侯朝宗又问他："昨日与柳兄一同离开阮大铖家的，是哪几位？"

　　"都已散去了，只有擅长昆腔的苏昆生，就住在附近不远。听说他在一家妓院教唱昆曲。"

　　侯朝宗表示："我们也要去拜访他，尚望柳兄与他同来赐教。"

　　柳敬亭应允道："自然是要奉访的。"送三人出了门，拱手而别。

CHAPTER THREE

Li's Adopted Daughter

On the bank of Qinhuai River, close to the Temple of Confucius, there is a brothel run by the famous prostitute Li Zhenli. Its front gate faced the Wuding Bridge and its back door Chaoku Street. The Examination Office was across the Qinhuai River so that men of letters often came to the brothel. Li Zhenli, a natural beauty, was good at entertaining her clients. Handsome scholars attracted by her beauty had often visited her. However, though still good looking, she was getting older; she was a middle-aged woman. She had adopted a graceful and charming girl who attracted many men but had not begun to accept clients. Of her admirers Yang Longyou adored her most.

Yang Longyou, a native of Guiyang in Guizhou Province, was once a successful candidate in the imperial examinations at provincial level; he later became a county magistrate. He was a brother-in-law of Governor Ma Shiying of Fengyang and was on friendly terms with Ruan Dacheng. After he resigned his post, he frequently visited brothels in Nanjing and had an affair with Li Zhenli. Having once caught sight of Li's adopted daughter he was determined to introduce her to a good man. On a spring day when plum blossoms withered and willow tree leaves turned green he headed for Li Zhenli's home.

As it was warm and fine, Li Zhenli had allowed the maids to roll up the curtains and clean the sitting-room. She was expecting Yang Longyou and soon he pushed the door open to walk in. Li Zhenli greeted him warmly. They exchanged words and she invited him upstairs where she hospitably burned joss sticks, served tea and invited him to view the inscriptions that celebrities had made on the four walls. However Yang Longyou, who was more interested in her daughter, asked where she was.

"She is making up in her room." Li Zhenli called out, "Daughter, Lord Yang is here."

The daughter hurriedly applied lipstick and rouge; her hair was done

第三章
命名香君

　　秦淮名妓李贞丽接客的青楼，坐落在夫子庙附近，前面对着武定桥，后门开在钞库街，与贡院隔着一条秦淮河。一些文人墨客经常是出了贡院就来到妓院。李贞丽自幼生长在此，擅于迎送，再加上天生丽质，更成为风月场上的名妓。在她梳妆楼中出入的文人墨客，颇多一时俊彦。然而岁月催人，尽管未谢铅华，风韵犹存，毕竟青春易逝，她不能不为后半生衣食着想。于是，收养了一个义女。这个义女一副温柔纤小的身段，宛转娇羞的神态，尽管尚未接客，却已令人倾倒，其中最数杨龙友对她赏识不已。

　　杨龙友名文聪，贵州贵阳人，以举人出身做到县令，是凤阳督抚马士英的妹夫，又与阮大铖交好。此时罢职闲居，便频频出入秦楼楚馆，尤其与李贞丽有染。见到贞丽义女，一心想为她第一次接客找个可意人儿。此日春光明媚，梅花已落，柳叶放黄。闲来无事，他又去李贞丽处闲话。

　　李贞丽见今日春阳醉人，也想到杨龙友会来闲耍，吩咐丫环卷起窗帘，打扫客厅，以便迎客。说话之间，杨龙友已是推门而入。李贞丽一见，随即热情地迎上前去，寒暄了几句，就邀他登楼，焚香煮茗，盛情招待，并请他赏鉴四壁上悬挂的名家题诗。哪知杨龙友却一心扑在贞丽义女身上，开口竟问："这是令嫒的妆楼，她却往哪里去了？"

　　"正在梳妆，尚未出卧房哩。"李贞丽随即高呼："孩儿出来，杨老爷在此。"

in a fashionable coil and she changed into new clothes and walked out of her room taking quick short steps.

With a cup of tea in his hand Yang Longyou viewed the poems and paintings on the walls. Seeing the inscriptions by Zhang Pu and Xia Yunyi, two famous scholars, Yang Longyou wanted to write a poem himself. He started composing one and heard a sweet voice saying, "Lord Yang, all blessings." He turned round and found a beautiful girl standing by him. He stared at her and said, "I only saw you a few days ago and now you are even more pretty. All these poems describe your beauty. Let me write one myself."

Li Zhenli brought a brush, an inkstone and a piece of paper. With a brush in hand, Yang Longyou was lost in thought. Finally he put the brush down and said, "My poem cannot compare with theirs. Let me paint some orchids to decorate the white wall."

"That would be better!" said Li Zhenli.

Yang Longyou looked at the poems and paintings once again. "Oh, there are jagged rocks painted by Lan Tianshu," he said. "Let me paint orchids beside them."

He raised his brush and drew the orchids with great care. When he had finished he put the brush down and stepped back to examine his work. "Though it cannot compare with the works of the famous painters of the Yuan Dynasty (1279-1368), a famous girl needs orchids as a comparison," Yang said proudly.

"It is excellent. It adds splendor to the room," Li Zhenli said enthusiastically.

"Please don't laugh at me." Yang was even more pleased with himself. He turned to the girl and asked, "What's your formal name? I would like to write an inscription for you."

"I'm too young to have a formal name," the girl answered.

"Would you please name her, Mr. Yang?" Zhenli cut in.

Yang Longyou wanted to show off in front of the two women; he had a fertile imagination. "There's a saying from *Chronicles* of the later Zhou Dynasty, 'The orchid has natural fragrance and people admire its enchanting beauty.' Let's name her Xiangjun (Fragrant Lady)."

"Wonderful!" Li Zhenli said. "Xiangjun, come here and thank Lord Yang."

"I also have a name for your building — The House of Enchanting Fragrance." So saying, Yang Longyou picked up his brush and wrote an

　　贞丽义女闻知杨龙友已来,随即重新点了唇,抹了胭脂,匆匆挽了一个流行的发髻,更换了几件新装,碎步迈出卧房。

　　此时杨龙友正捧着一杯香茗,欣赏四壁诗画,见到当代赫赫有名的大名士张溥、夏允彝等人都有题赠,益发知道她的身价,颇想和诗一首。正当他思索诗句时,"老爷万福"一声清脆呼声,杨龙友不觉回过神来,原来是女孩儿已走到身边。他不禁注视着这青春少女:"几日不见,益发标致了。这些诗篇赞美的丝毫不差。待下官也和韵一首。"

　　李贞丽闻言,亲自捧了笔、砚过来。杨龙友提笔在手,构思半晌,终于放下笔来:"做他们不过,索性藏拙,还是画几笔墨兰,点缀这白壁罢。"

　　李贞丽识趣地附合:"这样更妙。"

　　杨龙友又将四壁诗画再打量一番:"这不是蓝瑛蓝田叔画的拳石么!俺就将墨兰画在石旁,借他的画衬贴衬贴也好。"

　　说罢,他提起笔来,着意布置,潜心点染,一幅兰花顷刻画就。掷笔后退,审视再三,不无得意地说:"虽比不上元代著名画家画的,但名姬也正需要兰花相配。"

　　"真正名笔,为妆楼生色多多。"李贞丽自然称赞不已。

　　杨龙友更为得意:"见笑,见笑。"随即转向贞丽义女问道:"请教尊号,以便落款。"

　　"年幼无号。"义女老老实实回答。

　　贞丽颇善凑趣:"就求老爷赏她两个字罢。"

　　杨龙友自恃才思敏捷,在两个青楼女子面前自要逞能卖弄:"《左传》有云'兰有国香,人服媚之',就叫她香君如何?"

　　李贞丽连声称谢:"甚妙!香君过来谢老爷。"

　　杨龙友又笑道:"连这座楼名也有了,就叫媚香楼。"说罢,他

inscription on the painting which read: "In the spring of the year of Guimo of Chongzhen reign, I painted these orchids in The House of Enchanting Fragrance which won a smile from Xiangjun. — Yang Wencong from Guiyang."

"Both the painting and inscription are excellent," Li Zhenli said. When Yang Longyou sat down she served him a cup of tea.

Yang Longyou wished to know more about Xiangjun and said, "I believe that Xiangjun is the most beautiful girl in the country. How well developed are her entertainment skills?"

"My daughter is elegant, but has not learnt any skills yet. A few days ago she started to learn *kunqu* from Su Kunsheng."

Yang Longyou said that he knew Su Kunsheng, the famous actor, well and asked what she was learning from him.

Li Zhenli said that Xiangjun was learning *The Four Dreams of the Jade Tea Studio*,* and that she had just learnt to sing half of *The Peony Pavilion*. She let Xiangjun take out the script to see it. At that moment Su Kunsheng came in, saw Yang Longyou and said, "Lord Yang, I haven't seen you for a long time."

"Congratulations on having such a good student."

Yang Longyou stood up and saluted him and after the exchange of greetings, Su Kunsheng began to teach Xiangjun. "Today Lord Yang is here. We may follow his instructions."

Xiangjun began to sing an aria from *The Peony Pavilion* which she had learned. Sun Kunsheng often corrected her and taught her sentence by sentence. She also learned to sing a new scene from the opera. "Your daughter is very bright. She will surely be a famous entertainer soon," Yang said after hearing her sing. Then he turned to Su Kunsheng and said that he had met Hou Xun's son, Hou Chaozong, the day before. "He is rich and well known for his literary talents. This young man is looking for a beauty. Do you know him, Mr. Su?"

"He comes from the same town as me and he's from an old and famous family."

Yang Longyou said, "We should introduce Xiangjun to him." Li Zhenli happily agreed and asked Yang Longyou for his help. Yang Longyou promised to take the matter seriously. After drinking more tea they all left.

The Four Dreams of the Jade Tea Studio include four dramas: *The Purple Hairpin, The Peony Pavilion, The Story of Nanke* and *The Story of Handan*, written by Tang Xianzu (1550-1616), a famous dramatist in the Ming Dynasty.

又提起笔来,在画面上落款:"崇祯癸未仲春,偶写墨兰于媚香楼,博香君一笑。贵阳杨文聪。"

李贞丽又称赞道:"写画俱佳,可称双绝,多谢了。"题款已就,贞丽又请杨龙友落座奉茶。

"我看香君乃国内第一美色,不知技艺如何?"杨龙友为了替她拉客,真是要全面知晓她。

"小女一向娇美,不曾学习。前日才请了苏昆生来传她词曲。"

"苏昆生,倒是名手,是一向熟悉的。传的哪套曲?"

李贞丽说传的是《玉茗堂四梦》*,才将其中的《牡丹亭》学了半本。接着,又叫香君取出曲本来温习。正说着,苏昆生又来传曲了,见杨龙友在座,先行招呼:"杨老爷也在此,久违了。"

"恭喜昆老,收了个绝代门生。"杨龙友拱手为礼。

彼此寒喧几句,苏昆生叫香君取出曲本来,说:"趁大行家杨老爷在座,对对曲子,求得指教。"

香君唱起学过的《牡丹亭》片断,苏昆生逐句地指导和纠正。师徒二人就这么一支曲一支曲地对唱,学完了《牡丹亭》中的《惊梦》一出。"可喜令嫒聪明得很,不愁不是个名妓哩。"杨龙友听完后,对李贞丽称赞道。继而又向苏昆生说:"昨日会着侯恂的公子侯朝宗,客囊颇丰,又有文名,正在这里寻访名姝,昆老知道么?"

"他是敝同乡,世家大族,确是有名。"苏昆生应和着。

杨龙友接着这一话题:"这段姻缘,是不可错过的。"李贞丽立即欣然表示同意,并请求杨龙友极力帮衬,成此好事。杨龙友应允道:"自然在心的。"说定,又小酌一番,彼此散去。

---

*《玉茗堂四梦》:明代著名文学家,戏曲家汤显祖（1550-1616）创作的戏曲作品《紫钗记》、《牡丹亭》、《南柯记》、《邯郸记》合称《玉茗堂四梦》。

Chapter Four

Scholars Denounce Ruan

The sworn brother of Yang Longyou, Ruan Dacheng was hated and denounced by everyone. Ruan Dacheng (styled Yuanhai) was a native of Huaining in Anhui Province. He was good at writing *ci* (poetry written to certain tunes with strict tonal patterns and rhyme and rhyme schemes, in fixed numbers of lines and words) and *qu* (a type of sung verse). However he was overweeningly ambitious. To advance his career, he had thrown in his lot with Wei Zhongxian, the head of the eunuch clique. When the clique was crushed, he was cursed and hated by others and instead of repenting, he tried to seek another backer.

Every year, during the middle of spring, a memorial ceremony would be held at the Temple of Confucius. On the day, those who administered the temple rose early, cleaned the paths, set out sacrificial containers with meat, vegetables, fruit, wine and cakes, and lit candles and joss sticks. When all was ready, they waited for the officials in charge of the ceremony and other men of letters.

Amid the sounds of drums and music, officials of the Imperial Academy led many scholars in sacrifices to Confucius. In the Ming and Qing dynasties, the Imperial Academy was the highest educational body and, as Emperor Zhu Yuanzhang of the Ming had chosen Nanjing as the capital, the Six Boards and Imperial Academy were all located there. Later Emperor Zhu Di made Beijing the capital and founded another Imperial Academy there, but the one in Nanjing remained unchanged.

Ruan Dacheng attended the ceremony skulking among the men of letters and looking for a way of accomplishing his schemes. However the famous five scholars of the Restoration Society Wu Ciwei, Yang Weidou, Liu Bozong, Shen Kuntong and Shen Meisheng were there. After they had kowtowed to the statue of Confucius, scholars stood up and exchanged greetings. Ruan Dacheng went over to salute Wu Ciwei hoping that he would salute him in return; he would then be accepted by other scholars. However Wu Ciwei, an upright man, could not tolerate such a despicable

第四章
众士斥阮

正当杨龙友留连媚香楼之际,他的盟兄阮大铖却落在老鼠过街,人人喊打的处境。阮大铖,别号圆海,安徽怀宁人,极擅词曲,颇著文声。可惜名利心重,为了飞黄腾达,居然投靠阉党魏忠贤门下为干儿子。等到魏党事败,他就成了枯树林中的一头枭鸟,遭人唾骂,被人鄙视。但他又不自作忏悔,也不甘心寂寞,仍图另找依靠,他日东山再起。

眼看仲春已至,届时要在文庙祭孔。这一天,专事管理文庙的坛户绝早起来,清扫道路,布置祭器,安排荤、蔬菜肴,果酒点心,点燃香烛,专等主祭官员及众文士前来。

明清时代,国子监是朝廷的中央最高学府,只因明太祖朱元璋定都南京,六部以及国子监等机构自然设在南京。后来明成祖朱棣迁都北京,又在北京设立国子监及六部等中央机构,但南京的这些机构并未撤销。每年祭祀之日,由国子监的主管官员率领诸多文士在鼓乐声中行祭孔之礼。

阮大铖也混进祭拜的文士之中,悄悄四顾,窥测方向,以求一逞。哪里知道以吴次尾为首的复社著名的五秀才杨维斗、刘伯宗、沈昆铜、沈眉生也来参加祭孔。在排班跪拜之后,众文士立起身来一一相认。阮大铖厚着脸皮上前与吴次尾拱手为礼。心想,如果吴次尾能向他回礼,最好应答几句,那他又可被众文士所接纳。他哪里知道吴次尾是一条是非分明、铁骨铮铮的好汉,岂容得他这样

19

person. Instead of returning the salute, he denounced him: "You are Ruan Dacheng? How dare you come here to attend the sacrificial ceremony! You will offend Confucius and bring disgrace to our scholars! Get out of here!"

At this Ruan Dacheng became most irate and retorted, "I'm a successful candidate in the highest imperial examination, and a famous writer. What crimes have I committed? Why shouldn't I attend the memorial ceremony?"

"Your crimes are known to everyone. You're a person without heart. How dare you enter the temple and attend the ceremony?" Wu Ciwei scolded in a loud voice. "The notice to prevent insurrection, posted the day before yesterday, is directed at people like you."

Though discouraged, Ruan tried to defend himself. "I came to the memorial ceremony to lay bare my true feelings."

"Let me express your true feelings for you. You are Wei Zhongxian's adopted son, and a diehard follower of Cui Chengxiu and Tian Ergeng of the eunuch clique. You colluded with the Xichang secret service to arrest, torture and persecute upright men of the Donglin Party. All of your crimes are abundantly clear. Once the sun rises, the ice on the mountain melts. You have no way to go."

Wu Ciwei had exposed all of Ruan's crimes and Ruan Dacheng could not deny the facts. He looked for an excuse. "Brothers, you only curse me, you don't understand my predicament. You did not know that I was a student of Mr. Zhao Nanxing (a politician and literati in the Ming Dynasty and an important member of the Donglin Party) who was persecuted to death by Wei Zhongxian. When the Wei clique ran wild, I stayed at home to mourn my teacher's death. Have I hurt anyone?" He raised his voice. "You make groundless accusations. It's true that I was acquainted with Wei Zhongxian, but that was to prevent attacks on scholars of the Donglin Party. Why do you scold me?" He composed himself and pointed to Wu Ciwei and his friends. "How dare these frivolous young men start rumors here!"

On hearing this the young scholars at the ceremony became indignant. They shouted, "How dare this shameless man curse us at the Temple of Confucius. Let's teach him a lesson."

"Beat the traitor!"

"Slap his face!"

"Grab his beard!"

的卑污小人！非但没有还礼，还怒斥道："你不是阮大铖吗？你怎敢来参加祭礼！这不是冒犯夫子，玷辱斯文！快快出去！"

阮大铖见吴次尾如此不留情，也无名火升，怒气冲冲地说道："我乃堂堂进士，当代名家，有何罪过，不容我参加祭礼！"

"你的罪过，天下俱知。枉为人身，身无人心，还敢入庙，参加祭礼！难道前天贴出的防乱公告，还不曾说到你的病根吗？"吴次尾大声斥责。

阮大铖不禁有些气馁，辩白说："我正是为表白自己心迹，前来参加祭礼的。"

"你的心迹，待我替你说出来：你投拜魏忠贤为义子，你既和阉党崔呈秀、田尔耕结成死党，又和抓人拷人的西厂特务机构勾勾连连，专整正直的东林党人，你这些罪恶，昭昭在人耳目。一旦阳光出，冰山倒，你也就无处可逃了！"吴次尾不容他为自己狡辩，将他的劣迹倾箱倒箧地掀了出来。

阮大铖眼见自己的辫子捏在别人手里，无法否认，依然找借口，开脱自己："诸位仁兄，你们不谅解我的苦衷，一味辱骂。你们哪里知道俺阮大铖原来是被魏忠贤害死的赵南星先生门人。魏党横行时，我在家守丧，何曾伤害一人？你们这些话从何说起！"说到此际，他又张狂起来："你们指责的事情全是无中生有，捕风捉影。不错，我曾屈节结识魏忠贤，那全是为了援救东林诸君子，怎么倒责备起我来！"说着，又摆出他当年的气派来，手指着吴次尾一众："你们这般轻薄新进，也在此处放屁狂言！"

参加祭礼的秀才们早已围在他的四周，听见他这般狂言，人人发指，个个愤慨，一时七嘴八舌地嚷道："你这无耻之徒，敢在文庙中公然骂人，真是反了！"

"打这个奸党！""掌他的嘴！""扯他的胡子！"

The scholars surrounded Ruan Dacheng, grabbed his beard and beat him badly. Ruan Dacheng ran away, holding his head with his hands.

As he ran off Wu Ciwei raised his voice and said, "We did well today. We avenged the men of the Donglin Party and brought credit to the Imperial Academy. We are very happy. From now on we should work together with one heart to prevent such shameless people coming back." All the scholars supported him.

CHAPTER FIVE

Ruan Tries to Return

Ruan Dacheng was not an ordinary man. Although the scholars had beaten him at the Temple of Confucius he had no intention of changing his ways; instead he planned revenge. He knew that to achieve it he had to take up an official post and regain power. Night and day he thought of possible ways. Finally an idea came. Unlike his small hometown Huaining, Nanjing was a metropolis with a large population and many merchants. He rented a large mansion in Kusifang where he established an elegant garden with several pavilions. There he kept a number of well trained, young and pretty actresses.

The opera troupe was expensive to maintain but Ruan Dacheng planned to use it as a stepping-stone for his career. He curried favor with powerful officials by offering bribes to the greedy and providing actresses to those fond of beautiful girls. When the opportunity came he would regain power but for the moment he was cautious.

One day when he was lost in thought, a servant handed him a letter from someone wishing to hire his theatrical troupe. Ruan Dacheng looked at it and was surprised to find that the hirer was Chen Dingsheng, a famous young scholar in Nanjing. His servant said that Chen's messenger had told him that Chen Dingsheng, Fang Mizhi and Mao Pijiang were drinking wine at the Jiming Temple. The three young men wished to see Ruan's

　　霎时,他的胡子被扯,腰臂受伤,抱头鼠窜而去。

　　吴次尾见阮大铖已走,高声对与祭的秀才们说:"今日此举,替东林党人雪了愤,替南京国子监的读书人增了光,真是痛快。以后大家同心协力,不能容忍这类无耻小人再出头!"诸秀才莫不赞成。

第五章
借戏图进

　　阮大铖并非等闲之辈,虽然被众秀才在文庙中痛打一顿,依然没有任何醒悟翻悔之意,还在谋思如何报复。而要有能力报复,先要复官掌权。他日思夜想,终于想出一个办法。原来南京并非像他的故乡怀宁那样是个小地方,而是一座极其广阔的大城市。商贾云集,市廛辐辏,人口繁众。他在南京城西库司坊买了一座大院落,盖了极其精巧的园亭,养了一批歌儿舞女,悉心调教,终日竹歌不绝。南京士民鄙其为人,常将他所居住的"库司坊"用谐音称做"裤子裆",称他为"裤子裆里的软"——"软"乃谐"阮"也。

　　阮大铖这般作为,当然不是为了闲居纳福,而是为了今后图个进身之阶。他不惜财力、物力,一心攀结当朝有权之人,贪财的,贿以珍宝;恋色的,供以歌舞。一旦死灰复燃,起复有望,他便要倒行逆施。不过眼前,他还不敢冒失行事。

　　正当他左思右想的时候,忽然家人拿了一张帖子前来:"禀老爷,有帖借戏。"他接过帖子一看,借戏的人原来是陈定生,颇感诧异,心想这陈定生是个声名赫赫的公子,今日怎肯向我借戏?他从家人口中得知,那送帖子来的人说,还有方密之、冒辟疆两位,一

new opera *The Swallow's Love Note*. Ruan Dacheng realized that it was a good opportunity to show his talents. He said to the servant, "Go upstairs right away, pick out the best stage properties and tell the actors and actresses to make up immediately. Go with them to the temple to take care of everything."

Soon everything was ready. As the theatrical troupe was about to leave, Ruan Dacheng whispered to the servant, "You must listen to what the three scholars say and report it to me in detail." The servant, his reliable agent, nodded his head. After they had left, Ruan Dacheng went to his study and sitting at his desk, poured wine into a cup; he began to drink. He was in a good mood. The famous scholars still remembered him.

After a while Yang Longyou paid a visit. Ruan Dacheng was famous for his poetry and sung verse while Yang Longyou was good at painting and calligraphy; the two men of letters had a good relationship. Yang Longyou knew that Ruan Dacheng had written a new opera *The Swallow's Love Note* and was eager to read it. During the past few days he had been so busy that he had not had time to visit him. Now that he was free he had taken a leisurely walk to Ruan's residence. He passed the Yonghuai Hall before the janitor had time to tell Ruan that he had arrived; at the study he saw Ruan reading an article. "Brother Ruan, don't work too hard," Yang boomed, "You must take good care of yourself!"

"Oh, it's you, Brother Yang." Ruan Dacheng came out of the study to greet him. "Please take a seat."

"Why do you stay at home by yourself on such a beautiful spring day?"

"My new opera *The Swallow's Love Note* will be sent to the press soon. I'm proofreading it."

"Oh, I came here to see the same masterpiece."

"I'm sorry to say that my theatrical troupe is away right now."

"Where has it gone?" Yang Longyou was surprised.

"A few young scholars have hired it." Ruan Dacheng wanted to keep Yang guessing and Yang Longyou had no choice but to say, "Then let me read your script while we drink wine."

The suggestion made Ruan Dacheng very happy — he had wine and food prepared. Yang Longyou drank the wine and read the script. He lauded Ruan's work which made Ruan very happy, although he pretended to be modest.

齐在鸡鸣寺饮酒消遣,要看他的新作《燕子笺》传奇,所以特地让人持帖商借戏班。阮大铖虽感意外,但继而一想,这不正是我买女教戏的用意所在么?怎能不好好利用这一难得的机会,连忙应允,吩咐家人:"快去楼上,要挑最好的道具,让班里角色尽快梳洗,随道具一同前去。你也拿帖跟去,诸事都要仔细。"家人答应着,招呼戏班,正准备出门,阮大铖又将家人叫转回来,悄悄对他说:"你在他们席上,仔细听听他们看戏时有什么议论,速速报我知道。"家人与戏班走后,他不禁高兴起来,感到在这班名士的眼中还有自己的位置,便得意洋洋地走进书房,坐在小桌前自斟自饮起来。

正在他的兴头上,杨龙友前来拜访。他们两个一个极擅词曲,一个能书善画,彼此誉为绝技,互诩为一代传人,时相过从。阮大铖的《燕子笺》传奇刚刚写就,杨龙友就已知悉,一直想先睹为快,总未能脱身前来。今日无事,他便信步踱到库司坊石巢园来访阮大铖。不待家人通报,径自穿门入户,走过咏怀堂,就听到书房中隐隐有吟哦之声,他便高声招呼道:"大铖兄,稍稍歇歇,性命要紧呀!""我道是谁,原来是龙友兄。请坐,请坐!"阮大铖笑着迎了出来。

"春光如此美好,为何闭户独处?"

"只因传奇四种,正在付印;恐有错字,在此校对。"

"啊呀,小弟正是来欣赏大作《燕子笺》的啊!"

"真是抱歉,恰好今日戏班全都不在舍间。"

"哪里去了?"杨龙友有些诧异。

阮大铖又故意卖关子:"有几位公子借去,他们也要欣赏。"杨龙友无可无不可地说:"那就把稿本赐阅,权当下酒之物。"

阮大铖正想有个知己闲话,就吩咐家僮备酒。杨龙友一面小啜美酒,一面阅读剧本,看到情深处,不由不赞美几句,阮大铖听了浑身舒坦,口中却故作谦虚:

"Don't laugh at it. It's not good enough."

The servant from the Jiming Temple walked in and said, "The three scholars have watched three scenes and the wine has gone ten rounds. All of them are full of praise."

On hearing this Ruan Dacheng could not help shouting, "Wonderful! They really can appreciate good work! What else did they say?"

"They said Your Lord is a gifted scholar. Your work is extraordinary."

"Oh, they really said that? What else did they say?"

The servant added exaggerated details to please his master. "They said that, as for literary talent, Your Lord should rank first in the world of letters."

It made Ruan Dacheng happy, but he pretended to be unsatisfied. "They flattered me. You go back to the temple and continue listening to what they say." The servant left. Smiling from ear to ear, Ruan Dacheng gave a toast to Yang Longyou and said proudly, "It is surprising that these young scholars know me so well."

"Who are these scholars?" Yang Longyou asked.

"They are Chen Dingsheng, Fang Mizhi and Mao Pijiang, all outstanding scholars and they all admire me," Ruan Dacheng said delightedly.

"They never give praise without reason. *The Swallow's Love Note* is a good work indeed...." Before Yang Longyou had finished speaking, the servant returned. Ruan Dacheng was expecting more praise, but the servant said that though the young scholars praised his literary talents, they denounced him bitterly as an adopted son of the eunuch clique who used his powerful connections to bully people. Hearing this, Ruan Dacheng flew into rage and said, "Damn, how dare these young villains curse me?"

"Why do they pick on you?" Yang Longyou asked.

Ruan Dacheng did not know what to say. He chattered for a long time then said, "I must find a way out or I will never be able to face people." While speaking he stood up, rubbed his hands and walked up and down sighing, but could not find an answer. He turned towards Yang and said, "What shall I do then?"

"芜词俚曲,见笑大方。"

二人对饮,你一杯我一盏,兴致正浓。前往鸡鸣寺的家人急急回来报告:"那几个公子才看完三出,酒倒饮了十巡,不断击节称赞。"

阮大铖喜不自禁地高声道:"妙!妙!他们竟然也懂得赏鉴哩!他们可曾说些什么?""他们说,老爷不愧是才子,下笔确是不凡。"

"啊呀呀,也难得他们这样倾倒——还说些什么?"

家人趁着主人高兴,添油加醋地说:"他们说,论起文采来,简直是天仙下凡,好教老爷执文坛牛耳。"

阮大铖内心高兴非凡,却故作不满地说道:"这也过誉了,叫我难当。再往后看,还不知说什么话来哩——你再去打听,速速回来禀报。"家人奉命又去探听。阮大铖笑容满面地劝杨龙友再干一杯,不无自诩地说道:"不料这班公子,倒是知己。"

杨龙友摸不着头脑地问道;"请问借戏的是哪班公子?"

"陈定生、方密之、冒辟疆,都有了不得的学问,他们竟也服了小弟。"阮大铖沾沾自喜地回答。

"他们倒是不随便称赞人的,老兄这本《燕子笺》原写得极好……"话还未完,家人又来禀报,二人以为又是一片赞扬之辞,岂知这番家人所禀报的是:这班公子虽然称赞他的文才,却对他的为人极为不齿,痛骂他甘心做阉党义子,仗势欺人。阮大铖听了家人这番回话,洋洋自得的心情一扫而光,顿时火冒三丈:"啊呀呀,了不得,这班不识进退的轻薄,竟然骂起老夫来了!气死我也。"

"请问他们因何痛骂老兄?"

阮大铖只推说自己也不清楚原因,末后吞吞吐吐地说:"假若不想个办法,此后我如何出门见人?"他急得推开酒盏,立起身来,搓着双手,在书房中来回踱步,长吁短叹,眼看多日心血白白抛洒。想不出任何办法来,便有口无心地对着杨龙友说:"如何是好?"

CHAPTER SIX

Ruan Presents Dowries to Hou

The former county magistrate, Yang Longyou, knew that Ruan Dacheng longed for power and was down on his luck, but was wealthy. Some of the scholars belonging to the Restoration Society were keen on courtesans. Why not get him to use his money to curry favor with them? He saw an opportunity of convincing him.

"Brother Ruan, I have an idea that may solve your problem but I'm not sure that you will agree."

"If Brother Yang is willing to help, I'll agree," Ruan Dacheng replied.

"Brother Ruan, Wu Ciwei is the head of the young scholars and Chen Dingsheng is the leader of the young masters. If both Wu and Chen let the matter drop, all the others will end their nonsense," Yang said.

Ruan Dacheng rubbed the table and stood up saying, "That's a good idea! But who's going to convince the pair?"

"Only Hou Chaozong from Henan can do it. He is an intimate friend of Wu Ciwei and Chen Dingsheng. They always follow his advice."

"Who will convince Hou Chaozong then?" Ruan Dacheng asked anxiously.

Yang Longyou told Ruan Dacheng of his plan. "I discovered that Hou Chaozong was bored to death in Nanjing. He wants a beautiful girl to keep him company. I have found the right one for him. Her name is Xiangjun. She is both pretty and skillful. It's a certainty that Hou Chaozong will fall in love with her at first sight. If Brother Ruan is willing to spend money to establish a good relationship with him, he will argue your case to Wu Ciwei and Chen Dingsheng."

Ruan Dacheng clapped his hands and shouted, "Wonderful! A really good idea." After thinking for a while he said, "As a matter of fact, our friendship spans two generations. His father and I passed the imperial examination at the same time. I should do something for him. But how much money will be needed?"

第六章
赠奁结纳

杨龙友虽曾为官县令，但已罢职，闲居无事，专门寻花问柳，出入门户人家，为他人牵线作媒，倒也少有空闲。这次来访阮大铖，虽口称看戏，实是另有所谋。他深知阮大铖其人，终日企望出头，重新掌权，但受制于东林、复社文人。他知道，复社文人虽然负有清望，但大多社友也喜留连风情，阮大铖虽然一时缩头，但却广有家财。如何既能迎合复社文人的声色之好，又能对这个魏阉余孽援之以手，这岂不是两面讨好之事？

"阮兄不必烦恼，我倒有个办法，可为阮兄排忧解难，不知阮兄能否依从？"杨龙友见火候已到，缓缓说来。

"龙友兄肯援手，小弟怎会不依从？"阮大铖也急忙应允，顾不得身份了。

"阮兄可知道，吴次尾是秀才领袖，陈定生是公子班头，只要两将罢兵，千军就可解甲了！"

阮大铖闻言拍案大喜："对呀！但又有谁去劝说这两个为头的人呢？"

"别人无用，只有河南侯朝宗，他与这两个人乃文酒至交，言无不听，计无不从。"

"那又怎能说动侯某人呢？"阮大铖急不可耐地追问。

"这倒有个办法——前些时听说侯朝宗闲居无聊，很想寻一个秦淮佳人作伴。小弟已替他物色了一个，名唤香君，色艺双精，估计必定中他的心意。阮兄如肯为他出这一笔费用，与他结为友

"Two hundred taels of silver will be enough for dowries and a banquet," Yang Longyou replied.

Ruan Dacheng agreed readily. "No problem. I'll have 300 taels of silver sent to your residence and leave you to take care of it."

Yang Longyou thought that he had settled the matter and raised his wine cup. Ruan Dacheng, who finally saw a way out of his predicament, raised his as well. Both of them were very happy. After having drunk his fill, Yang Longyou took his leave.

好,得到他的欢心,然后再托他向这两个人说情,包管成功。"杨龙友终于将他深思熟虑的计谋出售给这个不齿的阉党余孽。

阮大铖由衷地表示佩服,不断拍手赞叹:"妙妙! 好个计策。"又侧头沉思一会儿, 说道:"这侯朝宗与我还有世交, 他的父亲原与我是同榜考取的, 他的事, 我料理料理, 也是应该的——但不知道需要多少银两? "

"嫁妆酒席,二百多两也就差不多了。"

阮大铖爽快地说道:"这个数目不难, 小弟就送三百两银子到府上,凭老兄安排。"

杨龙友见阮大铖已愿意出资, 认为此事定能办成, 情不自禁地举起杯来; 阮大铖也为找到一个摆脱窘境的办法, 减轻了心病, 也陪着举杯, 这两个难兄难弟不免为各自打算都能实现而高兴。尽情小酌后,杨龙友方告辞而去。

CHAPTER SEVEN

Hou Meets Xiangjun

The war in north China made it impossible for Hou Chaozong to return home. Lonely and bored, he wanted to visit the brothels in Nanjing but had no money. Although Yang Longyou had mentioned Xiangjun several times, Hou Chaozong had not dared visit the brothel to see the charming girl.

It was the time of the Pure Brightness Festival, which coincided with the warmth of spring, captivating scenery and a city transformed by the season. Hou Chaozong, fed up with loneliness, threw down his book and walked out planning to visit Xiangjun in a brothel.

On the street he heard someone calling from behind. "Master Hou, where are you going?" He turned and saw Liu Jingting walking towards him and invited him along. Soon they came to the bank of the Qinhuai River.

"That is the Waterside Pavilion and there is the Long Bridge. Let's slow down." Liu Jingting led the way. "The old brothel is quite close. A lot of famous courtesans live in that lane over there."

Following Liu Jingting's directions Hou Chaozong entered the lane. Red apricot branches spread over pink walls and he heard the cries of flower sellers. He could not help saying, "It is quite different. Each household has a black door and tender willow branches."

Liu Jingting pointed and said, "That taller house is Li Zhenli's home."

"Where does Xiangjun live?" Hou Chaozong asked.

"She is Li Zhenli's daughter. She lives there as well."

"Wonderful, I just want to see her now that we chance to be here." Hou Chaozong's spirits rose and he thought that it was a good omen.

Liu Jingting came to the door and knocked. Someone inside answered saying that Li Zhenli and her daughter had gone to a box party at Bian Yujing's home.

Hou Chaozong knew nothing about box parties and asked Liu about

第七章
侯李初会

　　侯朝宗乡试失手之后,北方烽火未靖,归家无望。寄寓在南京莫愁湖畔已非一日,虽有三五文友,不时或来寓所造访,或结伴畅游风景名胜,但终究掩抑不了寂寞之感。有心寻花问柳,总因囊中羞涩,不敢纵情冶游。尽管杨龙友在他面前一再夸赞香君妙龄绝色、天生丽质,但总未敢轻易去访,一直未能亲睹芳颜。

　　眼看清明已至,侯朝宗难耐独坐书斋的冷寂,信手抛开几卷残书,出门踏青,借此也顺路去秦淮河畔的旧院访访香君。出门行不数步,忽听身后传来一声呼唤:"侯相公何处闲游?"回头一看,原来是柳敬亭。他正苦无伴,乃相约柳敬亭一同往秦淮河畔走去。

　　"那是秦淮水亭,这是长桥,我们慢慢的走。"柳敬亭老马识途地引路。走了不远,他又向侯朝宗介绍道:"眼看就是旧院了,那边一条巷子里,都是有名的姊妹人家。"侯朝宗顺着他所指,缓缓步入巷中。眼前一带粉墙,偶露几枝红杏,耳边叫卖鲜花声不断,不禁应和着说:"果然不同,家家黑漆双门,户户高插嫩柳。"

　　柳敬亭说:"这边高门儿,便是李贞丽家。"

　　"香君住在哪个门里?"侯朝宗问道。

　　柳敬亭回答道:"香君是贞丽的女儿,自然就住在那高门儿里。"

　　"妙妙,俺正要拜访她,恰恰走到这里。"也许是好兆头吧,侯朝宗情绪顿时高涨。

　　柳敬亭走上台阶,敲动门环,不见人开门,只闻人答应,一问一答中方知贞丽母女二人都到姨娘卞玉京家做盒子会去了。

them. Liu Jingting was tired after the long walk and sat down on a stone block in front of the house. He said to Hou Chaozong, "Famous courtesans from various brothels are sworn sisters, just like some men are sworn brothers. On festive occasions the sworn sisters get together, each bringing a box of fresh food. They taste each other's food, exchange cooking skills and play musical instruments."

Hou Chaozong was pleased, "Oh, it must be interesting. Do they invite guests?"

"No, no!" Liu Jingting waved his hand. "They are afraid of the guests disturbing them. They lock the door and allow guests to watch performances from downstairs only."

"What would a guest do if he was fond of one of the courtesans?" Hou Chaozong asked.

"He may throw something upstairs. The courtesan he picks will throw fruit back to him. Then she will walk down to make an appointment," Liu Jingting explained.

"That's the way it is. We'd better go there and have a look."

Liu Jingting stood up and led the way. Hou Chaozong noticed that each household grew poplar and willow trees as well as colorful flowers. Limpid water ran under the bridges and the melodious sound of the *xiao* (a vertical bamboo flute) came from the deep lanes. The pair soon arrived at the Warm and Green Building, Bian Yujing's residence. In the doorway they ran into Yang Longyou and Su Kunsheng. "How could Brother Hou condescend to come here? It's most unusual, most unusual!" Yang Longyou pretended to be surprised.

"I heard that Brother Yang went to see Ruan Dacheng. It's a surprise to meet you here!" Hou Chaozong teased back.

"Brother Yang comes here for you, Brother Hou." Su Kunsheng answered for Yang Longyou. Liu Jingting, who knew nothing of the affair, interrupted and they sat down.

Soon Hou Chaozong stood up to look at the house, "How wonderful the Warm and Green Building is, but why can't we see Xiangjun today?"

Yang Longyou knew what Hou Chaozong was thinking. "Xiangjun is upstairs," he said.

"Listen," Su Kunsheng said. "They are playing musical instruments."

They also heard the elegant songs that the instruments accompanied. Hou Chaozong was so excited that he took a pendant from his fan and

　　侯朝宗不知道盒子会是怎么一回事，柳敬亭当然是知道的，见朝宗询问，自己腿又走乏了，索性在门口石磴上坐了下来，向侯朝宗说道："各院的名妓互相结为姊妹，就像男子汉结为兄弟一样，每逢佳节，大家聚会，各自携一副盒子，盛着各样新鲜食品，互相品尝，又彼此竞技，弹琴的弹琴，吹箫的吹箫。"

　　侯朝宗听到有这样的热闹事儿，兴致极高："啊呀，有这般有趣的事儿！允不允许客人参加？"

　　"不许，不许！"柳敬亭摇手答道："她们最怕就是客人前来混闹，都是锁住楼门，只许客人在楼下赏鉴。"

　　"赏鉴中意的，又如何会面？"侯朝宗不甘心地追问道。

　　"中意了，便将一样东西抛上楼去，楼上的也抛下果子来。如彼此相当，就下来捧酒相敬，再进而缔结密约。"

　　"既然如此，小生也好去走走了。"

　　柳敬亭连忙起身，在前面引路。一路上，家家杨柳，户户莺花，白板桥下，碧波荡漾，长巷深处，箫声悠扬。侯朝宗目不暇接地边行边看，跟着柳敬亭来到卞玉京的暖翠楼。刚刚进门，劈面就撞上杨龙友、苏昆生二人。杨龙友故作惊异地问道："侯世兄怎肯到这种地方来？难得，难得。"

　　侯朝宗也不让步："听说杨兄今日去看阮大铖了，怎想在这里遇着。"苏昆生不觉漏了底："杨兄特为侯相公喜事而来。"柳敬亭不知底里，只是招呼大家进去就座，一时打断了这一话题。

　　侯朝宗刚坐下又起立，端详此楼，窗明院敞，不禁脱口而出："好个暖翠楼。香君为何不见？"

　　杨龙友已窥悉朝宗内心，答道："香君正在楼上。"

　　苏昆生也说："你听，楼上开始演奏了。"

　　果然，笙、笛齐鸣，琵琶、筝箫竞起，云锣又响，歌声悠扬，声声

threw it upstairs. Soon cherries wrapped in a white silk scarf were thrown down.

"Who threw that?" Hou Chaozong asked anxiously. "How nice it would be if it were Xiangjuan."

Yang knew quite well who it was. "I guess this white silk scarf belongs to Xiangjun." No sooner had Yang Longyou said that than Li Zhenli appeared leading Xiangjun. Both gentlemen were surprised and overjoyed. Yang Longyou introduced them to Hou Chaozong.

Hou Chaozong said, "I'm Hou Chaozong from Henan and have long admired you. Today I'm truly fortunate to meet you." Hou Chaozong saw that Xiangjun was beautiful, and said over and over again, "Brother Yang, you have been a good judge."

Li Zhenli allowed the guests to sit down. They were served tea, dishes were prepared and they began playing wine-drinking games. Su Kunsheng let Li Zhenli take over while Xiangjun held the wine cup. Li Zhenli did not decline; it was a rule in the brothel that the procuress gave orders. Then she said, "We shall take turns to drink wine. Each person drinks all the wine in the cup and then shows their talents. Here are the topics: the first is cherry; the second, tea; the third, willow; the fourth, apricot blossoms; the fifth, the pendant of a fragrant fan; the sixth, a snowy silk scarf." Then she turned to allow Xiangjun to cater to Hou Chaozong. "Xiangjun, drink a toast to Master Hou." Xiangjun poured a cup of wine for Hou Chaozong and another for herself; both emptied their cup.

Li Zhenli threw the dice on the table and called, "It is the pendant of a fragrant fan." She stared at Hou Chaozong and said, "Master Hou, drink this cup of wine and then say something."

Hou Chaozong drank the wine and said, "Let me compose a poem." He stood up while the others clapped. In a low voice he recited:

The breeze of beauty in south China,
Does not hide in the sleeve.
Following the young man's fan,
It will sway and give out a fragrance.

"A good poem! A good poem!" Yang Longyou exclaimed.

Liu Jingting knew that Xiangjun's nickname was Lesser Fan Pendant and he teased her. "What a fragrant fan's pendant! Don't spoil it while swaying!"

撩人心肠。侯朝宗一时忍捺不住,取下扇坠向楼上抛去。接着,楼上就有一条白汗巾包着樱桃掷了下来。侯朝宗急不可待地问道:"不知是谁抛来的? 若是香君,岂不可喜!"

杨龙友心中有数:"看这洁白的丝巾,有九分是香君了。"话声尚未落地,李贞丽已领着香君冉冉而来。楼下的几位,有的惊异,有的欢喜。杨龙友连忙拉着侯朝宗向前说:"世兄认认,这是贞丽,这是香君。"

侯朝宗不等别人介绍,就自报家门:"小生河南侯朝宗,一向渴慕,今日方才如愿。"又看了香君几眼:"果然妙龄绝色,杨兄真有眼力。"

李贞丽忙着招呼大家坐下,先行奉上苏州的新茶,接着又命人滗酒上菜,彼此行令饮酒。苏昆生让李贞丽发令,吩咐香君把盏。李贞丽此时也不再推辞,因为院中旧例,由主人行令。她便宣令道:"酒要依次轮饮,每一杯干,各献所长,便是酒底。么是樱桃,二是茶,三为柳,四为杏花,五是香扇坠,六是冰绡汗巾。"她又回过头来,不无意思地吩咐香君照顾好侯朝宗,说:"香君,敬侯相公酒。"香君便为朝宗与自家各斟一杯,相对而饮,彼此照了酒杯。

李贞丽掷出骰子,呼道:"是香扇坠。"双眼注视侯朝宗道:"侯相公速干此杯,请说酒底。"

侯朝宗干了杯,说:"小生就做首诗吧。"在大家的叫好声中,他立起身来,低吟道:

"南国佳人风,休教袖里藏;

随郎团扇影,摇动一身香。"

杨龙友立即高声赞道:"好诗,好诗!"

柳敬亭凑趣儿地说道:"好个香扇坠,只怕摇摆坏了。"众人都知香君浑名小扇坠也。香君闻言,脸上也不禁一阵潮红。

Li Zhenli hurriedly changed the subject. "Xiangjun, prepare a cup of wine for Lord Yang!"

Yang Longyou took the cup and drank the wine. Then they drank in turn and enjoyed themselves.

But after a while Hou Chaozong stood up and said, "I've drunk enough wine. I must leave now."

Liu Jingting knew what Hou was thinking and stood up. "It's a rare chance for a gifted scholar to meet a beauty." Holding Xiangjun with one hand, and Chaozong with the other he said, "You're a born couple. Why don't you drink a cup of heart-to-heart wine?"

Su Kunsheng who also wanted to see the pair engaged stood up and said bluntly, "Xiangjun is very shy. I have to ask you, Master Hou, would you accept an engagement with Xiangjun? We spoke of it the other day."

"How can I refuse? Can a scholar refuse to be the best in the country?" Hou Chaozong answered excitedly.

When she heard that Hou Chaozong was to be promised to Xiangjun, Li Zhenli said, "If my daughter is to be united with the socially elevated could you please pick an auspicious day?"

Yang Longyou, who had already chosen a day for them, said that the 15th day of the third lunar month would be best. But Hou Chaozong said that it was very hard for him to arrange for a dowries in such a short time. "Don't worry," said Yang Longyou, "I've arranged for the dowries and an engagement banquet."

Everything was settled and they left.

　　李贞丽见状,连忙岔开:"香君,该奉杨老爷酒了。"

　　杨龙友接过香君敬的酒,一饮而尽,说出酒底。接着,苏昆生、柳敬亭一众相互你一杯我一盏地轮流畅饮,说笑打趣,闹做一团。

　　大家尚未尽兴,侯朝宗站起身,以退为进地说道:"酒已够了,就此别过。"

　　柳敬亭此时已明白聚会的用意何在,赶紧起身说道:"才子佳人,难得聚会。"他一手拉住香君,一手拉着朝宗,说道:"你们是天生的一对儿,吃个交心酒如何?"

　　苏昆生也不愿好人由柳敬亭一人做,更直截了当地对侯朝宗说:"香君面嫩,当面不好说。前日所说订情之事,相公意下如何?"

　　侯朝宗正巴不得有此一问,连忙应道:"秀才中状元,还有什么不肯!"

　　李贞丽见侯朝宗已允,趁热打铁地说道:"贱妾就要高攀了。既蒙不弃,还要择个日子。"

　　杨龙友早有安排,说三月十五,花月良辰,便好成亲。侯朝宗如实相告,只怕仓促之间,客囊羞涩,一时难以准备厚礼。杨龙友劝慰他说不须发愁,嫁妆、酒席所费,他早已备好。

　　至此,说定一切,各自方行散去。

CHAPTER EIGHT

Hou Marries Xiangjun

Time flew and the day came. Li Zhenli had waited anxiously. She was not young and would have to rely on her adopted daughter, Xiangjun, for the rest of her life. It had been hard to find the right man for Xiangjun who was beautiful but haughty. She would arrange everything with great care. But when she thought of the trouble of preparing a big banquet as well as inviting guests she was worried. She hurried to finish her make up and went into the sitting room shouting, "Bao'er (a male servant), where are you? Come here!"

Bao'er walked in slowly, waving a palm fan. His languor angered Li Zhenli.

"Today is a day of great importance for our young lady. Distinguished guests will arrive soon, but you're still dreaming. Roll up the curtains and clean the house right now." Then she walked around the house, instructing her servants on this or that. The House of Enchanting Fragrance bustled.

While she was occupied Yang Longyou walked in. He wore brand-new clothes and was followed by several porters carrying gifts from Ruan Dacheng. He had made up his mind not to mention Ruan Dacheng's name on this occasion. He was familiar with the building, pushed open the door, walked straight to the sitting room and asked in a loud voice, "Where is Zhenli?"

Li Zhenli was so busy that she had not seen him enter. Hearing his voice, she turned and said, "Lord Yang, I'm very grateful for your services as a go-between." She saw Yang Longyou had arrived alone and asked, "Why has Master Hou not come?"

"He will come soon," Yang Longyou comforted her with a smile. He beckoned the porters in and they carried cases of ornaments and clothes to the sitting room. "I have prepared several cases of clothes for Xiangjun as gifts. Please take them." The cases were sent to the bridal chamber.

第八章
定情之夕

　　转瞬之间，已是三月十五。自从侯朝宗去暖翠楼初会香君之后，李贞丽可是掐着指头等待这一天，因为自家已是半老徐娘，下半生就指望着义女香君。这孩儿虽然生的一副国色天香，但生性高傲，至今尚未找到可以以身相托的人。幸亏杨龙友为她物色了家道、才名皆属上乘的侯朝宗。今天乃是他俩初次定情的吉日，怎能不细心安排妥贴哩。匆匆梳洗过，就立即来到客堂，大声呼道："保儿，在哪里？快来。"

　　保儿闻得呼唤，并不急忙，手中摇了一把芭蕉扇，慢吞吞地踱了进来。贞丽见他一副慢条斯理的神态，顿时气不知从何处来："啐，今日是小姐的大喜之日，贵人将到，你还作梦哩。快快卷帘扫地，安排桌椅。"她四处察看着，吩咐着，媚香楼上下一片忙乱。

　　正当她么喝不断之际，杨龙友穿了一身簇新的时装，受阮大铖之托，押着几挑礼物前来。一路上，他已打好主意，今日送礼不能提阮大铖的名字。他是熟门熟路，推开掩着的院门，一路走向客堂，一边招呼道："贞丽在哪里？"

　　李贞丽忙乱之中未曾见他进来，听了这声招呼，回过头来方见到杨龙友，先行谢过："杨老爷，多谢您作媒，酒席俱已备齐了。"她只见杨龙友一人，不免有几分焦急："怎么新官人还不见到？"

　　"想必就要来的。"杨龙友安慰道。说着回转身来，招呼站在门口的杂役将内装首饰、衣物的箱笼抬了进来，对李贞丽说："下官备有箱笼几件，为香君助妆，盼笑纳。"说罢，吩咐杂役将礼品抬入洞房。

"You are extravagant. Thank you very much."

Yang Longyou took a red package from his sleeve and gave it to Zhenli. "Here are 30 taels of silver for the banquet. Please ask the kitchen to prepare their best dishes and supply wine." Li Zhenli was overjoyed and thanked Yang Longyou again and again. "We really don't deserve this.... Xiangjun, come here immediately!"

Xiangjun had risen early and taken extra care over her make up. She looked quite beautiful. Hearing her mother's call, she entered the room. "Lord Yang gave you many presents. You must thank him." said Li Zhenli. Xiangjun saluted Yang Longyou gracefully. Waving his hand Yang Longyou said, "They are mere trifles, hardly worth mentioning. You should not bother."

Just then Hou Chaozong arrived. He wore brightly colored clothes and Bao'er who saw him shouted in a loud voice, "The New Master has come!"

Yang Longyou walked to the gate to greet him. "Congratulations, Brother Hou. Xiangjun is an extraordinary beauty. I have prepared the dowry and banquet and hope you will enjoy yourself." Hou Chaozong was very grateful. "You're most considerate, Brother Yang. However can I thank you?"

Yang Longyou bowed and Bao'er came to serve them tea. Yang Longyou asked, "How is the banquet coming along? Is everything ready?"

"Everything is ready," said Li Zhenli. Yang Longyou was relieved. He stood up to take his leave. "Today is your happy day, Brother Hou. I must not stay long. I take my leave now and tomorrow I'll congratulate you on the happy occasion."

"Why don't you stay?" Hou Chaozong asked.

"It's not convenient, just not convenient." Yang Longyou stood up and walked towards to the door.

With the help of Bao'er, Hou Chaozong began to change his clothes. Li Zhenli excused herself saying that she had to prepare for the banquet and help Xiangjun dress.

After she had left, Ding Jizhi, Shen Gongxian and Zhang Yanzhu, some of the brothel's clients and their literary friends, entered the room. They saluted and congratulated Hou Chaozong. He returned the salute and said in a friendly way, "Please excuse me today."

Just then some of Nanjing's famous courtesans headed by Bian Yujing arrived. Bian Yujing was very fond of Xiangjun. When she saw the

　　"如何这般破费，多谢老爷。"不待李贞丽致谢，杨龙友又从袖内摸出一个红包，递给李贞丽说："这是酒席银三十两，请交厨房代办，一应酒肴俱要上等。"李贞丽更是高兴得再三致谢："真是不敢当了！"说罢朝楼上喊道："香君快来。"

　　香君清晨起来即仔细上妆，打扮得越发出众了，闻得妈妈呼唤，进了客堂。李贞丽指着杨龙友对香君说："杨老爷赏了许多东西，快上前拜谢。"香君缓缓作礼，杨龙友摇手推辞："这点薄礼，何须致谢，请回，请回。"

　　正当他们一边赠礼，一边谢礼时，侯朝宗穿着一身光鲜衣服，来到媚香楼。保儿一见，即向门内大叫："新官人到门了。"

　　杨龙友抢先迎了出来："恭喜世兄，得了青楼佳丽。小弟无以为敬，草草办了妆奁，粗粗陈设了筵席，以助一宵之乐。"侯朝宗不消自己操心，做了现成的新郎，得了个绝世佳人，自然感谢杨龙友："您安排得太周到了，教我何以承受得起？"杨龙友拱手谦逊。保儿捧上茶来，杨龙友问保儿："一应喜筵，都安排齐备了没有？"

　　不待保儿回答，李贞丽抢先说道："托老爷福，一切准备妥当。"杨龙友似乎这才放心，立起身来，向侯朝宗拱手为礼道："今天是吉日，小弟不便在此多坐，就此告辞，明天再来道喜。"

　　"同坐何妨。"侯朝宗无可无不可地挽留。

　　"不便，不便。"说着，杨龙友就出了客堂，向院门走去。

　　"请新官人更衣。"在保儿服侍下，侯朝宗脱了外衣。李贞丽还有事要张罗，就对侯朝宗告个失礼，说："妾身不在此奉陪，要替新官人打扮新妇，准备酒席。""请便。"侯朝宗应道。

　　李贞丽与香君方才转进里间，丁继之，沈公宪，张燕筑一班清客，彼此打趣着进了院门，与侯朝宗见面作揖行礼。口中嘈杂着一片："恭喜，恭喜。"侯朝宗也只得以礼相待，友好地说："今日借光。"

bustle in the hall she thought that the ceremony was being held up and shouted, "Master Hou is here. Let's ask Xiangjun to come out!"

Li Zhenli heard her in the backroom and hurried upstairs to help Xiangjun, who was already dressed, to come down. Shen Gongxian, Ding Jizhi and Zhang Yanzhu played music to welcome her. Suddenly the room was filled with the sounds of *sheng* (a reed pipe wind instrument), *xiao* and gongs and drums. Surrounded by happy music, Hou Chaozong and Li Xiangjun saluted each other.

It was a rule of the brothel not to have a formal ceremony and after the courtesan met her man there was a feast. Hou Chaozong and Li Xiangjun took the place of honor with men sitting to the left and women to the right. They sang, played musical instruments, recited poems and blew flutes while Bao'er served wine to everyone.

Smiling happily and holding wine cups Hou Chaozong and Li Xiangjun looked at each other. To the laughter of clients and friends and courtesans, Hou Chaozong and Xiangjun drank the first cups of wine. Hou Chaozong felt pleased and meditated. The scene reminded him of Du Mu, a famous poet of the Tang Dynasty (618-907). When Du Mu frequented the brothels in Yangzhou, he was very proud of his literary talents, and his beautiful women.

Li Xiangjun also reflected, "I'm only a girl driven to prostitution. Today I'm fortunate to receive a scholar as handsome as Hou Chaozong. He may not treat me as a concubine and I could become his wife eventually." She was both happy and concerned.

The clients and literary friends, who often visited the brothel, were fond of making fun of the courtesans. Today with plenty of wine and food they were too excited to pay attention to Chaozong and Xiangjun. Ding Jizhi reminded them, "Look out of the window, the sun is setting. It's late. Let's send the lovers to the bridal chamber."

Shen Gongxian disagreed, "There is no hurry. Master Hou is a gifted scholar. Today he gets an unrivaled beauty. He has drunk wine. Now he should compose a love poem." Zhang Yanzhu said that it was a reasonable idea. He spread a piece of paper on the table and began to rub an ink stick against an inkstone.

Hou Chaozong knew very well that he must comply and said, "I don't need the paper. I have a palace fan with me. I will write a poem for Xiangjun on it as a token of my love." "That's a good idea!" the others said. Hou Chaozong walked to the table, bent down and wrote a poem on

话声刚落地，卞玉京等一班秦淮名妓也摇摇摆摆地进了院门。卞玉京自是喜爱香君，见堂上一片吵闹，怕误了正事，便开口道："官人已来，还是快请香君出来吧。"

李贞丽虽在堂后，也已听到此话，连忙上楼去扶着已妆扮好的香君下来走进客堂。沈公宪见状，赶紧吩咐丁、张二位："我们做乐迎接。"一时笙箫并作，锣鼓齐鸣，在粗细十番*声中侯朝宗与李香君相互行礼。

按青楼规矩，不兴拜堂，见过面就吃喜酒。大家簇拥着侯朝宗、李香君二人上坐，男左女右地坐了满满一桌，吹的吹，弹的弹，吟的吟，唱的唱。保儿手执一把酒壶，向众人逐个斟酒。

侯朝宗与李香君两人举着酒杯，相视而笑，在清客、歌妓的哄笑劝酒声中彼此饮了第一杯酒。面对这一场面，侯朝宗既感慨万端，又感到满足，颇有唐代诗人杜牧当年在扬州出入娼楼妓馆的风流心态，以才情自负，以美女自诩。

而李香君也在自忖：自家不过是野草闲花，沦落风尘，今日居然也接待了雄姿英秀的侯公子，料想他也不会将自家看作侍妾相待，终究能有个夫人身份。想到这里，不禁有几分得意也有几分惶恐。

清客与歌妓，原就不时相聚，每一会面，必然笑闹，今日又有酒吃，更是尽兴畅饮，一时也顾不上这对新人了。倒是丁继之想着他们，对喧闹成一团的诸人说："你们看看窗外，太阳都下山了，时辰不早，快送新人进入洞房吧。"

沈公宪还不尽兴，连忙说："忙什么？侯官人是当今才子，今天又有了绝代佳人，合欢有酒，哪能定情无诗呢？"张燕筑附和声起："说的有理，说的有理。"并动手摊开诗笺，磨起墨来。

---

* 十番：一种民间音乐，乐队由十种乐器组成（包括管乐器，弦乐器和打击乐器），统称十番锣鼓。

the fan. It read:

> *A red building is located in a sloping lane,*
> *Where the nobility and scholars often go by cart.*
> *The Qingxi River is lined with lily magnolia trees,*
> *Which are not as attractive as peach and plum blossom.*

"A good poem! A good poem!" The guests were profuse in their praise and a bridal poem written by Yang Longyou was delivered to Hou Chaozong. Master Hou unfolded it and read:

> *Li Xiangjun was an unsurpassed beauty,*
> *And an elegant girl hidden by dress and sleeve.*
> *Just like the goddesses of Mount Wushan,*
> *Who waited to meet Prince Chu in their dreams.*

"Lord Yang is most affectionate," said Hou Chaozong, smiling.

Soon all the people at the banquet realized that it was late. Special music played by trumpeters sent the new lovers to the bridal chamber. Each of the other customers found his lover to enjoy.

CHAPTER NINE

Xiangjun Denounces Ruan

The following morning Yang Longyou went to The House of Enchanting Fragrance. The gate was closed, the courtyard silent; a male servant cleaned a stool outside. As a frequent guest of the brothel, Yang Longyou knew everyone, the procuress, courtesans and the servants. He shouted to the male servant, "Bao'er, go to the new couple's window and tell them I have come to congratulate them."

"They're not up yet. They went to bed late last night. Why don't

侯朝宗知道推辞不掉，只得说道："不用诗笺，我带了一柄宫扇，就题赠香君，作为订情之物吧。""妙呀，妙！"赞声四起，有的捧砚，有的捧笔。侯朝宗在一片哄闹声中站在案前，弯下身来，就在扇面上题诗一首，大家念道：

夹道朱楼一径斜，王孙初御富平车。

青溪尽是辛夷树，不及东风桃李花。

"好诗，好诗！"正在大家赞美不断之际，极会凑趣的杨龙友也派人送来一首催妆诗，侯朝宗展开一读，诗云：

生小倾城是李香，怀中婀娜袖中藏。

缘何十二巫峰女，梦里偏来见楚王。

阅罢，侯朝宗莞尔一笑："此老多情。"

大家又说笑一番，时辰确实不早，吹鼓手打起十番，送新人进新房去。众清客也都找着自家的相好，各寻乐趣去了。

第九章
却奁斥奸

杨龙友结好侯朝宗，是受了阮大铖的重托，自然是要用心用意地办好这桩喜事。因此，次日清晨，他就来到媚香楼，只见院门深闭，寂无人声，惟有保儿在门外刷马桶。杨龙友是常客，妓院中从鸨母、妓女到保儿、帮闲，谁个不识？此刻便托熟地叫道："保儿，你到新人窗外，说我前来道喜。"

保儿也打趣地说："昨夜新人睡迟了，今天怕起不来哩。老爷请回去，明日再来罢。"

you go home and come back tomorrow?" Bao'er teased Yang Longyou.

Yang Longyou didn't mind Bao'er's joke and said with a smile, "Stop the nonsense! Go quickly."

Li Zhenli, who was already up, called out, "Who's there Bao'er?"

"Lord Yang is here to offer his congratulations," Bao'er answered.

Li Zhenli quickly opened the door and went out to welcome Yang Longyou. "I'm most grateful to Master Yang for finding such a good man for my daughter."

Yang Longyou asked if the lovers were up. "No. They went to bed very late. Please take a seat, Master Yang, I'll wake them."

"Don't worry, it's unnecessary!" Yang Longyou said, but Li Zhenli woke them. While waiting in the sitting room Yang Longyou thought: They stick to each other like glue and want to stay in bed. I allowed them such pleasure.

"That's interesting!" Li Zhenli said as she walked in. "Lord Yang, don't you think it interesting? They helped each other to dress, then looked at each other in the mirror. They have washed and dressed but remain in each other's arms. Lord Yang, you're not a stranger. You go in and bring them out."

Without hesitation Yang Longyou followed Li Zhenli to the bridal chamber where he bowed to Hou Chaozong, congratulated him and asked, "What did you think of the bridal poem I wrote last night?"

"Wonderful!" Hou Chaozong said with a smile.

"You must have composed an excellent one yourself?" Yang Longyou queried.

"I wrote a hurried poem. I wouldn't dare to show it to you," Hou Chaozong said modestly.

"Where is it?" Yang Longyou had to praise the poem before broaching the subject.

Xiangjun took the fan out of her sleeve and handed it to Yang Longyou. "Oh, written on a fan." Yang Longyou sniffed the fan and said it smelled good. Then he unfolded it and read the poem. "It is wonderful. Only Xiangjun is worthy of it." He returned it to Xiangjun and told her to put it in a safe place.

Yang Longyou looked at Xiangjun and said, "Look, Brother Hou, Xiangjun is even more beautiful. You are blessed with good fortune, how else could you have such a beautiful lady?"

At first the young lovers flirted and ignored Yang Longyou, then Li

杨龙友知道他在说笑,不以为忤,也笑着说:"胡说,快快去问。"

李贞丽早已起来,听见门外人声,高声问道:"保儿,是哪一位?"

"是杨老爷来道喜了。"保儿不再胡扯了。

李贞丽听说是杨龙友前来,赶不及地开了院门,迎了出来:"真要多谢老爷,成了孩儿一世姻缘。"

"好说,好说。"杨龙友转而问道:"新人起来没有?"

"昨晚睡得很迟,却还未起哩。"说着,李贞丽让坐,"老爷先请坐,我去催他们。"

"不必,不必。"杨龙友口中虽如此说,却任由李贞丽去催唤,自家坐在客堂上不由不想:这对男女情如花酿,睡到这时刻还未曾起床。若非我从旁帮衬,怎能得如此美满!

"好笑,好笑。"李贞丽一路走来一路说着,打断杨龙友的沉思。"老爷,你看可好笑!他两个在那里恩恩爱爱哩。他替她穿衣,她替他扣扣,又在那里共同对着镜子照看,刚刚梳洗好,真是缠绵不清。杨老爷,你也不是外人,索性进洞房去唤他们出来。"杨龙友听得这一声,也就毫不犹豫地跟着李贞丽转身进房去。

杨龙友进得新房,先是一揖:"恭喜,恭喜!"继而又问道:"昨晚催妆拙句,可还说的入情么?"侯朝宗笑道:"妙极了。"

"夜来定情,必有佳作。"杨龙友问道。

"草草塞责,不敢请教。"侯朝宗谦虚地答道。

"诗在哪里?"杨龙友不得不先恭维朝宗的文才,方好谈出正事。

香君闻言,从袖中取出宫扇递给杨龙友,杨龙友接在手中,说道:"原来写在宫扇上。"又嗅了几嗅:"香的有趣。"再展开纸扇吟诗道:"妙,妙,只有香君不愧此诗。"将扇还给香君:"好好收藏。"

彼此称赞过,杨龙友又细细看了香君几眼,对朝宗称赞道:"香君比日前更觉艳丽了。不是世兄有福,怎能消受这绝色美人。"

Xiangjun said seriously, "Master Yang, though you're a relative of General-Governor Ma Shiying, you're not very well-off. How could you spend so much money to help someone in a brothel? I need to know so that I can repay you. I feel most uneasy accepting such expensive gifts" Xiangjun's words struck a chord with Hou Chaozong. "What she says is reasonable. We met by chance, like patches of drifting duckweed. I feel uncomfortable about accepting such generosity."

Yang Longyou had intended telling all and was not surprised. He said, "Let me tell you the truth. The dowries and banquet cost over 200 taels of silver. They were all paid for by a man from Huaining."

"Ruan Dacheng from Huaining of Anhui Province?"

"That's right." Yang Longyou felt embarrassed.

"Why did he spend money on me?"

"He only wants to be your friend."

Hou Chaozong recalled what he knew of Ruan Dacheng. "He passed the imperial examination at the same time as my father and knew him. But I despise him and have broken off relations for a long time. I don't understand why he did me a favor."

Yang Longyou hoped that his explanation would persuade Chaozong to forgive Ruan Dacheng and said, "Ruan Dacheng used to be a student of Zhao Nanxing and was one of us. Later for protecting the Donglin Party he sought refuge with Wei Zhongxian. To his surprise, when the Wei clique was crushed, members of the Donglin Party regarded him as an enemy. Recently the scholars from the Restoration Society fiercely attacked him. A few days back they even insulted and beat him; it has been like a family feud. Ruan Dacheng had many friends but no one has defended him; his background makes them suspicious. Everyday he has looked at the sky, cried bitterly and said, 'Brothers attacking brothers, how sad it is!' He says that you are the only one who can save him and earnestly wishes to make friends with you."

Yang Longyou was a good speaker and Hou Chaozong was moved. "So that is what it's all about! Ruan Dacheng appears to be sincere. I feel some sympathy for him even if he did belong to the Wei clique. If he repents and mends his ways, we should welcome him; his crimes can be forgiven. Dingsheng and Ciwei are intimate friends of mine. I'll discuss it with them when we meet tomorrow."

Yang Longyou was pleased. "If you do, it will be good for us all."

Xiangjun had listened to Yang Longyou carefully and realized the

　　李香君一本正经地对杨龙友说："杨老爷虽是督抚马士英的至亲，但作客南京，手头也不宽裕，如何花这么一大笔钱，填这烟花窟窿？在奴家受之有愧，在老爷用之无名，今天问个明白，日后也好报答。"香君此问，倒提醒了侯朝宗，也接着说："香君问得甚是有理。小弟与杨兄萍水之交，昨天承情太厚重，也觉不安。"

　　杨龙友原就有摊出底牌之意，因此对两个新人所问并不觉得意外，不用思索托辞就回答说："既蒙问及，小弟只得据实相告了。这些妆奁、酒席，大约费了二百余两银子，都是出自怀宁之手。"

　　"是那安徽怀宁阮大铖么？"

　　"正是。"杨龙友开始觉得有些尴尬了。

　　侯朝宗此际有些戒心："他为何这样周旋我？"

　　"不过是想结交足下。"

　　至此，侯朝宗才晓得几分，随即明白表示："阮大铖原与先父同年中式，是敝人年伯，但小弟看不起他为人，与他绝交已久。他今日无故用情，令人不解。"

　　杨龙友闻言，便拿出说客的本领："阮大铖原是赵南星弟子，也与我辈声气相求，后来之所以投靠魏忠贤，只是为了救护东林党。不料魏党一败，东林诸君子却与他反目。近日复社社友，又对他大肆攻击，甚至殴辱，岂非同室操戈？阮大铖虽然故交颇多，但只因这段经历被人怀疑，也无人代为分辨，每每朝天大哭，说同类相残，伤心惨目，非河南侯君，不能救我。所以今日才诚诚恳恳地来结交足下。"

　　杨龙友真善言词，娓娓说来，倒极动听，侯朝宗一时被他打动："原来如此，俺看大铖情辞迫切，也觉可怜，即便真是魏党，悔过来归，也不可绝之太甚。何况他的罪过也有可原谅之处。定生、次尾，都是我的好友，明日相见，就替他分解分解。"

　　杨龙友听罢大喜："果然如此，也是我辈大幸。"

true character of Yang Longyou, a hired agent speaking for Ruan Dacheng. She would not put up with it. She stood up and said to Hou Chaozong, "What did you say, my dear. Ruan Dacheng is a shameless cur of treacherous court officials. All the people, women and children included, spit on him and curse him. Others attack him and you want to protect and save him? I would like know where you stand, Master."

The more she spoke, the more excited she became. Undeterred by the men's responses, she continued, "He paid for the dowries and for personal gain you wish to act wrongly? These ornaments and costumes mean nothing to me." She removed her hairpins and silk garments and said indignantly, "We are not afraid of being poor, but our reputation counts for all."

Yang Longyou was taken aback by the elegant young woman's stand. He was embarrassed and said, "Alas! Xiangjun is too tough and vehement."

Li Zhenli picked up the things from the ground and said, "What a pity to throw out such fine goods."

Hou Chaozong felt ashamed. "All right! You have your own view and I have fallen below your standards, but we are friends and lovers." He turned to Yang Longyou. "I hope you understand me, Brother Yang. I do not like being looked down upon by women. If a courtesan of a brothel holds dear her reputation, how can I, a scholar, mix with treacherous court officials. I am loyal and enjoy great esteem from my friends in the Restoration Society. If I associated with an evil man, my friends would all turn their backs on me. I could not save myself, let alone others."

Left with no choice Yang Longyou said, "If that is so, I take my leave."

Hou Chaozong did not urge him to stay and said, "These presents belong to Ruan Dacheng. As Xiangjun will not use them there's no point in leaving them here. Please return them to him."

Hou Chaozong turned to Xiangjun who was still angry and said, "Xiangjun is a natural beauty. She'll look more lovely without pearl and jade ornaments or brocade garments." Xiangjun ignored him.

Li Zhenli was not happy. "Even so it is a great pity to give away precious things."

Hou Chaozong knew that the procuress loved money and comforted her. "Don't worry about those things. I will compensate you."

Li Zhenli was relieved and said, "That is good."

　　香君在旁静静细听，她对杨龙友的说客嘴脸倒看得清楚，听到此际，实在忍无可忍，怒气冲冲地对朝宗说："官人说的什么话！阮大铖趋附权奸，廉耻丧尽；妇人女子，无不唾骂。别人攻他，官人救他。请问官人，你又自处于何等地位？"

　　她越说越动感情，不顾在坐之人如何反应，继续数落："官人之意，无非是因他赠俺妆奁，便要徇私废公。哪知道这几件钗钏衣裙，原就放不到我香君眼里。"说着，就拔下头上的珠簪，脱下身上的绸衣，气愤愤地表示："为人穷不妨，只要姓名香。"

　　杨龙友未曾想到娇小的香君会如此发作，尴尬万分地说道："啊呀！香君气性也太刚烈了。"

　　李贞丽却舍不得财物："把好好的东西都丢在一地，可惜，可惜。"说着，又一件一件地拾起来。

　　侯朝宗不免有些愧色："好，好！这样见识，我倒不如，真是侯某敬畏的知已了。"便向杨龙友解释道："老兄休怪，弟非不领情，不承教，但恐为女子所笑。青楼女儿都能讲究名节，我辈读书君子岂能混淆贤奸！那些复社朋友之所以推重俺侯某，也只为这点儿义气。我若依附奸邪，那时群起来攻，自救不暇，还能救人？"

　　杨龙友此刻已无能为力，说道："既然如此，小弟告辞了。"

　　侯朝宗也不再挽留，对他说道："这些箱笼，原是阮家之物，香君不用，留之无益，还是取回去吧！"

　　侯朝宗对着尚在恼怒的香君说："俺看香君天姿国色，摘了珠翠，脱了绮罗，十分容貌又添了十分，更觉可爱。"香君仍未答话。

　　李贞丽在一旁倒说："虽然如此，舍了许多东西，到底可惜。"

　　侯朝宗知道鸨母爱的是钱钞，便说道："这点儿东西，又何须挂念！待小生照样赔你一份。"

　　李贞丽听了这话，方才放心："这样才好。"

CHAPTER TEN

The Dragon Boat Festival

How time flew! The Dragon Boat Festival which fell on the fifth day of the fifth lunar month was coming. During the festival it was the custom of each household to place cat tail leaves on their doors to keep away evil. Everybody, men and women, old and young, would view the lanterns along the Qinhuai River.

Chen Dingsheng and Wu Ciwei, two distinguished scholars of the Restoration Society, arrived at the Examination Office by the Qinhuai River. It was a scene rich in variety but they saw no members of the Restoration Society. Disappointed, Chen Dingsheng turned to Wu Ciwei. "Brother Ciwei, we were bored at the inn. We came here to enjoy the festival with other scholars. Why don't we see any?"

"Brother Dingsheng," Wu Ciwei replied, "I guess all of them are now on the lantern boats." Pointing to a pavilion by the river, Wu Ciwei said, "That is Ding Jizhi's waterside pavilion. Let's watch the lanterns from there."

At the pavilion they lifted the curtain and climbed the steps. "Is Mr. Ding Jizhi home?" Chen Dingsheng called.

A boy attendant came out and said, "Master Chen and Master Wu, my master has gone to the lantern fair. But we have prepared wine and dishes. My master said before leaving that his guests should drink wine and feel at home."

"That sounds interesting," the scholars said happily.

"Your master is in an esthetic mood." So saying the two young scholars sat down and the attendant placed wine and food on the table. Chen Dingsheng was about to drink then put down his cup. "This is a fine place to enjoy the lanterns but we are a select band and should keep unwanted people away." He turned and called, "Boy, bring me a lantern." He picked up a brush, dipped it into the ready-made ink and wrote eight Chinese characters on the lantern, "Only members of the Restoration

第十章
端阳游船

春去夏来，眼前已是端午佳节。南京的风俗，每到端阳，家家户户插上蒲叶，男男女女赏灯秦淮。

复社文人陈定生约了吴次尾也漫步至贡院附近、秦淮佳处，只见满眼繁华，不见社中文友，顿生寥落之感。陈定生不禁向吴次尾问道："次尾兄，我和你因不耐旅店抑郁，特来此赏节，怎的不见同社一人？"

吴次尾应声回答："定生兄，想来社友都在灯船上哩。"随即指着前边不远处的水榭，说道："前面就是丁继之水榭，咱们去那里看灯吧。"

二人走到水榭前，掀起下垂的灯帘，拾级而上，陈定生边走边喊："丁继老在家么？"

一个小书僮听到声音，走出来一看："原来是陈、吴二位相公。我家主人赴灯会去了。不过，家中备有酒菜，主人吩咐，只要有客来，可随便留坐、饮用。"

陈定生、吴次尾一口一声地赞叹着："这样有趣。"

"主人真好雅兴。"说着，也不再推让，随意拣了两个座位坐定，自有书僮搬上酒菜。陈定生方才举杯，又放了下来，面对吴次尾说："我们在此小聚，颇多雅兴，万一有一两个俗人闯了进来，多么扫兴。不如先设法拦一拦。"又回过头来招呼："书僮，拿个灯笼来。"随即取过桌面上现成的笔砚，在灯笼上写了"复社会文，闲人免进"八个大字，让书僮把它挂在水榭外边高处。

Society are admitted." The attendant hung it on a high spot outside the pavilion.

"If members of the Restoration Society arrive, we invite them in," said Wu Ciwei.

"That's right. The lantern keeps out unwanted people and invites friends in," Chen Dingsheng said proudly.

The attendant leant on the railing and viewed the river scene. On hearing the sounds of drums and musical instruments he went inside, calling, "The lantern boat is coming."

Chen Dingsheng and Wu Ciwei emerged, leant on the railing and looked out. Accompanied by melodious music a small boat came towards them. Dimly they discerned four people. Chen Dingsheng stared at them and suddenly turned to Wu Ciwei. "Look, on the lantern boat, it looks like Hou Chaozong."

"It is Hou Chaozong. He is a member, let him join us."

"The lady must be Li Xiangjun. Can we invite her as well?"

Wu Ciwei said without hesitation, "It is well known in Nanjing that Li Xiangjun refused Ruan Dacheng's dowries. She acted as a friend of our society and should be invited."

Chen Dingsheng agreed. He pointed to the others in the boat and said, "That's Liu Jingting and Su Kunsheng playing the musical instruments. They refused to be Ruan Dacheng's hanger-ons which also makes them friends of our society. It would be more interesting if we invited them too."

"I'll call them," Wu Ciwei said and without waiting for a reply shouted, "Brother Hou! Brother Hou!"

Hearing his name, Hou Chaozong raised his head and spotted Chen Dingsheng and Wu Ciwei. He placed his hands together and bowed. Chen Dingsheng invited them over saying, "We're on Ding Jizhi's waterside pavilion. Wine and dishes are prepared. Brother Hou, Xiangjun, Jingting and Kunsheng come and enjoy the lanterns with us."

"That sounds interesting," Hou Chaozong said, supporting Xiangjun as they climbed onto the pavilion. Liu Jingting and Su Kunsheng followed.

It was early summer, breezes blew from the river and laughter came from the pavilion as the occupants chattered cheerfully. The boy attendant, still leaning on the railing, saw dragon boats in the distance. He shouted to the people inside, "Lantern boats are coming!" As they came out he pointed and said, "They are magnificent with hundreds of people."

"如果真有复社朋友到了这里,便该请他入会了。"吴次尾问道。

"正有此意——这灯笼既可阻拦俗人,又可招呼友人。"陈定生不无得意地答道。

书僮去栏外挂了灯笼,就扶在栏上欣赏河面景色,此刻听到鼓吹之声由远而近,便返身对室内招呼道:"灯船来了。"陈、吴二人应声而出,也凭栏而望。远处确有一条小船顺水漂来,只听见吹弹鼓板之声,隐约可见船上四人身影,直到淌下一段水面,陈定生定睛一看,招呼吴次尾道:"你看,那灯船上好像是侯朝宗。"

"啊,是侯朝宗,他是同社,该请入会的。"

陈定生又看见李香君,"那个女客便是李香君,也好请她么?"

吴次尾毫不犹疑地说:"李香君不接受阮大铖赠送的妆奁,此事传遍南京城,她这般作为,可算得上是复社朋友,请她何妨!"

陈定生见此话有理,又指着小船说道:"那两个吹歌的是柳敬亭、苏昆生,他们不肯做阮大铖的门客,也都算得上复社朋友,一齐请上楼来,更是有趣。"

"待我唤他。"不待陈定生应允,吴次尾便探出身去,向河面小船上大声招呼:"侯社兄,侯社兄! "

侯朝宗听见有人招呼,抬头一看,见到陈、吴二位,立即拱手为礼。陈定生连忙说道:"这里是丁继之水榭,备有酒菜,侯兄快同香君、敬亭、昆生一齐上楼来,大家一道赏节。"

侯朝宗应声道:"这太有趣了。"说着,扶着香君,又招呼柳、苏二人,一同弃船登楼。

此时已是初夏季节,阵阵微风自河面上拂拂吹来,水榭中谈笑风生,彼此融洽欢快。书僮仍独自在栏上看船,看到远处又有一条烛龙顺流而下,便向栏内高呼:"灯船来了,灯船来了。"又指着远处的烛龙对已走到栏边的众人说:"你们看人山人海,真是好看。"

The visitors peered out. The large boats belonging to the nobility were decorated with five-color corner lanterns and equipped with large drums and trumpets. Rich merchants' boats had five-pointed gauze lanterns and carried a large number of musicians. The others with only a few musicians belonged to the men of letters from the National Academy.

Wu Ciwei sighed and said what the others were thinking. "Compared to the merchants and nobility we scholars are a miserable and shabby lot." They started to make fun of each other but Hou Chaozong changed the subject.

"It is about midnight, the dragon boats have passed by. Let's celebrate the festival by composing poems." The three scholars talked among themselves then each extemporized a four line verse. They drank a cup of wine, Liu Jingting beat his drum, Su Kunsheng played his *yueqin* (a four-stringed plucked instrument with a full-moon-shaped sound box), and Xiangjun linked the poems together singing them gracefully. Chen Dingsheng was so impressed that he said he would have them printed the next day.

In low spirits Wu Ciwei said to himself, "We sing about our feelings and they make sad music. Only a few people on the river can really understand how we feel."

Su Kunsheng tried to create a happy atmosphere and said to Liu Jingting, "An enjoyable event does not last. We should make the best use of time and enjoy ourselves. Brother Liu, let's sing a song together. Master Chen and Master Wu propose a toast to Master Hou and Xiangjun congratulating them on becoming a couple. What do you all think?"

The others supported him and Liu Jingting said that it was a good idea. On behalf of Wu Ciwei, Chen Dingsheng said, "Brother Wu and I intended inviting the new couple to a dinner to congratulate them. Today is as good a day as any." Everyone sat down.

Hou Chaozong was very pleased. Xiangjun was still indignant over the dowries and he wished to use the opportunity to comfort her. He smiled and thanked his friends, then he turned to Li Xiangjun and said, "It will be interesting to drink wine from one cup again." Xiangjun nodded her head gracefully.

Master Chen and Master Wu kept urging the couple to drink while Liu Jingting and Su Kunsheng sang. They were enjoying themselves.

大家放眼看去,只见有的船高悬五色角灯,大鼓大吹,显然是公侯显贵之家的船;有的船悬着五角纱灯,打着粗十番,这正是富商和书办之家的船;还有一些悬着五色纸灯,打着细十番的船,分明是翰林院的文人船。

看着看着,吴次尾不禁感叹地说出大家心底话:"我辈文士到底有些寒酸。"彼此不免自我解嘲说笑一番。

侯朝宗毕竟不愧为复社领袖人物,岔过这一令人沮丧的话题,说道:"夜也深了,龙船也过尽了,我们做篇诗赋,也算是会文了。"三人商议一番,还是即景联句,每成四韵,三人饮酒一杯,柳敬亭击锣,苏昆生弹月琴,香君则慢声一曲,倒也算得上文酒笙歌之会。不一会儿,联成十六韵,陈定生兴致勃勃地说:"有趣,有趣,明日就将它刻印出来。"

吴次尾情绪总不高,自言自语地说道:"我们唱和得许多感慨,他们吹弹出无限凄凉,楼下船中,大约也没几个人能理解!"

苏昆生有意打断这丧气的话语,对柳敬亭说:"闲话少讲,自古道良宵苦短,胜事难逢。老柳,我们两个唱个曲儿,让陈、吴二位相公劝酒。"又指着侯、李二位道:"让他们的名士、美人,另作一个风流佳会,如何?"

苏昆生这一提议,众人齐声赞同,柳敬亭首先说道:"使得,这是我们帮闲的份内事。"陈定生接着代表吴次尾说:"我与次尾兄原该做东请新人,正该表示表示。"吴次尾则招呼大家依次坐下。

侯朝宗见大家一片诚意,也十分高兴,借此佳会也可扫却香君前日被杨龙友激怒的一腔愤慨,便笑着向大家说:"承众位雅意。"又转向李香君说:"让我两个并坐牙床,再吃一回合卺双杯,倒也有趣。"香君微笑点头。

陈、吴二人劝酒,柳、苏二人唱曲,此刻可谓欢会之盛了。

It was midnight, the lantern boats had gone. Suddenly one appeared accompanied by songs and music played by professional musicians. The five people in Ding Jizhi's pavilion pricked up their ears and listened.

The boat was Ruan Dacheng's. His theatrical troupe played and sang — he could not resist joining in the fun, or taking his boat out for the festival. But he had been afraid of meeting the members from the Restoration Society and had waited until after midnight when all pleasure boats had gone. He had not expected to chance on them at Ding Jizhi's pavilion. When he saw the brightly lit waterside pavilion, he sent a servant ahead to see who was there.

The servant told him about the words on the lantern and afraid that he would meet his enemies in the narrow stretch, Ruan Dacheng exclaimed, "This is terrible!" He made his followers put out the light and stop playing. The boat turned and they moved away quietly.

On the pavilion Chen Dingsheng was very surprised at the change and Wu Ciwei asked the attendant to take a closer look.

Liu Jingting stopped him and said, "There's no need for that. Even with my blurred vision I see it clearly. It is Ruan Dacheng's boat."

"No wonder the music was professional," Sun Kunsheng said.

Chen Dingsheng flew into rage. "How dare that old reprobate turn up in front of the Examination Office to do his sightseeing!"

"Let me pull his beard!" Wu Ciwei tried to stand up but Hou Chaozong put out his hand to stop him.

"Let it pass. We should not push too hard, he tries to avoid meeting us."

Liu Jingting said that his boat was already far away.

Realizing that the boat had disappeared, Wu Ciwei muttered with feeling, "This time we have let him off lightly."

Xiangjun, who thought that it was very late, stood up and took her leave. They all left the pavilion.

　　不觉夜已三更,灯船渐渐散去。忽而又漂来一条灯船,细吹细唱,与前面那些灯船粗细十番又自不同,都是出自行家里手,颇引起丁楼上这班人的注意,个个凝神细听。

　　原来这条船乃是阮大铖所乘,吹拉弹唱的都是他的家乐班子,自然不同。他原是个老白相,买舟载歌,佳节游河,怎能轻易放弃?只怕遇着复社的人与他过不去,所以今日专等游船散去、夜深人静之时,方才放船出来。他哪里知道还有一班复社朋友正在丁楼上吟诗赏灯哩。当他看到丁继之的水榭上还有灯火时,连忙吩咐小厮上岸去看看何人在那里。

　　小厮回来禀报说,灯笼上写有"复社会文,闲人免进。"阮大铖顿时感到冤家路窄,连呼:"了不得,了不得!"向后摆手,吩咐随从赶快熄了灯火,停了笙歌,将船悄悄调头而去。

　　水榭上的陈定生看了这般光景,不觉诧异:"好好一只灯船,为何歇歌灭灯,悄然而去?"吴次尾也觉奇怪,吩咐家僮去看看。

　　柳敬亭接过话来,说道:"不必去看,我老眼虽然昏花,早已看清了,那便是阮大铖。"

　　苏昆生插话道:"难怪我觉得船上吹歌确是与众不同哩。"

　　陈定生闻言大怒:"好大胆的老奴才,这贡院之前也许他来游耍么?"

　　吴次尾也跃跃欲试:"待我前去,扯掉他的胡子。"

　　侯朝宗却伸手拦住他说:"算了,算了,他既然知道回避,我们也不要过份了。"

　　柳敬亭说:"船也划远了,丢开手罢。"

　　吴次尾见船确已走远,恨恨地说:"便宜了这胡子。"

　　李香君见夜色已深,表示欲回之意,大家也就各自散去。

CHAPTER ELEVEN

Zuo Threatens Nanjing

Hou Chaozong and Li Xiangjun were still intoxicated by the river of love months after their betrothal and remained unaware of the great changes in the external world. Marshal Zuo Liangyu, the military commander of Wuchang, had caused much unrest by threatening to occupy Nanjing.

Zuo Liangyu, a native of Liaoyang in Liaoning Province, had joined the army as a young man and achieved rapid promotion but had been dismissed for his mistakes. He sought and received refuge with Hou Xun, the Provincial Military Commander in Changping County, Hebei Province. Hou Xun thought highly of his talents and promoted him to officer in charge of the province's military affairs. Zuo Liangyu was only 32.

At the time Zuo Liangyu was military commander of Wuchang, a prosperous city with a large population and a place of great strategic importance in Hunan and Hubei; through it ran the roads to nine provinces.

As commander of 300,000 troops, Zuo Liangyu tended to be headstrong and only heeded Hou Xun, his benefactor. But the court had dismissed Hou Xun from his post as commander of the army and there was no one to offer him advice. He had reaffirmed his loyalty to the court, but stayed in Wuchang while others fought, claiming that treacherous court officials stopped him from performing a more active role.

The court, however, could not provide rations for the troops or forage for the animals and Zuo Liangyu had to support them himself. His officers and men had become restive.

As a born general, Zuo Liangyu was aware of the importance of discipline and training. When the roll was called, he would gather officers and men and train rigorously but the men had used the opportunity to ask for rations.

On one occasion when he was sitting in his office he heard a disturbance outside. "Who is making such a noise?" he asked angrily.

第十一章
就食南京

　　侯朝宗、李香君定情之后不数月，正沉醉在卿卿我我的爱河中，哪知外部世界形势大变，南京城中近日又骚动起来，纷纷传说左良玉要率众就食南京。

　　左良玉乃是镇守武昌的兵马大元帅。原籍辽宁辽阳，当兵出身，因从戎有功，官至辽东都司，后因罪失去官职，到河北昌平投靠军门侯恂，不断得到赏识和提拔，直做到掌握一省兵权的总兵官，那时也不过三十二岁，真可谓青年得志。

　　武昌为中部重镇，不仅城市繁荣，人齿众多，且自古有九省通衢之称，是攻战必争之地。朝廷因左良玉是员战将，便任令他为镇守武昌的兵马大元帅，指麾着三十万大军。

　　但左良玉也非驯良之辈，军权在握，并不完全听从调度，只有对他有大恩的侯恂的话，他还能听得进。但侯恂被朝廷任命督师不久，就被免职，从此更少有人能向他进言。因此，他坐镇武昌，虽一再申说要报效朝廷，但又说因"奸人忌功"，以致自己"报主无期"，占据这可战可守的湖南、湖北重镇，坐观成败。

　　岂知这如意算盘也不好打。三十万之众，要吃要活，朝廷早已无力支付兵饷粮草，要他自行就地筹划，广大兵众躁动不安，思有作为。

　　左良玉行伍出身，深知操弓试马不能稍为松弛。每逢点名之日，必集合麾下将士，训练一番。广大士兵也就选定此日，要向元帅讨饷。

　　这日左良玉刚刚升帐，尚未发号施令，就听得辕门外不像往日肃静，人声鼎沸，一片喧哗。便大怒问道："辕门之外，何人喧闹？"

"The soldiers are hungry and are asking for their rations," a deputy general replied.

"What? We borrowed 30 boats of grain from Hunan not long ago. Has it all gone in a month?"

The two deputy generals replied in unison, "Sir, we have 300,000 officers and men. Thirty boats of grain do not go far."

When Zuo Liangyu heard, he rubbed the table and murmured to himself, "What can I do?" He turned to the deputy generals and said, "Look, war leaves central China in a state of chaos. Jackals, wolves, tigers and leopards rise one after another, no one is willing to serve the court. Officials are incompetent, officers and men are in a state of disorder, unable to fight, we are short of provisions and the soldiers are stirring up trouble. What can I do?" Zuo Liangyu revealed his anger but the noise outside continued. He had to find a way of alleviating the situation. He turned to his two deputy generals. "Don't blame me. We all work for the court. Over the past 300 years the court has treated the army well. Soldiers should not make trouble. There is no grain in the depot and no money in the official warehouse. We sent people to fetch grain from Jiangxi again. Please tell them that we shall supply provisions and grain as soon as they arrive from there."

Holding an arrow-shaped token of authority the deputy generals walked out and spoke to the soldiers. "This is an order from the marshal. Because this is a large army it is difficult to pay for your provisions. It is a difficult situation, but you should not forget the court's kindness, and we must obey the marshal's orders. In a few days grain from Jiangxi will arrive and we shall pay you in full. Please be patient and accept this calmly."

However, the promise came too late and the soldiers had suffered from hunger too long; talk would not calm them. They continued shouting loudly, "Pay us our provisions and give us grain!" Instead of retreating, they moved towards the office.

As a marshal, Zuo Liangyu might have disobeyed a higher authority, but with thousands of restless soldiers he could not play games. He did not know what to do. It seemed that they might rebel. He had to allow the deputy generals to announce an emergency measure.

"This is an order from the marshal. As soon as Jiangxi's grain boats arrive we shall provide provisions. However, as Jiangxi is a long way away and all of you are hungry, the marshal has written an urgent letter to Nanjing. The military department of Nanjing is to convey a request to the

"那是饥兵讨饷,并非喧闹。"副将如实禀报。

"嗳!前不久刚向湖南借粮三十船,还不到一月,难道都支完了!"

两个副将异口同声地回答道:"禀元帅,本镇人马足足有三十万之众,那一些些粮食,怎够开销?"

左良玉闻言方知实际情况,无可奈何地拍案自言自语:"啊呀,这却难办了。"又对两个副将诉说道:"你们看中原大地,一片战乱,豺狼虎豹纷纷而起,有何人肯报效朝廷!做将官的都是些无能之辈,吃兵粮的又是不能打仗的乌合之众!这天下叫咱怎支撑得起?如今这军粮问题又爆发,辕门外闹得不可开交,叫我如何处理?"他思索了一会儿,对副将说:"朝廷三百年养兵,咱们也要讲个良心。目前粮库中无粮,官库中无饷,我们已向江西借粮,你们去宣告大众,一等江西粮到,立即支销。"

两个副将执了令箭走出辕门,对激动异常的饥兵宣告:"元帅有令,三军听着:目前军饷缺乏,是因帐下人马众多。朝廷深恩,不可不报。将军严令,不可不遵。江西粮食,不日就要运到。届时支销,请稍安勿躁。"宣告完毕,也不等饥兵有什么反应,便转身走入大辕向左良玉回话:"奉元帅军令,已告诫三军了。"

但远水救不得近火,画饼岂能充饥?辕门外的士兵挨饿已非一日,这番空话哪能就安定军心?他们仍然不断高呼:"发欠饷,要吃饭!"非但没有退去,反倒向辕门逼近了。

左良玉身为大元帅,对三十万鼓躁不安的饥兵饿卒,不能敷衍,一时真是束手无策,兵变是不可避免的了。万般无奈,他不得不许愿要两个副将去宣布这样的应急措施:

"元帅有令,三军听着:江西粮船一到,即刻开支粮饷。但恐转运困难,大家空腹难挨。现在宣告,元帅已用特快文件,呈请南京兵部转呈圣上,许可武汉三镇兵马撤离汉口,去南京附近屯驻,以

emperor that troops from the three towns in Wuhan withdraw and move to a place near Nanjing. There we could get food from the city. If allowed we may go to Nanjing, the land of rice and fish. All will have enough to eat. I hope all officers and men will heed the marshal and stop the disturbances."

The soldiers although hungry accepted this. They shouted, "Good! Good!" and "Let's prepare to go to Nanjing." Then they left.

Zuo Liangyu had dispersed the soldiers but he sent no letter to Nanjing. Without an imperial decree, he dared not take his army there. The emperor had always been kind; he would not be sentenced to death during a time of turmoil, but he would be denounced by people all over the country. He racked his brains, but there was no easy answer. He could not stay and it was unwise to go. Fortunately the hungry soldiers had withdrawn and there was time to think it over.

Though they had made no preparations, everyone now knew of the plan and soldiers expressed different opinions. One petty officer said to a group, "We should discuss it in detail. Wuhan now has the strongest force in the country. Tomorrow when we go east along the Yangtze River, no one would dare stop us. We'd better support Marshal Zuo, capture Nanjing, and holding high a yellow banner, move towards Beijing. It will certainly work."

Another soldier waved his hand. "No, that's not a good idea. Marshal Zuo is loyal to the court. Don't talk nonsense, we can't do it. In my view we should just move to Nanjing to get enough to eat."

A veteran said, "As soon as we leave Hankou for Nanjing, the country will be panic-stricken. Even if we didn't attack Beijing, they will say our force threatened the court."

The provisions and funds for the army were so important that both the marshal and soldiers were worried about them. There was chaos inside and outside of the court and the people in central China would suffer a disaster.

便就食。如能去南京,则永无缺粮之虞,全体将士可同饱饥肠。希三军将士静听元帅调遣,勿再喧哗!"

这些饥兵饿卒听了此令,虽然仍未能立即支领到半粒军粮,但想到这也许是目前可能找到的惟一出路,便你呼我吆,"好,好,好!大家收拾好行装,预备东去,到南京安营歇马。"便逐渐散去。

左良玉虽然万般无奈,用就食南京的话儿将这群饿了多日的将士搪塞回去,但自家何曾事先向南京禀报过此事呢?虽然事出无奈,但未有明旨允许,自作主张移师南京,这可是非同小可之事。圣恩虽然宽大,处此动乱时局,也未必加以死罪,但难免不受天下人的指责。左良玉前思后想,一时真不知如何行事,东下不得,留守不住,真难煞人也。好在饿卒已退去,撤师汉口之命暂时可不发下,再多考虑考虑。

撤师汉口之议虽尚未付诸实行,但当众已经宣布,在军营内已议论四起,各有各的想法,各有各的打算。有个冒失的将士居然对几个亲近的士卒说道:"老哥,咱弟兄好好商量商量。目今论起天下的强兵勇将,没有谁能超过武汉,明日顺流东下,有谁人能抵挡?不如大家簇拥着元帅,一直抢到南京,再扯起黄旗,往北京进取,有何不可。"

另一兵士慌忙摇手道:"不成,不成。我们元帅是有名的忠义之士。你这般发疯的话语,千万不要提起,这是做不到的。不如依我说,还是移家就粮,吃个饱饭为妙。"

一个年岁较大的军士说:"你们哪里知道!只要咱们队伍一离开汉口,东去南京,人心必是惊慌,就是不取北京,这个威逼朝廷的罪名也就套定在头上,还说什么!"

这正是粮饷难煞人:将也不知如何做,兵也不知如何当!朝廷内外,上下混乱,中原大地,万民遭殃。

CHAPTER TWELVE

Hou Writes to Zuo

Hou Chaozong was still intoxicated by his happy life in The House of Enchanting Fragrance. He enjoyed time with his lover, visited scenic spots and historical sites in Nanjing or drank wine and composed poems with his friends. Autumn came and one day he wanted to listen to the stories of Liu Jingting, the best storyteller in Nanjing.

Liu Jingting's talents were well known throughout southeast China. He had been an orphan and, although far from home and destitute, he was an exceptional person. Some high-ranking officials and noble lords had tried to engage him as a retainer, but he was very fussy about his master. If an official or a lord was an evildoer, he would rather tell stories on the street than be attached to their household. That's why he left Ruan Dacheng.

Liu Jingting used storytelling to sing the praises of national heroes and denounce arch careerists and evil cliques. He had experienced ups and downs himself and seen the inconstancy of human relationships. His stories gave dutiful sons and officials loyal to their sovereign a proud and dignified end; evil people met an ignominious fate. Only the perceptive really understood him. Most scholars in Nanjing loved to listen to him and showed great respect.

Hou Chaozong had made a reservation the day before by sending his servant boy to Liu Jingting with a deposit. After taking a nap he walked leisurely to Liu Jingting's home but at the door he heard the sound of drums and clappers. Hou Chaozong knew Liu well and, thinking someone had arrived before him, walked directly into the sitting room. To his surprise he found Liu Jingting telling a story to himself and beating the drums and clappers.

"There is no audience here. Why are you telling yourself a story?" Hou Chaozong asked.

"Telling stories is my job. I practice it whenever I can, just as you sit

第十二章
修书劝左

　　自从侯、李定情之后，侯朝宗一直流连在软玉温香的游冶生活中，终日面对美人佳酿，或是游览名胜古迹，或是与友人聚饮吟诗，好不自在。不觉已到了桂子飘香季节，他又动了个听书的念头。在南京，提起讲书的，还有谁能胜过柳敬亭？

　　说起柳敬亭，自幼无依无靠，流落江湖，靠说书为生。曾经有达官贵人愿他做门客，他却择人而居，宁愿闲坐街坊泡壶茶吃，也不愿投靠歹人，以求荣华。因此，当他得知才子阮大铖居然是阉党馀孽，便不告而别，仍在市井以说书为生。

　　柳敬亭说书自有一番苦心，他历尽了人生苦难，看透了世态炎凉，也就借说书这个行当还世界一个公平。每当他说到含冤的孝子忠臣，则必然说出个令人扬眉吐气的结局；说到得意的奸雄邪党，总要让他们落个可耻的下场！他哪里是说书，只不过借这个谋生的手段指点江山、评论人物而已。能听懂他说书的深刻含意的人也非同寻常，南京的士人大都愿与他往来，对他也十分尊重。

　　侯朝宗知道要听他说书得预先约定。昨天已令小僮送去茶资，约定今日午后去听书。中睡片刻之后，侯朝宗即独自信步踱至柳寓，尚未进门，就听见屋内鼓板声响，以为已先有人来听书了。侯朝宗与柳敬亭此时已十分熟悉，便不拘俗套，径自走入，只见柳敬亭一人在那儿打鼓板，说平话，不禁哑然，问道：

　　"听众还未到，你独自一人在此说书，又说给谁听？"

　　柳敬亭笑答道："这说书是老汉的本业，无事时也要操练操

in your study playing *qin* and composing poems. Do you have an audience then?"

"That sounds reasonable," Hou Chaozong said.

"Young Master Hou, what story do you want to listen to today?"

"Anything that is exciting and straightforward."

"Unfortunately, Master Hou, you don't realize," Liu Jingting said with meaning, "An exciting situation is the source of indifference and a straightforward one always has two sides. I'd better tell you a story about a conquered nation, homeless people, patriotic generals and traitors. That will make you shed tears."

Hou Chaozong remarked with admiration, "I did not expect you, Brother Liu, to see through the current situation. It worries us all."

While they were chatting they heard footsteps. Yang Longyou rushed in. "Brother Yang, you have come at the right time. Let's listen to Brother Liu tell a story," Hou Chaozong said.

"Don't you know what's happening? How can you calmly listen to storytelling?"

Hou Chaozong was astonished. "Why are you so frightened?"

"Alas! Don't you know? Zuo Liangyu is bringing his army to Nanjing. He will wait here for a decision to be made by Beijing. The Minister of War Xiong Mingyu has no idea what to do. He asked me to ask you for a plan of action." Hou Chaozong saw that the situation was critical. Yang Longyou continued, "The people, officials, gentry and merchants are panic-stricken. Minister Xiong expects you to come up with an answer." The minister had not thought of Hou Chaozong but Yang Longyou knew that Zuo Liangyu once took refuge with Hou Chaozong's father, Hou Xun, when he had been dismissed. It had been Hou Xun who promoted Zuo Liangyu to officer in charge of the province's military affairs and he had been his mentor.

Yang Longyou added, "I've known for a long time that your father is Zuo Liangyu's benefactor. If you wrote a letter to Marshal Zuo, I am certain he would give up his plan for attacking Nanjing. What do you think?"

Hou Chaozong said that it seemed a good idea but his father had resigned from his official post and stayed at home for a long time. He had no power and he didn't think Zuo Liangyu would take his advice. "Moreover, he lives in Guide, my hometown, over 3,000 *li* away from Wuchang. Distant water won't put out a fire close at hand."

练。就像相公,闲坐书房,弹琴吟诗,难道也要有人听么?"

侯朝宗连声道:"说得有理,说得有理。"

柳敬亭进而问道:"请问相公,今日要听哪一朝的故事?"

"不拘哪朝哪代,你只拣热闹爽快的说上一回。"

"啊呀呀,相公不知,"柳敬亭意味深长地回答说:"那热闹的局面就是冷淡的根芽,那爽快的事情却是牵缠的枝叶——倒不如把那些国破家亡、孤忠孽子的故事讲它几句,也让大家滴些伤心泪吧。"

侯朝宗顿时收敛起消遣寻乐的心情,十分钦佩地赞叹道:"咳! 真未想到您敬老也看清目前的局势——可真令人忧虑呀。"

两人正在闲话,说书尚未开场,忽听得一阵脚步声,杨龙友神色匆匆地闯了进来,侯朝宗连忙招呼道:"杨兄来得正好,一起听敬老说书!"

杨龙友却不无埋怨地答道:"现今是何等时候,还有心情听说书!"

侯朝宗一怔:"杨兄为何这样惊慌?"

"啊呀呀,侯兄还不知道么?左良玉领兵东下,要抢占南京,而且还有窥伺北京之意。南京的官绅士商闻知此事,莫不震动,惊慌失措。兵部尚书熊明遇熊大人束手无策,不知如何是好,特此要小弟前来恳请侯兄,赐以妙计。"听得此言,侯朝宗方知目前局势紧张的程度。其实熊大人何曾想到求救于侯朝宗? 乃是杨龙友献计方有此举。因为杨龙友知道侯朝宗的父亲侯恂是左良玉的大恩人。

此刻, 他向朝宗建议道:"久闻尊翁老先生乃左良玉之恩公,若肯给他一信,他必能退守武昌。不知吾兄意下如何?"

"这样的好事,怎能不做? 但家父已辞官居乡,并无职掌,纵然写信,未必能有作用。更何况家父身在故乡归德,与武昌相隔三千里之遥,又何能解眼前之危?"

Yang Longyou had already thought this out. "Brother Hou, you are a gallant man. Our country is in danger. How can you sit back and do nothing? Why not write a letter on behalf of your father? It is a matter of extreme urgency. You can report it to your father later — I'm sure he'll not blame you."

Hou Chaozong could not refuse and said, "All right. I'll go home and draft a copy which I'll submit to you for advice."

"It can't be delayed. You should write and deliver it now, otherwise it will be too late. There's no time for discussion." Yang Longyou feared that the situation could change.

"All right, I'll write the letter here." Hou Chaozong went to a desk, picked up a brush, wrote the letter and gave it to Yang Longyou.

Yang Longyou read it with great care. Hou said that Nanjing, the former capital of China, contained the mausoleum of Emperor Taizu which should not be wantonly trampled. Unless Marshal Zuo had good reason he should not move east but find another way of solving the problem of pay and provisions. He was known for his loyalty to the court and should reconsider twice before acting.

"It's an excellent and reasonable letter. I'm sure it will convince Zuo Liangyu. This letter shows how capable you are."

"It should be submitted to Minister Xiong for correction and polishing before being delivered," Hou Chaozong suggested. He looked worried.

"That's unnecessary. I'll tell him later," Yang Longyou said firmly. "There's something else...." Yang Longyou was concerned.

"What's the matter?" Hou Chaozong and Liu Jingting asked in unison.

"We need someone to deliver the letter to Zuo Liangyu," Yang Longyou said. "The letter is confidential. We need a proper person for the task."

哪知杨龙友早已胸有成竹,不慌不忙地说出一个主意来:"吾兄素称豪侠,当此国家危亡之际,岂忍坐视不管。何不代写一书函,暂解燃眉之急,他日再禀明尊翁,料想尊翁也不至于罪责吾兄。如何?"

侯朝宗被杨龙友一番话打动,应承道:"好吧,待我回寓所去起草一信,再请大家商量。"

"事不宜迟!即刻发信,犹恐不及,岂能再容商量?"杨龙友惟恐迁延多变,紧紧盯住侯朝宗。

侯朝宗只得应允:"既然如此,就在此处写信了。"说罢,就伏在案前,一挥而就,递与杨龙友过目。

杨龙友细细看过,信中无非是劝诫之语,说不可师出无名,南京为留都,太祖陵树尚在,哪能轻易践踏,至于兵饷不继,可善自安排,莫改一片忠心,希望将军善自裁度云云。

杨龙友读罢,连声赞叹:"妙妙,写得激切婉转,有情有理,叫他不好不依。此信足见世兄经世济民的才能了!"

侯朝宗不无顾虑地说:"此信还宜先送熊大人过目,细加改正,方为万妥。"

杨龙友却大包大揽地回答道:"不必如此了,待小弟与他说一声便可——只是有一件事尚无着落……"杨龙友不禁有些发愁。

"何事让杨兄为难?"侯、柳二人异口同声地问道。

"侯兄信已写了,还找不到一个妥当的人送信!"杨龙友又紧逼一句:"这紧要的密信,又怎能让不熟知的人去送?"

CHAPTER THIRTEEN

Liu Delivers the Letter

Liu Jingting, who had stood by and listened quietly, stepped forward and said, "Don't worry. Let me deliver it."

Yang Longyou was unsure. "It would be good if you could go but there are many passes on the way to Wuchang. It's not an easy route."

Liu Jingting pressed his case. "I not only have extraordinary physical strength but I am very resourceful in an emergency."

Hou Chaozong was also worried. "I know that Zuo Liangyu maintains good discipline. It's not easy for an outsider to enter his camp. You're old and it will be difficult for you to get access to him."

"Master, don't prod me. As a storyteller, I am very familiar with the method of rousing somebody to action. Though I'm old, I can do the job. You're good at writing a letter and I can deliver it as well as I can portray a battle with words or describe how to get pearls from the sea. I swear I'll deliver it into the hands of Zuo Liangyu."

Yang Longyou could not help admiring Liu Jingting's confidence. "Wonderful! But only if you can explain the contents of the letter clearly, can you do the job."

"I understand the letter pretty well. I could even fulfill the mission without it. I'll chide Zuo until he feels ashamed!"

"How would you chide him?" Hou Chaozong asked.

"I'll ask him how an army empowered by the court to stop thievery could be allowed to engage in it." Jingting replied with assurance.

Hou Chaozong felt great respect for Liu Jingting. "Wonderful! What you say is clearer than my letter. That is quite penetrating."

Yang Longyou felt relieved. "Pack up. I'll send you some silver. You must leave Nanjing tonight." Liu Jingting nodded, bowed and went to his inner room.

"I didn't realize that Liu Jingting was such a versatile person," Yang Longyou said.

第十三章
慷慨投书

当杨龙友与侯朝宗商量如何解南京之危时,柳敬亭在一旁专心聆听,并未插话,见他们二人因找不到可靠的送信人而犯难时,便挺身而出,自告奋勇地说道:"你们也不必发愁,让我走一遭,如何?"

杨龙友却有些不以放心:"敬老肯去,自然很好。只是一路关卡盘查,也是不好对付的。"经杨龙友一激,柳敬亭更是奋然而起:"我柳敬亭身高力大,有左冲右挡的膂力,也能随机应变说话。"

侯朝宗则有些担心:"听说左良玉管束甚严,军营以外的人不易入帐。你这般老态,怎能见着他?"

"相公,你也不必来激俺了,这是俺说书的惯用手法。我老汉要去就行,不去就止。哪在乎你的一激之力。你笔力能写信,俺胸中就能画策。俺老柳可舌战群雄,可下海探珠,定把书信送达。"

杨龙友不得不称赞:"果然好本领!不过,书信中的意思,你还要说得明白,方可起作用。""啊呀呀,这书中的意思还待细说?俺有何不明白?就是不用书信,凭俺一张口也会去当这回差!俺定将他的人马骂回八百里之外!""你怎样骂他?"侯朝宗倒有些惊讶。

"俺只问他朝廷要你防贼,你怎地自家做起贼来,该不该!"

柳敬亭理直气壮的快人快语,顿时令侯朝宗肃然起敬,刮目相待:"好,好,好!比俺的这封书信还说得明白,还问得透彻!"

直到此际,杨龙友方始放心:"你快快进去收拾行李,俺替你送一些银两来。今夜务必出城上路才好。"柳敬亭一面应承,一面拱手,回里屋去准备了。

"I always thought he belonged to our group. Story-telling is just one of his skills," Hou Chaozong replied.

Liu Jingting set out that very night. Braving the wind and snow he walked along the side of the Yangtze River. At Wuchang, instead of staying at an inn for the night, he found an empty place to change his clothes, and there he put on his boots and hat. He was ready to deliver the letter.

At the start he could not find the military camp and had to ask several people. He realized the importance of the letter; he could afford no mistakes and instead of going directly to the camp, he walked round inspecting it. Two soldiers approached and he quickened his steps to draw near and hear what they were saying.

The shorter soldier was singing: "Those who executed thieves got the thieves' wallets; And those who saved the people occupied the people's houses. An official is in charge of the granary; And one soldier gets the grain for three."

The taller soldier said, "That's wrong. It's out of date."

"Sing the right one for me then."

"The situation has changed. It should be like this: Thieves are fierce, leaving no wallets; The people run away leaving empty houses; The official is poor without grain to supply; Thousands of soldiers have no food to eat."

The shorter one agreed and sighed deeply. "It seems that poor soldiers like us will go hungry."

"It looks like that."

"When we appealed to the marshal for food, he said that we could go to Nanjing to get it. Nothing has been said about that in the past few days, maybe he has changed his mind."

"There's nothing to worry about. If he changes his mind, we shall go back and appeal," the taller one said.

Just then Liu Jingting came over and bowed by placing his hands together in front of his chest. "Excuse me, could you tell me where the marshal's office is, please?"

The shorter soldier whispered to the taller, "His accent is from the north of the Yangtze River. He must be a deserter or a rebel."

The taller had an idea. "Let's steal his money to buy a meal."

They agreed and went over to tie Liu Jingting up with rope. Liu Jingting had not expected this and shouted, "Alas! Why are you arresting me?"

杨龙友对朝宗说道:"咱们竟然不知柳敬亭是个有用之士。"

侯朝宗回答说:"我往常就夸他是我辈中人,说书不过是他的余技罢了。"

柳敬亭当夜出发,一路冲风冒雪,沿江而行,不止一日,已到了武昌城外。他也不去旅店投宿,就在城外无人之处脱下行装,换上靴帽,准备去辕门送信。

初来乍到,一时找不到大营驻地,只得东打听西寻问,好不容易找到大营附近。柳敬亭想:投书可是大事,切不可粗心冒失,得做到万无一失。因此,尽管大营就在不远处,他却不直接去闯营门,先在附近走走,察看一番动静。走不几步,他见前面有两个大兵一摇一摆地向营门走去,便快行两步,尾随在后,听他们两个在谈些什么。

一个稍矮的口中唱道:"杀贼拾贼囊,救民占民房,当官领官仓,一兵吃三粮。"

那个高个子的却反驳道:"你唱错了,如今不这样唱了。"

矮的不服气:"你说不这样唱,那么你就唱唱看。"

"形势变了,该这样唱——贼凶少弃囊,民逃剩空房,官穷不开仓,千兵无一粮。"矮的听高的这么一唱,也不得不服气,现状不就是如此么?他长长地叹了口气:"这样看,我们这穷兵当真要饿死了。""也差不多哩。""前日大家去辕门请愿,元帅答允我们就食去南京,这几天怎不见动静,想必又是变卦了。"

高的士兵好像有些主意:"怕什么?他变了卦,俺们依旧去请愿!"

柳敬亭听得这番对话,上前几步,向两个大兵拱了拱手:"两位将爷,借问一声,哪边是将军辕门?"

矮的对高的说:"这个老儿是江北口音,不是逃兵,就是流贼。"

高的一听,计上心来:"何不诈他几文钱,买顿饭吃。"

两人商议已定,就上前用绳索套住柳敬亭。事出意外,柳敬亭

"We're patrolling officers of the Wuchang military camp. Who else is there to catch besides you?"

Before they had finished, Liu Jingting shot out first with one hand, then with the other, throwing the two soldiers on the ground. He said with a smile, "You're two blind beggars, both famished."

"How did you know that we are hungry?"

Liu Jingting saw that the topic could be used as a way to see the marshal in person and replied, "I would not have come here if you weren't."

"Have you transported the grain from Jiangxi for us?"

"Of course. What else?"

"Alas! We are blind. We'll carry your luggage and send you to the marshal."

They arrived at the headquarters and the soldiers pointed to the mansion. One said, "That is the marshal's residence. You wait here and I'll beat the drum to announce you."

As soon as it was done, an officer walked out and asked if they had any military information. The soldier who had beaten the drum said, "We have a suspect. He said that he had escorted grain here but we're not sure that he's telling the truth. We escorted him here to let you deal with him."

The officer turned to Liu Jingting and asked, "You escorted grain here? Do you have an official document?"

"No, but I do have a letter," Liu Jingting answered calmly.

"That makes it suspicious. Without the document there can be no grain. You could be a deserter or a thief."

Undaunted Liu Jingting replied, "You are wrong. Would I dare come here if I were a deserter or a thief?"

The officer found this reasonable. "I'll present the letter to the marshal."

"It is confidential. I must present it in person," Liu Jingting replied. Given no option the officer reported to the marshal.

Zuo Liangyu sat lost in thought. The disturbance over food had been the day before. He knew that he could not lead his men to Nanjing and that he should wait for the grain to arrive from Jiujiang in Jiangxi. Just then he heard that the man who had escorted grain from Jiangxi had arrived which made him happy and he asked, "Which local government's document does the grain escort hold?" On hearing that the escort had only a letter, he thought that something was wrong. Officers and men

居然被他们套住,不禁怒叫道:"啊呀呀!怎么拿起我来了?"

"俺们是武昌大营专管巡逻的官兵,不拿你,又拿谁呀!"

他们的话声刚刚落地,好一个柳敬亭,左右开弓,顿时将这两个兵丁推倒在地,笑着道:"怪不得要饿得东倒西歪的,你这两个原来是没长眼睛的讨饭花子!""你怎晓得我们挨饿?""不为你们挨饿,我又如何来到此处?"柳敬亭借此话题以为求见之计。

"这样说来,你就是从江西运粮来的?"

"不是运粮的,又是做什么的!"

"呀呀呀,我们瞎眼了,快搬行李,送你老哥去大营。"

行不多时,三人来到辕门前。这两个兵丁指着辕门说:"这就是帅府了!老哥在此稍等,待我们击鼓传报。"

随着鼓声落地,中军官出来问道:"有何军情,速速报来。"那个击鼓的兵丁说道:"刚刚在防地捉到一个可疑的人,声称解粮来此,不知真假,已拿到辕门,听候发落。"

中军官转身对柳敬亭瞧了几眼,开口问道:"你解粮到此,有无公文?"

"没有公文,只有书信。"柳敬亭坦然回答。

"这就可疑得很了。既无公文,何来军粮?看你的神情不是逃兵也是盗贼!"中军官追问道。

柳敬亭毫不惧怯,反问道:"此话就差了!若是逃兵、盗贼,怎敢自寻辕门?"

中军官觉得此话有理:"你既有书信,让我替你送上去。"

"这是一封密信,一定要当面呈交元帅。"中军官无法,只得替他禀报元帅。

左良玉正坐在帐中,独自沉思:日前因饥兵鼓噪,一时许愿就食南京,众多士兵方才散去。但此举实不行:兵去就粮,何如粮来

were prepared and the visitor was allowed to enter.

Liu Jingting walked in to see two rows of guards holding weapons. Calmly and fearlessly he walked past the spears and battle axes. He bowed instead of kneeling to the marshal. "Please forgive me. I am not familiar with the military code. I have a letter for you and hope that you will read it carefully."

Zuo Liangyu, surprised at the man's equanimity, asked, "Who is it from?"

"It's a letter from Mr. Hou of Guide."

Zuo Liangyu said, "Mr. Hou is my benefactor. How do you know him?"

"I work at Mr. Hou's residence."

"I'm sorry I didn't recognize you. Where is the letter?"

Liu Jingting handed the letter to the marshal with both hands. When he saw the envelope, Zuo Liangyu invited Liu Jingting to sit and the gate of the mansion was closed. After reading it, Zuo Liangyu sighed. "I, Zuo Liangyu, am loyal to the court. I would never betray the court or let my benefactor down." He explained the circumstances. "You would not have known that, after roving rebel bands swept through and set fire to it, Wuchang became an empty city. My army is stationed here but hungry soldiers cause disturbances day and night. I have great difficulty keeping them under control."

Liu Jingting stood up. "That is quite unreasonable. Since ancient times the soldiers have always followed the general. How can a general be controled by soldiers? Who else makes a decision if you are not in a position to decide?" Liu Jingting threw down his teacup which made Zuo Liangyu angry.

"How dare you throw the teacup on the ground!"

Liu Jingting smiled. "I dare not be impolite. I threw it on the ground without thinking."

"Without thinking? Does your heart make decisions?" Zuo Liangyu was still angry.

"If my heart could make a decision, I would not allow my hand to do it."

Liu Jingting looked at Zuo Liangyu thoughtfully. Zuo Liangyu understood the point and said with a smile, "What you say is reasonable but my soldiers are so hungry that they have to forage for food themselves."

就兵！所以按兵不动,专等九江粮饷到来。正当此际,忽听有解粮之人前来,大喜过望,连忙问中军官:"解粮之人拿了哪处衙门的公文？"他听说只有私信,怀疑有诈,吩咐左右军士手执兵械提防。然后方传命进见。

柳敬亭进帐后,见左右卫士神情严厉,两排兵器交加,并不胆怯,从戈矛之中躬身安然穿过,上得大帐,一揖为礼,也不下跪:"请恕晚生不知军中礼数——有封书信,请将军仔细看视。"

来人居然毫无惧色,左良玉也有些惊异,问道:"是谁人书信？"

"归德侯老先生寄来奉候的。"

左良玉仍不失警惕之心,问道:"侯老先生是俺的恩师,你又如何认得他？""晚生现在侯府。""这就失敬了。信在哪里？"

柳敬亭双手呈上书信,左良玉一看信封,便吩咐军士关上辕门,重新请柳敬亭坐下。他仔细看过书信后叹息道:"恩师,恩师,你怎知俺左良玉也是一片忠心,哪能背弃深恩,有辱您的保举！"接着又解释道:"你可知道这座武昌城,自从张献忠焚掠之后,十室九空,俺虽镇守在此,粮饷缺乏,饥兵日日鼓噪不休,连俺也做不得主了。"

柳敬亭闻言勃然而起:"元帅说哪里话,自古道'兵随将转',哪有'将逐兵移'的！将军做不得主,谁人能做主？"说罢,就将手中茶杯摔在地上。

左良玉大怒:"啊呀！你这等无礼！竟然把茶杯摔了！"

柳敬亭莞尔一笑:"晚生怎敢无礼！一时说得高兴,顺手摔了。"

"顺手摔了,难道你的心做不得主么？"左良玉仍然气不消。

"心若做得主,也不让手乱动了。"

柳敬亭意味深长地看着左良玉。左良玉顿时醒悟,对他一笑说道:"你讲得有理,只因兵丁饿得急了,方许他们去内里就食,这也是无可奈何之举啊！"

"It was a long way here and I'm hungry myself. Why does Your Highness have to discuss it now?"

"Alas! I'd forgotten!" Zuo Liangyu asked his subordinates to set the table.

Liu Jingting kept touching his stomach saying, "I'm hungry! I'm hungry!"

Zuo Liangyu told his men to hurry up but Liu Jingting rushed towards the inner room. "I can't wait any longer. Let me go inside to eat."

Zuo Liangyu was very angry. "How can you go to my inner room?"

"I'm starving," Liu Jingting replied.

"You're starving. But who allows you to enter my inner room?"

Liu Jingting burst out laughing. "The marshal also knows that even if I'm starving, I should not go to your inner room."

Zuo Liangyu saw the parallel. "Ha, ha. You make fun of me. What a silver tongue! I really need a man who dares to criticize my faults frankly."

From that day on Zuo Liangyu let Liu Jingting stay in the camp and they discussed ancient and current affairs together. The question of going to Nanjing was put aside for the time being.

CHAPTER FOURTEEN

Ruan Frames Hou

After sending the letter to Zuo Liangyu, the authorities in Nanjing adopted other measures. The government submitted a petition to the emperor asking him to promote Zuo Liangyu and to appease him by offering official posts to his descendants. Also the governors and governors-general of nearby provinces and all of Nanjing's officials gathered at the Qingyi Hall to find a way of gathering sufficient food to feed the hungry soldiers at Wuchang.

Yang Longyou had been dismissed from office but was invited to

"晚生远来,也饿急了,元帅何以也不问我一声?"

"啊呀,我倒忘了。"他连忙吩咐左右快快摆饭招待。

柳敬亭不断摸着肚子,连声叫道:"真饿,真饿!"

左良玉不断催促开饭,柳敬亭却朝后面闯去,口中不断声言:"等不得了,等不得了,到内里去吃罢。"

左良玉不禁恼怒:"你这人怎的进我内里?"

柳敬亭只是答:"饿得极了。"

左良玉更加愤愤:"饿得极了,就许你进内里么?"

柳敬亭哈哈大笑:"饿得极了,也不许进内里——这道理,元帅竟然也知道!"

左良玉这才省悟:"哈哈,好个能言善辩之士。俺帐下倒少不得你这个敢于直谏的人哩。"从此左良玉就将柳敬亭留在帐前,早晚谈论古今,把那移兵南京之事暂时搁起。

第十四章
谗言陷侯

话说杨龙友奉兵部尚书熊明遇之命,请侯朝宗以他父亲侯恂的名义,修书劝左良玉不要东下南京之后,南京方面也同时采取了一些措施。一方面奏请朝廷加封左良玉官爵,连他的子侯也都封了官职,以安抚左良玉;另一方面又召集各处总督、巡抚以及南京城内大小文武官员,齐集在清议堂中,共同筹划粮饷以接济武昌,以稳定广大饿兵饥卒。

杨龙友因劝侯朝宗修书有功,虽是罢职闲官,也收到参加会议的通知;阮大铖同样是罢了职的人,但此人极会钻营,居然也收

attend because he had contributed by persuading Hou Chaozong to write a letter. Ruan Dacheng, who was skilled at ingratiating himself with those in authority, came also and they arrived at the Qingyi Hall earlier than the others.

Carrying his official notice, Ruan Dacheng was tremendously proud of himself and when he saw Yang Longyou he said excitedly, "Brother Yang we have been invited to discuss military affairs and we should have a say."

Yang Longyou said with indifference, "It is an important matter and we don't have official titles. We'd better listen to the discussion."

Ruan Dacheng appeared annoyed and raised his voice. "How can you say that? We must take state affairs most seriously. Emperor Taizu made Nanjing the country's capital. Now it is in great danger. We should look at the likelihood of hidden traitors when considering the troops of Wuchang."

Yang Longyou was astonished. "You should not make irresponsible claims."

Ruan Dacheng became more indignant. "I've heard about it. Why can't I mention it?"

Just then the Governor-General of Huai'an, Shi Kefa, and the Governor-General of Fengyang, Ma Shiying, arrived. The Minister of War, Xiong Mingyu, was absent because he had gone to the Yangtze River to call the muster roll of officers and assign tasks according an imperial decree. Ma Shiying was worried and said, "The military situation is critical but we can't discuss it without the minister. What shall we do?"

Shi Kefa was anxious also. He said that although old, weak and feeble he would defend Nanjing at any cost. Yang Longyou went over to comfort him. "Mr. Shi, don't worry too much. Zuo Liangyu used to be a subordinate of General Hou Xun. A few days ago General Hou wrote a letter to Zuo Liangyu to persuade him to give up the plan. I think Zuo Liangyu will accept his advice."

"I heard about that. Though it was Minister Xiong's idea, it originally came from you," Shi Kefa said.

Ruan Dacheng interrupted, "I haven't heard about it, but I have heard that there is a person in Nanjing who colludes with Zuo Liangyu."

Shi Kefa asked who it was and Ruan Dacheng replied that it was none other than Hou Chaozong, the son of Hou Xun. Shi Kefa did not

到会议通知。这两个人不像现职官员,有公务缠身,他们在收到会议传单后,便早早来到清议堂。

尤其是阮大铖,能被通知与会,顿时踌躇满志起来,一见到杨龙友,不无煽动地说:"龙友兄请了。今日集会商议军情,既然传我们到此,也不可默默无言。"

杨龙友虽与阮大铖交好,但也颇知其为人,听了这样言语,便淡淡地答道:"事情重大。我们无职之人,拿不得主意,与会听听就是了。"

阮大铖见杨龙友并不附和自己,未免有几分恼怒,反倒提高声音气忿忿地说道:"说哪里话!朝廷大事,怎能不认真对待!太祖曾定鼎于南京,如今局势岌岌可危,不要只考虑武昌兵顺流东下,只怕内里有人勾引!"

杨龙友乍闻此言,不免暗中一惊:"这话不可乱说!"

阮大铖更是愤然:"小弟实有所闻,岂能不说!"

正当此际,淮安督抚史可法、凤阳督抚马士英先后来到,但主持会议的兵部尚书熊明遇突然奉旨去江上点兵去了。马士英首先忧虑地说:"军情紧急,今日怕又商议不起来,如何是好?"

史可法也是忧心如焚,表示要拼衰病之身尽力保卫南京。杨龙友赶紧劝慰史可法说:"老先生不必过于忧虑,左良玉是侯恂大人的部下,日前已请侯大人发信劝阻,料想他也会听从的。"

史可法接着话题说:"我也听说了。此事虽出自熊大人的意思,其实都是你的功劳。"

这时,阮大铖忽然出语挑拨道:"这一节,我倒未曾听说,只知道左良玉发兵,实因此地有人暗中勾结。"

史可法不知底里,忙问道:"是何人?"

阮大铖见问,露骨地挑明是侯恂之子侯朝宗。哪知史可法深

believe him. He knew that Hou Chaozong, a distinguished scholar, belonged to the Restoration Society and would never do such a thing.

Ruan Dacheng tried to further implicate Hou Chaozong, "Your Highness would not have known that Hou Chaozong corresponded with Zuo Liangyu. If we don't do something soon, he will surely become an agent."

Ma Shiying, who was sitting nearby, agreed with him. "That sounds reasonable. We should not let him endanger the people of Nanjing."

Shi Kefa rejected the idea. "Mr. Ruan has been dismissed from his post and should not make irresponsible remarks. The story has been fabricated." He ignored them and went off in a huff.

Rebuffed, Ruan Dacheng said to Ma Shiying, "I have a conclusive evidence. I heard that the person who delivered the letter for Hou Chaozong is Liu Jingting."

At this, Yang Longyou stood up and said, "Please don't wrong an innocent person. It was me who invited Liu Jingting to deliver the letter. I stood by while Hou Chaozong wrote it. He wrote it with great sincerity. How can you suspect him?"

Ruan Dacheng knew that this was true, but he persisted. "You don't understand, Brother Yang. Hou Chaozong used a code in the letter."

Ma Shiying believed him. He nodded his head and said, "You're right. Hou Chaozong should be executed. As soon as I return to my office, I'll have him arrested." He beckoned Yang Longyou, "Brother-in-law, let's go together."

Yang Longyou declined, "You go first. I'll follow."

Ruan Dacheng, who wished to ingratiate himself with Ma Shiying, bowed at the waist and said, "I'm a good friend of your brother-in-law. I've heard much about your great political achievements and I'm fortunate to have met you. Could you please spare me a few minutes? I have much to tell you." Ma Shiying, who shared some of his interests, said happily, "I've admired you for a long time. I need your help." The pair went off together.

After they had left, Yang Longyou said to himself, "Ruan Dacheng makes a false charge against an innocent man." He remembered that Li Xiangjun had refused Ruan Dacheng's dowries. That was why he persisted; he was trying to destroy him. Yang Longyou decided to inform them immediately.

知侯朝宗乃复社中铮铮有名之士,绝不会做此事,因此并不相信。

阮大铖又进一步诬陷道:"老大人有所不知,他与左良玉相交甚密,常用密信往来。若不早除此人,将来必为内应。"

马士英居然赞同阮大铖之言:"说得有理,不能因他一人而陷全城百姓之命。"

史可法仍不以然:"这可是莫须有的事了——阮老先生乃罢职的人,国家大事不可乱讲。"说罢,就不再理会,拂衣而去。

阮大铖碰了个钉子,大为不满,恨恨地对马士英说:"小弟之言凿凿有据,听说日前捎密信的就是柳敬亭。"

阮大铖编造谎言,罗织罪状,杨龙友实在听不下去,乃申辩道:"这太委屈人了,敬亭送书,乃小弟所请;朝宗写信,小弟在旁。全亏他写的恳切,怎么反怀疑起他来?"

阮大铖明知此言不假,但执意要栽赃诬陷,便信口编造:"龙友不知,那信中都有字眼暗语,别人哪里晓得?"

马士英偏偏听得进这些谗言,点头称赞:"是呀,这样的人是该杀的。我回去,即派人访拿。老妹丈,咱们一同走吧。"

杨龙友推辞说:"请舅翁先行一步,小弟随后就来。"

阮大铖趋附马士英,躬腰说道:"小弟与令妹丈龙友就像同胞兄弟,常常说及老公祖令声政绩,难得今日会着大人,小弟有许多心事,请容小弟向大人诉说,未知可否?"马士英与他正是臭味相投,慨然应允:"久闻高雅,正要请教。"两人乃一同别去。

杨龙友待他们走后自言自语地说道:"这不是栽赃陷害么?"又一想,阮大铖之所以陷害侯朝宗,大约是因为香君辞谢妆奁一事,而侯、李结合是自家牵的线,向香君赠礼也是自己为阮大铖计谋的,如今阮大铖翻脸不认人,乃必欲置之死地。事态发展到这一步,他觉得对不起朝宗和香君,于是决心前往李贞丽院子报信。

It was dusk and the shadows had lengthened when he arrived at The House of Enchanting Fragrance. From the yard came the sound of traditional stringed and woodwind instruments. With all his strength he knocked on the door shouting, "Open up quickly!"

Su Kunsheng came to the door and was pleased to see him. "It is Master Yang. Why do you come so late to indulge in pleasures?"

Without replying Yang Longyou asked for Brother Hou.

"Xiangjun has learned a new *qu* (a type of verse for singing) and Mr. Hou is listening to her singing it upstairs."

"Tell them to come down immediately."

Yang Longyou was flustered and looked irritable. Su Kunsheng ran upstairs to ask Xiangjun and Chaozong to come down. Chaozong walked down smiling broadly. "Brother Yang, you're in such a good mood that you seek entertainment at midnight."

"Brother Hou, you haven't heard. You're in great danger." They all became alarmed.

"What's the danger?"

Yang Longyou told them about the meeting.

Hou Chaozong was frightened. "I've never had anything to do with Ruan Dacheng. Why does he do this?"

"You shamed him by refusing his dowries. He is angry."

Afraid that she may be incriminated, Li Zhenli urged him to go to somewhere far away. Hou Chaozong understood right away and said that it was a reasonable request, but he looked at Xiangjun and sighed. "How can I part with Xiangjun?" Unlike her adoptive mother, Xiangjun was not afraid. Her thoughts were of Chaozong's safety and she agreed that it would be best if he were to leave Nanjing. Earnestly she said that it was not the time to think of love.

"You're right," he said. She had earned his respect by refusing Ruan Dacheng's dowries and at this critical moment she calmly advised him to go away. Chaozong admired her even more. However, his hometown was far away, the flames of battle raged everywhere, and he said, "Where shall I go?"

Yang Longyou had thought about it and said that he had an idea. "The Governor-General of Huai'an Shi Kefa tried to defend you at the meeting and said that he had a good relationship with your father. Why don't you go to his residence to wait for the letter from home?"

Chaozong was most grateful and thanked him.

　　杨龙友乘着暮色急行，很快就走到媚香楼，只听见院内不断传出丝竹之声，便用力敲门，大叫："快快开门。"

　　苏昆生应声而出，打开院门一见是杨龙友，兴致颇高地问道："原来是杨老爷，天色已晚，还来此闲游。""啊呀，你不是苏昆老么？"杨龙友不待他答话又问："侯兄在哪里？""今日香君学完一套新曲，都在楼上听她演唱。""快请他们下楼。"

　　苏昆生见杨龙友气急败坏、神色张皇，也不敢怠慢，立即转身上楼，招呼朝宗、香君等人一齐下楼来。侯朝宗满面春风地问道："杨兄高兴，也来消夜？""侯兄还不知，有天大祸事要落在你头上了！"这冒冒失失的一句话，可把大家吓了一跳。

　　"有何祸事？""今日清议堂议事，阮大铖对大家说，你与左良玉有交往，常通私书，将为内应。那些主事的官儿，都有捉拿你的意思。"杨龙友慌不择言地一口气说完原委。

　　侯朝宗惊怕起来："我与阮大铖素无深仇，他为何下这毒手？"

　　"还不是却奁一事，他恼羞成怒，方有此着！"

　　李贞丽在旁听到此事，深怕连累自家，劝侯朝宗赶紧远走高飞，侯朝宗听话听音，已知其意，便立即接答："说的有理。"继而又看了香君几眼，叹息道："只是才与香君成婚，如何舍得？"香君倒不像她的义母李贞丽那样怕连累自己，而是为朝宗设想，如今也只有远远避开才是上策。她严肃地对朝宗说："官人素以豪杰自命，为何学儿女子态？"

　　"说的是，说的是。"自从香君却奁以后，朝宗一直视她为畏友，此时形势危急，香君却处变不惊，劝他出走，确有识见。但继而一想，家乡路遥，烽火连天，欲归不得，不禁脱口而出："走到何处去？"

　　杨龙友一路上来此倒替他考虑过，此时便建议道："侯兄也不必惊慌，小弟倒有个主意。"接着面对在场诸位说道："会议时，凤

Xiangjun went upstairs to pack for him then returned. Chaozong tried to comfort her, "It is only a temporary parting. You must take care of yourself, we'll meet again."

Xiangjun wiped away her tears and said, "The flames of war are everywhere. We may never meet again."

Li Zhenli saw their reluctance to part and urged Chaozong to leave; the soldiers could arrive at any time. Su Kunsheng knew where Shi Kefa lived and volunteered to escort Chaozong to his home at Yinyuan Garden in the city proper.

After they had gone, Li Zhenli held Yang Longyou's sleeve. She said that together with Master Hou he had brought about the situation and asked what would happen if the soldiers came to arrest Chaozong the next day.

Yang Longyou comforted her, "Don't worry. Hou Chaozong has gone and it has nothing to do with you."

CHAPTER FIFTEEN

Changed Situation Shocks Zuo

Zuo Liangyu stayed in Wuchang for two reasons. The first was that the emperor sent an imperial envoy, Huang Shu, to make him a grand mentor and his son, Zuo Menggeng, a regional commander. The second was that the Governor-General of Jiujiang, Yuan Jixian, had personally escorted 30 boats of grain to Wuchang and the troops remained peaceful.

He was very pleased to see Huang Shu and Yuan Jixian and arranged a banquet for them at the Yellow Crane Tower. As host, he went there early, surrounded by his subordinates. Huang Shu and Yuan Jixian had not arrived and Zuo Liangyu leant on the railing enjoying the scenery. Dongting Lake looked vast and in the distance stood the majestic Mount Yunmeng. The three towns of Wuhan were the doors to southwest China and he felt proud of being charged with defending such an important place.

阳督抚、舍舅马士英也在坐,他的话不怎么友好,倒是淮安督抚史可法为侯兄大力分辨,并且说与尊府有世谊。这样,何不随他去淮安暂避,再等家信。"

"好,好呀,多谢指引。"侯朝宗绝处逢生,连连称谢。

香君闻言急忙上楼去为朝宗准备行装;又下楼来,朝宗安慰她说:"暂时分别,多多保重,后会有期。"香君闻言,揩去眼泪,哽咽着道:"满地战火,能否重见,也太难说了。"李贞丽见他们难分难舍,心急火燎,催促朝宗道:"怕有巡兵前来,你快走罢。"苏昆生知道史可法来南京常在市隐园居留,便主动护送朝宗前往。

李贞丽见侯朝宗已去,便拉着杨龙友衣袖说:"这桩祸事,都是杨老爷引起的,还要杨老爷来收结。明日果真来拿人,怎么办?"

"贞娘放心,侯朝宗人都走了,与你就全无干系了。"杨龙友劝慰李贞丽后,也自行离开媚香楼而去。

第十五章
武昌惊变

侯朝宗背负着为左良玉内应的罪名被迫出走,离开南京。但左良玉其实并未撤兵武昌、就食南都。一则是朝廷近日特派巡按御史黄澍前来武昌宣旨,加封他为太傅,他的儿子左梦庚为总兵;二则九江督抚袁继咸又亲自押运三十船粮食前来接济,将兵心都稳定下来。

当黄、袁两位大人来到武昌后,左良玉大喜过望,吩咐从人在黄鹤楼摆设宴席,招待两位同僚登楼饮酒、观看江景。黄、袁两人尚未到,左良玉独自一人凭栏四眺,周围景色,尽收眼底,那洞庭

He wanted to speak to someone and turned to said to a soldier, "It's dull having to wait for them here! Please ask Master Liu to come to the tower for a chat."

Liu Jingting was waiting below. When he heard Zuo Liangyu call him, he immediately climbed up the tower. Zuo Liangyu asked an attendant to serve the storyteller a cup of good tea. Liu Jingting began to beating his drum and took up his clappers to continue a story that he had started the day before. When Liu Jingting told the story about Qin Qiong, a hero of the Tang Dynasty, Zuo Liangyu sighed with emotion. "I rendered meritorious service in the border areas. I was very brave — the equal of 10,000 men. Now I am getting old and grey, but the roving bandits have not been wiped out. The thought of it makes me uneasy."

Just then a soldier called out, "Marshal, the two lords have arrived!"

Liu Jingting withdrew quietly as Huang Shu and Yuan Jixian climbed up the tower. Zuo Liangyu met them at the entrance. They bowed to each other and Zuo Liangyu said, "We are greatly honored to have you here. Food and wine have been prepared and I invite you to enjoy the river scenery."

Huang Shu and Yuan Jixian said together, "I've long been looking forward to meeting you. I'm very happy to meet you now."

After the exchange of conventional greetings, they sat down. They were about to raise their wine glasses when a man who specialized in reporting state affairs ran in.

"A report for the marshal, an imminent disaster!"

The three immediately put down their wine and stood up. "What's the matter?"

"A report for the marshal. For three days a large group of roving bandits have surrounded the capital. There were no relief troops and they broke through the city gate. They set fire to the palace and the emperor hanged himself on Coal Hill."

They were shocked, "When did it happen?"

"On the 19th day of the third lunar month."

When they heard the report, the attendants in the tower knelt facing the north and wailed bitterly. Zuo Liangyu, who had just found favor with the emperor, was devastated. He stood up, wringing his hands, then walked back and forth shouting, "Your Majesty, my master! I, Zuo Liangyu, am far away. I should have lead my troops to save you. I am guilty of a crime for which I deserve to die 10,000 deaths!" All his subordinates shed tears.

浩浩,云梦苍苍,返顾武汉三镇,正是控西南之险,当江汉之衢。他颇为自己能镇守如此重要之地而感到自豪,不禁要找人谈谈,便对随从说道:"快请柳相公上楼来闲谈。"

柳敬亭早已在楼下专等召唤了。左良玉吩咐从人泡上好茶,柳敬亭打起鼓板,将昨晚未说完的书再接着说,当说到秦叔宝被罗公看重时,左良玉不禁感慨万分,自言自语道:"俺左良玉立功边塞,有万夫不当之勇,也算得上是天下一个好健儿。如今白发渐生,杀贼未尽,怎不令人生恨!"

叹息未止,从人已禀报:"元帅爷,两位老爷已到楼下。"

"快请!"柳敬亭此刻知道自己事儿已毕,从旁悄悄退下。黄、袁二人已拾级而上,左良玉迎至楼口相接,彼此作揖,左良玉欢迎道:"二位先生俯临敝镇,无胜荣幸,聊备水酒,请二位先生同看江景。"

黄、袁二位齐声说道:"久仰感望,今日喜见,大快生平。"

彼此寒暄已罢,依次入席,举杯欲饮之际,突然一个专报军国大事的报子急步跑上楼来:

"禀报元帅爷,大事不好了,大事不好了!"

左、黄、袁三人掷下酒杯,立起身来,连连问道:"有什么紧急军情,这等喊叫?"

"禀报元帅:大伙'流贼'北犯,层层围住京城,三天未有救兵,城门已破,宫殿被烧,圣上已自缢煤山。"

三位文武大官大惊失色:"有这样事,是哪一天?"

"就是这,这三月十九日。"

三人带头,随从等人一齐向北跪下,顿时一片哭声,尤其是左良玉,新近恩宠有加,哭罢立起身来,搓着双手,来回跳步,嚎叫着:"我的圣上呀,我的主子呀!小臣左良玉,远在此地,不能率一旅之众以勤王室,罪该万死了!"周围将佐闻言莫不齐声泪下。

At this moment Yuan Jixian, who had kept calm, waved his hand and said, "Stop this behavior! There are important things to be discussed."

Zuo Liangyu did not understand the sudden change and Yuan Jixian said forcefully, "Beijing is lost. The country has no emperor. If Marshal Zuo had not kept the flag flying, the country would be in chaos. How can we regain control of the nation?"

The gravity of the situation dawned on Huang Shu, who nodded his head and pointed to the area stretching out beyond the front of the tower. "Jiujiang, Wuchang, Jingzhou and Xiangyang make up half of the country. If roving bandits capture them, they will be very hard to recover."

Yuan Jixian and Huang Shu convinced Zuo Liangyu who said that it would be his responsibility to appease the local people. He said, "As a marshal I am duty bound, but I hope you will help me defend the country's territory."

They both agreed to follow him.

A memorial ceremony for Emperor Chongzhen was then held on the orders of Zuo Liangyu. The three formed an alliance in front of the emperor's memorial tablet. Marshal Zuo announced, "Today an alliance is formed and we become sworn brothers. Lord Yuan will be my military counselor, and Lord Huang will be the army supervisor. I, Zuo Liangyu, will work hard, train my troops and defend the territory with my life. Once the crown prince, or another prince, is restored at the imperial court, I will go north to support him." The others backed him and agreed that they would go to Wuchang, if required, at any time to discuss state affairs. Then Yuan Jixian left for Jiujiang and Huang Shu for Xiangyang.

　　此刻惟有九江督抚袁继咸方寸未乱,摇手止住大家:"且莫举哀,还有大事商量。"

　　左良玉一时不解,问道:"有何大事?"

　　袁继咸慷慨道来:"北京既失,江山无主。将军若不早举义旗,顷刻乱生,那时如何安抚天下?"

　　黄澍也恍然大悟,连连点头称是,并指着楼前旷野说道:"这江、汉、荆、襄,也算是半壁江山,万一失守,也难以收复了!"

　　两人之语点醒左良玉,他立即表示要以安抚地方为己任,责无旁贷地说道:"小弟滥握兵权,职责难辞——不过,也望二公协力,共保疆土。"

　　袁、黄二人异口同声地表示:"敢不随从。"

　　左良玉得到他们的支持,乃下令先行祭拜崇祯皇帝。并在皇帝灵前与二人结盟,说道:"我等三人如今拜盟,义同兄弟。今后请袁爷督师,黄爷监军,我左良玉操练兵马,死守疆土。一旦有太子诸王出来中兴王室,我等再北上勤王,恢复中原。"袁、黄二人都表示同意。继而又约定,若有国家大事,袁、黄二人仍来武昌商议。说定之后,袁继咸回九江,黄澍返襄阳。

CHAPTER SIXTEEN

Ma Supports Prince Fu

After Hou Chaozong had sought refuge with Shi Kefa the two of them left Nanjing for Huai'an. Time flew! It was six months since Hou Chaozong had arrived there. Shi Kefa, a townsman of Hou Chaozong and a former student of his father, was very kind to him.

Shi Kefa had been a successful candidate in the highest imperial examination in the last year of the reign of Emperor Chongzhen when there was much unrest in the country. He had once served as provincial intendant. Finally he had been promoted to governor-general of Huai'an. A month earlier he was appointed Minister of War for Nanjing to replace Xiong Mingyu who had been summoned to Beijing. After the promotion Beijing fell to the "roving bandits". Fortunately the Yangtze River to the north of Nanjing acted as a natural moat and was safe for the meanwhile. However, with no emperor there was utter confusion. Some supported one prince and others would have welcomed another. One day Shi Kefa drilled his troops by the river then returned to his residence where he was chatting to Hou Chaozong. "Brother Hou, today I heard what could be good news. Though Beijing has fallen, the emperor is safe. He went south by sea and the crown prince traveled south by backroads. Whether it true or not I do not know."

Chaozong was not convinced. "If it is true, it is fortunate for the country."

Just then a soldier reported that a letter had arrived from Ma Shiying and a messenger waited for a reply. Shi Kefa took the letter, opened it and began to read. He frowned and said to Hou Chaozong, "Ma Shiying wishes to support Prince Fu, Zhu Yousong, as emperor." He sighed and continued, "He says that it was true that the emperor hanged himself. No one knows where the crown prince is. Even if I don't support him, he will encourage Prince Fu to ascend the throne." He thought for a moment and said, "Allowing him to be emperor would accord with the imperial family's

第十六章
拥立邀功

侯朝宗自从避难投奔史可法后，不久就随他离开南京前往淮安。岁月荏苒，不觉已有半年。亏得史可法与他是河南同乡，又是乃父侯恂的学生，对他颇加青睐。

史可法崇祯末年考中进士，正值天下变乱之际，做过部曹、监司，好不容易才做到淮安督抚。一月前南京兵部尚书熊明遇被召至北京，就任命他升任南京兵部尚书。哪知接任以来，北京失守，留都南京幸在天堑长江之南，暂时无事。不过朝中无君，不免人心惶惶。朝中大臣有的议立某王，有的议迎某王，众说纷纭。今日他从江上操练军兵归来，又听到一些传闻，便请侯朝宗出来，说道："侯兄，今日听得一喜信，说北京虽然失守，但圣上无恙，早已航海到了南方；太子也从小道奔至东边。就是不知道这一消息是否准确！"

侯朝宗将信将疑地说道："果真如此，乃天下百姓之福。"

正当二人闲谈时，忽报凤阳督抚马士英处有人前来投信，并立等回书。史可法从随从手中接过信来展视一番，双眉立即皱起："这个马士英，又讲什么迎立之事了！"嗟叹数声后对侯朝宗说："看他来信意思，颇有意迎立福王。他信中说圣上确确实实在煤山缢死，太子也下落不明。果真如此，即使俺不依，他也会自行迎立。"停顿片刻，沉吟一番，又接着说："按照皇室辈份排行，立福王也无不可。罢，罢，罢，给他回信，一同列名算了。"

rules of seniority. I'll write saying that I agree to the proposal."

Hou Chaozong stood up, stepped forward and said firmly, "What you say is not right. Prince Fu's fief is my homeland. I know him well and he is not the right person."

When Shi Kefa asked him why, he said that Prince Fu had committed three major crimes: "For a start he once plotted to murder the crown prince which would have allowed him to succeed to the throne himself. He would have already usurped it if high-ranking officials had not stopped him. Secondly, he extorted a large amount of gold and silver but when the 'roving bandits' were approaching Henan, he gave nothing to help the army and the country was conquered. He also seized the palace's property and treasure to feather his own nest. Thirdly, Prince Fu took refuge in Huaiqing when his father Changxun was killed. During the chaos he forced a girl to marry him. How could such a person ascend the throne?"

Shi Kefa nodded. Hou Chaozong gave an analysis of the situation: "First, it is not known whether the emperor is alive or dead; second, even if the emperor had died, the crown prince may be alive; third, if the imperial family's rules of seniority are not adhered to in selecting an emperor we must choose a person of extraordinary ability; fourth, Prince Fan is very powerful and may declare himself emperor while the country is in a state of confusion and fifth, evil officials could manipulate the new emperor because of their support. Therefore, we should not decide rashly."

Shi Kefa was convinced. "Brother Hou, your opinions make sense. Could you please write a reply to Ma Shiying giving the three major crimes and the five reasons?"

Hou Chaozong took little time writing the reply which was handed to Ma Shiying's messenger.

At this moment a servant walked in to announce the arrival of Ruan Dacheng. It had been Ruan Dacheng's idea that Prince Fu should be the candidate. He had sneaked out of Nanjing during the chaos to see Prince Fu in Jiangpu. Then he crossed the Yangtze River to return to Nanjing the same night and had lost no time in promoting the advantages of Prince Fu becoming the emperor to Ma Shiying. What worried him was that the Minister of War, Shi Kefa, would not agree. He allowed Ma Shiying to write the letter and came himself at midnight to convince him.

He had tried many times to get the doorkeeper to report his arrival and finally the doorkeeper had given in.

"Master. Ruan Dacheng has come to see you."

　　侯朝宗听说后,立即站了起来,上前半步,斩钉截铁地对史可法说道:"老先生之言差矣。福王封地正是晚生家乡,晚生对他的情况极其了解。断断立不得。"

　　史可法闻言乃问其底里,侯朝宗说:"他有三大罪,人人皆知:第一,当年谋害太子,欲行继位,若无大臣阻挡,早将帝位争去;第二,搜刮金银无数,'流贼'逼近河南,他竟然不拿出一文助饷,以致国破家亡,满宫财宝,全饱贼囊;第三,福王朱由崧,在乃父常恂被杀之际,逃到怀庆去避难,还乘乱离之际,强娶民女——有这三大罪,怎能继承皇位?"

　　史可法连连点头称是。侯朝宗又进而分析当前局势,说明有五不可立之理:第一,圣上存亡,传说不一;第二,即令圣上殉国,尚有太子;第三,中兴之主,虽可不拘辈份,但必选英杰;第四,藩王势众力强,可能趁乱自立;第五,奸邪之臣又将以拥立之功挟持新主。有鉴于此,不可匆忙议立议迎。

　　这篇透彻的分析终于说动了史可法,连连称是,说道:"世兄高见,考虑深远。就烦世兄以这三大罪、五不可立的原由,写信回他便了。"侯朝宗即时写好回信,交与马士英家人持去。

　　正当此际,家人又报称阮大铖前来求见。原来迎立福王之议,正是出自此人。阮大铖为了再次出仕,趁这人慌马乱之际,悄悄溜出南京,到江浦寻着福王朱由崧,以为奇货可居;又连夜渡江回到南京,与马士英商定迎立福王朱由崧。他担心兵部尚书史可法从中掣肘,所以先由马士英写信商量,自己又深夜前来史可法寓所求见,欲说服史可法赞同迎立福王。

　　家人在他一再要求下,进去禀告:"老爷,有阮大铖到门求见。"

　　史可法问:"如此深夜,他来干什么?"

"Why does he come so late at night?" Shi Kefa wondered.

"He must be here to discuss the new emperor." Hou Chaozong said.

Shi Kefa resolutely refused to meet him. "He is the man who accused you of spying last year in the Qingyi Hall. He is a former member of the eunuch party and a real villain. Let him go."

A soldier drove Ruan Dacheng away which upset him and he said to himself, "Shi Kefa holds the seal of the Ministry of War. He is so stubborn. What on earth can I do to convince him?" Suddenly he recollected with a smile, "Hah, no one knows where the emperor's jade seal is. What use can the seal of the Ministry of War be?" He looked at Shi Kefa's residence and shouted, "Old Shi, I came to send you a plate of buns stuffed with meat, but you refused them. You'll regret it some day!" He burst out laughing and left.

Ruan Dacheng reported to Ma Shiying as soon as he returned. Ma Shiying was worried over whether his backing of Prince Fu as emperor would succeed or not. Shi Kefa had military power and could cause difficulties. He would not let the matter drop and with Ruan Dacheng's agreement decided to contact generals Liu Zeqing, Huang Degong, Liu Liangzuo and Gao Jie. The four were so eager to take the credit that they agreed to gather their military troops at Jiangpu on the 28th day of the fourth lunar month. Ruan Dacheng also convinced officials such as Duke Wei, Xu Hongji, Director of Ceremonies, Han Zanzhou, and the Supervisor of the Ministry of Personnel, Li Zhan, and Chief Investigating Censor, Zhu Guochang. They appointed Ma Shiying as their leader and misrepresented certain officials and officers by adding their names to the list of those who supported Prince Fu. On the day that Prince Fu ascended the throne Ma Shiying wore court costume and Ruan Dacheng served as temporary master of ceremonies. They had ridden their horses directly to Jiangpu to welcome Prince Fu to Nanjing.

On the first day of the fifth lunar month in the 17th year of the Chongzhen reign, Prince Fu went to pay homage at the mausoleum of Zhu Yuanzhang, the first emperor of the Ming Dynasty. As soon as he returned to the palace, he found officials and officers in court costume, led by Ma Shiying, Huang Degong and Liu Zeqing, who held a petition and advised him to ascend the throne. Supported by Ma Shiying and his followers Prince Fu, Zhu Yousong, became the regent emperor.

As it was a fait accompli, Shi Kefa fell into line with other court officials. Prince Fu was very pleased; he would supervise the court and

侯朝宗说:"不用说,又是讲迎立之事了。"

史可法断然拒绝:"去年在清议堂诬害世兄的便是他。这人原是阉党,真正小人,不见。"立即叫家人将他拒于门外。

阮大铖气丧地搓手自语道:"这史可法掌着兵部大印,如此执拗,迎立之事,怕也为难,如何是好?"忽而又脸露笑容,自语道:"咦!如今皇上的玉玺尚无下落,你那一颗兵部的印章又有何用?"不禁指着史府大门,恨恨地说道:"老史,老史,一盘大好的肉包子送上门来,你不会吃,反去送了他人,日后你可不要后悔!"说罢,哈哈大笑,自行离去。

阮大铖归去后,自然向马士英一五一十地诉说。马士英闻知掌握兵权的史可法作梗,对迎立之事能否行得,便犹疑起来。但迎立之功又诱使他不甘罢休,便与阮大铖谋计,由阮大铖出面,绕开兵部,直接与掌管重兵的武臣刘泽清、黄得功、刘良佐、高杰等人串联。这四个武将邀功心切,欣然赞同,相互约定四月二十八日,带着全副仪仗到江浦聚集。同时,阮大铖又约会了魏国公徐鸿基、司礼监韩赞周、吏部给事李沾、监察御史朱国昌等几个文官参与。他们一致公推马士英领衔迎立,又将当朝大臣的名字写了一些在迎立表上,也不怕他们到时推辞。一切准备停当,到了那天马士英身穿朝服,阮大铖暂时充做奉礼官,跟随在马士英身边,分别上了坐骑,马不停蹄地赶去迎接福王来南京即位。

在这班宵小之徒的拥戴之下,神宗皇帝之孙、福王朱由崧成了监国之主,于崇祯十七年(1644)五月初一拜谒了乃祖朱元璋的孝陵。回宫后,早有马士英率着黄得功、刘泽清等人身着朝服,捧着表文,前来劝进,继登大位。

史可法见事实既成,也只得厕身其间,一齐上朝迎立。此举正中朱由崧下怀,虽说"暂以藩王监国",但却"照常办理一切政务"。

handle all state affairs.

Ma Shiying and his followers did not care whether Prince Fu called himself regent emperor or the new emperor. Their only concerns were their own interests and they all conveyed the same message to him. "A long life to Your Majesty! Now that you are emperor we will faithfully follow your orders. However, we are faced by a formidable foe and should recover the lost land as soon as possible. There is much to do and Your Majesty must appoint all officials and officers without delay."

Prince Fu knew perfectly well what they were after and said, "Your concerns over the recovery of land indicate your loyalty to the court. As to filling official posts, I have already made arrangements. They will be given in an imperial decree announced later." The officers and officials left the palace.

Soon an eunuch came and read the decree in a loud voice: "Ma Shiying, Governor-General of Fengyang, who proposed the new emperor's accession to the throne, has rendered outstanding services. He is promoted to Grand Secretary of the Grand Secretariat and Minister of War. He will enter the Grand Secretariat to handle these affairs. Minister of Personnel, Gao Hongtu, Minister of Rites, Jiang Yueguang, and Minister of War, Shi Kefa are all promoted to members of the Grand Secretariat, and still hold their own posts. Gao Hongtu and Jiang Yueguang will enter the Grand Secretariat to handle state affairs, and Shi Kefa will go to the north of the Yangtze River to serve as the chief military commander. Other officials and officers will be promoted by three classes. The regional commanders of the four towns Huang Degong, Gao Jie, Liu Zeqing and Liu Liangzuo will be promoted from counts to marquises, and go back to their respective posts. All those who contributed to the emperor's coming to the throne may be enrolled in different ministries."

The promotions made the officials and officers very happy. Shi Kefa, who thought he could contribute by recovering lost land, spoke to Huang Degong and Liu Zeqing.

"As Minister of War I am ashamed that we cannot recover the central China. Now that the emperor puts me in charge of troops north of the Yangtze River, I will use the opportunity by rendering services to the court. I wish to see both of you. Let's get together at Yangzhou on the 10th day of the fifth lunar month to discuss relevant affairs. We cannot delay it and we should work hard." The new marquises happily agreed. Shi Kefa headed for his new post.

马士英等人由着朱由崧自称监国之主也好，或即称新皇帝也好，随他说去。他们只重视自身的加官进爵，齐声称颂："万岁，万万岁！真是仁群圣主之言，臣等敢不遵旨。但大仇当报，失地当收，文武官员不可或缺，宜即时设置。"

朱由崧也不是个糊涂主子，自然知道这班官员拥立自己的用心，开口说道："你们以报仇复国为请，足见忠心。至于设立将相，寡人早有计划，请稍待听旨。"这班文武臣子退出宫外。

不一会儿，有太监捧旨出来，高声宣称："凤阳督抚马士英，倡议迎立，功居第一，升内阁大学士，兼兵部尚书，入阁办事。吏部尚书高弘图、礼部尚书姜曰广、兵部尚书史可法，均升补大学士，各兼本衔。高弘图、姜曰广入阁办事，史可法去江北督师。其余部院大小官员，各加三级。迎驾人员论功选补。四镇总兵黄得功、高杰、刘泽清、刘良佐，都由伯爵进封侯爵，各归防地驻守。"

这班大小官员人人欢喜异常，但各有各的打算。史可法以为可一展收复中原之志，首先对黄得功、刘泽清二人说道：

"老夫掌管兵部，每以不能克服中原为耻，圣上命俺督师江北，正好报效朝廷，今与两位侯爷约定，五月初十齐集扬州，共商复仇之事。各须努力，不得迟延。"黄、刘二人新晋侯爵，自然应承。史可法随即走马赴任去了。

黄、刘二人也准备归去，马士英却连忙招呼道："二位将军请转来。"黄、刘二将只得停步。马士英上前几步，拉着这两个新侯爷的手，别有用心地说道："圣上看重咱们迎立之功，拜相封侯。我等都是朝中勋旧大臣，比不得别个。此后内外消息，需要相互照应，千秋富贵，方可常保。"

这两个人自然心领神会，感激不尽地连声承诺："蒙大恩携带，方有今日，敢不听从吩咐。"说罢，别去。

As Huang Degong and Liu Zeqing were about to leave, Ma Shiying called them back. He walked up to them and holding their hands said, "The emperor was kind enough to offer us high official posts. As senior officials and officers, we should be in contact with each other often and exchange information. Only by doing this can we guarantee our wealth and rank."

The two generals understood him and promised to do what he told them.

After the officials and officers had gone Ma Shiying started laughing. "I'm the prime minister. What a happy event!" Though he had driven Shi Kefa out of Nanjing, Gao Hongtu and Jiang Yueguang would be in the Grand Secretariat and he would have to take care that they could not seize power. He decided to go to the Grand Secretariat rather than return home.

He was still happily reflecting on his success when he heard, "My congratulations to you on becoming prime minister." He looked up and saw that it was Ruan Dacheng.

"Where have you been?" he asked.

"I stayed in the court to hear the news."

Since his wish had come true, Ma Shiying saw no further use for Ruan Dacheng and said, "Ordinary people are not allowed here. Today is the most important day for the new emperor and you should not stay. You'd better go."

Ruan Dacheng was cunning and calmly said that he had a few words to say. He walked up and whispered, "You were promoted to prime minister because of your contribution in the emperor's accession to the throne. I also rendered services. Why didn't the emperor promote me?"

Ma Shiying had no choice but to say, "An imperial decree was announced. Those who rendered services in welcoming the new emperor may be enrolled by different ministers."

Ruan Dacheng was happy to hear it. "Wonderful, I hope Your Highness will recommend me."

"Don't worry. I'll take care of you." Ma Shiying made a few casual remarks and prepared to leave but Ruan Dacheng said, "It should not be delayed. I'll come with you to the Grand Secretariat to see if I have a chance."

Ma Shiying found that he could not get rid of him and said, "As a new member of the Grand Secretariat, I am not familiar with my work. You could give me a hand, but you must be careful."

　　眼看众官儿一时走散，这马士英方始放声大笑："想不到，俺今日也做了堂堂首相，好不快活呀！"笑声刚落地，他又想到：史可法这个倔老，虽被自己略施小计，排出京城，但高弘图、姜曰广却与自家一同入阁办事，可得小心，不要让这两个家伙夺了权去。说不得，今日只能暂缓回府，先入阁办事去。

　　正当他得意非凡之际，忽听得："老公祖，恭喜了，果然登了相位。"

　　他抬头一看，原来是阮大铖，不知什么时候踅了进来，连忙问道："你从哪里来？"

　　"晚生藏在朝房里，打听新闻哩。"

　　马士英宿愿已偿，觉得此人如今已无大用，不无嫌弃地说："此处是禁地，今日立法之始，你青衣小帽，一无官职，在此不便，还是请出去吧。"

　　阮大铖为人深沉，多有心计，也不是三言两语可以打发的人，听了马士英这番言语，立即明白他的心意，不紧不慢地说道："晚生有要紧话说哩。"不待马士英答话，他便趋前半步，附耳说道："老师相叙了迎立之功，获此高位。晚生奉表迎立，也有微劳，如何不见提起？"

　　马士英被他追问，不得不说："方才宣旨，各部院缺员，可将迎驾之人按功选补。"

　　阮大铖方露喜色："好，好，这得看老师相的荐拔了。"

　　"你的事，何须谆谆嘱咐！"马士英敷衍几句，又待转身入内。哪知阮大铖不容他就此走脱："事不宜迟。晚生权当跟班，随师相入阁，看看机会如何。"

　　马士英见摔不脱他，干脆做好人，说道："俺初入内阁，事务尚不熟练，你来帮帮忙，倒也不妨，只是要小心在意。"

Ruan Dacheng was eager to start his official career again and was pleased. Acting like Ma Shiying's footman, he wormed his way into the Grand Secretariat; power would make him arrogant again.

CHAPTER SEVENTEEN

Four Generals Compete

After the 10th day of the fifth month of the lunar year, Shi Kefa sent for Hou Chaozong to get his opinions and suggestions on the reorganization of his forces for a plan to restore the state. Hou Chaozong naturally went along with Shi's plan, but warned that Gao Jie, the general garrisoned at Yangzhou and Zhengjiang, worried him. Gao was arrogant and his men conceited. The other generals Huang Degong, Liu Zeqing and Liu Liangzuo resented him deeply. If they were at odds it would be to the enemy's advantage. Shi Kefa knew of the friction and was ready to mediate.

While Shi Kefa was exchanging opinions with Hou Chaozong, the four defender-generals came to pay their respects to him. Shi saluted each in turn and said to them, "I have been asked to command the forces in the area. You are marquises not ordinary soldiers." After saying this, he gestured for them to take their seats.

Gao Jie who was very self satisfied took the first seat so that Huang Degong, Liu Zeqing and Liu Liangzuo had to sit down one by one. Huang scowled at Gao. Shi saw the incident, but continued persuading them to make a joint effort.

Huang became enraged as he listened to Shi. "With the marshal here, I should not quarrel...." He pointed his finger at Gao and rebuked him. "You are a solider, surrendered to the imperial court. Why did you take the first seat today?"

Gao took umbrage at his words and said, "I was the earliest to come over to the imperial court and am the oldest. Why should I come after

阮大铖为了一官半职，也顾不得自家身份，替马士英捧着笏板，俨然一个跟班模样，摇摇摆摆地混入内阁去了。

第十七章
四镇争位

眼见五月初十已至，史可法在与高杰、黄得功、刘泽清、刘良佐四总兵齐集议事之前，请出在帐前效力的侯朝宗来先行商量，听取侯朝宗对于整顿军旅、雪仇复国的见解和主张。侯朝宗自然赞成史可法的规划，但又提醒史公："只有一事堪忧，高杰镇守扬州、镇江一带，兵骄将傲，那黄得功、刘泽清、刘良佐三镇，每每有不平之恨，今日相聚，万一四人不和，怕要被敌人利用。"史可法自然明白这四镇之间的摩擦，已准备为他们当面调停。

史可法与侯朝宗商议已定，四镇侯爷鱼贯而入，齐来叩见阁部大元帅史公，史可法拱手还礼："列位请起。"继而又严肃地说道："本帅以阁部督师，君命隆重，大小将军均在指挥之下。四镇乃堂堂列侯，不同寻常武夫。"边说边举手："请四位坐下，共商军情。"四镇乃作揖告坐。

高杰自视甚高，也不谦让就坐了首位，黄得功、刘泽清、刘良佐只得依次而坐。但黄得功满脸怒容地盯住高杰。史可法看在眼里，口里却劝说四镇"同心共把乾坤造"。

黄得功听得这番言论，反而怒气上激，开口说道："元帅在上，小将本不该争论……"用手指着身边的高杰斥责道："这高杰乃是流贼投诚，有什么战功？今日公然坐在俺三镇之上！"

高杰闻言勃然大怒："我投诚最早，年岁又大，怎能居你辈之下？"

you?"

Liu Zeqing joined in the fray saying to Gao, "We are guests in your land. If you don't know how to treat guests how can you command your forces?"

Liu Liangzuo said bluntly that Gao had enjoyed the fruits of his high position in Yangzhou; it was their turn today.

Gao roared that he would give more than he received, if they dared take him on.

Huang immediately stood up. "Who wouldn't dare." He gestured to Liu Zeqing and Liu Liangzuo. "Come on, let's compete with him and see who is the better." He stepped forward angrily.

Shi Kefa attempted to defuse the argument and said to Gao, "They are right. You ought to humor them a little." Gao refused, saying, "I would rather die than make a concession."

Shi Kefa felt angry and discouraged. "You are wrong. I am depending on you to recover the land but you wish to compete among yourselves. It is ridiculous to engage in an internal struggle before repelling invaders. I find this very discouraging." Shi ordered the three governors to return to their stations and wait for further commands. He said to Gao, "You are garrisoned in this station and will act as my vanguard. In these circumstances they would not dare return for a further quarrel." Gao Jie had no option but to comply.

Before this had been announced there was a disturbance outside. Huang Degong had taken the lead and backed by Liu Zeqing and Liu Liangzuo called for Gao Jie to come out.

Without a word to Shi, Gao Jie went out and strongly rebuked them, "You come in daylight with swords, you rebels."

Huang answered, "Why are we rebels? We've just come to kill you, a discourteous man."

"You dare take liberties in front of the residence of our marshal. You are the discourteous ones." Gao refused to back down but the swords of the three generals convinced him and he retreated inside the inner gate crying for help. "Help me, Master Shi. The three have entered your residence to kill me." The generals came to the outer gate and stopped. Shi Kefa heard the cry and knew that the generals were at each other's throats. He felt it would be easier to eliminate the Manchu Army than to unite his generals. He asked Hou Chaozong to read an official proclamation and Hou went to the outer gate:

　　刘泽清也忍耐不住,斥责高杰说:"此处是你防地,我们都是客,你连一个宾主之礼都不晓得,还要统兵!"刘良佐更是急不择言地反对:"你在扬州享受荣华,尊大惯了。今日也该咱们来享受享受。"

　　高杰针锋相对地吼道:"你们敢来,我就奉让。"

　　黄得功顿时站了起来:"哪个是不敢来的。"又招呼刘泽清、刘良佐:"两位刘兄同我出来,与他见个高下!"说罢,怒冲冲地走了出去。

　　史可法眼见这四镇争得不可开交,首先对高杰说:"他们讲得也有理,你该谦让点儿才是。"高杰毫不听史可法劝诫:"小将宁死,也不屈居他们之下!"

　　史可法既有些怒气又不免灰心:"你这就错了。本拟倚重你们收复地方,哪知你们四个为了争坐首位,相互吵嚷,还未上阵,却已同室操戈,可笑如此!老夫满怀壮志,已灰冷了一半。"事到如今,只得命令他们三镇,各回防地,听候调遣。又指着高杰说道:"你既然驻扎本境,就在本帅标下做个先锋。如此,你们各有执掌,他们也不敢来争闹了。"高杰也只得听从这样安排。

　　岂知这一告示尚未写好,外面已传来喧嚷之声,黄得功一马当先,刘泽清、刘良佐紧随左右,齐声高呼:"高杰快快出来!"

　　这高杰也不向史可法告辞,一头迎了出去,毫不示弱地斥责道:"你们青天白日,持刀呐喊,竟是反了!"

　　黄得功申言:"我们为什么造反?只不过要杀你这个无礼贼子!"

　　"你们敢在帅府门前这般放肆,难道不是无礼贼子?"高杰似乎得礼不让人。这三镇更不答话,各自提起刀来追杀高杰,高杰抵挡不住,逃进辕门,大声呼救:"史大老爷救命!这三个贼人杀进帅府来了!"这三人赶至辕门,也不禁止步而立。史可法听得呼救之声,方知四镇已相互残杀。此时,明崇祯皇帝自杀后的北京城已由入关的满族建立了清王朝,史可法真正感到"清贼易讨"而部将难

"Your attention, I am an advisor to the marshal and have been commanded by him to warn the three generals. There have been changes at the imperial court but enemy forces have not been eliminated. We should work for the benefit of the imperial court. If you do not keep this in mind, it will destroy the overall plan. After the central plains are recovered, you will be rewarded. Today the situation is urgent and you must keep the overall plan in mind. You should understand this and unite with each other. General Gao Jie was originally stationed in Yangzhou and Tongzhou. Today he will stay here and be the vanguard of the marshal. General Huang Degong goes back to Luzhou and Hezhou, General Liu Zeqing goes back to Huaiyin and Xuzhou and Liu Liangzuo goes back to Fengyang and Sizhou. You will wait there for further commands. This is an order and you will obey it, or be punished according to military law."

When he had finished, Huang declared, "We just came to kill a discourteous man; we did not intend breaking any of the marshal's military laws."

"Your action in coming to the outer gate with swords today cannot be tolerated by military law," Hou Chaozong answered.

Liu Zeqing said that that was how it was. They would have to be off, but Liu Liangzuo was angry and said, "We will kill Gao Jie in his own house tomorrow." The three left.

Hou Chaozong returned to the hall and reported that although they had left, it was not over.

Shi Kefa wrung his hands, "What can I do?" He turned and saw Gao Jie who was in low spirits and standing nearby. "General Gao, you are too full of your own importance and the cause of these quarrels; they threaten the plan to recover the central China."

"Don't worry, marshal. Tomorrow I will fight them and win their forces over. Then I will assist you to recover the central China. It is not difficult."

Shi stopped him. "Invaders are coming from the north and will soon cross the Yellow River. The regional commander, Xu Dingguo, has reported an emergency. He cannot stop them. I wanted to talk to all of you about dispatching a force to help him. Today you fought each other and ruined the plan. I am extremely worried about the situation."

"In fact, the three generals came for nothing but the prosperous and bustling city of Yangzhou. I refused to give it up." Gao Jie still refused to admit that any blame lay with him.

114

调了。不得已,请侯朝宗出去告诫四镇。

侯朝宗拿着告示走出辕门,大声喊道:"小弟乃本府参谋,奉大元帅之命,告知三镇:当今新主坐朝,清贼未讨,我辈当思报效朝廷,不可各怀小忿,致乱大谋。一旦中原收复,自会赐宴太平,论功行赏。目今军机紧急,凡事当以大谋为重,相互谅解,无失旧好。高杰将军,原来镇守杨州、通州,今即留在本帅标下,委作先锋。黄得功将军,仍回庐州、和州驻地。刘泽清仍回淮阴、徐州。刘良佐仍回凤阳、泗州。静听调遣,不得违抗。军法整肃,本帅不能徇情。"

侯朝宗刚刚念完告示,黄得功赶紧申明:"我们只要杀无礼贼子,怎敢犯元帅军法。"

"目今辕门截杀,这就是军法难容的事了。"侯朝宗回答道。

刘泽清接口说:"既然如此,不要惊着元帅,大家暂且散去。"刘良佐仍不解恨:"明日杀到高杰家里去。"说罢,各自散去。

侯朝宗回到大堂,面复史可法:"三镇听了告示,虽然一时散去,但明日还要厮杀呢。"

史可法闻言,搓着双手:"这却怎么好?"回头见高杰垂头丧气地立在一边,指着他责备道:"高将军,你也妄自尊大,太不谦让了。这般争去,恢复中原的事业不要全丢了!"

"元帅不必着急,明日我和他们见个输赢,把他们三镇的人马全都并了过来,再随元帅收复中原,大约也不难。"高杰此刻倒又逞强起来。

史可法见他又想到歪处,断然喝住:"你说的是些什么话!'清贼'北来,将渡黄河,总兵许定国抵挡不住,连夜告急;我正要与你们四镇商议,发兵支援。今日你们也动了干戈,坏了大事,怎不令人忧心!"

"他们三个其实也不为别的,只因杨州繁华,要来夺取,俺怎肯让他!"高杰犹不认错。

"Your words are ridiculous," Shi said and sighed. He had no choice but to defend the imperial court even with his life, but it was difficult to get these arrogant generals to give way.

Hou said, "Marshal Shi, let's wait. Perhaps we can discuss it again." They went to the inner room leaving Gao alone.

The next morning Gao took his forces to the Golden Dam. The forces of Generals Huang Degong, Liu Liangzuo and Liu Zeqing went there too and, uttering cries, the two sides fell on one another. Accompanied by several soldiers, Hou mounted a platform where he held high the marshal's arrow-shaped token of authority. He cried out: "An edict from Marshal Shi. The revolt of the four generals results from my weak leadership. Please come to kill me in my residence and then occupy the imperial court in Nanjing. It is not necessary to fight here or cause difficulties for the local people."

Liu Zeqing immediately replied, "We are not rebels. We fight because Gao is discourteous, self-important and occupied the first seat. We want to make that clear and then see the marshal."

Gao Jie argued saying, "I'm the marshal's vanguard. Would I dare rebel? They came first and tried to kill me. I had to defend myself."

Hou Chaozong ignored their arguments. "When you fight you are breaking an order from the marshal, which makes you rebels. Tomorrow I will report it to the imperial court and you will go there to explain yourselves."

Liu Zeqing's anger evaporated and he said, "The marshal was appointed by the imperial court which was established with our approval. We rebel against the imperial court if we disobey a military order. We cannot do this. I would rather admit that we were wrong and allow our marshal to cool his anger."

"General Gao, what about you?" Hou asked.

"I am a general under the command of the marshal. I have violated military law and will submit to the punishment of the marshal."

"As you agree, go to the outer gate of the marshal's residence and ask for his forgiveness." Because Huang Degong and Liu Liangzuo had returned to their defense sectors after they were defeated, Liu Zeqing and Gao Jie went to the marshal to be punished by him.

Hou Chaozong asked the two generals to stay outside the outer gate while he went to report to the marshal. He returned and said, "All four generals used their forces without permission from a higher authority and

"你这话更可笑了!"史可法说罢,又长叹数声,心知这一班桀骜不驯之徒是不会认输的,只得自己拼命一死,效忠朝廷,也别无良策了。

侯朝宗劝说道:"史公,且看局势发展,再做商量。"说罢,两人也不理会高杰,径行入内。

次日清晨,高杰点齐兵马在黄金坝上布好阵势。这边黄得功、刘良佐、刘泽清也率领三镇所部迎上前来,两边混战一场,呐喊之声不断。侯朝宗在几个兵丁簇拥之下,登了高台,手持元帅令箭,高声喝道:"我大元帅有令:四镇造反,都是元帅督师不力之过。请先到帅府,杀了元帅;再到南京,抢了宫廷。不必在此混战,骚扰百姓。"

刘泽清闻令,大声辩解:"我们并不要造反,只因高杰无礼,妄自尊大,强占首座,我们要争个明白,日后也好参见元帅。"

高杰也不反省,仍然强辩道:"我高杰乃元帅标下先锋,怎敢造反?他们领兵杀来,俺也只能上前迎敌。"

侯朝宗不和他们正面辩论,只是说道:"不奉命令,妄行厮杀,都是反贼,明日奏闻朝廷,你们自去分辩罢。"

刘泽清被这番言语镇住,赶紧表态:"朝廷是我们迎立的,元帅是朝廷派来的。我们违了军令,便是叛了朝廷,如何使得的。俺情愿认罪,只求元帅饶怒。"

"高将军,你又如何说?"侯朝宗见刘泽清已伏输,乃逼问高杰。

"我高杰是元帅兵马,犯了军法,只听元帅处分。"

"既然如此,你们速与黄得功、刘良佐二镇,同去辕门,央求元帅。"因黄得功、刘良佐已败回防地,刘泽请、高杰二人乃同去元帅帐前听凭发落。

侯朝宗让这二镇在辕门外歇着,自己先走入帐去禀报。不一会儿,又返身出来,大声说道:"四镇擅自用兵,相互争夺,都该军

should be punished according to military law. But Gao holds the main responsibility because he was discourteous. He should apologize to the other three generals. The punishment will be announced after the four generals are reconciled."

Gao Jie became angry. He had thought that as he was the marshal's vanguard he would have been protected. Instead he had been asked to apologize which made him feel ashamed. He felt that he did not have the marshal's trust and decided to leave and carve out his own territory. Without letting the others know, he commanded his forces to cross the Yangtze.

Liu Zeqing saw him and knew that he would join forces on the southern bank to fight against them. He left the marshal as soon as possible and joined Huang Degong and Liu Liangzuo to confront him.

Hou was shocked by the turn of events. He could not stop it and reported to the marshal.

After crossing the Yangtze, Gao planned to occupy Suzhou and Hangzhou, but the provincial governor Zheng Xuan defended the river with boats and guns. They stopped him and he had to retreat to Yangzhou. During the withdrawal he learned that Huang Degong, Liu Zeqing and Liu Liangzuo had arrived at Gaoyou to fight his force. Gao was shocked and could neither advance nor retreat. He had to request help from Marshal Shi Kefa.

Shi told him sternly that in the past he had been a mutinous soldier. "Later you surrendered and were granted a title and territories. The imperial court treated you generously. Why did you rebel just because of a few words? When you found that you could not cross the river, you came to me to ask for help. You rebel then surrender as if you were playing a game. You should be punished according to military law. As it's not too late for you to repent, I will forgive you once again." Gao kowtowed and the marshal told him to apologize to the three generals as a way of defusing the situation. The generals, persuaded by Shi, ended the quarrel and left Huaiyin and Yangzhou.

Shi ordered Gao to defend the river but he was still anxious. He said to Hou, "The fate of the state rests on these defences. General Gao is brave but not astute and we cannot afford to make a mistake. Once you often visited your home in Henan, why not go with the forces? You could supervise the river defenses and please your parents."

The arrangement suited Hou and he agreed. Shi Kefa emphasized

法从事。但其事乃因高将军不知礼体而起,要负主要责任,着其先向三镇赔礼。四镇和解之后,再议处分。"

高杰一听此令,大为恼怒,心想:自己为元帅标下先锋,元帅却不加庇护,倒让自家向三镇赔礼,可不羞死。看来元帅也不用自家,索性离他而去,领兵渡江,另做一番事业。想罢,也不告辞,径自率领部众渡江而南。

刘泽清见他要渡江,知道他要纠合江南党羽再来厮杀,便也趁早抽身,前往约会黄得功、刘良佐,好调遣人马,预做准备。

被冷落在一旁的侯朝宗,目瞪口呆地见他们纷纷走散,再也未曾想到局势竟然发展到这种地步,终于明白无力挽救,只得去回复史可法。

高杰打的是如意算盘:渡江而南,抢占苏杭。岂知巡抚郑瑄守江有责,操舟架炮,堵住江口。他怎能飞渡?事出无奈,前进不得,只得退回扬州。行不数里,忽有报子禀报,黄得功与二刘三镇人马已至高邮,前来厮杀。高杰大惊,此际方知进退两难。不得已,他只有率领兵众再向史可法求救。

史可法升帐,他急不可待地小跑上前跪求元帅开恩。史可法义正词严地斥责道:"你原为一介乱民,朝廷许你投诚,加封侯爵,不曾薄待了你。为何一言不合,竟自反去?渡江不得,又来求饶。忽而造反,忽而投诚,如同儿戏,岂不可恨!本该军法从事,姑念你悔罪还不迟,暂且饶恕一回。"高杰只得叩头称谢,并进而要求元帅为他解危。元帅要他向三镇赔礼,他执意不从。侯朝宗乃出谋划策,建议史可法派他率众前往开封、洛阳一带加强河防。高杰不得已,只得接受这一任务。三镇眼见高杰已离淮杨,又经史可法劝说,方才罢手。

史可法虽然命高杰前去防河,但并不放心,对侯朝宗说道:

119

the conditions. "You will be on your own and the situation could change; you will have to be careful. I will wait for news from you." Hou understood what Shi meant and after thanking him for his help left with General Gao and his force for the home that he had left three years earlier. He went first to Huai'an where he inspected the river defenses and visited his parents on the way.

"防河一事,乃国家重要一着,我看高将军勇多谋少,倘有疏失,老夫罪过甚大。仔细想来,河南是你故乡,吾兄又每每要回家乡,如今何不随营前往,既遂了还乡之愿,又可监军防河,还能造福故土,可谓一举而三得。吾兄以为如何?"

侯朝宗闻言,正合私意,自然应允,史可法又再三叮嘱:"吾兄此去,便如同老夫亲身防河。只怕局势变化难以测度,需要十分小心。老夫专听好消息。"侯朝宗深深领会史可法此意,谢过史可法多时照顾,便随着高杰人马起程,向别了三年之久的故乡而去。

CHAPTER EIGHTEEN

Yearning for Hou

Xiangjun was still lived in The House of Enchanting Fragrance, but no longer wore her dancing costume, played the flute or sang. She remained upstairs waiting for Hou Chaozong.

She did not care what people thought of her or what happened. But people remembered her. After Zhu Yousong became emperor, he granted titles to those who pleased the imperial court. (In small hills even a monkey can become the king.) Those who received them still enjoyed liquor and the company of beautiful women. Yang Longyou was promoted to director of the Ministry of Rites for his services. Ruan Dacheng resumed his position as the chief minister of the Court of Imperial Entertainments.

Tian Yang, a townsman of Yang Longyou, was promoted to grand coordinator of the Transport Office and intended leaving the imperial court for this position. Before he left, he sent 300 taels of silver to Yang Longyou asking him to find a beautiful prostitute along the Qinhuai River to accompany him.

Although Yang was the director of the Ministry of Rites, he continued serving the rich through literary work. Tian Yang was a townsman and a powerful official who he could not refuse.

He thought of all the prostitutes along the Qinhuai River and believed none compared with Li Xiangjun for beauty or singing. He decided to go to the old brothel by himself but realized that it was not a good idea. He had recommended Xiangjun to Chaozong not long ago. How could he recommend Xiangjun to another man? He thought of asking for help from his literary friends Ding Jizhi and Bian Yujing from The House of Enchanting Fragrance. He called in his head servant.

"What can I do for you?"

"Ask my friends Ding Jizhi and Bian Yujing to come to my study. We have important things to discuss."

The head servant hated his employer having anything to do with

第十八章
守楼待侯

话说侯朝宗先去淮安，随即又去防河顺道返乡。那香君却仍在媚香楼中讨生涯，不过已尽洗粉黛，脱去舞裙，丢了箫笛，歇了歌喉，长斋礼佛，轻易不下楼，专一等待朝宗归来。

虽说香君忘却世俗，但世俗之人并未将她丢开。自朱由崧登基后大封有功之臣，群小沐猴而冠，粉墨登场，须臾离不开酒食美色。媚香楼的常客杨龙友也因迎驾有功，补了礼部主事；阮大铖官复原职，仍为光禄寺卿。

杨龙友的同乡田仰也提升为漕运巡抚，即将离开朝廷前去赴任。临行之前，送了三百两银子给杨龙友，托他寻找一个绝色的秦淮歌妓携往任所。

杨龙友虽官礼部主事，依旧脱不掉帮闲习气。田仰既是同乡，又是高官，他怎能不允其所请？自然是尽心尽意去办了。

他将秦淮名妓一一排过，论色艺之精者，无人比得上李香君。拿定主意，他决定立刻去旧院走一趟。继而又一想：不成。将香君推荐给侯朝宗的不正是自家？时隔不久，怎好当面让香君另事他人？对了，此事还得麻烦那些清客。"长班过来！"

"老爷有何吩咐？"

"你去把清客丁继之、女客卞玉京找到我书房中来，有事要办。"

这长班倒有些脾气，看不惯这个杨老爷常与这班人往来，回话道："禀告老爷，小人是长班，只认得名位官府，那些唱戏的、卖身的，倒不知去何处寻找。"

these literary friends and refused. "Master, I am your special servant and know famous officials. I do not know any prostitutes. Where could I find them?"

Yang Longyou was not embarrassed and said, "Around the Qinhuai River." The head servant left to look for them but as he approached the door he heard a knock.

There were men and women at the door and when he asked who they were and what they wanted, an old man answered, "I am Ding Jizhi. These are my friends, Shen Gongxian and Zhang Yanzhu. We would like to see your master."

A woman standing by them said, "I am Bian Yujing and with me are Kou Baimen and Zheng Tuoniang."

The servant was glad. They were the people he had been sent to fetch. He went inside to report to his master who was very pleased.

"We wouldn't have bothered you, but we come to ask for help." They all knelt down.

Yang left his seat to help them up. "Be seated, please. What can I do for you?"

"Is Master Ruan Dacheng of the Court of Imperial Entertainments a close friend of yours?" Ding Jizhi asked.

"Yes."

Ding Jizhi saw that Yang was candid. "We heard that when the new emperor ascended the throne, Master Ruan presented four operas to him. The emperor was very pleased and planned to choose some of us to give a performance inside the imperial court. Is that true?"

"It is true." Yang Longyou thought it a great event and there was no reason to keep it secret.

Zhang Yanzhu continued, "You know that we earn a living by singing. If we are chosen to sing inside the imperial court, who will support our families?" Zheng Tuoniang also tried to say what he had heard.

Yang Longyou understood why they had come. He smiled and said, "Don't worry. Dancing for officials and urging them to drink are the business of those in the Music Office. Your are famous and nobody would dare ask you to do such a thing."

They expressed their thanks together and asked to be put under his protection.

"That's all right. Tomorrow I will send your names to Ruan Dacheng and ask him to free you from the event."

　　杨龙友倒不以为忤，丝毫不感到难堪，反而指点说："就在秦淮河旁嘛。"长班只得奉命去寻。

　　岂知长班刚走到大门前，就听到一阵敲门声，打开大门一看，有男有女，三五成群，问他们是何人。只见为首的一个老者答话道："老汉是丁继之，这两个是沈公宪、张燕筑，有事求见杨老爷。"

　　那边为首的一个半老徐娘答话道："我是卞玉京，这两位是寇白门、郑妥娘，也有事要找杨老爷。"长班闻言，不由得有几分高兴，正要去找他们，他们却自行前来，也免得自己跑一趟了，便立刻返身进去禀报。

　　"如何来得这么巧？"杨龙友见他们陆续进来后也有几分高兴。

　　"无事不敢随便来麻烦杨老爷，今日特有要事来恳求杨老爷施恩。"男女老少一齐叩拜。

　　杨龙友倒也不摆架子，将他们拉起："请坐，请坐，有何事见教？"

　　丁继之首先开口："新光禄寺院阮老爷是杨老爷至交么？"

　　"是呀！"丁继之见杨龙友并不回避，接着说下去："听说新皇帝登位，阮老爷进献了四种传奇，皇上十分高兴，要挑选我们入宫内教习演出，有这么事么？"

　　"果真有这事儿。"杨龙友认为此举乃盛事，倒也没有必要隐瞒。

　　张燕筑接话道："不瞒老爷说，我们靠这张唱曲的嘴，养活一家子哩。这一入宫，不是让我们灭门绝户了，谁来养活一家子呢？"郑妥娘等人也七嘴八舌地诉说着同样的事儿。

　　杨龙友总算明白了大家的意思，笑着对大家说："不必慌张，陪舞劝酒一类差事，自有教坊中的一班男女去应承，你们也算得上是名士了，谁人好拿你们去应差！"

　　众人齐声致谢："只求杨老爷多多庇护。"

　　"好说，明日开个名单，送给阮大铖，叫他一概免拿就是了。"

"Thanks for your help and sympathy. You are a person of great worth."

"But, you can return a favor."

"What can we do for you?" Ding Jizhi was surprised.

"My friend Tian Yang will take up his position as the grand coordinator of the Transport Office soon. Recently, he sent 300 taels of silver for another wife."

Ding Jizhi asked, "Have you someone special in mind?"

"I have thought of one but I need your help."

Bian Yujing asked who and Yang Longyou said that it was Li Xiangjun.

Ding Jizhi shook his head and said, "No. I couldn't do it."

"Why?" Yang Longyou could not understand.

"She is Hou's lover. How could you ask her to marry someone else?" Ding was angry.

Yang Longyou persisted, saying, "Hou is not serious about Xiangjun. He has gone and left her behind, he doesn't miss her. Go ahead, it's all right."

Bian Yujing demurred. "Since Hou left Xiangjun has refused to go downstairs. There is no reason for her to marry someone else. It is pointless talking to her."

"That is true, but if the man were a better person than Hou, she would, wouldn't she?"

Ding Jizhi still had reservations. "You get along with her mother. It would be better if you talked directly to her."

Yang was embarrassed and said, "You know that it was me who introduced Hou to Xiangjun. How could I suggest another person to her mother? It would be far better for you to do it, and you'll be paid."

Ding Jizhi and Bian Yujing thought for a while and finally agreed; they farewelled the others and left for The House of Enchanting Fragrance. On the way they recalled that when Hou Chaozong and Xiangjun were engaged, they had sung and played musical instruments at the banquet. Today they were going to ask her to marry someone else which was shameful.

"We should not go," Bian Yujing said but Ding Jizhi was older and saw that it was more complex. "If we did not, Lord Yang as director of the Ministry of Rites could make us servants in the imperial court. We would be asking for trouble."

　　"多谢老爷可怜,这功德不小。""不过,下官也有一事要借重。"杨龙友答应得爽快,要求也直捷。丁继之一惊:"老爷有何见教?"

　　"舍亲田仰,近日就要升任漕运巡抚,刚才送到聘金三百两,让俺为他寻一小妾。"丁继之问道:"老爷意中可否已有人选?""人,倒想好一个,但要你去作媒说合。"卞玉京抢先问道:"是哪一个?"杨龙友此刻方揭了底:"便是李家的香君。"丁继之摇头如摆鼓:"这办不成,这可使不得。""如何使不得?"杨龙友不解。

　　"她是侯公子的情人,怎能叫她改嫁!"丁继之已有些不满。

　　杨龙友还不识相,进一步劝说丁继之去作媒,说:"侯公子与香君之事,不过是他一时高兴罢了,现在避祸远去,哪里还想着香君哩,你去说,不碍事。"卞玉京也表示不妥:"香君自侯郎去后,不肯下楼,哪有嫁人之理,去说也无用。"杨龙友仍坚持要办,说道:"话虽如此说,但只要有个比侯公子强的人,香君难道不肯?"

　　丁继之在杨龙友追逼之下,仍然不肯,设法推脱:"香君之母,原来就与老爷交好,还是老爷去当面讲更好。"

　　杨龙友不无尴尬地表示:"你是知道的,侯郎与香君交好,原就是下官作的媒。如今面对面怎好讲这椿事?还是请二位走一趟,自有重谢。"

　　丁继之与卞玉京碍于情面,只得应承,两人别过大众,向秦淮河旁媚香楼走去。一路上,两人絮絮叨叨地谈起往事。丁继之说道:"记得当初侯公子与香君定情,俺们也从旁帮衬过;也曾替他们吹弹拉唱。如今倒好,又去替她说合别人,这种迎新送旧的勾当,令人多难为情啊!"

　　"我们就不去说罢!"卞玉京想得太简单。丁继之到底年岁长些,考虑问题要复杂些,回答道:"俺们要是不去呵,杨老爷是现任礼部主事,把俺们一齐硬送入内宫当差,岂不是自讨苦吃!"

Bian Yujing asked what they could do.

Ding Jizhi had a plan and said that they should discuss it with Xiangjun. They walked and talked until they came to the outside gate of The House of Enchanting Fragrance. Zhang Yanzhu, Shen Gongxian, Zheng Tuoniang and Kou Baimen, who had come another way, had arrived before them. They had come to make sure that Ding and Bian shared the fee and followed them in.

There was no one in the courtyard and Ding Jizhi raised his head and called out, "Aunt Li, please come out."

Xiangjun was sitting alone in her room lost in thought. When she heard somebody calling her adoptive mother, she walked out and leaned over the railing.

"Who's downstairs?"

Bian Yujing answered, "Official Ding."

"Aunt Bian and Uncle Ding, here? Please come up."

"Where is your mother?"

"She has gone to dinner with her friends. Please be seated." Xiangjun gave them a cup of tea.

Bian Yujing asked, "Who were you chatting and playing with in the room?"

"Aunt, don't you know? Myself, I remain alone."

"Why don't you find yourself a husband?"

Xiangjun was amazed, "Official Hou and I are engaged. Can I change my mind?"

Ding Jizhi could not refrain from saying, "We all know your mind. Today Lord Yang entrusted us to ask you if you will agree to marry Tian Yang, a grand coordinator, who will pay you 300 taels of silver."

After hearing this, Xiangjun said sternly, "Don't mention this, the love poem written by Hou should be valued at 10,000 taels of silver."

Bian Yujing knew that Xiangjun would not change her mind and said that she should forget it. She turned to Ding Jizhi and said, "Since it is so, let's go to tell Lord Yang."

Ding Jizhi felt uneasy and said to Xiangjun, "I hope your mother won't be bribed."

Xiangjun replied with confidence, "My mother loves me and would not force me to do what I don't want to do."

Ding Jizhi said, "That is good and worthy of respect." Then he and Bian stood up to go.

卞玉京这才觉得事儿不那么轻易:"那怎么办才好呢?"

丁继之回答说:"到那里好言好语与香君细细商量。"两人边谈边走,方才走进了媚香楼院门。那张燕筑、沈公宪、郑妥娘、寇白门也从另一条路赶来,这四个男女却是怕丁、卞二人得了好处瞒着大家,特地前来要均沾利益的。不由丁、卞二人分说,一齐涌进门去。

丁继之见院中无人,不免仰起头来对楼上叫道:"贞娘出来。"

香君正独自坐在卧房中沉思,听见有人招呼义母,便走出卧房,探身问道:"楼下是哪位?"

卞玉京抢先答道:"丁相公来了。"

"啊,原来是卞姨娘和丁大爷光临,快请上楼。"

"令堂怎的不见?"

"去参加盒子会去了。——请坐。"香君一面让坐,一面捧上茶来。

卞玉京问道:"香君闲坐楼窗,和谁人顽耍?"

"姨娘不知,只俺独自一人,守此空楼而已。"

卞玉京慢慢逗起话题:"为何不找个女婿?"

"奴家已嫁给侯郎,怎能改变主意?"香君有些愕然。

丁继之此刻再不能不说话了:"我们晓得你的苦心。今日礼部杨老爷说,有一位大老爷田仰,肯出三百两银子,娶你作妾,让俺来问一声。"

香君立刻变容,正色回答道:"这个话题再甭提起。侯郎的定情诗,比万两雪花银还有价值!"

卞玉京知道香君之志不可更移,便不勉强,说道:"这桩事全由你自己拿主意,你既不肯,那就算了。"又掉转头来对丁继之说:"既然如此,回绝杨老爷吧。"

丁继之还有些不放心,对香君说:"令堂回来,不要见钱眼开才好。"香君颇有自信地说:"妈妈疼我,也不会强迫的。"丁继之连

But Shen Gongxian and the others were worried over their failure to persuade Xiangjun. Shen said abruptly, "How could you refuse Lord Yang's kindness?"

Xiangjun was resolute. "I don't care if the suitor is poor or rich. It is for me to make up my mind."

The unexpected rejection infuriated Zhang Yanzhu, Kou Baimen and Zheng Tuoniang who threatened Xiangjun but she stood firm. Ding Jizhi saw that they were unreasonable and said, "She has made up her mind. Let's go."

Bian Yujing said, "Although she is young, she has high principles." They had come on a shameful task and left feeling unworthy.

Ding and Bian turned to comfort Xiangjun. "Set your mind at rest. We will refuse Lord Yang and we will not do this again."

"My thanks to both of you," Xiangjun said and Ding and Bian left.

CHAPTER NINETEEN

Seeking Favor and Abusing Power

Zhu Yousong had been excessively fond of leisure before he became emperor but once on the throne he spent far more time with prostitutes and other diversions. Ma Shiying was happy that the emperor took little interest in imperial court administration; it allowed him to do what he wanted. He placed trusted subordinates in important civil and military posts and enjoyed power. Others looked on him with fear.

Although the rebels were moving continuously southward, Ma Shiying believed the small imperial court south of the Yangtze River was stable and that they could live in peace. When the plum in the Wanyu Garden was in blossom, he ordered his servants to prepare a family banquet and invited friends so that they could share his enjoyment of the flowers. The banquet kept them together and gave him the opportunity to flaunt his power and accept their flattery.

声说："如此甚好,可敬,可敬!"丁、卞二人站起身来,准备告辞。

哪知其他几个男女,生怕此事不成,沈公宪迫不急待地说:"杨老爷的好意,如何拒绝得?"

香君坚决地回绝:"奴家不希罕富贵!"

未曾料到,香君坚辞却激怒了张燕筑、寇白门、郑妥娘三人,对她威吓有加,香君抵死不从。丁继之见这三人的表现太不像话,便劝他们道:"吓她不动的,走罢走罢。"

卞玉京也称赞道:"看她小小年纪,倒有志气。"这几个人讨了场没趣,也只得耷拉着脑袋,走出门去。

丁、卞二人又回过头来安慰香君:"香君放心,我们回绝杨老爷,再不来找你麻烦。"

"这就要谢谢二位了。"香君拜了几拜。丁、卞二人就此别去。

第十九章
媚上压下

朱由崧在藩邸为世子时,原就贪鄙无厌,如今登上皇位,更是沉沦淫乐。马士英以迎立之功,官居首辅。他倒高兴朱由崧闭目拱手,不理朝政,自己就可任意胡为,呼朋引党,重用同类,满朝文武要职,全由他心腹充任。一时权倾朝野,时人侧目。

近来"流贼"虽然不断南侵,但小朝廷尚可偏安江南。马士英以为天下太平,正可享福,正值万玉园中红梅盛开,便命家人设宴,邀些亲朋旧友前来赏梅,一则彼此拉拢,固其权势;一则受他们奉承,也显示自己尊荣。

Ma Shiying went into the sitting room and asked his head servant who had been invited that day.

"The guests are your townsmen: the director of Ministry of Rites, Yang Longyou; Capital Censor, Yue Qijie; the newly appointed grand coordinator of the Transport Office, Tian Yang and chief minister of the Court of Imperial Entertainments, Ruan Dacheng."

"Ruan Dacheng is not my townsman," Ma Shiying said.

"He always says that he is a close relative of yours."

"We get along quite well. All right, I'll make him a relative. It's already noon, bring them in."

"They are waiting in the sitting-room, all you need to do is ask them in," the servant said rather distainfully.

Yang Longyou and Ruan Dacheng entered the Plum Study and Ma Shiying said, "Brother-in-law Yang, you are a relative. Why didn't you come straight in?"

"Today a relative is the same as a friend in need," Yang said sadly.

Ma Shiying knew what he meant but asked him what he was talking about. Then he turned to Ruan Dacheng, "You are close to me, why were you waiting for my invitation?"

"It is a custom of your family. Who am I to break it?" Ruan said obsequiously.

"Don't regard yourselves as outsiders. Please be seated."

Yue Qijie and Tian Yang were not there. A servant said that Master Yue was sick and Master Tian was leaving for his new position tomorrow; he was helping his family board a boat and would come to say farewell in the evening.

Ma ordered the banquet to be set out and sat at the head of the table. Yang and Ruan sat in the guests' chairs.

Feigning modesty, Ruan Dacheng said to Ma, "You have had several family banquets. Who were invited?"

Ma answered ambiguously, "Some of my generation, but no more elegant than you."

Yang Longyou understood the purpose of Ruan's question and pressed Ma Shiying. "Who were they?"

Ma sent his servant for guest list and Ruan read it carefully. It included Zhang Zhensun, Yuan Hongxun, Huang Ding, Zhang Jie, Yang Weiyuan and others. Yang Longyou intentionally flattered Ma by remarking, "They are really talented people who have experienced great

"长班,今日请哪几位可人?"马士英走进客堂来问道。

"都是老爷同乡。有兵部主事杨龙友,金都御史越其杰,新任漕抚田仰,光禄寺卿阮大铖这几位老爷。"

马士英不无怀疑地问道:"那阮大铖可不是同乡呀。"

长班回答道:"他常对人说,他是老爷至亲。"

马士英无可无不可地笑道:"相处还说得过,就算个至亲吧。天已过午,快去请客吧。"

"哪还用去请,他们早在门房里坐等哩,只要传叫一声,便齐齐整整地来叩见了。"长班答话中不禁流露出鄙夷语气。

随着长班的传呼,杨龙友与阮大铖二人卑恭万状地来到梅花书屋。马士英招呼杨龙友:"杨妹丈是咱内亲,为何不直接进来?"

"如今亲不敌贵了。"杨龙友有些酸溜溜地答道。

马士英听出其中醋意:"说的哪里话。"又朝着阮大铖说:"阮老一向走熟的,为何也等人传呼?"

"府上规矩,哪敢冒昧。"阮大铖卑躬屈膝地回答道。

"这就见外了,坐,请坐。"

闲谈半晌,不见越其杰和田仰二人到来。马士英问了家人,家人禀报说:"越老爷发了痔疮,不能来了;田老爷明日赴任,打发家眷上船,夜间才能来辞行。"

马士英听说,吩咐道:"如此,就安排酒席罢。"马士英坐了主位,杨、阮二人依次坐了客位,三人对酌起来。

阮大铖装出一副谦恭样子,心机却十分深沉,向马士英问道:"相府连日开宴,不知请的是哪几位客人?"

马士英含糊地答道:"总是吾辈中人,但总不如二公风雅。"

杨龙友听出了阮大铖问话的用心,追问道:"究竟是哪几位?"

马士英吩咐家人取来一份宾客名单。阮大铖伸手从家人手中

events in the world and done good things for the people."

"I promoted all of them to higher positions," said Ma.

Ruan Dacheng immediately stood up and bowed to Ma. "We are younger and look forward to promotion. You have chosen talented people for the imperial court and have shown excellence in this field."

Ma was very proud. "You are different from the others. Tomorrow I will tell the Ministry of Rites to promote you."

Yang Longyou immediately stood up and thanked him. Ruan Dacheng knelt down and did the same. Ma Shiying stretched out his hands to help him up. After a few cups of liquor, he was very happy to receive their flattery. The servants cleaned away the dishes and they talked freely, more like close friends.

After dinner there was to be a performance. Yang and Ruan overwhelmed by the unexpected favor signaled their boy servants. The servants immediately realized what was meant and took out money wrapped in red paper to hand to Ma's servant. Ma said that it was unnecessary, "The artists are not from the Palace Theatre so formal rules don't apply."

Ruan Dacheng was pleased and said, "My group of artists have nothing to do, why not ask them to perform here?"

Ma answered, "Forget it today. Next time when I treat guests I will borrow your group for a performance."

Yang Longyou joined in saying, "Today the plum is in blossom. Since ancient days men have appreciated flowers and beautiful girls. If the performance is not to be by artists from the Palace Theatre, we require a beautiful girl to sing for us."

Ma could not refuse this time. His servant would have to fetch a singer prostitute. The servant asked who and Ma turned to Yang and said, "Brother-in-law Yang, it is your choice."

Yang Longyou said unhurriedly that there was no absolute best but added that Li Xiangjun had recently learned extracts from *The Peony Pavilion* and they were good.

Ma sent his servant to fetch Li Xiangjun and Ruan Dacheng asked if it was true that she had turned down the newly appointed grand coordinator of Transport Office, Tian Yang, who had offered 300 taels of silver for her.

Yang Longyou reluctantly admitted that it was.

取过名单仔细看过,原来是张振孙、袁宏勋、黄鼎、张捷、杨维垣等人。杨龙友有意恭维道:"这些人果然是大有经世济民之才的。"马士英颇为受用,说:"个个都是我提拔的,如今都居高位了。"

阮大铖赶紧离席,一揖到底,趁机进言:"晚生等都是闲废之员,还蒙相公起用,老师相为国谋才,功劳大矣。"马士英更是得意非凡:"岂敢,岂敢。二位不比他人,明日嘱托吏部,还要破格擢升。"

杨龙友赶紧立起身来,作揖致谢。阮大铖干脆跪下磕头,感恩不尽地说道:"多谢提拔。"马士英伸手拉了他一把,几杯下肚,又受到这两人恭维,心情舒畅,吩咐左右家人撤了大席,安排小酌,促膝谈心,更显知己。

杨、阮两人见马士英如此垂爱,受宠若惊,各自以目示意立在身后的家僮。家僮立即从身边抽出红包,献给马府家人。马士英嘈嘈杂杂地念叨:"不必,不必。我们小酌,也无梨园艺人,不必行如此官礼。"

阮大铖闻言大喜,献媚道:"舍间戏班,倒日日闲在那里,何不传来演出?"马士英答道:"今日算了,改日请客,当向贵府借来。"

杨龙友却凑趣地说道:"从来名花、美女并提,缺一不可。今日红梅盛开,梨园演出可以省却,倒不可少一美人清唱。"

马士英也不好意思再拒绝,说道:"这也容易。"随即吩咐家人传歌妓伺侯。家人便问要哪班歌妓,马士英则转向杨龙友,说道:"请杨姑爷定。"

杨龙友不慌不忙地说:"小弟物色已多,总难寻到可意的。只有旧院李香君,新学得几出《牡丹亭》,倒还可听。"马士英不假思索地吩咐家人去传唤。

阮大铖却节外生枝地故意向杨龙友问道:"听说前些时候,新任漕抚田仰用三百两银子要娶她做妾,她不肯去。可有其事?"

"正有其事。"提及此事,杨龙友也有些不快。

Ma Shiying was interested. "Why did she refuse?"

Yang Longyou remembered how he had acted as matchmaker, failed, and lost face to Master Tian Yang. He said angrily, "She is a silly girl. She will not marry because of Hou Chaozong. I went to see her several times and she even refused to come down the stairs. I was most disappointed."

"Is she that audacious?" Ma Shiying asked angrily. Ruan Dacheng remembered that she had refused the gifts he sent her on her engagement and had shown little respect for his feelings. He said, "It is Hou Chaozong's fault."

Hou Chaozong's name reminded Ma of Shi Kefa's opposition to the new emperor through the "three crimes" and "five nos"; Hou's objections could well have damaged his career. He cried, "That is impossible. The newly appointed grand coordinator unable to buy a prostitute with 300 taels of silver. It is ridiculous."

Ruan Dacheng added, "Tian Yang is a townsman of yours. It is well known that a prostitute humiliated him."

"When she arrives, I will do something," Ma said, but a servant came in and reported, "Master, I have been to The House of Enchanting Fragrance and told Li Xiangjun that you asked her to come. She said she was sick and refused."

Ma was angry but thought of his position — a prime minister angry with a singing prostitute. He calmed down and said, "If she will not come to sing for us, you will go with some clothes and gifts to marry her."

The Ma family servants liked to stir up trouble and hurried away to prepare clothes and gifts; they wanted revenge for Xiangjun's refusal. Ruan grinned broadly. "Good, good. Your decision is most gratifying to all."

Li Xiangjun had nettled Yang Longyou but he disliked the idea. He stood up and told them that it was late and he would have to leave. Ruan wanted to stay and see what would happen, but he had to follow Yang. Ma Shiying did not ask them to stay and stood up to send them off. Yang Longyou and Ruan Dacheng made three bows with their hands clasped in front of them, then left for home.

After they had left, Ruan Dacheng said to Yang Longyou, "It was difficult for Ma to take such strong action. You'd better help him."

Yang Longyou asked him how and Ruan, who could not see Yang's face said, "You are familiar with The House of Enchanting Fragrance. You could go there right away, pull her down the stairs

　　马士英也感兴趣地问道:"为何没有去?"杨龙友恨恨地说道:"可笑这个傻丫头,要为侯朝宗守节,竟然不肯下楼,令我扫兴而回。"

　　"有这样大胆奴才?"马士英大怒。阮大铖想到当年他好心送去一副嫁妆,也被李香君退回,毫不为他留点儿情面,不禁在马士英面前挑拨道:"这都是侯朝宗教坏的!"

　　马士英听得"侯朝宗"三字,顿时想到迎立福王朱由崧时,他曾在史可法面前倡言"三大罪"、"五不可立"之说,差点坏了自家大事,大声吼道:"了不得,了不得! 新任漕运巡抚花三百两银子居然买不到一个妓女,岂有此理!"阮大铖又进一步煽动:"田仰是老师相乡亲,被妓女羞辱,并非小事!"

　　马士英果然发话:"正是,等她来时,我自有处断。"他的话音刚落地,前去传唤的家人回来禀报:"老爷,小人去旧院,寻着李香君,说老爷传她。她却声称有病,不肯下楼。"

　　马士英闻言,十分恼怒,正要发作,转而一想,自己身居相位,与一个歌女斗气,未免有失身份,因而强行咽下这口气:"好吧! 既然她不肯来陪酒清唱,你们就携带些衣服、财礼,干脆将她娶来!"

　　马府家人连忙奉命去准备衣物财礼,好去报复一下刚才碰的钉子。阮大铖也拍手笑道:"妙,妙! 相公此举,大快人心!"

　　杨龙友虽然对季香君回绝田仰亲事有些气恼,但见马士英如此作为,也觉得有些过分,便立起身来说:"天色太晚了,我们告辞罢。"阮大铖虽然还想等待"好戏",也只得随着立起身来。马士英也未强留,起身作送客姿态,杨、阮二人连忙作了三揖,口称"不敢",告辞而退。

　　出得门来,阮大铖又撺掇杨龙友说:"难得令舅老师相看在乡亲面上,动此义举。龙友,你也该去帮一帮。"

　　杨龙友反问道:"如何去帮?"阮大铖并未窥视到杨龙友此时

and tell her to come."

"We can't put too much pressure on her."

"Longyou, from what you say, you would let her off lightly. I hated her because she refused my gifts and I need revenge."

Yang Longyou said nothing. They farewelled each other and went home.

CHAPTER TWENTY

Zhenli Stands in for Xiangjun

Although Yang Longyou was annoyed with Li Xiangjun, he was angry at Ruan Dacheng's and Ma Shiying's high handed attitude. What Ma Shiying proposed was unreasonable and unfair to Xiangjun. He had introduced her to Chaozong and now it appeared that he would be responsible for their separation. He turned and walked towards The House of Enchanting Fragrance.

On the way he met two servants who came out of the Ma mansion, one carrying gifts and clothes, the other holding a candle lantern. One said, "Both mother and daughter are alike. How will we know which is Li Xiangjun?"

"You can follow me," Yang Longyou said.

The servants were pleased and followed him. When they arrived one stepped forward and knocked. The door was opened by Li Zhenli who was shocked to see them. She asked, "Where have you been, Lord Yang?"

Yang Longyou replied, "At my brother-in-law Ma's place. I have come to congratulate you."

"Congratulate me? For what?"

"An official wishes to marry your daughter." He pointed to the servants and said quietly, "You see, there are 300 taels of silver and an embroidered suit...."

心态，只顾一时痛快地说："旧院是你熟游之处，你可径去把她拉下楼，打发她起身便了。"

"也不可太难为她。"

"啊呀呀，龙老，你说的什么话！这还便宜她。想起日前却奁之恨，就处死这婊子，也难泄我之恨！"

杨龙友也不再答话，彼此分手而去。

第二十章
将李代桃

杨龙友虽然对李香君不为他留点儿面子，拒绝给田仰作妾有些气忿，但过后一想，此事原也不能过于怪罪香君。当年为朝宗说合的是自家，如今拆散他们的也是自家，因而对阮大铖这般谗言、马士英如此霸道也微有不满，觉得这样对待香君，也未免太过分了。因此，走不几步，又折过身来，岔向去旧院的路上。

正遇上马府两个家人一个捧了衣服、财礼，一个提了灯笼，边走边说："李家母子两个，长得也差不多，也不知哪个是香君。"

杨龙友接口道："你们就跟我去吧。"

这两个家人自是高兴："杨姑老爷肯去，定然不会娶错人。"他们跟着杨龙友，不一会儿就到了旧院李家门前。马府家人上前把黑漆大门敲得山响，李贞丽连忙开门，见灯笼火把、骄马人夫，不禁问道："老爷从哪里赴席回来？"

杨龙友连忙说道："刚刚在马舅爷相府，特来报喜。"

李贞丽倒丈二金刚摸不着头脑了，忙问道："有什么喜？"

"有个大老官来娶你令嫒哩。"指着站在身后的马府两个家

As he was speaking, Li Zhenli, who also kept her voice down, asked, "Who wants to marry her and why have the family not mentioned it earlier?"

Yang Longyou pointed at the writing on the lanterns and said, "Can you see the lanterns? They are from the Ma family."

Li Zhenli saw the two lanterns outside the gate and asked, "Does Master Ma himself want to marry my daughter?"

"No, it is Tian Yang, grand coordinator of the Transport Office and a townsman of Master Ma. Today he left for his post. Master Ma wants to choose a beautiful girl for him."

"A marriage to the Tian family has been turned down. Why do you come again?" Li Zhenli was surprised.

The servants saw that Li Zhenli was beautiful and thought that she was Li Xiangjun. They handed her the silver. "You are Li Xiangjun, aren't you? Please accept the money and gifts."

Li Zhenli was crafty and said, "Let me think inside."

The servants still thought that she was Li Xiangjun and said, "The Ma family does not give you time to think. Accept the silver, come out and get into the bridal sedan chair."

Yang Longyou realized that the servants believed that she was Li Xiangjun but did not disabuse them. He said, "She would not dare refuse. Wait outside the gate and I'll take the presents upstairs and persuade her to hurry up." The servants were glad to let him take over and relaxed outside.

Yang Longyou followed Li Zhenli into The House of Enchanting Fragrance. Li Xiangjun did not know what was happening and when Li Zhenli told her, she was quite frightened. Li Zhenli was angry and said, "Lord Yang, I thought you loved both me and my daughter. Why have you helped the others?"

"You are mistaken. It has nothing with me. After Ma Shiying heard that you had turned down Tian Yang, he flew into a rage and sent servants here to force your daughter to comply. I was afraid that you would be bullied and came to protect you."

Li Zhenli was immediately thankful. "That's so and I should thank you. Please help and protect us."

Yang Longyou, who had no idea what to do, tried persuasion. "To me, 300 taels of silver is not a bad price and it wouldn't be too bad if Xiangjun married the grand coordinator of the Transport Office. You're

人,悄悄地说道:"你看,这三百两银子,一套绣衣……"

不等杨龙友把话说完,李贞丽问道:"是哪家来娶,怎不早说?"

杨龙友指着那对灯笼说:"你不看这是马中堂府上的灯笼么?"

李贞丽见门外果然是一对相府灯笼,开口问道:"是内阁老爷自己娶么?"

杨龙友回答道:"不是。漕运巡抚田仰,与相爷同乡至戚,如今赴任而去,相爷为他讨娶一房佳人。"

"田家亲事,不是已经回绝,怎么又来纠缠?"贞丽有些意外。

那两个家人见贞丽楚楚动人,以为她就是李香君,拿出银子来递过去:"你就是香君了?请受财礼。"

李贞丽是个玲珑剔透的人,不置可否地说:"待我进去想想。"

马府家人闻言,更以为他就是香君无疑了:"相府要人,还等你想?快快收了银子,出门上轿吧!"

杨龙友见状,知道家人误认了,也不说破,只是劝说马府家人:"她怎敢不去?你们先出去歇歇,待我将财礼拿上楼,催她梳洗罢了。"两个家人见杨老爷出面张罗,落得到外面寻乐去。

杨龙友紧跟着李贞丽上了媚香楼,李香君还不知内情,听李贞丽说出此事,不禁惊恐万分。李贞丽对杨龙友也十分不满,质问他:"杨老爷从来疼俺母女,为何帮他们来下毒手?"

"啊呀呀,你可误会了。这不干我的事。那马士英知道你拒绝了田仰,大发脾气,动了真怒,差了一班恶仆登门强娶。我倒怕你们受气,特地跟着前来保护的。"

贞丽立即改容致谢:"这样,真要多谢你了,还求老爷始终救护。"

杨龙友此际也并无良策,只得劝说道:"依我说,三百两财礼,也不算吃亏;香君嫁给漕运巡抚,也不算失所。你有多大本事,能对抗他两家的势力?"

not strong enough to resist Tian and Ma, are you?"

He made it seem sensible. Li Zhenli thought for a while and said that he was right. She turned to Li Xiangjun. "Look at the situation. You cannot make them change their minds. It would be better if you packed your things and went downstairs."

Li Xiangjun had waited for Li Zhenli's response and became very angry. "What are you saying? Lord Yang acted as matchmaker and you held a ceremony betrothing me to Master Hou. Friends were present and know of the marriage. The gift that marks my betrothal is here...." She took the paper fan from the inner room and showed the poem on it to Yang Longyou. "This poem was written to mark the event. Lord Yang, you read it, didn't you? Have you forgotten?"

Yang deflected the question. "Master Hou has fled and you do not know where he is. If he does not come back in three years, will you wait for him?"

"I will wait three years, even 10 or 100. I will not marry Tian Yang."

Yang Longyou respected her and said, "How strong you are! You still have the same resolution as when you rejected jewelry and wedding clothes and so severely scolded Ruan Dacheng that year."

The name of Ruan Dacheng made Li Xiangjun angry again. "Ruan Dacheng and Tian Yang are followers of Wei Zhongxian. I refused to accept a dowry from Ruan but today I am expected to marry Tian Yang."

As they talked the two servants resumed their call for the bride to go downstairs. Li Zhenli had to persuade Xiangjun to go and moved forward to help her make up her mind. Xiangjun kept her mother away with the fan, but she was a thin girl and the man-servant, Bao'er, held her so that she could not move. She banged her head against the floor; blood spurted out spotting the paper fan. Then she fainted and Zhenli, shocked, asked Bao'er to prop her up and take her to the inner room to lie down. The servants again urged them to hurry up. After trying to assure them, Yang Longyou said to Zhenli, "You know how powerful Master Ma is. If you made him angry, how would you and your daughter survive?"

"Please help us," Li Zhenli was flustered.

"We have to think of a compromise."

"Please tell us what you think," Li Zhenli pleaded.

Yang Longyou spoke slowly, "It is good for a prostitute to have a family. After marrying into the the Tian family, you would have no more worries. Xiangjun has refused. Why should you not go instead?"

144

这番话说得既委婉又符合实情,李贞丽低头沉思,答道:"杨老爷说的有理。你看这局面,拗不下去了。还是收拾收拾下楼吧。"

李香君一直在注视着李贞丽,看她的态度如何,听得此话,不禁大怒:"妈妈说的什么话!当日杨老爷作媒,妈妈主婚,把奴家嫁与侯郎,满堂宾客,谁人没看见?当年定婚之物还在……"说罢,急急从内房中取出一把纸扇,指着扇面题诗对杨龙友说道:"这首定情诗,杨老爷不是也看过,怎么忘了?"

杨龙友无法正面回答,只是说:"那侯郎避祸逃走,不知去向。假若三年不归,你也等他么?""便等他三年,等他十年、等他百年,只是不嫁田仰!"李香君坚决地答道。

"啊呀呀,真好性气!又像当年摘除首饰、脱却衣裳痛骂阮大铖那样了!"杨龙友不无钦敬地说道。

李香君听得"阮大铖"三个字,满腔怒气兜底升上:"那阮大铖与田仰不同是魏忠贤党徒!阮家的嫁妆,俺尚不肯妥收,倒去嫁给田仰!"

他们三人在媚香楼上说个不停,那两个家人却已寻乐返来,不断在楼下催促。李贞丽不断劝说,香君却自是不从。贞丽事出无奈,强行为她梳洗。香君贞节自守,用扇子前后乱打。但她毕竟是一个弱女子,被保儿强行抱住,行动不得,拼命挣扎,以头撞地,顿时血喷而出,溅湿纸扇,晕倒在地。贞丽见状,十分惊恐,忙叫保儿扶起香君,进到内室安歇。楼下不管楼上发生什么事情,只是一味催促。杨龙友先行答话,稳住马府家人,又对李贞丽说:"那宰相的权势,你是知道的,这次又羞辱了他,你母女不要性命了!"

"求杨老爷救俺两个。"李贞丽倒真地慌张起来。杨龙友此际已成竹在胸,说道:"没奈何,只有想个变通的方法了。"

"杨老爷快说,有什么变通之法?"李贞丽迫不及待地询问。

杨龙友缓缓道来:"娼家从良,原是好事,况且嫁给田府,吃穿

"Would that be all right?" Li Zhenli had not expected this.

"The servants are waiting, what can you do?"

There was no other way out and Li Zhenli agreed, but thinking again she cried out, "No, no. It won't work. I'm afraid I will be recognized." Yang thought otherwise. He patted his chest and said, "I told them you are Xiangjun. Who knows any better?"

He was right. Only Hou Chaozong and Yang Longyou were allowed access to The House of Enchanting Fragrance. No one else could tell the two apart. Li Zhenli agreed. She prepared herself and went downstairs. The servants said, "Good, you are here. Please get into the bridal sedan chair."

"Lord Yang, we have to say good-bye." Li Zhenli was very sad and bowed her body to express her thanks.

Yang Longyou felt depressed and said, "Take care of yourself. We will meet again."

"Lord Yang, please stay here for the night and take care of my daughter." Li Zhenli still cared for Xiangjun.

"Certainly. Don't worry." Yang Longyou was a sentimental man. Assured, Li Zhenli stepped slowly out of the gate.

CHAPTER TWENTY-ONE

Painting a Fan

A month after Li Zhenli married Tian Yang it was winter. Leaves fell, a cold wind blew and few travelers were seen. Li Xiangjun had cut up her dancing shoes and ripped her dancing dress apart. The House of Enchanting Fragrance was cold, quiet, and bleak, only a white cat slept on a pillow.

Upstairs Li Xiangjun waited hopelessly for her fiance. She was forever thinking of her time with Chaozong and was depressed. She had no idea where he was. Her mother had left and she did not know when

不愁。香君既然没有这福气,你何不替她去田府?"

"呀,这怎能?"贞丽乍闻此言,也出乎意外。

"相府等着拿人,你看怎么办?"杨龙友又逼了一句。李贞丽一时别无他法,只得应允。继而一想,又惊呼道:"不好,不好,只怕有人认出。"杨龙友却心中有数,轻轻拍着胸脯说:"我说你是香君,又有谁人可以辨别!"此话倒也不错,当年只有侯朝宗与杨龙友两个可以径直上得媚香楼,如今又有谁人可以分清她们母女二人呢?李贞丽终于答允,梳洗妆扮一番,下得楼来,马府家人看见了,连声说:"好,好,新人出来了,快请上轿。"

"杨老爷,今日相别了。"李贞丽不禁十分伤感,深深一拜。

杨龙友也神色黯然,叮嘱道:"前途多加保重,后会有期。"

"老爷今日就暂时住在院中,照管一下孩儿。"贞丽放心不下香君,请求杨龙友关照。"自然,放心。"杨龙友也有些伤感。李贞丽见杨龙友应允,才慢慢迈出院门。

第二十一章
画扇寄扇

自从李贞丽被马相爷府中娶走转赠田仰以后,已经月余,时届冬令,落叶敲窗,寒风飒飒,冻云残雪,冶游人少。香君自家剪碎了舞鞋,裂破了舞裙;媚香楼上,炭冷香消,只有一只白猫依偎在枕边,自在安稳地睡着。

香君困居在楼上,无望地等待侯郎。整日闲闷,只是回想当日与朝宗相聚的岁月。每当念及侯郎匆匆避祸远走天涯,便不禁悲从中来,也不知如今流落何处,令人断肠。又想起马府恶仆,前来

she would come back. Grief overwhelmed her and tears rolled down her face. She had no sisters to confide in and the only sound she heard was the clack of curtain hangers as the wind blew. She took out the fan that Master Hou had given her and folded it, determined to wait for his return.

One afternoon after looking at the fan with its bloodspots she felt depressed and tired. Leaning over her dressing table she fell into a deep sleep with the fan spread nearby. Su Kunsheng, an old artist who taught Xiangjun to sing local operas, was very fond of his female student. After Li Zhenli married, he was worried about Xiangjun and, as he approached The House of Enchanting Fragrance, he saw a young man walking in front of him. He recognized him as Yang Longyou and caught up with him. He said, "You're Lord Yang, aren't you?"

Yang Longyou turned his head and said, "Su Kunsheng, you're here too. I have been busy with my work at *yamen* and have been away for several days. Today I was with a friend in East City and came to call in on my way back."

They entered The House of Enchanting Fragrance and Su Kunsheng said that they should go up as Xiangjun refused to come downstairs. The pair made their way up quietly and saw Xiangjun sleeping at her dressing table. They tried not to wake her and sat on nearby chairs.

Su Kunsheng saw the fan and asked Yang Longyou why it had blood spots. Yang told him that it had been a gift from Brother Hou and told him how the spots had got there.

Yang picked it up, looked at it carefully and said, "The spots can be made into a picture by adding branches and leaves. But I have no green color."

Su Kunsheng said, "I'll pick leaves from potted plants and squeeze the juice which can be used as a substitute."

Yang Longyou said, "Wonderful! That's a good idea."

Su Kunsheng went downstairs and returned a few minutes later with a wine cup of leaf juice. Yang Longyou took up the brush thoughtfully, added branches and leaves around the spots and in minutes a beautiful fan picture emerged. Su praised it saying, "Excellent! Excellent! It is a perfect picture of peach blossom."

Yang Longyou was excited by the result and cried out, "It is really a peach blossom fan."

Their laughter woke up Li Xiangjun who opened her eyes and called

逼娶，自家矢志不从，可怜妈妈当灾，顶替前往，飘然而去，竟不知何日归来。想东想西，肝肠寸断，泪水不淌自流，独坐无聊时，就取出当日侯郎送她的定情扇来展开，权当作与侯郎相守。

这日午后，又取出诗扇展开，只见扇面上点点血污，这是她以头撞地喷溅出来的。看了又看，伤心异常，不觉困倦上来，就伏在妆台上睡着了，任那柄扇子摊开在一旁。老艺人苏昆生一向教香君唱曲子，对这个女弟子颇有情谊，如今贞丽从良，他放心不下。这日午饭后，他信步蹀到旧院，见前面走的一位官人好似杨龙友，不免紧走几步，上前招呼："前面可是杨老爷？"

杨龙友应声回头："呀，原来苏昆老也来了。下官自从那天打发贞丽起身之后，守了香君一夜。这一阵衙门有事，不能脱身。方才去东城拜客，就便来此看看。"

两人说罢，已进旧院。苏昆生说："香君不肯下楼，我们就上楼去谈谈吧。"两人轻手轻脚地上楼，只见香君伏到妆台上打盹，竟未察觉有人登楼。他们不忍心唤醒她，随意坐在两张靠椅上。苏昆生忽然看到那柄诗扇，上面有许多血污，不知何故，乃向杨龙友询问。杨龙友说："这乃是侯兄定情之物，香君一向珍藏，轻易不肯示人。这血污乃是她的头面碰破溅出来的，今日想必取出摊在此处晾晾。"说着，他轻拿起扇子看了看，向苏昆生说道："几点血痕，正可添些枝叶，装点装点。"沉吟一番，又自言自语地说："只是没有绿色，怎么办？"

苏昆生已走拢来，接口答允道："此事不难，待我去盆中摘几片叶子，拧出鲜汁，可当绿色颜料使用。"

杨龙友称赞道："妙极，妙极！就有劳苏昆老了。"

苏昆生下楼去，不一会儿就用小酒杯盛了一些叶汁上来。杨龙友提起案上画笔，将纸扇打量一番，以血污为主，刷刷几笔已成了一帧扇画，苏昆生赞不绝口地说："妙，妙！竟然是一幅折枝桃花画面哩！"

out in alarm, "Oh, I am so sorry. I did not know that you were here." She stood up and asked them to be seated.

Yang Longyou did not sit but looked closely at Xiangjun. "I have been too busy to see you. The wound on your forehead has healed." He said that he had a picture fan for her and handed over his work. Xiangjun put it into her sleeve saying that it was an old fan that had been spoiled by blood spots.

Su Kunsheng smiled and said, "Without looking, you folded it. There is a picture on it that you have not seen."

"How did it get there?" Xiangjun was confused.

Pleased with himself Yang Longyou said, "I am so sorry for altering it."

Xiangjun opened the fan and saw a peach blossom branch on it. It depressed her and she said, "The peach blossom has a short life. Thank you Lord Yang for a portrait of my life."

Yang tried to comfort her. "With this peach blossom fan in your hand you will be sought after by a handsome young man. Unlike Chang'e* you will not wait years for a husband."

His words were well intentioned but they saddened Xiangjun. "You are wrong. Few prostitutes live to marry their lover."

Su Kunsheng knew what she was thinking and asked if she would still refuse to go downstairs if Hou came back the next day.

The question cheered Xiangjun who raised her voice and said, "Then I would have a happy and comfortable life. I would go anywhere, including downstairs."

Yang Longyou praised Xiangjun's loyalty and asked Su Kunsheng if he could do him a great favor — find out where Hou was so that the lovers could be reunited.

Su Kunsheng had thought about it before. "I have tried to find Hou. I know he left for Yangzhou with Shi Kefa. Today he was sent to supervise the river defenses with Gao Jie. I'm going home in a few days and will look for him on the way. When I know where he is I'll let Xiangjun decide what to do." He asked Xiangjun if she would write a letter; it would make the task easier.

Li Xiangjun said that she was a poor writer and asked Yang to write

---

*Chang'e, the goddess of the moon who in a legend, swallowed elixir stolen from her husband and flew to the moon.

杨龙友也得意忘形,高声呼道:"真是一柄桃花扇!"

伏在妆台上的香君,被二人的笑声惊醒,睁开惺忪睡眼,惊呼道:"啊呀,杨老爷、苏师父来了。"连忙起身让坐。

杨龙友且不坐下,在香君身边左看右看,说道:"这一阵子没空来看你,额角伤痕也渐渐平复了。"又笑着说道:"俺有画扇一柄,奉赠妆台。"说着,将那柄扇子递了过来。

"这是奴家的一柄旧扇,已被血迹所污,看它怎的?"香君说着,就放进袖中。

苏昆生笑道:"你且打开看看,扇面有妙画呢。"

"几时画的?"香君倒有些不解。

杨龙友不无得意地说:"得罪得罪,方才让俺点坏了。"香君打开扇面,只见上面画着一枝折枝桃花。她不禁流露出无可奈何的悲戚,长叹一声说:"咳,桃花薄命,扇底飘零。多谢杨老爷替奴家写照了。"

杨龙友听得此言,不得不加以劝慰:"你有这柄桃花扇,总会有英俊青年来求,不会像月中嫦娥般长年守寡。"

这番话语,虽属好意,反而引得香君十分的不快:"说哪里话!烟花场上也有为人守节到老的!"

苏昆生知道她的心思,问道:"明日侯郎重到,你也不下楼么?"这才逗起香君兴头,声音也不自觉地高了起来:"那时锦绣前程,尽俺享用,哪处不可游耍,何止下楼!"

杨龙友不觉赞叹道:"香君守节这段苦情,真是今世少有。"又向苏昆生建议:"昆老何不看师弟之情,寻到侯郎,将她送去?"

其实,苏昆生何尝不作如此想,连连说道:"杨老爷说的极是!我一向留心访问侯郎消息,知道他随史可法去两淮赴任,自两淮来京,又从南京去杨州,今又同总兵高杰去防河了。晚生不日返乡,顺便找寻,得到确信,再作区处。"又向香君说:"须得香君一封书信方好。"

one for her. Yang was not keen and Xiangjun did not insist. "This fan explains what I am thinking. Please take it to him."

Su Kunsheng thought it an excellent substitute for a letter and Xiangjun put it in a box. Su packed it carefully and said that he would do his best to get it to him.

Xiangjun was eager for him to start and Su said that he would leave as soon as possible. The two farewelled Xiangjun.

Yang asked Xiangjun to look after herself and said that if Hou knew how faithful she had been, he would certainly come to marry her.

After seeing them off, Xiangjun felt sad. She refused to go down the stairs and remained by herself.

CHAPTER TWENTY-TWO

Xiangjun Speaks Her Mind

Ruan Dacheng's fawning behavior earned him promotion from Ma Shiying and he became a palace provisioner. Some poets also secured important positions and to stay in favor, they did what the new emperor wanted.

Ruan Dacheng knew much about opera and selected four to be performed for the emperor. Emperor Zhu Yousong was very pleased and asked the Ministry of Rites to select singers to rehearse *The Swallow's Love Note*. Ruan Dacheng thought that they might not be good enough and suggested that they invite singers, who had performed the opera, from outside the palace. The emperor agreed and asked him to find literary men and singers from the old brothels along the Qinhuai River. With the emperor's backing Ruan Dacheng selected prostitutes who were beautiful and sang well. When Yang Longyou asked him to leave them alone, he had to comply, but he appealed to Ma Shiying who found in his favor arguing that the emperor eagerly anticipated the new opera and that they could not select poor singers.

李香君自然愿意，便向杨龙友求道："奴家出言无文，还是杨老爷代写罢。"杨龙友以为不可，香君不好勉强，寻思半晌，忽然想起一个主意："罢，罢，罢！奴的千愁万苦，都在这柄扇子上了，就请师父把这扇子寄去罢。"

苏昆生立即同意："这封家书，倒也别致。"香君见师父同意，随手就把这柄扇子装在盒子里，交给苏昆生。

苏昆生接过扇盒，仔细包好，说道："老汉一定设法替你送到。"

杨龙友一边告辞，一边劝慰："香君保重，你这段苦节，说给侯郎知道，他自然要来娶你的。"

苏昆生也说："我也不再来告别了，就此别过。"香君此刻见二人又将离去，倍感凄凉，索性闭了楼门，独个儿去挨那寂寞之苦。

第二十二章
香君骂筵

阮大铖百般谀媚马士英，不久就得到马士英的破格提拔，作了内廷供奉。他原就擅长戏曲，进贡了四种传奇，朱由崧看了十分高兴，立即传旨礼部，采选官人，先行将《燕子笺》排练演出。阮大铖生怕这部精心撰制的传奇，被不懂戏的凡庸教手教坏，有损自己文名，便向朱由崧启奏说："生口不如熟口，清客强似教手。"朱由崧觉得有理，就让他在秦淮旧院中搜罗会唱曲的清客、妓女。但这些妓女，色艺平常，虽有几个佼佼有名的，又被杨龙友求情，只得将她们的名字勾去。不过，阮大铖并不情愿，见到马士英时，就特意把这事儿说了出来，马士英不满地说："教演新戏是圣上的心事，怎能不选好的演员倒拣差的演员？"

Ruan Dacheng selected whoever he wanted and for a while well-known prostitutes and literary men were recruited by force.

On the seventh day of the first lunar month in 1646, Ruan Dacheng and Yang Longyou invited Ma Shiying for a drink in the Shangxin Pavilion where they could appreciate a snow-covered scene. There they asked Ma for a final decision about the singing prostitutes. As newly promoted officials, they wished to ingratiate themselves with higher officials and enjoy themselves despite the hardship they caused. Literary men and singing prostitutes were sent for or caught. The well-known prostitute, Bian Yujing, who had no wish to take part, said good-bye to her friends that evening and changed into Taoist clothes. She left the old brothel and became a Taoist nun in the Dongyun Mountains.

Ding Jizhi was one of the literary men. He was about 60 and had not sung for a long time. How could he sing again? He had asked for Yang's help several days before and had been excused. He was wondering why he had been asked again when he was joined by Shen Gongxian and Zhang Yanzhu. When they learned of his plight they said, "We were excused too. We don't know why we are being called up."

Ding Jizhi looked at them and said, "You are young and talented and should go. I am old and in poor health. I can't expect to improve and must avoid this. I need your help." They offered it and Ding, who knew that he would be caught if he stayed at home, changed into Taoist clothes and left for a Taoist temple.

After he had gone, Shen Gongxian and Zhang Yanzhu joined others from brothel and went to the Ministry of Rites to be examined. While they were there they saw Kou Baimen and Zheng Tuoniang arriving accompanied by a magistrate. The magistrate saw three names on the summons and asked, "Why isn't Ding here?" Shen Gongxian answered, "He has become a Taoist priest." The magistrate checked the singing prostitutes and was told that Bian Yujing had left to be a Taoist nun. He asked about Li Zhenli who should have been there and Kou Baimen said that she was married.

"That's strange. When I pulled her down the stairs, she said she was Li Zhenli. She cannot be anyone else, can she?"

Zheng Tuoniang said, "Most probably that's her daughter. She took her place by assuming her name."

The magistrate, who was just doing his job, said, "Mother or daughter, it's all the same. As long as we have the right number of people,

　　阮大铖正等着这句话，就此完全按照自己的心意去挑选，一经挑中，立即去传，一时旧院中有名的清客、妓女，尽数被他强行征来。

　　转眼已是南明弘光新年（1646）正月初七，阮大铖约好杨龙友一同敦请马士英去赏心亭饮酒赏雪，同时也请他验看新挑选的这批歌妓是否中意。这些新贵们只知讨好主人，寻欢作乐，哪管骚扰百姓？一时之间，秦淮清客、歌妓被传的传，捉的捉。名妓卞玉京不愿趋奉这为人不齿的新贵，趁夜与众姊妹告别，清晨换上道服，逃向城东云山深处，从此出家做了道姑。

　　丁继之也在勾传之列，他自忖，年过六旬，歌板久已抛在一边，哪能再去弹唱？前些日子托了杨老爷，已经免了，怎的今日又传起来？正当他自言自语时，沈公宪、张燕筑两人也走来，听了丁继之的话，接着说道："俺两个也是免了的，不知又传，有何话说。"

　　丁继之抬头，见是他们两个，便说道："二位年青有为，该去走走。我老汉年衰多病，也不指望有什么发达机会。今日就躲了这份差事，还求二位代为遮盖遮盖。"这两位满口答允，丁继之也知道呆在家中是避不开的，索性换了道妆，出家去了。

　　沈公宪、张燕筑见丁继之出了家，只得会齐院中姊妹一同去礼部过堂。不一会儿，寇白门、郑妥娘在差役伴同下走来。那差役见传票上有三个名字，便问道："那姓丁的为何不来？"沈公宪回答说："他出家去了。"差役又取出歌妓的传票来验看，一问之下，方知卞玉京也出了家。差役又问："后面来的想必就是李贞丽了。"寇白门回答说："不是，李贞丽从良去了。"

　　"又是奇事了！出家配对儿。这个，我拉她下楼时，她自称是李贞丽，怎的又不是了？"

　　郑妥娘说："想必是她女儿冒名顶替的。"

　　那差役不过应付差事，倒也好说话："母女一样，只要人数不

it's all right." He asked a woman to hurry up. It was Xiangjun who had been pulled down the stairs. She had been told that she would be sent to learn opera singing, something she looked on as the work of prostitutes. At Shangxin Pavilion they heard shouting and saw Ma Shiying arrive followed by Ruan Dacheng and Yang Longyou on horseback. Their heads were held high. They dismounted and walked into the pavilion where a banquet was laid out. Ma Shiying took his seat and Yang Longyou asked for wine. Ruan Dacheng asked the singing prostitutes to step forward, but Ma Shiying didn't appreciate their presence. "They are out of place at such a banquet. Let the Ministry of Rites do the work of selecting them."

Ruan Dacheng said, "They are only here for your pleasure." Ma Shiying didn't want to disappoint Ruan and said, "Please ask the youngest to stay." Li Xiangjun, who had come in her mother's name, was the youngest. Ruan, who couldn't tell her apart from her mother, shouted, "Come here, pour wine and sing." Xiangjun shook her head and refused.

Ma Shiying had not expected this and said, "You know no songs and yet you are reputed to be a well-known prostitute?"

"I am not a well-known prostitute," she said and cried.

"Say whatever is on your mind, you are allowed to speak out," Ma said, feigning magnanimity.

"I am nervous. I have been forced to leave my husband and my mother."

"Oh, that's what you think."

Yang Longyou was afraid that something might happen and said, "Today the masters wish to enjoy themselves. It's not appropriate for you to tell us about your woes." Xiangjun continued and said frankly, "Lord Yang, you know of injustices but it is pointless talking about them here. You are government officials and are expected to administer the southern areas. You neglect these duties and seek pleasure. You want me do your bidding in the cold wind and sing a song for you while you drink."

Her words touched a raw nerve and Ma shouted angrily, "Get out of here. You talk nonsense and deserve to be punished."

Ruan Dacheng added fuel to the flames. "I heard that Li Zhenli was a famous prostitute much appreciated by members of the Restoration Society. Naturally, she is unrestrained and should be punished."

Yang Longyou interceded, "She is so young and she is not the Li

少就行了。"同时大声催促她快些赶上来。这落后的正李贞丽的养女香君,她是被差役强行捉下楼来的,说是送去学习唱曲。她想:唱曲乃是烟花女儿本该做的行当,倒也无妨。她们到了赏心亭后,忽闻一阵喝道之声,只见马士英当先,阮大铖随侍其后,趾高气昂地跃马而来。他们进了赏心亭,酒席早已备好,马士英上坐,杨龙友招呼敬酒。阮大铖立刻传过一旁听从使唤的歌妓。马士英也不甚领情:"今日雅集,用不着他们,叫他们礼部过堂去吧。"

阮大铖仍不心甘,再三进言:"是特地唤他们来此伺候酒席的。"听了这话,马士英不便太扫阮大铖的颜面,便说:"那就留下那个年小的吧。"这个年小的正是李香君,是顶着其母李贞丽之名,好在阮大铖并分辨不清李贞丽与李香君母女两个,只是嘈杂地唤道:"你过来,斟酒、唱曲!"香君只是摇头口称"不会"。

马士英倒有些诧异:"啊呀,样样不会,怎能称作名妓?"

"奴家原就不是名妓。"说罢,掩面抽泣。

"你有什么心事,容许你说来。"马士英故作大度地说道。

"奴家心中好乱,俺夫妻被拆散,母女被分开!"

马士英却不知就里:"啊,原来有这样的心事。"

杨龙友知道香君性格,惟恐闹出事来,有意岔开说:"今日老爷们在此行乐,不必只是诉冤。"哪知香君直截了当地说道:"杨老爷,你是知道的,奴家冤苦原本不值得在此诉说。只是堂堂列公,这南半边的江山望你们撑持振兴,岂知你们不问朝政,一味寻欢作乐,却把奴家任意摆弄,要俺在寒风冰雪之中陪你们饮酒唱曲!"

这番言语句句直戳马士英的心窝,不禁勃然大怒:"啧,这小丫头胡言乱语,该打嘴!"

阮大铖见马士英恼怒起来,更是火上加油地说道:"听说李贞丽原是复社那班人赞赏的名妓哩,自然是放肆的。该打,该打!"

Zhenli you talk about."

Li Xiangjun ignored him and said angrily, "I am Li Zhenli. Do what you can with me. Members of the Donglin Party and the Restoration Society are scholars and we singing prostitutes respect them. If you have taken up office, you are followers of the eunuch Wei Zhongxian."

Ruan Dacheng flared up first. "How dare you speak to us like that." He ordered the magistrates to push her onto the snow and shouted at her, "Your bitch, you show no restraint in front of Grand Secretariat. You are detestable." He left the table, walked down from the pavilion and kicked Xiangjun.

Yang Longyou stood up and went to help her up. Ma Shiying said, "Such a bitch. It would not be hard to have her put the death, but it would damage my reputation."

Yang took the opportunity to speak out. "Your reputation counts for far more than this lowly prostitute."

Ruan Dacheng was not satisfied and suggested to Ma that they keep her in the palace to perform an unpleasant role. Still angry, Ma Shiying, agreed. Yang Longyou was afraid that Xiangjun would suffer again and asked somebody to take her away.

Ma Shiying said, "She has destroyed good banquet. How detestable she is."

Ruan Dacheng bowed and apologized. "Please forgive me. I will have another banquet for you some day." After farewelling Ma Shiying, Ruan and Yang left.

On his way home, Yang Longyou thought that without his help, Xiangjun would suffer more. Today, she had been selected to perform in the palace and he need not worry about her. But no one was taking care of The House of Enchanting Fragrance. He remembered that his friend, the painter Lan Ying, had asked him to find a place for him to live. He could live in The House of Enchanting Fragrance and wait for Xiangjun to return.

杨龙友赶紧为她遮掩,说:"看她年纪很小,恐怕不是阮公所说的那个李贞丽。"

谁知香君竟不顾及杨龙友话中维护之意,反而恨恨地说道:"就是那个李贞丽又怎么样!东林、复社,尽是读书君子,俺们青楼女子也知道敬重他们。你们这些阉党的徒子徒孙,即使重新上台,但总是魏忠贤的孽子孽孙。"

阮大铖不待马士英发作,先行斥责道:"好大胆,骂的是哪个?"命令左右差役将她推倒在雪地上。他怒吼道:"这奴才,居然当着内阁大老爷面这般放肆,可恨!可恨!"说着走下席来,狠狠踢了香君几脚。

杨龙友赶紧离席,将香君拉了起来。马士英这才开口道:"罢,罢!这样的奴才,处死她也不难,只怕有妨俺宰相大度!"

杨龙友趁机缓解道:"是,是!以丞相之尊,不必介意这个娼贱之女。"

阮大铖不甘心放过,想出一个恶毒主意来,向马士英建议道:"也罢!启禀老师相,将她选入宫中,拣一个极苦的角色,让她去扮演。"马士英正在愤恨之际,自然应允。杨龙友怕香君再当面受苦,赶紧叫人将她带走。

马士英兴味索然地说:"好好一个雅集,被这奴才搅坏了,可恨,可恨!"

阮大铖连忙作揖,陪不是:"得罪,得罪,望师相海量包涵,他日再竭诚相请。"送走马士英,阮、杨二人各自散去。

杨龙友在回寓所的路上忖思:今日这场是非,若无自己遮盖,香君性命恐怕难保。如今选入宫中,倒也省了几日悬挂,只是媚香楼无人看守,如何是好?低头沉思半晌,忽然想起画友蓝瑛曾托他找一个临时寓所,何不就让他暂住媚香楼,等香君出宫后再说。

CHAPTER TWENTY-THREE

Absurd King and Happy Officials

Ruan Dacheng knew of the emperor's liking for spectacles and prostitutes. He looked on his group of literary men and singing prostitutes as "capital" with which, with Ma's approval, he could curry favor from the emperor. Shen Gongxian, Zhang Yanzhu, Kou Baimen and Zheng Tuoniang were not allowed to go home where they could have waited before being summoned to sing for the emperor.

Two days later Ruan Dacheng sat in the Xunfeng Hall where the imperial music was performed and asked the singers to come in. They entered one by one but Li Zhenli was not there. He asked curtly, "Is everybody here? Where is Li Zhenli?"

Kou Baimen replied, "She couldn't move after falling down in the snow. She is lying in the corridor and finds it too painful to get up."

Ruan Dacheng intended punishing Li Zhenli and thought that she was malingering. It angered him and he shouted, "The emperor is coming to select roles for an opera. Can she be that stupid?"

Those who were there saw how angry he was and said that they would bring her in.

Ruan Dacheng's hatred persisted and he said to himself, "What a detestable woman. Today, I will ask her to play an unpleasant and heavy role."

Two eunuchs with dragon fans in their hands came in. They were followed by two more each with a kettle and a box in their hands. Zhu Yousong was coming to court.

Ruan Dacheng knelt to welcome him. He hoped that the emperor had had a good day and wished him a long life. From the corner of his eye he saw the emperor frown and realized that he was unhappy. He said, "Your Majesty, there is peace and you should be enjoying pleasure. Why are you worried?"

"There is something on my mind and I think you know what it is."

第二十三章
君荒臣嬉

阮大铖见马士英已有吩咐，而且他也深知朱由崧这个皇帝老儿又是一个喜爱热闹的角色，平日追逐声色犬马之事，尽人皆知。这班清客、歌妓不正是自己献媚皇上的"本钱"？于是再也不放沈公宪、张燕筑、寇白门、郑妥娘这几个人回去，以便随时召唤进奉。

过了两日，阮大铖进宫来了，在皇家奏乐之所薰风殿坐定，命人将这班人传了进来。见他们一个个顺序而入，独独少了一人，便没好气地问道："你们都来了么？怎的不见李贞丽？"

寇白门忙为李贞丽解释说："她在雪中跌了一跤，至今还疼痛不过，躺在走廊那里不能动弹哩。"

阮大铖原就要整治李贞丽，不信她摔跤，认为她装病，勃然大怒，发作道："圣驾将到，要选定角色，以便串戏，怎能让她任性胡为！"

这几个清客、歌妓见阮大铖动了怒，赶紧说："是，是，俺们拉她过来。"说罢，就一齐去走廊那头。

阮大铖仍不消恨，喃喃自语道："李贞丽这个奴才，如此可恶，今日一定派她一个又苦又重的净、丑角色。"

他沉思方罢，两个太监执掌龙扇前引，又有两个太监提壶捧盒紧跟，朱由崧前来坐朝了。

阮大铖赶紧跪迎，口呼万岁，恭请圣安。他用眼角偷觑几眼，见这个皇帝老儿双眉紧凑，满脸不悦，乃明知故问地谀媚道："圣上安享太平，正该及时行乐，如今厌倦游要，不知何故？"

"朕有一桩心事，料你也应该知道。"

Ruan Dacheng pretended not to and asked, "Are you afraid of invaders from north?"

"No, the invaders are as far north of the Yangtze River, even the Yellow River, as they are from heaven."

"Are you worried about a shortage of soldiers or grain?"

"No, that is all taken care of. There are four battalions from northern Jiangsu stationed in Huaiyin supplied by the Jiangling grain fleet."

"As you are not worried by military affairs I thought that you may be unhappy because you have no wife and there is no woman in your house."

"I have no concerns there. The Minister of Rites, Qian Qianyi, is busy selecting concubines for me. I will have them within days."

Ruan Dacheng took a step forward, knelt down and asked in a low voice, "Is it because the traitors Zhou Biao and Lei Yanzuo plot and scheme to make King Lu the emperor?"

"You are wrong. They caused trouble and have been arrested."

"Then please say what is the matter."

"You are Palace Provisioner and one of my trusted subordinates. Don't you know what is on my mind?" Zhu Yousong said.

"Excuse me, I am ignorant and wait for Your Majesty to tell me. Let me share your burden."

Zhu Yousong said, "The opera *The Swallow's Love Note* which you recommended is good. To perform it in the palace would be the most important thing that has happened since I came to power. Today is the ninth day of the first lunar month and the roles have not yet been decided. I am worried that it won't be ready before the Lantern Festival of the 15th day of the first lunar month."

"Oh, that's how it is. The opera is no better. It was my fault recommending it to you." Ruan Dacheng knelt down, saying, "I will do my very best to show my gratitude to you." He moved forward and added, "But I need to know what roles the palace has not been able to fill."

"Most are filled, but we need satisfactory male and female leads as well as clowns."

Ruan replied, "That's easy. The Ministry of Rites sent in a team of literary men and singing prostitutes. They are waiting outside for you to choose." Zhu Yousong nodded his approval and Ruan asked them to come in. The literary men and singing prostitutes knelt in a row waiting to be selected. Zhu Yousong said to Shen Gongxian and Zhang Yanzuo who

　　狡诈的阮大铖故作不知,回答道:"想是怕'流贼'南犯?""不是。那般贼子尚在北边,隔着滔滔黄河、长江,哪怕他从天上而降。""是否愁兵弱粮少?""也不是。俺有江北四总兵坐镇淮阴一带,有江陵大粮船接济,还怕什么!"

　　至此,阮大铖方始渐渐逼近话题:"既然不为内外兵马之事烦神,想是正宫娘娘未立,后宫无人?"

　　"也不为此。那礼部尚书钱谦益正在采选淑女,不日册立。"

　　阮大铖真是狡诈异常,又松弦放开:"又不为此,臣晓得了——"故意跪上一步,悄悄说道:"想因叛臣周镳、雷缜祚,倡导邪说,制造阴谋,想迎立潞王登大宝。"

　　"说得更错了,那般倡言惑众的奸人,早已收拿!"

　　"这却又是为了什么?"阮大铖不想担待引诱皇上嬉乐的罪名,不主动说出皇上的心事。

　　朱由崧带着几分埋怨的情绪说:"卿供奉内廷,是朕的心腹之臣,怎会不知晓朕的心事?"

　　阮大铖仍然故作糊涂地说:"微臣愚昧无知,伏望皇上明示,以便微臣为皇上分忧。"

　　朱由崧说道:"你献上的《燕子笺》乃是一代中兴之戏乐。朕立位以来,点缀升平,当是第一要事。今天已是正月初九了,角色尚未选定,万一正月十五灯节不能演出,岂不可恼!"

　　"原来如此!微臣所作,无非俚俗之曲,有损圣怀,真是罪过!"说罢,又叩头道:"微臣哪敢不鞠躬尽瘁,以报圣主知遇。"又跪前半步奏道:"但不知内廷女乐,还少什么角色?"

　　"别的角色,也还能用,只有生、旦、小丑,不合朕意。"

　　阮大铖答道:"这也容易,礼部送来一些清客、歌妓,正在外面听候拣选。"朱由崧微微点头示意,阮大铖立即将这批人传了进

were in front, "You are literary men, aren't you?"

"I'm afraid not, we earn a living by performing."

"You are opera performers. Have you performed roles in the new operas?"

Shen and Zhang replied carefully, "We have played roles in *The Peony Pavilion, The Swallow's Love Note* and *The Story of West Building*."

Zhu Yousong was pleased and said that they could teach the roles to those in the palace. Shen and Zhang kowtowed several times to express their thanks.

Then Zhu asked the three singing prostitutes whether they could sing *The Swallow's Love Note*. Kou Baimen and Zheng Tuoniang said that they had once learned it which pleased Zhu Yousong. He turned and said to Xiangjun, "You are young, why don't you answer my question?"

Xiangjun was unhappy but knew that she would have to reply and said honestly that she did not know the opera.

Ruan Dacheng used the opportunity to suggest that those who had learned the opera should play male and female leads. "She hasn't learned the opera so she can play the clown as it is traditionally done."

Zhu Yousong felt sorry for her, but he had to say that there were rules that had to be followed. He asked them to rehearse the opera.

Ruan Dacheng picked an act from the opera and told them to try it while he directed it. The performance elated the emperor who asked the eunuch to fill his wine cup many times, indicating his approval.

When the performance was over, Zhu Yousong was still elated and stood up. He walked towards the group and said, "We will all share the pleasure together. Let's have a musical performance. What do you think?"

Ruan Dacheng, fearful that he had not tried hard enough to please the emperor, agreed. Ten types of musical instruments joined in. Zhu Yousong had the eunuch fill his wine cup three times and danced for joy, exulting in the performance. "Girls from Suzhou, prostitutes from Yangzhou, music performers from Kunshan and singers from Wuxi gathered in my beautiful hall, all for my enjoyment. I have not a worry in the world. It is, indeed, a most happy event."

He stepped forward to look at the singing prostitutes, then pointed to Xiangjun and said to Ruan Dacheng, "This young prostitute is very beautiful. It is wrong to make her the clown." Without waiting for a reply he spoke directly to Xiangjun, "You are young and do not know this opera but have you learned others?"

来，跪成一排，听候朱由崧亲自审视。朱由崧先问跪在前边的沈公宪、张燕筑二人："你二人是串戏的清客么？""不敢。小民串戏为生。""既会串戏，新出的传奇也曾串过么？"沈、张二人恭谨地回禀道："新出的《牡丹亭》、《燕子笺》、《西楼记》都曾串过。"

朱由崧听罢，倒有几分高兴："既会《燕子笺》，就做个内庭教习罢。"沈、张二人连忙叩头谢恩。

朱由崧又问三个歌妓道："你们三个也会《燕子笺》么？"

寇白门、郑妥娘齐声回答道："也曾学过。"朱由崧高兴非凡，又问"李贞丽"道："你年龄小，怎不答应？"

"李贞丽"一肚子不高兴，又不敢顶撞皇上，回答说："没学。"

阮大铖趁机进谗言道："臣启奏圣上，那两个学过的，按惯例该派为生、旦，演主角；这个没学过的，按规定只能演丑角。"

朱由崧虽十分惋惜，但也只能说："既然有定例，那就依你所奏。"随即吩咐这些清客歌妓准备演戏。

阮大铖摘出《燕子笺》中一出曲辞，让这班人演唱，并且亲自指点，把个皇帝老儿哄得心花怒放，不断令太监进酒，再三庆贺。

戏唱完了，朱由崧还不尽兴，立起身来，离开御座，向前踱了两步，对阮大铖及这班清客歌妓说道："我们君臣同乐，打一回十番如何？"

阮大铖正惟恐献媚不足，哪会不尽力奉承？一时丝竹齐奏、钟鼓和鸣。朱由崧又吩咐宫监再次斟酒，又痛饮三杯，高兴得手舞足蹈，全无个君王的样子，得意非凡地自语道："苏州的姑娘，杨州的妓女，昆山演奏乐器的能手，无锡唱歌的艺人，都聚集在俺这红楼翠殿中，侍奉俺这个无愁天子，真是人生快意之事。"

想到此处，朱由崧又向前几步，仔细看视几个歌妓，指着"李贞丽"对阮大铖说："这个年小的歌妓，美貌非常，派她做丑角，未

"I know *The Peony Pavilion*."

"That's good. Could you sing it?"

Xiangjun paused. Although Zhu Yousong had a poor grasp of government affairs he was skilled at seeking pleasure from prostitutes. He said to an nearby eunuch, "She is shy. Give her a peach fan. She can cover her face with it."

Xiangjun could not remain silent. She accepted the fan and started singing conscientiously. She had learned the opera under the guidance of famous singers and her singing was excellent. It delighted Zhu Yousong who praised her. He took several cups of wine and pointed at her saying, "This singing prostitute has a good voice and body. Her talent is wasted as a clown. She should take the female lead."

Ruan dared not disagree. He had planned to cause trouble for her and was thwarted which increased his dislike.

Emperor Zhu Yousong, who was not sensitive to the feelings of others, said, "The prostitute with the dark skin, Zheng Tuoniang, she can be the clown. Take her and Kou Baimen to the dramatic troupe and put them under the guidance of two literary men. You should give them some instructions too." Ruan Dacheng dared not disobey and left immediately with the literary men and singing prostitutes.

Only Xiangjun remained and Zhu Yousong said to her, "You stay in Xunfeng Hall for three days and learn the opera thoroughly. Then you can join the dramatic troupe." The emperor went back to his living quarters and Xiangjun was left with tears in her eyes. When could she leave the palace? She had no alternative but to recite the script. Who knows when she would be out of the palace to meet her fiance?

免太委屈她了。"不待阮大铖回答,又直接向"李贞丽"发问道:"你这么年青,既然没学过《燕子笺》,有没有学过别的戏?"

"学过《牡丹亭》。"

"这也好了,你唱唱看。"

"李贞丽"却未遵旨立刻演唱。朱由崧正经事不在行,怜香惜玉的本领倒还有几分,对身边的宫监说:"你看她粉面发红,不好意思——赏她一柄桃花扇,也好遮掩遮掩。"

"李贞丽"至此也不能再不搭理了,接过桃花扇便认真唱了起来。她原来得到过名师指点,自然是字正腔圆,合节合拍,十分动听。唱得朱由崧圣心大悦,击节称赏,连饮数杯,指着"李贞丽"对阮大铖说:"看此歌妓,声容皆佳,派做丑角,是大才小用,还是应派做正旦。"

阮大铖敢不遵旨?——他一心想陷"李贞丽",却也未能尽如他意,从此对她更是愤恨不已。

朱由崧哪会理会阮大铖高兴不高兴?又指派着:"那个黑皮肤的可是叫郑妥娘,她该演丑角,你把她和演生角的寇白门带出去派在班里,叫两个清客用心教习,你也抽暇亲自去指点指点。"阮大铖哪敢不应命,立即带着这几个清客、歌妓退出。

惟有"李贞丽"还站在一旁,朱由崧发落了那班人后,方对她说:"你就留在薰风殿中,限你三天之内学会《燕子笺》,好去入班。"交代完毕,就回后宫去了。只留下香君一人独自垂泪,自忖既入深宫,何年才能出去?无可奈何,只得先去将脚本念熟,好应付目前,或许有朝一日能放出宫,与侯郎相会也未可知。

CHAPTER TWENTY-FOUR

Meeting in a Boat

After Su Kunsheng left Nanjing, he went to Henan to look for Hou Chaozong. At Henan he came to the banks of the Yellow River where he saw retreating soldiers everywhere. A donkey driver told him to move away but he did not listen and they were encircled by soldiers. The donkey was driven off and Su, an old man, was pushed and pulled by soldiers. Finally he fell into the river, which fortunately was not deep, and he held up the package with the fan crying for help. It happened that it was not far from a dock. People on a boat heard his cries and asked the boat's owner to help him. At some risk the owner pulled the boat towards Su Kunsheng, "Hurry up and climb in."

He extended a pole and Su climbed up, cold and wet. The owner found him dry clothes and Su, very grateful, kowtowed to him. The owner said, "This woman asked me to help you, you owe her your life."

Su Kunsheng looked up and received a shock. "You are Li Zhenli, aren't you? What are you doing in a boat?"

It was a surprise for Li Zhenli. "It's Master Su. Where have you been?"

"It is a long story," Su Kunsheng heaved a deep sigh.

"Please sit down and tell me what has happened."

The owner saw they knew each other and left them chatting while he pulled to the shore and left to fetch wine.

Su Kunsheng sat down and told Li Zhenli about Xiangjun pining day and night and his search for Hou Chaozong. When he had finished he heaved a deep sigh and said, "Aunt Li, if you are married to Tian Yang, what are you doing here?"

Li Zhenli cried and said, "Fate has been unkind. I have left the Tian family."

"Why? What happened?"

"After I arrived at the Tian family, I became the pet of Tian Yang.

第二十四章
巧遇河船

　　且说当日苏昆生携了一柄桃花扇离开南京，前往河南寻访侯朝宗。行到河南地面、黄河堤上，只见乱兵鼠窜。赶驴的要他暂时躲过一阵，他却不听，行不多远，果然被一群乱兵围住，将他一推，夺走驴子。苏昆生跌入河中。幸亏近岸处河水不深，他赶紧擎起包袱，高呼救命。此处正是泊船的码头，正有一只船撑近来。船上的人听见呼唤"救命"之声，就吩咐船家撑船过去。船家冒着风险将船撑近，对着苏昆生叫道："快快上来！"说着，将篙子伸出。

　　苏昆生借着这一篙之力，攀上船来。被河水浸透，他冷得直打颤。船家取出一身干衣，让他换下湿衣。苏昆生感激不尽，叩头称谢，船家忙称："不干老汉事，全亏这位娘子叫我救你的。"

　　苏昆生抬头一看，惊呼道："你不是李贞丽么？怎的在这船上？"

　　李贞丽也惊讶万般："原来是苏师父，你从何处来？"

　　"一言难尽。"苏昆生不禁长叹。

　　船家见这两人原来是旧相识，一任他们畅谈，便将船拢岸，自去买酒吃了。苏昆生坐稳后，便将李贞丽走后的情况细细说来："自从你嫁了田仰，香君独自一个人生活，收拾起舞裙，锁了楼门，终日思念侯郎，泪无干时。你看，我这不是受她之托前来寻找侯郎么？满地征尘，路途茫茫，叫老汉我何处去访呢？"说罢，叹息不止。继而又问："贞娘，你不是嫁到田府去的么？怎么来此？"

　　李贞丽未语泪先流，哽咽道："奴家命苦，如今不在田家了。"

　　"怎的？怎会发生变故？"

But his first wife was cruel and pulled me out of the bridechamber and beat me severely." Tears trickled down her face.

"Why did Tian Yang not stand up for you?"

"He was too frightened to say anything and gave me to an old soldier," Li Zhenli said angrily.

"What are you doing on a boat?"

"The old soldier was in charge of boats used for messages. He was carrying a message when I was in the bow of the boat that saved you."

As they spoke to each other, they became unaware of their surroundings. A small boat approached the dock and pulled in beside them. On it was Hou Chaozong. He was asleep in the cabin and heard voices in the night. He took no notice but listened after he realized that the man's voice sounded like Su Kunsheng. The woman's voice was familiar too. He shouted Su Kunsheng's name.

There was an immediate response. Su Kunsheng was most surprised and asked Hou Chaozong to come over. Chaozong stepped aboard carefully. Before he sat down, Su Kunsheng said, "There is another person here that you know."

Hou Chaozong looked up with excitement. "It's Aunt Li, isn't it? How did you get here? This is marvelous. Where is Xiangjun?"

Li Zhenli told him how Ma Shiying tried to force her to become Tian Yang's concubine. Hou Chaozong was shocked when he heard how Xiangjun had hit her head against the floor but was reassured when Li Zhenli said that she was still alive. Li Zhenli then gave an account of her own experiences. Hou Chaozong expressed sympathy and turned to Su Kunsheng.

"Why are you here?"

Su Kunsheng told him about the letter.

"Where is it?" Hou was impatient.

Su Kunsheng took out the fan and told Hou how Xiangjun had given it to him. Hou Chaozong wept.

Su Kunsheng gave him the fan and asked him why he was there. Hou Chaozong sighed deeply. Recalling the events made him angry.

Last autumn he had gone to supervise the river defenses with Gao Jie. Gao Jie had turned out to be a despot who treated people badly. He had insulted Xu Dingguo, the regional commander, by cursing him and Xu and his wife had plotted to kill him. They invited

　　"想起那天晚上,匆忙中替香君出嫁,到了田府,倒受到田仰的宠爱。谁知他的嫡妻,十分悍妒,生性残暴,把奴家揪出新房,打个半死。"讲到伤心处,李贞丽更是泪流满面。"田仰怎不出来说话相救?""那田仰哪敢说话?竟然把奴家赏给一个老兵。"李贞丽想起此节,恨恨不已。"既然转嫁,又怎么在船上?""老兵是在田仰标下专管报信的,此刻他上岸送公文去了,奴家独坐船头,哪想到救了你。"

　　这时正有一只小船驶来,傍着他们这艘船泊定。船上乘的不是别人,正是侯朝宗。那侯朝宗正半靠在舱中打盹,听到隔壁船上一男一女絮絮叨叨谈话。觉得那汉子的声音好像是苏昆生,闲着也是没事,不如高叫苏昆生试试。呼声才落,苏昆生果然答允。问答之间苏昆生知道是侯朝宗,惊讶不已,便让侯朝宗过船来叙谈。侯朝宗小心翼翼地跨过船来,苏昆生便说:"这里还有老熟人。"

　　侯朝宗抬头一看,惊喜万分:"呀,这不是贞娘么?你怎么到这里?香君在哪里?"李贞丽乃细说前情:"官人不知,自你避祸走后,香君待你回来,不肯下楼。后来马士英差些恶仆,拿了三百两银子,硬要娶香君送给田仰作妾……"

　　"啊呀,我的香君,怎么改嫁了?"侯朝宗大惊。

　　李贞丽接着说:"嫁是未曾嫁,不过香君一头碰死在地。"

　　侯朝宗闻言大哭道:"我的香君,怎么碰死了!"

　　"死倒未曾死,碰的血流满面。出于无奈,妾身只得替她嫁了田仰。"苏昆生又把贞丽嫁到田仰家后的不幸遭遇告诉了侯朝宗,侯朝宗同情地说:"可怜,可怜。"又转向苏昆生:"你又为何到此?"

　　"香君独自在媚香楼上,天天盼你归来,托俺寄书来的。"

　　侯朝宗急不可待地问道:"书在哪里?"

　　苏昆生取出一柄桃花扇,将扇上桃花的来历说明,侯朝宗不禁放声哭了起来:"香君,香君,教小生如何回报你呀!"

Gao Jie to a banquet in Suizhou City where he was slain. Hou Chaozong had known that they had a scheme and tried to persuade Gao Jie not to go but he would not listen. Xu later surrendered to the Qing Dynasty in the north and moved his forces to the southern bank of the Yellow River. Hou Chaozong had left for his hometown before Gao Jie was killed.

Hou Chaozong felt sad too and pointed to the soldiers on the road. "Look at them. They are defeated and are looking for a way out. How can I face Marshal Shi Kefa?"

"Where are you going now?"

"I cannot stay at Henan. I have to go eastward and I don't know where I will end up."

"So that's it. Why don't you go to Nanjing and see Xiangjun? Then we can talk about where to go."

Hou Chaozong thought about it and decided to go back. He told the owner of the boat that they would leave and said good-bye to Li Zhenli. Li Zhenli had happened to meet two folksmen but would have to leave them soon. She was sad and said, "It would be wonderful if we could live together again in the old brothel. Xiangjun is the only person absent here. When will we meet again?" Tears coursed down her face.

Hou missed Xiangjun but he had other things to think of. He and Su Kunsheng said good-bye to Li Zhenli and went back to the boat.

CHAPTER TWENTY-FIVE

Arrested While Visiting Friends

As he approached Nanjing, Hou Chaozong felt a sense of urgency. He and Su Kunsheng had traveled day and night. They stayed at a hotel and in the morning Hou Chaozong went in search of Xiangjun while Su Kunsheng looked after their luggage.

Hou Chaozong walked to her former dwelling and saw the old

苏昆生寄扇大事已交代过，不禁诧异侯朝宗怎的会来到此处，便问道："还没有问相公因何南下？"

侯朝宗长叹一声。原来他去年秋季，随高杰来防河。高杰为人性气乖张，无端责骂总兵许定国。许定国怀恨在心，设下圈套，请他进睢州城饮酒。侯朝宗深知许定国有诈，劝高杰不要进城。高杰恃强逞胜，不听劝告，入城赴宴。许定国命令部将将他杀害，又投降北朝，率兵南下。侯朝宗见高杰不听劝说，知道前景不妙，就告辞返乡了。说到此处，不禁悲伤起来，指着岸上对苏昆生说道："你看，大路之上，纷纷乱跑的都是败兵，叫俺有何面目去见史可法元帅！""那么，侯相公要去哪儿哩？""河南不能存身，只能顺流东下，现时还不知飘泊何处。""既然如此，相公何不先到南京，去看看香君，再作商量。"苏昆生竭力敦促他去南京与香君团聚。

侯朝宗凝神细想目前处境，便欣然同意。贞丽一时见了两个故人，片刻相聚，又将分手，黯然神伤，说道："想起从前，我们几个一起住在旧院，多么难得；此刻船上，只少了香君一人，不知今生还能不能相见！"说着泪水又不断流下。侯朝宗念着香君，也顾不得李贞丽的无限伤感，便与苏昆生一起向李贞丽作别，跨过船去。

第二十五章
访旧被逮

越是快到南京，侯朝宗的心情越是急迫，他与苏昆生二人不辞辛劳，日夜兼程，到了南京，找了一家旅店安顿下来。次日清晨，留下苏昆生看守行李，他便独自一人去旧院寻访香君。

courtyard covered with moss. Birds sang noisily and the window coverings were partly rolled up. No one was around and he walked straight into The House of Enchanting Fragrance. Climbing the steps he saw that the balustrade had been damaged and the staircase leaned to one side. Dust had gathered everywhere; there were cobwebs and when he entered a room he was surprised to find paintings hanging where rouge boxes once stood.

A man walked up the stairs and asked him who he was and what he was doing there.

"This is my Xiangjun's dressing room. Why are you living here?"

"I am Lan Ying, a painter," Lan Ying said. "My friend Yang Longyou said that I could live here."

Lan Ying was well known and Hou Chaozong said, "So you are Master Lan. I have heard of you. I'm pleased to meet you."

"May I know who you are?"

"I am Hou Chaozong from Henan Province. I am also an old friend of Yang Longyou."

"Oh, I have heard of you. It's a pleasure to meet you. Take a seat and have a cup of tea with me."

Hou Chaozong was worried and upset about Xiangjun and unable to drink tea. Lan Ying told him that he heard that she had been picked to serve in the imperial court but he could not give any details.

While they were talking Yang Longyou arrived. He was surprised to see Hou Chaozong and could only add that it was not known when Xiangjun would be allowed to leave.

The news grieved Hou Chaozong who wept and sighed. He stood up and saw the broken window papers and torn curtains. The dressing table was empty — no silk handkerchief or ornaments. The flute that hung on the wall was missing; the red silk bed roll was rolled up to one side and the water chestnut shaped mirror had fallen on the rack. The place had gone to rack and ruin; he felt saddened. He remembered that when they made their vows, the peaches were in full bloom and the building had been new. Now although the peaches were blooming, the place was dilapidated and Xiangjun was not there. Unable to suppress his feelings, Hou Chaozong wept. He said to Yang Longyou, "I will stay here and wait for Xiangjun."

Yang Longyou knew how complex the situation was and said, "Brother Hou, there is nothing to wait here for. It would be better to seek

行不多时，侯朝宗便来到旧院。只见一院苍苔，满树雀喧，寂无人声，窗帘半卷。他无心细究，径自走到媚香楼前，拾级而上，栏坏梯偏，尘封网结。他上了楼进了房，却见当年摆着脂粉香盒的地方，全都挂上画幅，使他感到意外惊奇。

这时一人上楼来问道："你是何人，怎么上我寓楼？"

"这是俺香君的梳妆楼，你为何住在此地？"侯朝宗反问道。

"我乃画士蓝瑛，是杨龙友让俺在此寓居的。"

蓝瑛本不是无名之辈，侯朝宗听罢，连忙说道："原来是蓝田老，一向久仰。"

"请问台兄尊号？"

"小生河南侯朝宗，也是龙友的老朋友。"

"啊呀，文名震耳，如今才得会面，请坐用茶。"

侯朝宗哪有心情用茶，连忙问香君下落。蓝瑛告诉他，只听说香君已被选入宫去，详情不知。

正当侯、蓝二人谈话之际，杨龙友也前来看望蓝瑛，见到侯朝宗，感到十分意外。侯朝宗乃向他细细打听，才知道香君正月里被选入宫中，不知何时才能出宫。

侯朝宗听了杨龙友叙述的详情，不禁伤感万分，掩泪叹息，再也坐不住了，立起身来，环顾四周，只见窗纸破碎，幔纱开裂；再看妆台上，香君用过的罗帕，戴过的首饰，一件也无，墙上原来挂着的箫管，也无所存；红锦被早卷在一边，菱花镜也倾复案头，一片萧索景况，更是伤感。他想起定情之日，正是窗外桃花盛开，簇新簇新的一座妆楼，岂料香君去后零落至此。今日重来，又逢桃花盛开，人去楼空，对景伤情，泪水再也止不住了，便向杨龙友表示："俺只有在此等待香君了。"·

a beautiful woman somewhere else."

"How could I betray my vow. I shall not rest till I find out what has happened to her."

Yang Longyou saw that he could not persuade him and changed the subject.

"Don't worry. Let's first look at the works of Lan Ying."

Lan Ying had started a picture earlier and when he heard Yang, he began adding details. The painting had been commissioned by a veteran imperial guard official, Zhang Yaoxing, and was called *Picture of a Peach Orchard*. He intended hanging it in his newly built pavilion, The Pavilion of Pines in the Wind.

Hou Chaozong looked at it for a while. He liked it and said that it was a unique and great piece of work.

Lan Ying said modestly, "I hope an expert won't laugh at my poor effort." He asked Hou to write an inscription which would make the picture look complete.

"If you are not afraid that my writing will spoil it, I will. But don't laugh at my poor performance." Hou Chaozong took up the pen and wrote:

> *One who originally was a man in the cave,*
> *Finds a labyrinth that puzzles him when he returns.*
> *The fisherman points to an empty mountain path,*
> *He lingers in the peach cave to avoid the Qin.*

He signed his name as Hou Chaozong of Guide.

Yang Longyou studied it carefully and said, "An excellent piece. An excellent piece. The inference, however, is that I am to blame." He then described how Xiangjun had been rebuked at the banquet and how he tried to defend her. He said that her life was spared as long as she served in the inner court. "Ma Shiying and Ruan Dacheng are in power. Although I am a friend and relative, I cannot influence them. You are a friend of Xiangjun so it would be inadvisable for you to stay here."

Hou Chaozong knew of Ma Shiying's and Ruan Dacheng's cruelty and thanked Yang Longyou for his advice. They left together after farewelling Lan Ying.

Back at the hotel, Hou Chaozong told Su Kunsheng of Xiangjun's fate and they moved through fear of being tracked down. Su Kunsheng gave a thoughtful account of their situation. "Society has changed. Court

杨龙友知道目前城中情况复杂,便劝道:"侯兄,此处已无可留恋,还是去别处另寻佳人吧。"

"小生怎忍负约?只有得到她的确实消息才放心。"

杨龙友见劝说无效,只得岔开话题,说道:"世兄不必愁烦,俺们先欣赏蓝瑛作画吧。"侯朝宗自然不好拂意。

蓝瑛出门之前原就在作画,听杨龙友一说,便又继续在画上点染。这幅画是应大锦衣张瑶星之请,为他修建的松风阁所画的《桃源图》。侯朝宗看了一会儿,十分赞赏,说道:"妙,妙,位置点染,别开生面,确是大手笔。"

蓝瑛谦和地说:"见笑,见笑,就求侯兄题咏几句,为拙画生色。"

"不怕写坏,小生就献丑了。"朝宗也不推让,提起笔就写道:

原是看花洞里人,重来哪得便迷津;

渔郎诳指空山路,留取桃源自避秦。

并落款"归德侯朝宗题"。

杨龙友细玩诗意,不无解释地说道:"佳作。寄意深远,不过有微怪小弟之意。"接着,他便将当日香君骂筵一节细细说来,并表明自己如何委婉维护,如今虽选入内廷,但却保得性命。又说道:"如今马士英、阮大铖当道,自己虽与他们为至亲好友,也不敢谏言。世兄既与香君有旧,此处也不宜久留。"

侯朝宗曾经领教过马、阮的手段,知道他们狠毒异常,听杨龙友如此劝说,也表示同意:"是,是,承指教了。"杨龙友又对他说:"我们就此别过蓝兄,一同出去罢。"

侯朝宗回到旅店,将香君近来的遭遇告诉苏昆生。两人随即更换住处,怕被宵小之徒侦知踪迹,多有不便。苏昆生细想目前局势,对侯朝宗建议道:"我看人情已变,朝政日非。如今当道的人,

politics have become more corrupt and those in power exert a malignant influence. They seek revenge by maliciously inflicting harm. It would be better to stay away for the meanwhile and receive news about Xiangjun later."

Hou Chaozong agreed saying, "We have no relatives or friends in the prefectures or counties near Nanjing. Chen Dingsheng, an old friend of mine, lives in Yixing and Wu Ciwei is at Guichi. We could pay them a visit and avoid those who seek us out." Su Kunsheng agreed and they left at once.

Crossing the city, they approached Sanshan Street, a densely populated place. Su Kunsheng urged Hou Chaozong to hurry but Hou pointed to a signboard, Cai Yisuo Study, and said, "Dingsheng and Ciwei always stay there when they come to Nanjing. Let's ask the proprietor about them."

The study's manager told them that Chen Dingsheng and Wu Ciwei were living in a room at the back of the study. He went inside to tell them and after greeting each other, they sat down to talk and drink tea.

Ruan Dacheng, the newly appointed minister of the Board of War, arrived in Sanshan Street at about the same time. He rode in a big sedan chair and his official robe, bestowed by the emperor, was decorated with a jade python. He looked haughty and rolled up the curtain of his sedan chair so that the people could see him. It gave him great satisfaction. Looking around he saw the posters in the Cai Yisuo Study and asked his subordinates to bring them to him.

When he saw that intellectuals of the Restoration Society were choosing books there, he was outraged. "The Restoration Society is a remnant of the Donglin Party. They are sought by the imperial government which want to arrest them. How audacious they are!" He got down from the sedan chair, walked into the study and asked his subordinate to summon the prison guard to search it and arrest anyone there. The official walked into the back apartment and dragged out Cai Yisuo. Ruan Dacheng yelled at him,

"I am here to arrest rebels. Rebellion is a serious offence. How dare you give them shelter and allow them to choose books? Confess your crime."

"Its none of my business. They came themselves. They are in the back room," Cai Yisuo said.

Ruan Dacheng had trouble suppressing his glee when he learned

想的是如何加害正人君子，大肆报复。侯公子，咱们不如暂时避让，香君消息，再慢慢打听。"

侯朝宗答道："你说的极是。只是南京附近的州县，又无相知。只有好友陈定生住在宜兴，吴次尾住在贵池。不如寻访他们，既可避人，又会晤故人。"苏昆生表示同意，二人立即上路。

他们穿城而过，不觉走近三山街。此处人烟稠密，二人不敢怠慢，苏昆生要朝宗快快离开。侯朝宗却指着蔡益所书坊的招牌说："定生、次尾每次来南京，都住在此处，何妨问主人一声。"

二人向书铺掌柜询问，得知陈、吴二位果然住在店馆后间，掌柜进去通报后，陈、吴二人迎了出来，四人乃得相聚，一同饮茶细谈。

正当此际，新升兵部侍郎阮大铖来到三山街拜客，乘着大轿，穿着钦赐的蟒玉，耀武扬威，显荣逞贵，轿帘高高卷起，一任百姓仰看，好不得意。他四处观望，偶见蔡益所书坊前的招贴，立即叫长班将它揭来细看。

见到复社这班文人在此选书，他不禁怒叫："复社乃东林后起，朝廷正在访拿。还敢留这等人选书，这个书店掌柜也太大胆了。"他吩咐落轿，走入店铺，命令长班速传坊官前来，叫他搜查书铺，捉拿乱党。坊官急忙走进后间，一把将蔡益所拽了出来。

阮大铖大喝道："咦！目下访拿逆党，法令森严，你怎敢容留他们选书？快快招来！"

"不干小人事，是相公们自己来的，现在后间。"

阮大铖听说陈定生、吴次尾这两个当年羞辱过自己的人正在里面，报仇有望，喜不自禁，随即传知镇抚司，让他们派校尉前来捉人。

that Chen Dingsheng and Wu Ciwei were in his hands. They had once humiliated him and now he could reap revenge.

Chen Dingsheng, Wu Ciwei and Hou Chaozong were dragged before him shouting, "We are innocent, we've committed no crime."

Ruan Dacheng received them angrily. "You had better first realize who I am." He spoke to Wu Ciwei, "Have you forgotten that when we offered sacrifices to Confucius you chased after me and struck me?" He turned to Chen Dingsheng. "Why did you insult me on the day of theatrical performance?" Lastly he said to Hou Chaozong, "I provided money for Li Xiangjun to buy a dowry. Why did you let her throw away the ornaments?"

Hou Chaozong realized that it was Ruan Dacheng and shouted at the top of his voice, "So you are Ruan Dacheng. Today you wish to get revenge."

Chen Dingsheng and Wu Ciwei suggested that they take him outside to let others know about his embarrassing past. However, circumstances had changed and four prison guards arrested them. The three scholars were sent under escort to the *yamen*.

Cai Yisuo was unable to do anything and Su Kunsheng said, that they should follow them to see what happened.

CHAPTER TWENTY-SIX

A Trial and a Resignation

After their arrest a report was compiled for the Imperial Bodyguard, the *yamen*, which could arrest and imprison people. The head of the *yamen* was Zhang Wei (styled Yaoxing). He had served with the unit in Beijing and after Zhu Yousong ascended the throne he retained his post. The new court was corrupt, dishonest officials held power and, one by one, honest people were ousted from positions. Ma Shiying and Ruan Dacheng had people with dissenting views executed. Zhang Yaoxing felt that he could not stay in office any longer. As the head of the Imperial Bodyguard, he

　　一时之间,陈定生、吴次尾和侯朝宗一同被缉拿出来。三人一齐大叫道:"我们有何罪过?"

　　阮大铖怒气冲冲地说道:"你们这三人,今天都来认认下官!"他对吴次尾说道:"你忘了丁祭之日如何追打下官?"又问陈定生道:"你借戏之日为何要羞辱俺?"接着对侯朝宗说:"俺替你出妆奁之资,你为何让李香君将裙钗乱抛?"

　　侯朝宗方知此人就是阮大铖,高呼道:"你就是阮大铖,今日来报仇了!"

　　陈、吴两人接着叫道:"好,好,好!大家把他扯到朝门外边,揭揭他平素的老底!"这三人哪知如今形势大变,说话之间,镇抚司的四个校尉已赶来,从坊官手中将他们三个秀才一齐扭住,押往衙门。

　　蔡益所自然无力解救,苏昆生则表示:"我们跟着去,打听一个真信,也好设法营救。"

第二十六章
审案弃官

　　侯朝宗与陈定生、吴次尾三人被镇抚司冯可宗属隶缉拿之后,具文解送锦衣卫。锦衣卫衙门专管侍卫、缉捕、刑狱等事,现任仪正之职的张薇,字瑶星。原在北京就担任此职,自从离开京师南下以后,正值福王朱由崧即位,仍任命他担任原职。不过,他见朝政混乱,权奸当道,一味排挤正人,所以并不安于此位。马士英、阮大铖因迎立之功,把反对者定为逆党,如周镳、雷缜祚等,并欲置他们于死地。张瑶星身为锦衣,明知这两人冤枉,全是马、阮二人

knew that men, such as Zhou Biao and Lei Yanzuo, were innocent. In their case it was simply a matter of revenge but he could not save them. This was why he wanted to retire to his pavilion, The Pavilion of Pines in the Wind, where he intended to live.

Four guards brought in Hou Chaozong, Chen Dingsheng and Wu Ciwei. Zhang Yaoxing held a court hearing. He had read the official report and said, "According to this you formed a society that planned insurrection. You intended to bribe officials and free Zhou Biao and Lei Yanzuo. You have been caught and unless you confess you will be flogged. By telling the truth you will be spared much pain."

Chen Dingsheng and Wu Ciwei said, "We are guilty of nothing. We were originally members of the Restoration Society and were looking at manuscripts. There is no such insurrection." Hou Chaozong said that he had come to see a friend and had just sat down when he was arrested.

Zhang Yaoxing did not know the men and their denial angered him. He hit the table with a gavel saying, "According to your pleas, you have done nothing wrong. Does this mean that I am guilty of making false charges of insurrection?" He told his men to get the instruments of torture ready. "This will make them confess," he said.

Chen Dingsheng prostrated himself saying, "Please do not be angry with us. I am Chen Dingsheng, a native of Yixing. I should not have chosen books in the Cai Yisuo Study. Apart from that I have done nothing wrong."

Wu Ciwei also kowtowed and made the same plea.

After studying the case carefully, Zhang Yaoxing saw that there was very little evidence against them. He spoke to the prison guards, "If these men intended bribing bureaucratic officials, or planning insurrection and forming a society for that purpose in the Cai Yisuo Study, Cai would know about it. Why did you not summon Cai Yisuo to the court?" The guards went off to fetch him.

Hou Chaozong used the opportunity and kowtowed to Zhang Yaoxing. He said, "I am Hou Chaozong of Guide, Henan Province, and am in the capital to study. I am an intellectual friend of Chen and Wu and had come to see them when I was arrested. I have really done nothing wrong."

Zhang Yaoxing remembered the inscription on Lan Ying's painting, *Picture of a Peach Orchard*. He recalled the name and asked, "Are you Hou Chaozong?"

挟仇报复,但又无力解救,早就萌发退隐之志,在城外修起了松风阁,以为日后归老之所。

当他闻报升厅后,四个校尉押着上了锁的侯朝宗、陈定生、吴次尾上大堂来。张瑶星看了文书,对这三人说道:"据坊官报单,说你等结社聚谋,要替周镳、雷缜祚行贿,因而被该司捕拿。——快快从实招来,免受皮肉之苦。"

陈定生、吴次尾大呼:"冤枉!此事从何而起!我辈本复社文士,在此评选文稿,哪有结社聚谋之事?"侯朝宗也上前辩明:"俺来此访友,刚刚坐下,并未在此多留,怎被一齐网罗?"

张瑶星也不知道这三人是何等样人,只见他们异口同声地否认其事,不禁有些发怒,将惊堂木一拍:"据你等所供,全无其事,难道本衙门诬良为盗不成?左右预备刑具,叫他们一个个招来?"

陈定生上前跪了一步,说道:"老大人不必动怒,犯生陈定生乃直隶宜兴人,不该在蔡益所书坊选书,并未有其他事情。"

吴次尾也前跪一步,说道:"犯生吴次尾,直隶贵池人,不该与陈定生一同选稿,也无别情。"

张瑶星听到这两个秀才的辩解,细细思索,也觉得此案有些不实,便向押解的镇抚司吏役问道:"既然这三人在蔡益所书坊结社聚谋,行贿上司,打通关节,蔡某人必然知情,为何不将他拿到?"说罢,就抽出一根签来掼与解役:"速将蔡益所捉来审问!"解役只得奉命而去。

趁解役下堂去后,侯朝宗赶紧跪前半步口称:"犯生侯朝宗,河南归德府人,游学到京,与陈定生,吴次尾是文字旧交,才来拜望,就被一同拿来,其实别无他事。"

张瑶星听到"侯朝宗"三个字,蓦然记起蓝瑛给他画的桃源避世图,图上有"归德侯朝宗"所题诗句,便问道:"你就是侯朝宗么?"

"Yes, I am."

"Sorry. I did not recognize you. You wrote an inscription on *Picture of a Peach Orchard*, and the verse showed much depth. I am obliged to you for it." He bowed slightly saying, "You are not involved. Take a seat and wait."

Hou Chaozong sat down and thanked him.

The prison guards returned and reported to Zhang that they could not find Cai Yisuo. He was at large and the door of his study was locked.

Zhang Yaoxing berated them. "You say that they plot an insurrection but offer no proof. How can I pass judgement on that?" He was thinking about it when his domestic servant came in with letters from Wang Juesi, a cabinet minister, and Qian Muzhai of the Ministry of Rites.

The letters asked him to treat Chen Dingsheng and Wu Ciwei, leaders of the Restoration Society, with leniency. Zhang Yaoxing did not wish to harm the prisoners and said in a gentle voice, "I have been discourteous to you, brothers Chen and Wu. Are you a good friends of Wang Juesi and Qian Muzhai?"

"We don't know the ministers."

Zhang was surprised and asked, "If you don't know them, then why do they commend you and asked me to set you free?"

Chen Dingsheng and Wu Ciwei said in one voice: "They must be doing this for the sake of justice."

Zhang understood and said, "Yes. Yes. Although I am a military official, I read poetry and history. How could I sentence innocent men to death just to please others?" Then he turned to the prisoners and asked them to wait. To the guards, he said, "I shall ask the prison guards to release them at once." But it was not so easy. As he was writing his conclusions he received a court bulletin, an urgent imperial edict. He knew that it would have something to do with the case and read it quickly. Ma Shiying, the Grand Academician, had submitted a report to the crown, claiming that Zhou Biao and Lei Yanzuo had maintained illicit relations with Prince Lu. The evidence against them was clear. Ma urged the crown to execute the men at once. The bulletin likened the Donglin Party to a swarm of locusts that should be dealt with before they caused disaster. The bulletin gave the names of members of the Restoration Society, asking the emperor's permission to arrest them. The emperor had agreed and asked all *yamen* or government official to implement the order.

"犯生便是。"

"啊呀,失敬了!日前所题桃源图,大有深意,领教,领教!"又半欠身说:"这桩事与你无干系,请一边坐候。"

侯朝宗立起身来,就坐在大堂之侧,连声谢道:"多谢超脱。"

解役匆匆赶回,交回签子,禀告道:"禀知老爷,书坊大门紧闭,蔡益所也不知逃到何方去了。"

张瑶星高声说道:"你们说他们聚谋打点,全无证据,这案如何审处?"说罢,低头沉思,正在考虑如何周全地处理此案,家人却送来内阁王觉斯、礼部钱牧斋的书信。

他接过二封来信,当堂拆开,将信浏览一遍。原来王、钱信中都说陈、吴二人乃复社领袖,劝他不要为难他们。他原也不想为虎作伥,自然乐于从命,便和颜悦色地说道:"陈、吴两兄,方才得罪了。"又问道:"二位与王觉斯、钱牧斋两位老先生一向交好么?"

两人齐声回答:"并无交往。"

张瑶星有些诧异了,问道:"既然素不相识,为何二公极其称道两兄文名,吩咐俺开释二位?"

陈、吴二人争相说道:"大约是二公主持公道。"

张瑶星终于明白,连声称赞:"是,是极了。下官虽是武官,也颇读诗书,岂肯滥杀无辜讨好他人?这事冤屈,三位请在一边稍候。"又对解役交代:"待俺批回镇抚司,速速释放。"岂知张瑶星存心救助无辜的人,也非易事。正当他批文时,家人送上朝报,上有紧急旨意,他接过朝报,匆匆阅过,只见上面刊着马士英的奏本,意谓"犯官周镳、雷缜祚"等私通潞王,"叛迹显然";东林奸党,如同蝗声蔽日;复社文人乃是幼蝗,如不及时除净,必为将来大患云云。他还将东林、复社首领名单,编了一本《蝗蝻录》,请求皇上按名搜捕。皇上居然准了这奏本,要求各衙门奉行不误。

Alarmed and surprised, Zhang Yaoxing sighed. Ma and Ruan had given a false report to the crown to back up their claim. From then on any honest person could be executed.

He paused for a while then said to the prisoners, "You have my sympathy. I was going to release you but have received this edict. Not only will Zhou Biao and Lei Yanzuo be given death sentences but no one in the Donglin Party and the Restoration Society will escape punishment."

"We beg your excellency to save our lives," the three pleaded.

Ma's and Ruan's perversity galled Zhang Yaoxing. After some thought he said, "If you are released now, you will be arrested by another official and will certainly die. But don't worry. I have an idea." He wrote a report saying that since the charges had not been substantiated, the prisoners should be held in custody until Cai Yisuo was arrested. Then he said to the three, "The prison guard, Feng Kezong, is ambitious and wants to climb the ladder of officialdom. But he has a conscience. I shall write to him asking him not to be harsh." His letter advised the prison guard to use his common sense and not be too rigid. Zhang Yaoxing placed his hands together before his chest and said to the prisoners, "I am sorry but you will have to stay in prison for a while. I hope that your names will be cleared some day." He then withdrew and the three were sent to the cells.

When he thought about the corrupt politicians, Zhang Yaoxing felt that he could no longer stay in office; he would be ridiculed for supporting autocratic officials. He left the *yamen* and rode on a horse to convalesce in his pavilion, The Pavilion of Pines in the Wind.

The colors there were a luxuriant green; when he opened the windows, pines were everywhere; it was a haven away from the workaday world. He took off his official robe, put on clothes of a Taoist and said good-bye to feudal bureaucracy.

His guards arrived a few hours later. They had arrested Cai Yisuo and he was with them. The turn of events surprised Zhang Yaoxing and he realized that once Cai had been arrested, the other three could not escape punishment. He sent the guards and his personal attendant on another mission and then privately told Cai Yisuo what had happened. Cai asked for his help. Zhang suggested that he became a priest in the Taoist faith with him. Cai agreed and they hid in the mountains.

　　张瑶星看罢，大惊失色，继而又叹息不止："不料马、阮二人又有这番举动，从此正人君子将被诛尽杀绝矣！"

　　他沉吟半响，走下公堂，对侯、陈、吴三人说道："下官怜尔等无辜，正欲开释。忽然奉到这道严旨，不但周、雷二公定了死案；从此东林、复社，怕也无有漏网之人了！"

　　"千万请大人超脱豁免。"三人一齐恳求。

　　张瑶星对马、阮的倒行逆施，也颇为不满，沉思片刻，计上心来，说道："俺若放了诸兄，倘若被别人拿获，再无生理，且不要慌，我自有主意。"又提笔批道："据送三犯，朋谋打点，俱无实迹，待拿到蔡益所时，再行审明定罪。"批完，放下笔来，对三人说："那镇抚司冯可宗，虽然功名心重，但也良心未丧，待俺另写一书给他，劝他不必诛求。"说罢，又立时写书一通，无非是劝诫他：职司风化，不可偏倚，更不可替人操刀；希望他重视公论，自留地步。处置已毕，拱手为礼："诸兄暂时屈居狱中，老夫深信自有昭雪之日。"说罢，便退堂而去，解役押了三人回镇抚司。

　　张瑶星回到后堂，心想朝政如此，不可再留居此任，以免受助纣为虐之讥，吩咐家僮，牵出马来，立即乘骑离衙，往松风阁养病去了。

　　松风阁在一片苍翠之中，有清泉汩汩，松涛阵阵，推窗四望，满目松阴，正是一派世外桃源风光。他索性脱去衣冠，换上道装，彻底离开官场。

　　他方换装不及半日，衙役便追踪而来，说是解到蔡益所，听候发落。张瑶星闻报，倒吃惊不小：捉到蔡益所，那侯、陈、吴三人怎能开脱？他干脆支走衙役、随从，把利害对蔡益所一一剖明，蔡益所求他超脱。他乃劝说蔡益所也跟从自己出家，蔡益所为了求生，自然应允。两人就一齐悄悄往白云深处、万山丛中行去，一个命官，一个书商从此成了出家道人。

CHAPTER TWENTY-SEVEN

Seeking Help in Wuchang

Su Kunsheng was one of the people who worried about Hou Chaozong's safety and wanted to help. Although a resident of Nanjing he came from the same hometown and was an *kunqu* opera singer, like Liu Jingting the storyteller. He was over 50 and had a generous nature. He decided to seek help from Marshal Zuo Liangyu at Wuchang and arrived there after a long and arduous journey.

At Wuchang he stayed in a small hotel in the main street but was unable to gain admittance to the marshal's headquarters. At the time, Zuo Liangyu was on a mission to train 300,000 troops with Yuan Jixian, the governor-general, and Huang Shu, the imperial envoy. When he returned to his barracks he would pass the hotel so Su Kunsheng ordered a cup of wine and waited for his arrival.

As he drank, he became anxious and sang to an improvised *kunqu*. The hotel manager feared that the marshal might hear him and asked him not to sing which gave Su Kunsheng an idea. He ignored the manager's advice and sang louder.

Marshal Zuo Liangyu heard him as he rode back to the barracks and Yuan Jixian, the governor-general, asked, "Do you allow song and dance to be taught here?"

"The military code is strict. Who dares sing here?" roared Zuo.

The voice went higher just as Huang Shu pointed out that someone was actually singing.

The marshal said angrily, "The curfew is in force. Anybody who sings at the dead of night should be arrested." Su Kunsheng was dragged before the marshal by guards who had traced his voice to the hotel.

"Was that you singing?" Zuo Liangyu asked.

"Yes."

"The military code is strict. How dare you sing in such a high voice?" Marshal Zuo was very angry.

第二十七章
武昌求救

　　侯朝宗虽然被马、阮党徒缉拿在狱，但仍然有关注他命运的人。与他同为河南人又同寄寓南京的苏昆生便是其中一个。别看苏昆生是个唱曲的人，而且年已五十多岁，却与说书的柳敬亭一般，都是慷慨仗义之士。自从侯朝宗被拿，他日夜焦愁，眼见他们要拿侯公子开刀，救援无门，只得远走湖广，去向左良玉元帅求救。

　　苏昆生不辞辛劳，跋山涉水，终于来到武昌，在通衢大道附近找了一家小客栈住下，可是一连三天，都进不了大营之门。今日听说左良玉元帅会同督抚袁继咸和巡按御史黄澍在江上操练三十万军马，回营时要路过此地。他便要了壶酒，自斟自酌，等待机会。

　　几杯浊酒下肚，不免更添几分愁闷，索性敲起鼓板来，信口把自家编制的曲子低吟浅唱。店主人闻声，告诫他切不可出声，免得元帅路过听见不便。他听了此言，倒有了心计，越发放声唱了再唱，正好被回营的左良玉元帅听见，袁继咸不无意外地问道："咦，将军，贵镇也教起歌舞来了？""军令严肃，民间谁敢如此！"左良玉不免有些恼怒。黄澍也接着说道："真的有人唱曲。"

　　此时，曲声却越来越高，左元帅怒喝道："目下戒严之时，不遵军法，半夜唱曲，快快锁拿！"左右军役，随即循声寻着客店，一把铁索将苏昆生拽到元帅马前跪倒。

　　"方才唱曲，就是你么？"左良玉问道。

　　"是。"

　　"军令严肃，你敢如此大胆！"左良玉大怒。

Su Kunsheng was not afraid and was rather pleased to be before the marshal. He said, "There was no other way. I risked death to sing that song. I beg your pardon, will your lordship please forgive me?" Yuan Jixian was puzzled. "He must be drunk." Huang Shu thought that it had been rather good and said that he had sung beautifully.

Marshal Zuo did not know what to do and ordered Su to be brought to the headquarters for interrogation. Su Kunsheng was overjoyed. There was no need to force him and he willingly followed the supreme commander back to the army barracks where they decided to start on him straight way.

Zuo Liangyu ordered the soldiers to bring him in and when Su was asked why he sang, he said calmly, "I came from Nanjing to see the supreme commander. I had no choice but to sing loudly."

This angered Zuo Liangyu who rebuked Su but Yuan Jixian tried to calm him and allow the singer to tell his story; they soon realized that Su Kunsheng had come to seek help for Hou Chaozong. Zuo Liangyu, however, was not fully convinced. "Hou Chaozong is a member of a family closely related to mine for generations. Why hasn't he written to me?"

Su Kunsheng went down on his knees and said, "Ruan Dacheng led the arrest himself. There was simply no time to write a letter."

Yuan Jixian also was not sure. "Why should we just take your word for it?"

Zuo Liangyu realized the need for urgent action and said, "I have a man here who is an old friend of Hou Chaozong. I'll ask him if he recognizes you."

The man was none other than Liu Jingting, who recognized Su Kunsheng at once; they were glad to see each other and Liu Jingting told Zuo Liangyu that Su was a star of the kunqu opera and known by all. When they heard who he was, they all nodded their approval and Zuo Liangyu thought it worthy that a singer should be so brave for a righteous cause. He told Su Kunsheng to sit down and relate in detail what had happened to Hou Chaozong.

Su's story outraged him and he said to Yuan and Huang, "Should we not be angry when we hear how corrupt the imperial government has become?"

Yuan Jixian said that other people were being persecuted besides

苏昆生倒毫不惧怕，回道："无可奈何，冒死唱曲，只求老爷饶恕。"袁继咸有些奇怪："听他说话，像是醉话。"黄澍却赞赏地说："唱的曲子，倒是绝妙。"

元帅左良玉一时拿不定主意，吩咐军役："这人形迹可疑，带入帅府，细细审问。"苏昆生正怕进不了帅府，闻得左帅此言，正中下怀，也不待军役拖拽，大步跟着一彪军马顺顺当当地走进了大帅府第。左良玉令军役将犯人押上来，审问道："你把犯法情由，从实说来。"苏昆生毫无惧色，从容回答道："小人来自南京，特投元帅，因无门可入，故意犯法，以求见元帅一面。"

左良玉勃然大怒，连声呵责，倒是袁继咸劝左良玉不要发怒，听他细细说出缘故。苏昆生乃将来此求救之情和盘托出，左、袁、黄三人方知来人是苏昆生，为的是救援已被马、阮下狱的侯朝宗。左良玉心知此事非同小可，追问道："那侯公子，与俺世交，他既来求救，必有亲笔书信，拿出来让我看看。"

苏昆生叩头答道："那日阮大铖亲领校尉，立时拿走侯公子，哪有时间写信？"

袁继咸也不无怀疑："凭你口说，如何作数？"

倒是左良玉救人心切，细细想了一番，说道："有了，俺幕中现有一个侯公子旧交，烦他出来一认，便知真假。"

这个侯公子旧交不是别人，正是说书的柳敬亭。他一向与苏昆生熟稔，被左良玉请出后，立刻认出苏昆生来，彼此惊喜不已。柳敬亭对左良玉说："他是河南苏昆生，天下第一个唱曲名手，谁人不认得他！"听柳敬亭这么一介绍，在座之人无有不相信的，左良玉也不禁赞叹道："想不到一个唱曲的人，倒是个肝胆义士。"立即让他坐下，从头说起侯公子下狱经过。左良玉听知详情，气愤填膺，对袁、黄二公说道："二位盟弟，朝政如此，怎不令人气愤！"

members of the Donglin Party and the Restoration Society. Ma Shiying and Ruan Dacheng had prevented Concubine Tong from becoming a queen. They intended installing another concubine. Huang added that Emperor Chongzhen's son was now in prison although the emperor had chosen him to be the crown prince, and he was acknowledged by all the ministers. Ma and Ruan treated him as an impostor.

These events made Zuo Liangyu even more irate and he cried out, "We have fought on battlefields to safeguard the state, but the crown itself will ruin the country. Only Marshal Shi Kefa is honest. He is hampered by Ma Shiying and Ruan Dacheng, and is unable to do anything about it. How can I alone beat off the Qing Army and restore Chinese rule in the central China?" He stamped his feet and said, "I am at the end of my tether and now I shall have to offend the crown."

He asked Yuan Jixian to write a report to the crown denouncing Ma and Ruan for misgovernment. Yuan Jixian wrote it immediately and after reading it Zuo said to Huang, "This must be made an official document if we are to get rid of Ma and Ruan who are too close to the emperor."

Liu Jingting voiced his support which surprised Zuo Liangyu. He said, "You asked me not to use the army a few days back. Why do you agree with its use now?"

"Zhu Yousong is now emperor. The times are different."

Zuo Liangyu signed the completed document and Yuan Jixian said, "This is a very important matter. It would be better if He Tengjiao, the newly appointed Huguang governor, signed it as well."

Zuo Liangyu knew what sort of man he was and said, "He is an obstinate character. There is no need to tell him in advance. Just put his name down, that's all." Yuan followed Zuo's instructions and signed his own name. Huang also signed. Zuo Liangyu told him to write the document that night. He would sent it to the crown by special mail and launch a punitive expedition. Yuan thought this unwise.

"The post may be delayed and Ma and Ruan are searching the capital for documents. If it falls into their hands they will destroy it and no one will read it."

"In that case we will have to get someone to carry it," Zuo Liangyu said.

"It's a bad situation. I have heard that Ma and Ruan secretly ordered General Du Hongyu to build defences in Anqing to stop our army coming down by the east. If the document falls into their hands, the messenger

袁继咸接着说，不仅东林、复社受到摧残，就连原来的皇妃童氏，不辞辛苦寻来，也被马、阮奸党阻拦，要为当今另选妃子。黄澍说，崇祯帝立有太子，大臣共认，马、阮却认为是假冒，将他拘于牢狱。

左良玉听得袁、黄二人你一言我一语，更是愤怒之极，大声叫道："我辈在战场上拼死拼活，为的是报效朝廷。岂知奸党当道，正人遭屠，日日卖官鬻爵，演舞教歌，一代中兴之君，行的全是亡国之政。只有一个史可法颇为忠心，又被马、阮之辈处处牵制，也不能有所作为，教俺独自一人，怎能杀退北兵，恢复中原！"说罢，气得直顿足，又叫道："罢，罢，罢！俺也无法，只得对君上不客气了！"便向袁继咸拱手为礼："请继咸替俺写一参本。"

袁继咸问道："如何写？""你只痛斥马、阮之罪好了。"袁继咸一挥而就，左良玉看过，又对黄澍说道："还要写一道声讨文书，说俺要发兵进讨，清除君侧。"

柳敬亭大声赞同，左良玉倒有些奇怪，问他："你前日劝俺不可用兵，今日又为何赞成？"

"如今是朱由崧做皇帝，彼一时，此一时也。"

说着，黄澍已将声讨文书写好，左良玉先行具名，袁继咸却说："这样大事，还该请新任湖广巡抚何腾蛟也具名方好。"

左良玉深知何之为人，说道："他生性固执，不必事先告知，就替他写上名字。"袁继咸也只得如此，并将自家名字列上，黄澍也签上名字。左良玉说："今夜誊写好，明早飞递投送，俺随后就发兵。"

袁继咸独有识见，说："只怕传递文书的驿站误事。京中匿名文书极多，马、阮奸徒每天令人搜寻，一旦获得，随即烧毁，并不过目。"

"如此，只有派人专送了。"

黄澍说道："这也不便。听说马、阮密令安庆将军杜弘域在板子矶地方构筑防御工事。防我兵马东下。声讨文书落入他手，送书

will definitely be killed," Huang Shu Said.

"What can we do, then?" asked Zuo.

Liu Jingting spoke up, "I can act as the messenger. I will go."

Yuan Jixian and Huang Shu respected Liu Jingting's offer. "He acts like Jing Ke who made an attempt on the life of Emperor Qin Shihuang. We shall farewell you as people do."

Liu Jingting said, "My life is really worth nothing. As long as I can help the Marshal Zuo to achieve great deeds, I shall be happy."

Zuo Liangyu was very pleased and said, "I bow down to such a righteous man." He ordered a bottle of wine to be brought in and knelt down saying, "Please drink this!"

Liu Jingting also knelt and in a ceremony, similar to that accorded to a departed soul, they farewelled each other. They all wept; Liu Jingting said good-bye and left without looking back.

Zuo Liangyu said loudly, "A righteous man. A chivalrous man who upholds justice."

CHAPTER TWENTY-EIGHT

Zuo's Army Goes East

The punitive expeditionary force led by Zuo Liangyu drove eastward but the government of the young emperor, Zhu Yousong, knew nothing of it. The emperor and the bureaucracy in Nanjing City were obsessed by power, wealth and their own existence.

The year was 1646, the second anniversary of the reign of the Qing Emperor, Zhu Yousong. It was the first anniversary of the death of Emperor Chongzhen of the Ming Dynasty (who hung himself when Beijing fell on March 19). The new emperor was required to mark the occasion and an order had been given for an altar on a raised platform to be set up on the outskirts of the city. For the ritual ceremony offerings, such as joss sticks, flowers, candles and wine were laid on the long table.

之人就死多活少了！"

"那怎么办呢？"左良玉倒一时束手无策。柳敬亭见他们无计可施，便挺身而出："倒是老汉走走吧。"

袁、黄二位闻言肃然起敬："想不到这位柳先生，倒是荆轲之流的侠义之士。我辈当以白衣送行。"

柳敬亭慷慨说道："我这条老命值什么？只要能办好元帅的大事。"

左良玉大喜，钦敬地说道："有你这样忠义之人，俺左良玉要下拜了。"并立即吩咐左右取来一杯酒，左良玉竟然跪下："请尽此杯。"柳敬亭见状，也赶紧跪下干了杯，彼此行礼告别。

临行之际，无异死别，各自垂泪，柳敬亭拱手作别，头也不回而去，左良玉大呼："义士，义士！"

第二十八章
左兵东下

左良玉率师东下，朱由崧小朝廷尚不知晓。南京城里，君臣上下只知争权夺利，全不思收复北方城池，一味寻欢作乐，醉生梦死。

眼前已是乙酉之年（1646），清帝福临建都北京已有二年之久，朱由崧也在这年改历为弘光。三月十九这天是崇祯皇帝自缢煤山的忌辰，新主子不能不祭拜。事先传旨在太平门外设坛祭祀。老赞礼＊绝早赶到，排好长案，供奉香、花、烛、酒，在坛前等候。

＊ 赞礼：旧时举行婚丧、祭祀仪式时，在旁宣读仪式项目，或从事此事之人。

Ma Shiying and Yang Longyou arrived in mourning clothes. As grand academician, Ma virtually held all the reins of power and he was obliged to attend the ceremony, but he was there to enjoy a spring outing rather than to pay respects to the late emperor.

Marshal Shi Kefa, who was also in mourning and stricken with grief, asked the old ceremonial official whether all the civilian and military officials were present. Although there were only a few minor officials besides Ma and Yang he was told that everyone was there.

Ma Shiying, who wanted the ceremony over and done with, said, "Since everybody is here, let's start." The old ceremonial official began and the only sound heard was that of people going down on their knees to prostrate themselves before the late emperor. The ceremony ended quickly and Shi Kefa felt sad and wept bitterly. The old ceremonial official also wept.

Ruan Dacheng arrived when the ceremony had ended and pretended to weep. He said, "On the anniversary of the death of the late emperor, Ruan Dacheng is here in tears to kowtow to the emperor." As there was no response from the others, he quickly regained his composure, and asked Ma Shiying whether he had performed the ceremony.

Ma said that he had and Ruan Dacheng walked to the altar and kowtowed four times, crying loudly, "The late emperor left the country in ruins like a family split up. The people responsible are members of the Donglin Party. We are the few surviving loyal officials. The others have scattered. I weep for you, emperor. Why did you realize the fact so late in your life?"

Ma Shiying thought that Ruan was making a spectacle of himself and displaying hypocrisy. He dragged him to one side saying, "Do not overdo it. It would be better if you stood up and took a bow."

Shi Kefa saw this, sighed, and shook his head in disapproval. He said in a low voice, "This is a farce." He made his farewells and left the scene.

After the ceremony Ma Shiying said to Yang Longyou and Ruan Dacheng, "We are all going to the city the same way, why no go together?" They swapped their mourning clothes for official robes, then slowly rode back to town, enjoying the spring scenery and praising each other's achievements.

When they arrived at Ji'e Lane, Ma Shiying invited them into his house to look at the peonies.

不一会儿，马士英与杨龙友穿着素服，首先来到。马士英身为内阁大学士，执掌朝纲，不能不来。不过，他也正好借这个名儿到郊外春游，哪里是哭奠旧主的？

接踵而来的史可法，一身缟素，满脸悲戚，一到就问老赞礼："文武百官到齐了没有？"因为眼前除了马、杨而外，只有零零落落地几个不起眼儿的官儿，老赞礼明白不可能再有官儿来，乃回答说："到齐了。"

马士英恨不得早早收场，连忙说："既然如此，就开始祭礼吧！"于是，在老赞礼"兴"、"伏"声中，草草礼毕。只有史可法一人心酸，放声痛哭，老赞礼也忍不住大哭了一场。

直到祭祀完毕，阮大铖方才赶到，故意放声嚎叫："我的皇帝呀，今日是你周年忌辰，俺旧臣阮大铖来哭拜了！"吼罢，见周围没有什么反响，于是擦干挤出来的眼泪，向马士英说："祭过没有？"

"方才礼毕。"

阮大铖小步行至坛前，匆匆四拜，又嚎丧地哭道："先帝先帝，你国破家亡，总是吃亏在东林党人身上。那般小人都各自走散，只剩下我们几个忠臣，今日还想着来哭你，你为何至死不悟呀！"

马士英也觉得阮大铖有些作戏，过来拉了他一把："大铖，不必过哀，起来作个揖罢。"史可法不禁摇头叹息，低低地自言自语："可笑！可笑。"并对这般人拱手为礼，先行去了。

马士英对杨龙友、阮大铖说道："我们都是回城的，就一同走吧。"这几个人立即脱下素衣，穿起官服，上马缓缓而行，趁着这良辰美景，一路观赏春色，一面讲些体已话儿。

不觉间进了城，已近鸡鹅巷，马士英便邀杨、阮二人道："已离小寓不远，请二位到荒园同看牡丹如何？"

Yang Longyou realized just how close the other two were and did not want to be with them; he left saying that he had an appointment. Ruan Dacheng, on the other hand, delightedly seized the opportunity and said that he would be honored.

The pair went straight into the garden and Ruan Dacheng gushed that the peonies were truly beautiful. Pleased, Ma called his attendants to lay the table and prepare a feast so that they could eat and enjoy the flowers.

As they drank and talked, they became boastful. Ma Shiying laughed as he said, "We bid farewell to Emperor Chongzhen today. Tomorrow we shall ask the new emperor to sit on the throne. This accords with the saying: 'When a new king is crowned he brings to the court his own favorites and expels those of his predecessor'."

Keen on gathering information, Ruan Dacheng asked if the court had taken any new measures; he had been busy making an inspection along the river.

"We have been considering the case of the crown prince. What do you think about it?"

"The case is obvious. It should be easy to handle," said Ruan Dacheng who liked to think that he was astute.

"Why is it so easy?"

Ruan Dacheng mumbled, "Why is it that as veteran chief minister your power is so great that you can subvert the kingdom from within and without? Doesn't this stem from flattery and patronage?"

Although Ma Shiying could not hear what he said, he nodded and replied, "That is true. That is true."

"Acclaim and approval are important. If the crown prince is acknowledged as the real son of the later emperor, what will become of the new king who we have supported?"

Ma Shiying understood. "Yes. yes. The crown prince should be kept locked up so that he won't have a chance to mislead the masses. What about Concubine Tong? She is mounting an appeal and demanding to be made queen."

"She is Emperor Chongzhen's concubine. Her appeals must be rejected."

"Yes. Yes. I have already selected another beauty for the court. Concubine Tong must not be allowed access to it." Ma Shiying asked Ruan about members of the Donglin Party and the Restoration Society who had been arrested but not questioned.

杨龙友在路上见他们二人谈话甚密，不愿与他们裹得太紧，乃借口还要拜客，先行辞过。阮大铖正巴不得有这一机会，连声说道："晚生趋陪。"

说罢，已到马府门前，直趋花园。入得园门，阮大铖先奉承起来："果然好花。"马士英高兴非凡，立即命家人速摆酒席，与他赏花。

几杯醇酒下肚，两个人忘了形，无话不说。马士英放下酒杯，得意地大笑道："今日了结了崇祯旧局，明日请圣上坐朝，我们真是'一朝天子一朝臣'了。"

"卑职连日在江上巡查，不知近日朝中有何新举措？"阮大铖忙于探听动静。

"现在假太子一案，正在商量如何处理，不知你有何高见？"

"这桩事情太明白不过，不难处置。"阮大铖故作高明。

"怎么容易处置？"

"老师相之所以权倾中外，全因'推戴'二字……"又故意含而不发。

"极是，极是！"马士英连连点头。

"既因'推戴'二字，若承认太子的确是崇祯之子，那把俺们推出拥戴的新主放在哪里？"

马士英方始大悟，极表同意："是！是！就把假太子监禁起来，不可再惑乱人心！"此事商定后，马士英又向阮大铖说："还有那旧妃童氏，在朝门哭诉，要求迎立为正宫娘娘，这事又如何处置？"

"这事更加行不得了。自古君王爱美人！"

"对，对，俺已另选美女入宫，这个童氏自然不许她入宫的。"马士英问了此事，又问一事："那些东林、复社党徒，已被缉拿起来，如何审问？"

Ruan Dacheng showed his true nature by arguing that they were natural opponents who could not be tolerated. They should be weeded out and killed.

Ma Shiying agreed that this seemed a sensible solution and turned to an attendant. "Get extra large cups. We shall drink to our heart's content."

A guard appeared and said that Zuo Liangyu had sent a petition to Zhu Yousong. Ma Shiying read it carefully. He noted with anger that it said that they were to be impeached. Zuo had listed seven crimes and demanded that the new emperor order their execution. Another guard came in with the request to launch a punitive expedition against them. Ma Shiying had calmed down but the second message frightened him and he turned to Ruan Dacheng. "The eastward drive by Zuo's troops is terrible. We will not be able to resist them." He rubbed his hands and said, "Must we stretch out our necks so that Zuo can cut off our heads?"

Ruan Dacheng thought and said, "We have no choice but to ask the three generals, Huang Degong, Liu Liangzuo and Liu Zeqing to dispatch their troops to the riverside. There they can block the Zuo's advancing army."

"But if the Qing army crosses the river, who is to resist them then?" Ma was puzzled.

Ruan Dacheng quietly asked, "If the Qing army comes, do you still wish to make a stand against them?"

"What else can I do but resist?"

"You have two options."

"What are they?"

Ruan stepped forward and said "run" then knelt down saying "surrender". Ma Shiying understood and agreed. "You are right. I would rather kneel down before the Qing army than to be killed by Zuo." He added that he would send the three generals to the riverside to resist Zuo, but it occurred to him that he needed a plausible reason for this.

As usual Ruan Dacheng had a ready answer. "The three generals are loyal to Prince Zhu Yousong. Tell them that Zuo comes to support Prince Lu. This should alarm them enough to send troops to fight him."

"Yes, we are all in this together. You must urge the three generals to resist Zuo or our fate will be sealed."

Ruan Dacheng agreed to go at once but Ma Shiying said in a

阮大铖真是心狠手辣:"这班人,天生与我们是对头,岂可容得?捉到之后,一齐杀尽,不可剪草留根!"

"有理,有理!确是老成之见,句句合着鄙意。"马士英高兴地回过头来,对家人说:"拿大杯来,痛饮三杯!"

家人尚未取来酒杯,长班却闯了进来,急急禀报:"左良玉有参本,送来请大人过目。"马士英连忙接过文书细细看了一遍,不禁拍案大怒:"呀,呀!这是参咱们的奏疏,说咱们有七大罪状,要皇上立刻赐死,好不恨人!"话音刚落地,又有长班送来讨伐公文。文中将他们痛骂一番,并说即日发兵前来,取他们人头以谢天下。马士英看了参本倒还镇定,见了这讨伐公文却慌了手脚,惊恐地问阮大铖:"左兵东下,如何抵挡?难道咱们伸长颈子,等他来割不成?"

阮大铖想了片刻,回答说:"没有别的法子了,只有将黄得功、刘良佐、刘泽清所部,调来沿江堵截。"

"倘若北兵渡河,又教谁迎敌?"马士英有些不解。

阮大铖附着他的耳根轻轻问道:"清兵一到,你还要迎敌么?""不迎敌,又有何法?""有两种办法。""哪两种办法?"

阮大铖拎起外衣下摆,大步向前,口中称"跑";又止步下跪,口中称"降",原来是非跑即降。马士英终于明白阮大铖的主意,居然表示赞同:"你说的也是。大丈夫轰轰烈烈,宁可向清兵下跪,也不可试左贼之刀。我的主意已定,调三镇人马迎截左兵。"说罢,又突然顿住:"呀,调之无名,三镇兵马未必肯去,这又怎么办?"

老奸巨滑的阮大铖主意颇多:"只说左兵东下,要立潞王,三镇是拥立福王朱由崧的,自然着忙,哪有不肯出兵的!"

"对,对!就烦你亲自去一趟,劝得黄、刘三镇同舟共济,抵住左兵,方能保住身家性命。"

阮大铖说道:"辞过老师相,晚生立刻出城去。"

low voice, "Wait. The cabinet ministers, Gao Xintu and Jiang Yueguang, have colluded with the insurgents. They have been removed from office. Zhou Biao and Lei Yanzuo are in prison but we must not allow them to become agents who could help the forces outside. Should we kill them at once?" "Yes. Yes." Ma Shiying excused himself for not personally seeing off Ruan, said good-bye to him at his garden gate and went into his study.

The guard asked Ruan Dacheng what should they do with the messenger. "Send him to the ministry to be executed." After saying that, Ruan Dacheng was about to mount his horse when it occurred to him that this would not look good if the three generals failed in their stand against Zuo. If the messenger were killed it would close the way to negotiations. He told the guard to ask Feng, the prison guard, to lock him up, then he left the city.

Liu Jingting, the messenger, was dragged to the cells. He was a brave man and it was the first time that he had been behind bars. Shackled hand and foot he found it unbearable, but in the night he heard Hou Chaozong's voice and in the moonlight saw him in the next cell. "Is it really you, Mr. Hou?"

"Is it you, Liu Jingting?"

Hou Chaozong had been imprisoned two weeks and as there was no evidence against him, no verdict had been given. He was anxious and each day had seemed a year; seeing Liu Jingting was like meeting an old friend in a strange place. They spoke about what had happened before they were imprisoned. Hou was grateful when he heard of the efforts made on his behalf but he also felt that he was the cause of much trouble.

When Hou Chaozong, Chen Dingsheng and Wu Ciwei learned of Zuo Liangyu's advance, they were worried. Chen pointed out that if the army arrived the three of them would have less chance of survival. Wu Ciwei thought that a military officer such as Zuo Liangyu could not really help them.

While talking they heard footsteps and voices. The prison guard was rounding up men for execution. Zhou Biao and Lei Yanzuo were to be executed that night. The three actually felt a sense of security when they realized it was not their turn. They pumped Liu Jingting for news but he only knew that officials were rounding up men everywhere. Chen Dingsheng and Wu Ciwei were surprised.

　　"请慢走一步,还有一事相商。"马士英低低对阮大铖说:"内阁高新图、姜曰广二人袒护逆党,都已罢了官。惟有那周镳、雷缤祚还在牢中,不要让他们做为内应,趁早处死,如何?""极该,极该。"马士英听罢,拱手作别,说道:"恕不送行了。"

　　门前那个役吏直截向阮大铖请示:"那个送公文的人还押在下面,怎么发落?""拿送刑部处决罢了。"说罢,出了门,正准备上马,忽然想到:"且不可鲁莽行事,这黄、刘三镇,怕不是左兵对手,万一斩了来人,日后也难于挽回,还是留一退步为好。"立即唤住役吏:"你速到镇抚司,拜上冯老爷,将送文书的人好好看押起来。"吩咐已定,乃上马急速出城而去。有了阮大铖的意旨,役吏自然照办,拽着柳敬亭直押到镇抚司大牢中。

　　柳敬亭虽然为人豪迈,胆识过人,但被捕下狱,还是第一次,尤其是手足上了锁,行动极不便利,感到万般难受。半夜里,他忽听得隔壁牢房里有人声,聆耳细听,竟然好像是侯相公的声音,不免挣扎起来,向外看去,借着满天明月,倒也认得不差,脱口惊呼:"真的是侯相公。"侯朝宗闻声也进前一步:"原来是柳敬亭!"

　　侯朝宗被捕后,一直关在牢狱中,只因找不出证据,既未定案,又不释放。身陷囹圄,却遇到旧时相识。从柳敬亭自述中,侯朝宗才知道他是因为替左良玉传书而被捕的。侯朝宗为自己连累柳敬亭而感到深深歉疚,也对苏昆生不畏艰险,救援自己而感激万分。

　　当侯、陈、吴三人知悉这一番情节后,反倒忧虑起来。陈定生首先说道:"只怕左兵一来,我辈倒不能苟全性命了。"吴次尾也附和道:"正是,左良玉不学无术,如何能收拾这一局面,救援我等性命!"不禁相对叹息起来。叹息未已,忽听得人声嘈杂,一阵杂乱的脚步声接踵而至,原来是狱卒半夜前来提人处决。及至报出姓名,方知今夜处死的是周镳、雷缤祚二人,心才定下来,也才有精神向

"Who are they rounding up?"

"I've heard they were arresting Huang Shu, the imperial envoy, Yuan Jixian, the governor-general, and Zhang Yaoxing, the veteran imperial guard official. Many scholars have been arrested, but I can remember only a few names."

Hou Chaozong was concerned. "Why don't you try?"

"There were so many. I can recall only those with familiar names, Mao Xiang, Fang Yizhi, Liu Cheng, Shen Shoumin, Shen Shizhu and Yang Tingshu."

"So many!" Chen Dingsheng was shocked. Wu Ciwei said that the prison would become the gathering place for intellectuals.

Zuo Liangyu met with Huang Shu, and He Tengjiao to urge them to join with him in the drive eastward. Yuan Jixian had already arrived at Hukou and they were discussing how to take Nanjing. They did not know that Ma Shiying and Ruan Dacheng had sent Huang Degong to block their advance at Banji. He Tengjiao, who was a fellow townsman of Ma Shiying, advanced half way and then returned to where he came from. Zuo Liangyu's son, Zuo Menggeng, intended seizing cities and townships to take more territories but disobeyed orders for troop deployment. As a result Huang Degong defeated the army's vanguard and retreat followed. A large fire broke out in Jiujiang, which Zuo Menggeng was occupying, cutting off the retreat of Yuan Jixian. Zuo Liangyu could neither advance nor retreat and had no explanation for the harm done to Yuan Jixian. He pulled out his sword and wanted to take his life but was stopped by Huang Shu. He suffered a sudden heart attack, spat blood and died instantly. News of his death spread and the army dispersed. Yuan Jixian did not know what to do and Huang Shu, aware that they would be sought by the court in Nanjing, said that they stood no chance of survival if arrested. Their best chance lay in returning to Wuchang with He Tengjiao. Yuan Jixian agreed and they went there together.

Su Kunsheng was the only person left in the army barracks. He stood by the dead supreme commander, Zuo Liangyu, weeping over the body and burning candles and joss sticks waiting patiently for Zuo's son to come and mourn over his father.

柳敬亭打听外边的新闻。柳敬亭答道:"我来的匆忙,未曾打听,只见校尉到处捉人。"

"啊呀呀,又捉人了! 不知捉的哪些人?"陈、吴两位异口同声地惊问道。

"听说要拿巡抚黄澍、督抚袁继咸、大锦衣张瑶星。呵,对了,还有几个公子秀才,想不起来了。"

侯朝宗倒又关心起来:"你想一想。"

"人多着哩。只记得几个熟识的,有冒襄、方以智、刘城、沈寿民、沈士柱、杨廷枢。"

陈定生惊呼道:"有这么多人!"吴次尾不无自嘲地说道:"俺这牢里,倒要变成一个文士大聚会了!"说罢,大家叹息不止。

果然不出陈定生、吴次尾所料,左良玉约会巡抚黄澍、何腾蛟,一同出兵东下,船泊九江,知会督抚袁继咸齐集湖口,共商下南京之计。哪知马、阮已调遣黄得功驻扎坂矶堵截;巡抚何腾蛟又因与马士英同乡,出兵半途就返回原地;左良玉的儿子左梦庚不听调派,一心想占城掠地,妄思进取;先锋败在黄得功手下,无功而退;左梦庚占了九江,城内一片大火,又断了袁继咸的退路。左良玉顿感前进不得,后退不能,又有负于袁继咸,无颜相对,拔出剑来欲求一死,虽被黄澍抱住,却又气急攻心,呕血不止,顷刻而亡。消息传出帐外,人马霎时溃散。袁继咸不知如何筹措,黄澍建言说:"我们原就是被南京朝廷缉拿的人,今又失陷城池,拿到京中,再无生理。不如转回武昌,同着巡抚何腾蛟另做一番事业去。"袁继咸觉得这未尝不是一条出路,乃结伴而行。

此刻,大帐中只剩下苏昆生一人守着左良玉尸首,怜惜油然而生,点起香烛,哭奠一番,耐着性子,等他儿子前来奔丧,然后辞归。

CHAPTER TWENTY-NINE

Nanjing in Disorder

The army commanded by Huang Degong, Liu Liangzuo and Liu Zeqing abandoned their defensive positions along the Yellow River. It had been deployed to block the advance of Zuo Liangyu but the Qing army took advantage of the situation and crossed the Yellow River on April 21, 1645 and marched on to Huaiyang. Marshal Shi Kefa defended Yangzhou with fewer than 3,000 men. Their morale was low and many thought of deserting. Shi, a great patriot, wept. Blood flowed from his eyes and stained his armor. Deeply moved by his patriotism his troops resolved to make a stand and defend Yangzhou.

Panic and confusion reigned in Nanjing even before the Qing army crossed the Yellow River. Rumor had it that the Qing army had surrounded Yangzhou and army intelligence revealed that the riverside of the city had no defences. With the collapse of Nanjing imminent, Emperor Zhu Yousong expected to see Ma Shiying and Ruan Dacheng, but they were not to be found. The emperor knew that he could no longer retain the throne. He gathered the royal treasure, his favorite concubines and prepared to flee. The city gates were opened to allow him passage to a safe haven. He had not told his officials that he was leaving.

At night the streets were quiet. Ma Shiying was still in the capital, hiding in his backyard. He asked his favorite concubines to pack and went to the palace where he learned that the emperor had already gone. He later tried to flee the city with 10 cartloads of possessions.

Many of those who had suffered persecution or exploitation under his corrupt rule waited for him, some with clubs in hand. He had not gone far before the hostile crowd confronted him and accused him of causing poverty and wasting the national treasury. There were cries of, "stop him" and he was beaten with clubs. He fell to the ground unable to move. Young people stripped him of his robes while others plundered his possessions.

第二十九章
南都大乱

　　且说黄、刘二镇，被马士英、阮大铖调遣堵截左兵之后，丢下黄河一带河防，千里空营，清兵乃于四月二十一日渡河，直抵淮扬一带。驻守扬州的史可法，兵卒不足三千，且又军心浮动，众心思离。史可法忠义过人，面对如此局面，痛哭失声，双眼喷血，湿透战袍，终于感动三千士卒，决心与他同守扬州。

　　岂知清兵尚未渡河，南京城内的小朝廷却已乱作一团。弘光皇帝听说清兵围住扬州，史可法连夜告急，人心惶惶；且得密报，江防已无兵力镇守，南京城破，只在旦夕。他欲找马士英、阮大铖商量对策，这两个家伙却躲得无影无踪，心想这宝位是坐不稳了，如今千计万计，走为上计。于是收拾了宫中珍宝，携着几个爱妃，趁天色未明，街上寂静之际，也不通知任何臣子，匆匆逃出南京城。

　　其实，马士英当时尚未离京，只是躲在家里收拾细软，吩咐姬妾做好应变准备。安排好这一切，方才去上朝，看看动静。岂知进得皇宫，得知弘光帝比他逃得还早。他也赶紧踅回私宅，指挥亲信家人，押着一队姬妾、十车细软，准备逃出这座乱了套的南京城。

　　岂知他空打如意算盘，左近百姓平日遭他凌辱欺压，满腔积愤，无可渲泄，时至今日，早有一班市民手执棍棒，守在他的房宅左右。马士英的人马行不多远，就被百姓发现，将他们围困在街心，纷纷喝责："这奸贼马士英，弄得民穷财尽。要往哪里跑？"众棒齐下，一阵乱打，不几下马士英早已跌倒在地，不能动弹。

　　马士英去观察弘光动静，阮大铖却来了解马士英行踪。他比

Ruan Dacheng wished to know what Ma Shiying planned. He was more cunning than Ma and had already packed his possessions and prepared his womenfolk. He had planned much earlier to flee from the invading Qing army but wanted to know whether Ma had chosen to surrender or leave.

Passing the Ji'e Lane he tripped over Ma who was lying on the ground. They spoke to each other and when Ruan Dacheng learned that Ma had lost his money and position he deserted his mentor and hurried back to his valuables and family. To his dismay he found that a crowd armed with clubs had already dragged away the women and plundered his wealth. They were shouting that the spoil should be divided equally when Ruan shouted, "How dare you steal my personal possessions!"

The crowd then realized that he was Ruan Dacheng and beat and stripped him. They spared his life but decided to burn down his house. Ma Shiying and Ruan Dacheng were left where they lay.

At the time Yang Longyou wearing simple clothes rode a horse into the street. It was May 10th, a good day for him to start an inspection as the newly appointed governor of Suzhou and Wusong. He had left his books, paintings and curios at the painter Lan Ying's place — The House of Enchanting Fragrance; Lan Ying had been instructed to bring them to him later. He was feeling pleased with himself when a servant told him about the rumors. The military situation in the north was critical and the emperor and prime minister had fled in the night. He deplored the situation and decided that he would have to leave the city.

But his horse was held by two men in the street. They were groaning and the servants pointed out that it was Ma Shiying and Ruan Dacheng. Yang Longyou looked at them and dismounted. "What happened to you?"

Ma Shiying managed to say that he had been robbed and beaten. Ruan Dacheng claimed that he had come to his rescue and met the same fate.

"Your servants should have looked after your property and wives. What happened to them?"

Ma Shiying said, "They scattered. They were no help at all."

Ma and Ruan were naked and Yang ordered the servants to unpack clothes for them. Then he gave them a horse to share and they left the city.

The servants told Yang not to go with them as they had too many

马士英更狡诈，事先已将妇女、财帛安排好，紧紧跟在他的身后，他自己早就选好"跑"的对策，还想去看看马士英究竟是"跑"还是"降"。

哪知道在转过鸡鹅巷的大街上，他就被卧倒在地的马士英绊倒。当他得知马士英已是人财两空，立刻想到自己的家眷细软都在后面，于是再也顾不得这个"恩公"了，急冲冲地往回跑。走不两步，只见一群市民持着木棒，拽着妇女，抬着箱笼，嘈嘈杂杂地嚷道："这是阮大铖的家财，方才抢来，大家均分罢！"阮大铖听得，无明火高三丈，高喝道："好大胆的奴才，怎敢抢我阮老爷的家财！"

"你就是阮大铖么！来得正好。"一阵棒子顷刻将他打翻在地，剥去衣服，抛在一旁。众人叫道："且饶他狗命，去烧他的房子！"众人一哄而去，只留下马士英、阮大铖两个奸贼分在两处躺在地上挣扎。

此时，杨龙友兴冲冲地骑马而来，他新近被任命为苏松巡抚，今日五月初十是出行吉日，他将书画古玩寄存在媚香楼画家蓝瑛处，让他随后捎来，自家则简装先行上路。正当他兴高采烈之际，家人上前禀告："街头传说纷纷，北边军情紧急，皇上、宰相连夜都走了。"

"呀，有这样的事，快快出城！"说罢策马急驰，岂知胯下之马却止步不前，原来马蹄被地上两个人先后绊住。突然，这两个人又发出呻吟之声，家人蹲下去仔细一看，"啊呀，好象是马、阮两位老爷！"杨龙友低头仔细端详，果然是马、阮二人，连忙下马，问道："二位怎么弄到这个地步？"

马士英挣扎着回答道："被那乱民抢劫一空，仅留得性命。"阮大铖此刻又不免要讨好了："我来救马师相，不料也遭到同样命运。"

"护送的家丁现在何处？"杨龙友问道。

马士英说道："他们也趁机拐骗，四散逃去了。"

杨龙友见他们衣冠不整，连忙吩咐家人取出一些衣服，叫他们两个胡乱穿了，腾出一匹马来，让他们共骑，一同向城外奔去。

enemies. Yang took their advice, tightened the reins and galloped quickly away. Ma and Ruan were left to their own devices. On his way Yang Longyou saw Kou Baimen, Zheng Tuoniang, Shen Gongxian and Zhang Yanzu who were fleeing from the palace. They told him that Li Xiangjun had gone to The House of Enchanting Fragrance in a sedanchair. Yang Longyou gave up any thought of taking up his new post and made his way to The House of Enchanting Fragrance. He intended to collect his pictures and books and flee to his hometown, Guiyang. When he arrived, he banged on the door, crying, "Open up, Open up."

Lan Ying opened the door and was surprised to see him. "Why have you returned, Your Lordship?"

"The situation in the north is critical. The emperor and his officials have fled. I no longer have a job and am collecting my things to return to my hometown in plain dress."

"Li Xiangjun has just returned and told us of her experiences." He turned his head and said, "Xiangjun, look who is here."

Li Xiangjun was surprised to see Yang and asked him how he was. Yang Longyou had no wish to speak to her and said that he was there to say good-bye; he would be away for a long time.

Xiangjun was astonished. "Where are you going?"

"Guiyang, my hometown."

Li Xiangjun's face fell, tears trickled down her cheeks and she sighed. "Hou Chaozong is still in prison and you are going home. I am alone and there is no one to help me."

Yang felt no sympathy and said, "It is a time of confusion and disorder. Even father and son are not able to look after one another. It is dangerous and you will have to make your own decisions. No one can help you."

At this moment Su Kunsheng arrived at the courtyard and pushed open the door. He saw Yang Longyou and Li Xiangjun and asked Yang if he knew where Hou Chaozong was.

Yang, who was in a hurry to leave, said, "Brother Hou is still in prison."

Li Xiangjun asked Su Kunsheng where he had been. Su told her about his trip to Wuchang. He had returned the night before and after hearing about the unrest went to the prison. The gates were open and it was empty. He was worried that Hou Chaozong might have been executed.

杨府家人悄悄说道:"老爷,切不可与他们二人同行,万一遇着他们的仇家,还要连累我们。"杨龙友觉得此言有理,趁马、阮赶路之际,勒着缰绳,向另一边奔去。哪知当头又遇到寇白门、郑妥娘、沈公宪、张燕筑一行,他们眼见皇上出宫,也各自逃出宫来。李香君雇了轿子先自回媚香楼去了。杨龙友闻知,再也不做赴任之想,立即转向媚香楼,准备取了书画古玩回老家贵阳去。到了李家院门,跳下马来,急急敲门:"开门,快开门!"

蓝瑛打开门一看:"啊!是杨老爷,为何又转来?"

"北方吃紧,君臣逃散,苏松巡府是做不成了,转来收拾行李,换上便服好还乡去。""原来如此。刚才香君回来,也说朝廷偷偷逃走了。"又回过头来唤道:"香君快来,你看谁来了。"

李香君应声而来,见是杨龙友,有些意外,也有几分高兴,连忙拜道:"杨老爷万福!"杨龙友此刻无心与她周旋,敷衍道:"多日不见,今天匆匆一叙,就要远别了。"

香君诧异地问道:"要向哪里去?""回敝乡贵阳去。"

李香君先前的几丝高兴情绪顿时消失得无影无踪,泪水不禁淌了下来,叹息道:"侯郎关在狱中还未出来,老爷又要还乡去,丢下奴家孤单单的一个,有谁人照顾哩。"

杨龙友此时再也没有什么怜惜之情了:"如此大乱,父子也不相顾的。只得自拿主意!"

正当此时,苏昆生知道城中大乱,特地来到李家院子打听侯朝宗信息。走到院门前,见院门半掩,便推门而入,看到杨龙友,便招呼道:"杨老爷在这里!"继而又看到香君:"香君也出来了,侯相公怎的不见?"

杨龙友急着要离开,也不想多叙谈,只是答道:"侯兄不曾出狱来。"

Li Xiangjun wept bitterly, tugged at his clothes and said, "Please help me to find him." Su did not know what to say.

Yang Longyou was about to leave and said, "Xiangjun, your old teacher is here, everything will be all right. I am leaving now." He turned to Lan Ying. "Do you want to come?"

"My home is in Hangzhou. Why should I go to Guiyang with you?"

"In that case, good-bye." Yang mounted his horse and left.

李香君急着问道:"师父从何处来？"

"俺为救侯公子，远走武昌，求左良玉元帅援手，哪里知道左帅中途身亡。俺便连夜赶回，听到城中大乱，急忙寻到大牢，只见狱门洞开，囚犯一个也不剩，正不知侯郎是否遇害哩！"苏昆生不无忧虑地说道。

李香君听说狱中也没有找到侯郎，不禁嚎啕大哭，拽着苏昆生袖子，求道:"师父快快替俺找来。"苏昆生不知如何作答。

杨龙友对他们二人说:"好好好，有你师父作伴，下官便要出京了。"又转身对蓝瑛说:"蓝田老要不要同俺一路去呢？"

"小弟家在杭州，怎能去贵阳？"

"既然如此，就此作别便了。"杨龙友匆匆换上行装。出门上马而去。

CHAPTER THIRTY

Collapse of the Emperor

After the emperor left Nanjing, his attendants disappeared one by one and he was left with the eunuch Han Zanzhou. They traveled to the Duke of Wei's residence but were not recognized and were thrown out. They went on to the army barracks of Huang Degong in Wuhu.

In the Battle of Banji, Huang had defeated Zuo Liangyu. He was now defending Wuhu, aided by his trusted lieutenant, Tian Xiong. When a soldier announced the emperor's arrival, Huang had to go and see for himself. He went out of the barrack gate and was greeted straight away by the emperor who asked, "How are you, General Huang?" Huang lifted his head and saw that it really was the emperor. He knelt down at once and said, "Long live Your Majesty! Please come inside. Allow me kowtow to you."

The eunuch, Han Zanzhou, saw that the emperor would not be rejected and escorted him into the camp where he sat him on a chair. Huang Degong kowtowed nine times and knelt three times in accordance with the proper ceremony. He asked the emperor why had he been traveling incognito and the emperor told him about the dangerous situation in Nanjing. "Things have come to such a sad state that my only hope is that you will protect me."

Huang Degong found this difficult to accept. He wept bitterly and said, "If you were in the palace I could fight for you in the name of the crown. As you have left, you have given up power. I am not equipped to prosecute war and I cannot retreat. When you left the palace, the reasons for the empire went out of the door with you."

Emperor Zhu Yousong, however, was not really concerned about the empire, said, "It is my own wish to abdicate the throne."

Huang was astounded. "How could you abandon the throne? The empire belongs to all ancestral emperors."

Emperor Zhu Yousong attempted to shift the responsibility to him.

第三十章
弘光复亡

话说弘光皇帝逃出南京城后，随侍太监渐渐散去，身边只剩下太监韩赞周一人，昼夜奔走，寻到魏国公徐宏基宅第，哪知徐宏基装作不相识，将他们逐出府去。君臣二人不免凄凄惶惶，继续向前奔逃，来到芜湖黄得功大营。

坂矶一战，黄得功大败左良玉，现正与心腹之将田雄据守芜湖。忽听守门军卒报称万岁爷来了。黄得功不得不出去一认。他刚出营门，弘光迫不及待地开口："黄将军一向好么？"他抬头一看，显然是当今皇上，扑通一声跪倒尘埃，口称："万岁，万岁，万万岁，请入大帐，容臣朝见。"

韩赞周听得此言，心知不会遭到在魏国公处的命运了，就扶了弘光进入大帐坐定。黄得功重新行了三拜九叩之礼，又问皇上因何不辞旅途辛苦，微服私访到此。韩赞周乃将京城危在旦夕，不得不连夜出奔的经过说了一遍，弘光长叹道："事到如今，也只能望你保护朕了！"

黄得功感到此事万难，跪在地上以手拍地痛哭不已，继而又奏道："皇上深居宫中，臣好拼力效命，今日离宫出走，大权已失，叫臣进不能战，退不能守，十分事业，已去九分了。"

弘光这个皇帝原就不是中兴之主，居然表示："不必着急，寡人只要保得性命，那皇帝一席，也不愿再做了！"

这倒出乎黄得功意外，高声回道："啊呀呀，天下者乃祖宗之天下，圣上如何能放弃？"

"Whether I abandon it or not depends on you entirely." Huang Degong was left with no choice. He felt obliged to protect the emperor. He arranged for the emperor to stay in the back camp and sat in the barracks thinking about his responsibility. To protect 15 provinces and the 300-year-old Ming empire was no small task. How could he live up to it?

The entire army was put on alert and a messenger went round the camp with a bell and wooden stick to warn of an emergency. Huang Degong consulted his trusted lieutenant, Tian Xiong, who, on this occasion, disagreed. He said to Huang, "I think this emperor is unlucky. If the Qing army crosses the river, everyone will surrender. You must see how the wind blows, so to speak, and hoist your sail accordingly." Huang would not accept this and Tian said nothing.

A soldier announced the arrival of Liu Liangzuo and Liu Zeqing and their army. Huang greeted them. As the two Lius dismounted they said, "Big brother, you have a treasure, but you are keeping it a secret."

"What treasure?" Huang did not know what they were talking about.

Liu Zeqing said openly, "Emperor Zhu Yousong."

Lowering his voice Liu Liangzuo asked, "When will you present it — why not today?"

"If we sent the emperor to the Qing army, we would be given dukedoms, wouldn't that be marvelous?"

Huang Degong realized their intentions and beat them soundly with his double whip shouting, "Traitor! Renegade!"

Liu Liangzuo tried to calm him. "We are brothers, don't rebuke us."

Huang Degong cried, "You don't even recognize the monarch. How can I recognize you as a brother?" He held his whip high.

Tian Xiong who was standing behind Huang ridiculed him in a low voice saying that he was a stupid ass who did not know when and how to act. He took a bow and shot Huang in the lower leg saying that he had come to end the argument. Huang had not expected to be shot from behind and fell to the ground. Tian Xiong returned to the back camp and carried out the emperor who protested and beat him with his fists. He threw the monarch on the ground before the two generals, saying, "I present to you the emperor."

The generals thanked him and took the emperor away. Tian, ignoring Huang's abuse, followed taking a bag of personal belongings. Huang

　　弘光皇帝趁此将天下兴亡的责任一股脑儿推卸给黄得功：
"弃与不弃，全看将军了！"黄得功无可奈何，只得表示报效朝廷，
鞠躬尽瘁，死而后已。他先安排皇上于后帐安歇，自己却坐在大帐
上沉思，心想三百年国运，十五省版图，就全在这大帐之中，自家
如何承担得起这天大的责任呢！

　　他一面命令三军马不卸鞍，人不解甲，一面又传进心腹田雄
将军，商量此事。哪知田雄却另有一番识见，悄悄建言道："元帅，
俺看这个皇帝，也不像有大福之人，何况清兵过江，人人投顺。元
帅你需要看风行船才好。"黄得功不以为然，田雄只好缄口不语。

　　忽然报子进帐禀报，说两镇刘良佐、刘泽清率了一彪人马前
来，黄得功赶紧出门迎接。那二刘跳下马来，刘良佐劈口说道："哥
哥得了宝贝，竟然瞒着两个兄弟！"

　　"什么宝贝呀？"黄得功有些丈二金刚摸不着头脑。

　　刘泽清快言快语："宝贝就是弘光呀！"刘良佐放低了声音问
黄得功："今日还不献宝，等到几时呢？"刘泽清紧接着说："把弘光
送与北朝，赏咱们大大一个王爵，岂不是好？"

　　黄得功这才明白二刘的用意，立时大怒，持起双鞭痛打二刘，
口中大呼："反贼，反贼！"刘良佐仍然劝他："不要破口，好好兄弟，
为何厮闹？""你这狗才，连君父都不认，我和你还认什么弟兄？"手
中的鞭子又高高举起。

　　站在黄得功身后的田雄低低讥诮道："好个笨牛，到了这个地
步，还不见机而作！"正当这三镇酣战时，田雄倒戈了，拉起了弦，
说道："俺田雄替你解围罢。"说罢，对准黄得功小腿射去。黄得功
何尝想到背后有人放冷箭？顿时跌扑在地。田雄返身进了后帐，背
了弘光，也不管这个皇帝在背上捶打狠咬，旋风般地冲到二刘面
前，将弘光掼下地来，对二刘拱手说道："皇帝一枚奉送。"

Degong, who knew that the cause was lost and that he was unable to do anything, killed himself with his own sword.

After Huang Degong's death Marshal Shi Kefa committed suicide by jumping into the river. Earlier he had resisted the Qing assaults but the city fell after they ran out of provisions. Shi had intended committing suicide then, but thought of the Ming Dynasty and what he could do for its survival. Dead, he would have been no use to the cause. He decided to go to Nanjing to help prop up the regime. He escaped from Yangzhou by lowering himself down the city wall on a rope and crossed the river on a small boat. At Longtan, he met the old ceremonial official, who had fled from Nanjing. He told Shi of the confusion and disorder in Nanjing and said that the emperor had already fled. Shi Kefa had come to the end of his tether. He did not know where the emperor was and wept bitterly. He took off his cap and gown and ended his life by jumping into the river.

The old ceremonial official wept as he stood by his clothes. Several men appeared. They were Liu Jingting, Hou Chaozong, Chen Dingsheng and Wu Ciwei who had all escaped from jail after the collapse of the Ming regime. Liu Jingting and Hou Chaozong had decided to return to their hometown in Henan on the central China; Chen Dingsheng and Wu Ciwei were sending them off. When the old ceremonial official told the four what had happened, grief overtook them and they paid homage to Marshal Shi Kefa. Chen Dingsheng went down on his knees to pay his last respects while Hou Chaozong thought of the good services Shi had rendered. He wept bitterly and after some time Liu Jingting persuaded him to go.

Hou Chaozong looked at the currents in the river and asked where they could go. In the north there were columns of smoke; there was no point in setting out that way.

"As you are not going north, why not come with us to south China?" Chen Dingsheng suggested.

Hou Chaozong saw the situation clearly. "This is a time of turmoil. We cannot depend on one another forever. It would be far better if each of us went his own way, for there is no peace in the country."

"What are your plans?" Wu Ciwei asked.

"I have discussed it with Liu Jingting. We shall seek an ancient temple deep in the mountains somewhere and from there see what happens, then return home later."

二刘连声称谢,拽了弘光就走,田雄不顾黄得功求救叫骂,背着一包细软也跟着而去。黄得功见眼前局势如此,无能为力,自刎而死。

黄得功死后不久,史可法又沉江自溺。他原率兵坚守杨州,抗击清兵,只因力尽粮绝,外援不至,城池终于被攻破。欲自尽孝忠,想到明朝三百年天下,只靠自身撑持,徒死无益,决心奔走南京,力求能维持半壁江山。他从城南挂下绳索出了扬州,直奔仪征,寻得一只小船,渡江而南。到了龙潭地面,遇到一个老赞礼背着一个小包袱落荒逃来,撞了一个满怀。史可法扶住他,问他何事如此慌张。老赞礼说南京城内大乱,皇帝老子也逃走了二、三天了。说话之间,老赞礼认出了史可法,原来在太平门外祭奠先帝时曾打过照面。史可法也细细说了杨州城破、自家赶来南京扶持皇上的经过。如今他听说弘光远遁,下落不明,顿时前后失据。不容老赞礼再三劝解,他双手摘下衣冠,投江而亡。老赞礼抱着他的衣冠放声痛哭。

哭声惊动了走近的几个人,原来是从镇抚司大狱中逃出来的柳敬亭、侯朝宗、陈定生和吴次尾。江南小朝廷已土崩瓦解,柳敬亭与侯朝宗原是中原河南人氏,决定北归故土。陈定生、吴次尾与侯朝宗为莫逆之交,乃结伴送他们一程。如今见一老者抱着衣冠痛哭,诧异万分,上前询问,方知史可法在此自沉大江。大家也悲恸不已,陈设好衣冠,祭奠了一番。侯朝宗想到史可法知遇之恩,更是放声大哭。柳敬亭在一边劝解,说道:"大家快走吧。"

侯朝宗指着大江,说道:"你看,对江烟尘满天,从哪里能回家乡?"

陈定生说道:"今既不能北上,何不随我们南归?"

侯朝宗看得清楚:"这纷纷乱世,何处有太平可寻?又怎能始终相依?还不如各人自便吧!"吴次尾问道:"那么,侯兄有何打算?"

侯朝宗回答道:"俺与敬亭已商议过,要寻一深山古寺,暂时避一避,看看形势再图返乡。"

The old ceremonial official said that he was going to Qixia Mountain, a secluded place, and suggested that they went with him.Hou Chaozong decided to try it and when Chen Dingsheng and Wu Ciwei saw that they had settled on a plan, they made their farewells.

The old ceremonial official intended taking Marshal Shi Kefa's clothes to Meihua Hill where Shi used to inspect his troops. They would bury the clothes and erect a memorial later. Hou Chaozong thought that he was a worthy person and asked him why he was going to Qixia Mountain.

"Officials held a funeral service in memory of the late emperor a few days ago. It was done in a perfunctory manner so I asked the city fathers for donations of money and food for a proper service; the confusion stopped us holding it. I am taking the food and money to the high priests in Qixia Mountain to perform the service there."

His good intentions won the respect and admiration of Hou Chaozong and Liu Jingting. The three started their journey to Qixia Mountain.

CHAPTER THIRTY-ONE

Entering the Priesthood

After Yang Longyou left, Li Xiangjun begged and implored Su Kunsheng to take her with him on his search for Hou Chaozong.

Su Kunsheng thought about it and said, "It is difficult. Hou Chaozong did not go to The House of Enchanting Fragrance after he left jail which means that he went out of town; he could be anywhere in the country."

Xiangjun said firmly, "I shall go to the four corners of the earth to find him."

Lan Ying interrupted them. "The army is in the northeast. Hou would not go there. He could only go to the southeast which is mountainous."

老赞礼接着说："我正要去栖霞山,那里十分幽僻,尽可避兵,何不同行?"侯朝宗连忙应允。陈、吴两位,见侯、柳两位已有去向,就此拱手作别。

老赞礼先将史可法的衣冠仔细收拾好,准备大兵退后,送至扬州梅花岭,那里是史可法点兵之处,将来在那里筑一衣冠冢,也好让后人瞻仰。侯朝宗赞道："难得你有此心,如此义举,实属难得。"又问道:"你到栖霞山中又有何事?"

老赞礼说:"当年在太平门外祭奠先帝时,文武百官只是虚应故事,敷衍场面,令人气愤!我已约定村中父老,捐施一些钱粮,七月十五那天替先帝做个水陆道场。不料城中大乱,好事难行,因此带着钱粮,去栖霞山中请高僧做法,了此心愿!"他这番举动,自然更受到侯、柳二人的钦敬。三人见陈、吴两位相公已经别去,也不再停留,便结伴向栖霞山行去。

第三十一章
栖真入道

杨龙友匆匆忙忙离开媚香楼之后,李香君再三纠缠苏昆生去寻找侯朝宗,断断续续地哭诉道:"杨老爷就这样去了,只有师父知道俺的心事,体谅俺的苦楚。前些时日,累得师父千山万水,寻到侯郎;哪知俺又被迫进宫,侯郎入狱,两不见面。今日奴家离宫,侯郎出狱,又不得相见,还求师父可怜,领着奴家各处去寻找侯郎才好。"

苏昆生感到此事难办,说道:"侯郎从大牢中出来,不到此处来,大概是出城去了,到哪里去寻找?"

香君却坚决表示:"便是走到天涯海角,也定要寻到侯郎。"

"I will travel across mountains and along unknown paths to find him."

Moved by her determination, Su Kunsheng said that he would take her along. He was looking for somewhere to go himself but he had no idea where they would end up.

Just then Lan Ying walked to the balustrade, pointed to the east and said, "Qixia Mountain is a secluded place where we can all avoid the army. I am going there to study Taoism under Zhang Yaoxing, the veteran imperial guard who abandoned his career to enter the Taoist priesthood. We could go together and perhaps we might find Hou Chaozong."

Su Kunsheng thought that it was a good idea and asked Xiangjun to pack. She followed them out of the town.

When they came to Baiyun Temple, Lan Ying found Zhang Yaoxing. He stayed there and Su and Xiangjun traveled on asking about Hou Chaozong at all the temples. At dusk they came to the Baozhen Nunnery where Su Kunsheng knocked on the door. He was surprised and delighted to meet Bian Yujing, the head of the nunnery and an old friend. The happy encounter was like a miracle. Bian Yujing asked them both to stay and as they had nowhere else to go; they were pleased.

Dressed in a straw hat, coat and sandals, Su helped out by gathering firewood. Xiangjun saw him take on the menial task and asked Bian if she could sew or mend.

Bian Yujing did not have anything for her but said that on July 15th they were holding Zhong Yuan Festival and the people of the village wanted to hold a ceremony in honor of Empress Zhou. She could help them make the banners.

Li Xiangjun was eager to help. After she had washed her hands and burnt incense, she began sewing the banners.

There was a knock on the door and someone asked who it was. Outside were the old ceremonial official, Liu Jingting and Hou Chaozong, who had gone to the nunnery to ask for accommodation.

Naturally, the nuns were cautious about receiving guests at such an hour and, when the old ceremonial official asked permission to stay, they told him that a nunnery could not allow male travelers to stay overnight.

Liu Jingting pointed out that they were not priests, but the nuns were adamant; the rules laid down by ancestral nuns did not allow travelers to stay in the nunnery.

站在一旁的蓝瑛插话说："西北一带都是兵马，侯兄也无法渡江北去。若要去寻找，大约只有东南方向，不过那全是山间小路。"

"就是荒山野道，奴家也要去寻找。"

苏昆生听得香君这番言语，倒也颇为感动，便答允道："你既一心要寻侯郎，我老汉索性领你去吧。只是不知朝何方向去为宜？"

蓝瑛说："那栖霞山中，人迹稀少，大锦衣张瑶星弃职修仙，俺正要去拜他为师。何不结伴同行，或者因缘凑巧，找到侯相公也未可知。"

"妙，妙。"苏昆生吩咐香君收拾行包，一齐离开旧院，出城而去。

蓝瑛先找到白云庵，张瑶星正在庵中，便留了下来。苏昆生则领着香君沿着山路，见着庵观寺院或是山村人家，就打听侯朝宗的消息。眼见天色渐晚，山色中隐约出现了一座庵观，近前一看，是葆真庵，苏昆生前去敲门，哪知天缘奇巧，原来是老相识卞玉京在这里做了庵主。彼此又惊又喜，相互诉说分手后的情景，各人叹息不已。

卞玉京热忱地挽留，师徒二人便寄住在庵中。苏昆生眼见一时无法寻到侯公子，不能坐吃山空，便每日清早爬山越岭，采伐些松柴，供庵中烧饭之用。李香君见师父如此谋生，也不好空手闲坐，就对庵主说："俺闲居此处，也觉无聊，你何不找些旧衣裳，让俺替你缝补缝补。"卞玉京没有旧衣裳让她缝补，想了想说道："七月十五中元节即将到来，村中男女要在白云庵中为皇后周娘娘做一场法事，悬挂的宝幡尚未做成，就烦你妙手缝制，也算一件大功德呢。"

李香君欣然同意："有这等好事，情愿效力。"说罢，就洗手薰香，细心缝制起来。

正当此时，一阵敲门声，庵内有人问道："哪个敲门？"原来是老赞礼、柳敬亭、侯朝宗三人。"俺是南京来的，要借贵庵暂时安歇。"

听得是男子声音，庵内立即回绝："这里是女道院，从不留客的。"

柳敬亭道："我们不是游方僧道，暂住一宿又有何妨！"

They were unyielding and Hou Chaozong, without realizing that he had missed his chance of seeing Li Xiangjun, said that they should look elsewhere.

They went their way and came upon a Taoist priest, who the official greeted. "We are on Qixia Mountain to hold a sacrificial funeral offering. Can we leave our bags in your temple for the night?"

The priest looked hard at Hou Chaozong and recognized a familiar face. He called out, "Are you Hou Chaozong of Henan?"

"If he is not Hou Chaozong, who else could he be?" Liu Jingting replied.

The priest heard Liu's voice and said, "Could that be Liu Jingting?"

"Yes."

Hou Chaozong recognized Ding Jizhi. "Why have you become a Taoist priest?"

Ding Jizhi explained why he had left the court and gone to the nearby Caizhen Temple, which was close to the place where he would enter the priesthood. He invited them to stay at the temple and they accepted. They farewelled the old ceremonial official who went on to arrange the ritual service for the Zhong Yuan Festival on July 15th in the White Cloud Temple. Hou and Liu followed Ding Jizhi to the Caizhen Temple.

At the festival, Zhang Yaoxing, head of the White Cloud Temple, intended erecting a large alter for the service in honor of the late Emperor Chongzhen.

On the day he told Cai Yisuo and Lan Ying to be ready and the old ceremonial official came as well. Villagers, men and women, young and old brought joss sticks, incense, sacrificial wine, sacrificial paper money and embroidered banners for the occasion. They filled the square. Cai and Lan had asked Zhang to supervise the service. Dressed in a Taoist robe, Zhang climbed to the alter on which there was a wooden tablet with the name of the late emperor. On the left were tablets with the names of civilian officials who had died during the fall of Beijing. Tablets on the right bore the names of military officials. To the sound of music, Zhang Yaoxing read the funeral oration and villagers burst into tears. The old ceremonial official remarked that the people were showing their true feelings unlike the officials outside the Taiping City Gate. The service ended; villagers ate the funeral meal and then dispersed.

Bian Yujing had brought Li Xiangjun and a few nuns to decorate banners in honor of the Empress Zhou. They greeted Zhang Yaoxing in

"谨奉祖师清规,不能留客!"仍无商量余地。侯朝宗见状,就对老赞礼说:"她们既然谨守清规,不必再强求了。"老赞礼点头说道:"前面还有不少庵观,俺们再去找吧。"哪里知道,阴错阳差,侯朝宗与李香君又错过一次聚首的机会。

三人只得继续前行,走不多远,老赞礼看到前边来了一位道人,便迎上前去,拱手为礼,说道:"老仙长,我们是上山来做好事的,要借个道院寄放行李,敢求道长方便一二!"

这位道长未即答话,倒仔细端详起侯朝宗来,觉得好面熟,不禁问道:"此位相公,好像是河南侯公子。"柳敬亭赶紧答话:"正是侯公子。"听见柳敬亭的声音,那道长盯了一眼,又问道:"你可是柳敬亭?""便是呀!"侯朝宗此刻方才认出眼前这位道长,不胜惊异:"啊呀,丁继之,你为何出家了?"

丁继之答道:"侯相公,你不知道么?俺不愿被强征入宫,就来到此处。前面有座采真观,是俺修炼之所,如三位不嫌弃,就一同去住下。"侯朝宗自然求之不得,老赞礼则要去白云庵商量设醮﹡事儿,便告别三人,独自去了。丁继之则领着侯、柳二人回采真观而去。

转眼之间,已到七月十五日中元节。栖霞山白云庵主张瑶星要大建经坛,广延道众,追荐先帝崇祯皇帝。这日凌晨,张瑶星吩咐蔡益所,蓝瑛铺设坛场,准备斋供。从南京城里逃出的老赞礼也来搭醮,一同祭拜。山中村民,或顶香捧酒,或携纸钱绣幡,从四面八方赶来,挤满了白云庵广场。蔡、蓝两人乃恭请法师张瑶星登坛祭拜。张瑶星换了法衣,上了拜坛。坛的正中供着崇祯皇帝牌位,左坛供着甲申殉难的文臣牌位,右坛供着甲申殉难的武臣牌位。在细乐声中,张瑶星读罢祭文,献酒烧纸拜奠。老赞礼说道:"今日不比当时太平门外,那般文武臣子尽是虚情假意,大家今日哭个尽情。"众民哭奠。

﹡ 醮:指古代结婚时用酒祭神的礼,也可泛指其它祷神祭礼。

the lecture hall.

Hou Chaozong came to the service with Ding Jizhi and spotted a familiar figure in the corridor. There were many people there but he looked more closely and realized that it was Xiangjun. He pushed through the crowd and pulled her out.

"Brother Hou, it's you. I have longed for you."

Hou Chaozong pointed to the fan and said, "Look at the peach blossom on the fan. You wrote it in blood, how can I ever repay you?"

The couple spoke of their yearning for each other but Ding Jizhi tugged at Hou's arms. Bian Yujing warned Xiangjun, "You must not show your feelings in this way. The supervising priest is at the altar." But the couple would not be parted and ignored her. Zhang Yaoxing saw what was going on and became very angry. Banging the table with a wooden gavel he said, "How dare you flirt here?" He walked down from the altar, took the peach blossom fan, tore it apart, and threw it away. "The altar is a sacred place. How dare you express your love to each other here?"

Cai Yisuo, who was standing behind Zhang Yaoxing, recognized Hou and Li. He said to Zhang, "It is Hou Chaozong. You know him."

"Who is this woman?"

Lan Ying identified Li Xiangjun and described how the couple had been living apart. Hou Chaozong recognized Zhang and thanked him sincerely for his help.

"So you are Mr. Hou. I am pleased that you escaped from jail. I became a priest on your account, I hope you realize that."

"I knew nothing of this."

"I had a similar experience," Cai Yisuo said, "But I'll tell you about it at a better time."

Lan Ying told Hou Chaozong how he and Li Xiangjun had searched for him. Hou Chaozong said that he and Xiangjun were deeply grateful and he again thanked Su Kunsheng and Liu Jingting.

"After we return home to Henan we shall surely pay back our debt."

When Zhang Yaoxing heard this, he said loudly, "Why are you talking in this manner? This is a time of supreme crisis and you talk of love, it is ridiculous."

Hou Chaozong refuted him, "The bond between a man and a woman is a most important human relationship. Separations and reunions are critical moments in life. To be sad or happy on such occasions is natural

此时，葆真观主卞玉京领了李香君等人在周皇后坛前挂了宝幡，也来到讲堂参见法师。哪知侯朝宗也随着采真观主丁继之一同前来参加大法会。他四处张望，见廊下站着一个年轻女子，身段十分眼熟，分明是李香君！他也无暇细想，分开众人，大步向前，走到李香君面前，香君突然一惊："啊呀，你是侯郎，想煞奴家也。"

侯朝宗指着纸扇说道："看这扇上桃花，全是你鲜血点染，教小生如何报答你！"

说着，两人一同对着这柄桃花扇，诉说别后情怀。丁继之急得拉着侯朝宗，卞玉京拽住李香君，告诫他们两个："法师在坛，不可只顾诉情了。"他们两个好不容易见面，哪会听从。坛上张瑶星看见了，不禁大怒，喝道："咦！哪里来的一对男女，敢在这里调情！"说罢，快步急行至侯、李面前，不容分说，伸手夺过桃花扇，撕作两半掷于地上，斥责道："我这清净道场，哪容谈情说爱的男女在此戏嬉！"

紧跟在法师张瑶星身后的蔡益所、蓝瑛二人已认出侯、李来，对张瑶星说："啊呀，这是河南侯朝宗相公，法师原是认得的。""这个女的是谁？"蓝瑛赶紧回答："是侯兄聘娶的妾香君。"经过众人说明，张瑶星才知道侯、李二人现在分别住在采真观和葆真庵中。

张瑶星说道："你是侯世兄，幸喜出狱了，俺原是为你出家，你可知道么？"侯朝宗自然不知道。蔡益所上前半步，对侯朝宗说："贫道也是因你才出家，这些缘由，待有机会慢慢对你说罢。"

蓝瑛对侯朝宗说："贫道蓝瑛，特领着香君来山中寻你，谁知果然遇上了。"

侯朝宗十分感动，说道："丁、卞二师收留之恩，蔡、田二师接引之情，俺与香君世世图报。"待咱夫妻还乡，对诸位都要一一报答的。"

张瑶星听得此话，喝道："你们絮絮叨叨，说的是些什么话！当此地覆天翻之时，还眷念情根欲种，岂不可笑！"

to all people."

Zhang Yaoxing said that he was stupid. "At this time of crisis where is our nation? Where is our home? Where is the emperor? Where is our father? Why do you only think of the flesh or the petty short life of man and wife?"

Zhang's concerns struck a chord with Hou and he thanked him for enlightening him. His views changed and he decided to follow Zhang's teaching and forgo earthly pursuits. He became an ascetic and entered priesthood as the pupil of Ding Jizhi while Li Xiangjun became a daughter of the Taoist faith and the pupil of Bian Yujing. Their romance ended.

CHAPTER THIRTY-TWO

Search for the Hermits

Three years after these events Su Kunsheng earned a living as a firewood man, and Liu Jingting worked as a fisherman. The old ceremonial official lived near Yanziji where he acted as a ritual master of ceremonies. This involved drinking and dining at sacrificial offerings.

One day he went to the mountain where he met Su and Liu and gave them the wine and food obtained from one of these ceremonies. They drank three cups of wine and became merry, each singing a song to the accompaniment of a stringed instrument.

They were becoming sentimental, applauding their own performances and talking non-stop when a policeman from the Shangyuan County magistrate arrived. The policeman, Xu Qingjun, was the son of the Duke of the State of Wei, Ming Dynasty. Born into an aristocratic family he had not fared well after the collapse of the Ming regime. He became a sort of local policeman and had been ordered to search out and call on hermits, who were formerly officials of the Ming Dynasty.

When he saw the revelers, one dressed as a fisherman and another as firewood cutter, he realized from their stance and dignity that they were

侯朝宗却不以为然,反驳道:"此言差矣! 从来男女婚嫁,人之大伦,离合悲欢,人之常情,先生如何管得?"

"啊呸,你这两个痴虫! 现今之世,国在哪里,家在哪里,君在哪里,父在哪里,偏是点儿女私情割不断么?"

听了张瑶星一番话语,侯朝宗如同醍醐灌顶,连忙作揖致谢,正色道:"法师几句话,说得小生冷汗淋漓,如梦方醒。"便遵法师之命,拜丁继之为师。李香君也晓得此理,拜卞玉京为师。侯、李二人终于了却这段尘世姻缘,头也不回地各随其师出家而去。

第三十二章
深山搜隐

转瞬之间,早已三年过去。苏昆生在栖霞山中以打柴为生,柳敬亭也在此处江边捕鱼为生。老赞礼却在栖霞山附近燕子矶边栖身,凡是祭赛之处,他都到场图个醉饱。

这日他来到山中,正好遇着苏、柳二位,就将分得的福酒取出,与他们二人席地而坐,同饮三杯。一时高兴,老赞礼弹唱了一曲[问苍天],柳敬亭唱了一曲[秣陵秋],苏昆生也唱了一曲[哀江南],无非是感叹兴亡而已。三人唱罢,拍手称快,继而又闲谈起来。

正当他们谈得投机时,上元县一名皂隶循声而来。这个皂隶是明朝魏国公嫡亲公子,名叫徐青君,可谓生来富贵,享尽荣华,哪知国破家亡,只剩下孤身一人。迫于衣食只得屈就皂隶。今日奉了本官之命,前往深山老林访拿前朝遗老、隐逸之士。

徐青君远远见到这三个老者在山头闲话,虽然穿戴着樵夫、

not ordinary laborers. He was sure they must have been men of high calibre, who were now living as hermits. He asked them if this was the case. The three denied it and asked Xu Qingjun why he was looking for hermits.

"Don't you know that the Ministry of Rites have filed a report to the crown to look for hermits — men who were formerly officials of the Ming Dynasty. A proclamation have been issued. No hermits have reported so far and we have been sent to take them to a government office. I think you are hermits and I would like you to accompany me."

The old ceremonial official said, "Only literary men live on the mountain and they will not leave it."

Su Kunsheng and Liu Jingting added that they were singers of *kunqu* opera who had become fishermen and firewood cutters. They would be of no use to the government.

Xu Qingjun said, "Literary men have talents and have to submit to circumstances. Some left the mountain three years back to become officials. Now I am looking for people like you."

The old ceremonial official was outraged. "Looking for hermits for the benefit of the court! They should be invited to work for the court instead of being hunted down. You are merely an underling engaged in an unworthy task."

"This is not my doing. Here is a warrant." Xu Qingjun took out the warrant and after reading it Su Kunsheng said that it looked genuine. Liu Jingting thought that they should leave and ignored the policeman's request.

They walked rapidly away in different directions. Xu Qingjun did not know who to follow and could not catch any of them. He left the mountain, but did not give up hope. He went to the woods and streams again, looking for them. The story ends with the policeman looking for the hermits but he was unsuccessful. The search goes on still.

渔子的服饰,气度却是不凡,认准他们是隐居山中的高士,劈面就问他们可是山林隐逸之士?三人一齐立起身来,连声说:"不敢!"他们又问他为何问起此事?

徐青君说道:"三位不知道么?现今礼部上本,搜寻山林隐逸,巡按大老爷张挂告示,布政司行文已有月余,并无一人前来报名。府里县里忙了,派遣我们各处访拿,三位一定是了,快快跟我回话去。"

老赞礼抢先说道:"老哥差矣,山林隐逸乃是文人学士,不肯出山的。老夫原是一个假斯文的老赞礼,哪能去得?"

苏、柳二人更说道:"我们两个是说书唱曲的朋友,如今又做了渔夫、樵夫,更不中用了。"

哪知徐青君却说:"你们不晓得,那些文人名士都是识时务的俊杰,三年前早就出山做了官了。现今正要访拿你们这等人的。"

老赞礼不禁恼怒起来:"啐,征求山林隐逸,是朝廷盛典,官应当以礼相聘,怎么要访拿?定是你们差役狐假虎威,奉行不善。"

"不干我事,有本官牌票在此,你们看。"说着,徐青君取出牌票。苏昆生一看,倒是真的。柳敬亭则说咱们走开不理,老赞礼也赞同。

霎时之间,三人分头走散,徐青君不知追逐谁好,也赶不上任何一人,只得听任他们散去。但仍不甘心就此罢休,仍然在林下水边,信步寻找。至于他是否能找到愿意出山的人,那就不得而知了。

图书在版编目（CIP）数据

桃花扇：英、中文对照／（清）孔尚任著；陈美林改编.
－北京：新世界出版社，1999.1
ISBN 7－80005－432－2

Ⅰ.桃…　Ⅱ.①孔…②陈…　Ⅲ.戏剧－中国－清代
－英语－对照读物，英、汉　Ⅳ.H319.4:I
中国版本图书馆 CIP 数据核字(98)第 34348 号

桃 花 扇

原　　著：孔尚任（清）
改　　编：陈美林
翻　　译：匡佩华　任玲娟　何飞
责任编辑：张民捷
版式设计：李　辉
出版发行：新世界出版社
社　　址：北京阜成门外百万庄路24号　　邮政编码：100037
电　　话：0086－10－68994118
传　　真：0086－10－68326679
电子邮件：nwpcn@public.bta.net.cn
经　　销：新华书店、外文书店
印　　刷：北京外文印刷厂
开　　本：850×1168(毫米)　1/32　　　字数：160 千
印　　张：8
版　　次：1999 年 3 月(英、汉)第 1 版　2001 年 1 月北京第 2 次印刷
书　　号：ISBN 7－80005－432－2/I·022
定　　价：22.00 元